# The Old Kingdom Ardänia

## Volume 2:
## Shattered Memories

By Preston Robison

Copyright © 2015 by Preston Robison
Cover art copyright © 2015 by Chelsey Fallis

Bison Publishing

ISBN-13: 978-0692493670

ISBN-10: 0692493670

www.bisonpublishing.info

bisonpublishing@gmail.com
www.facebook.com/shatteredmemories1

# Table of Contents

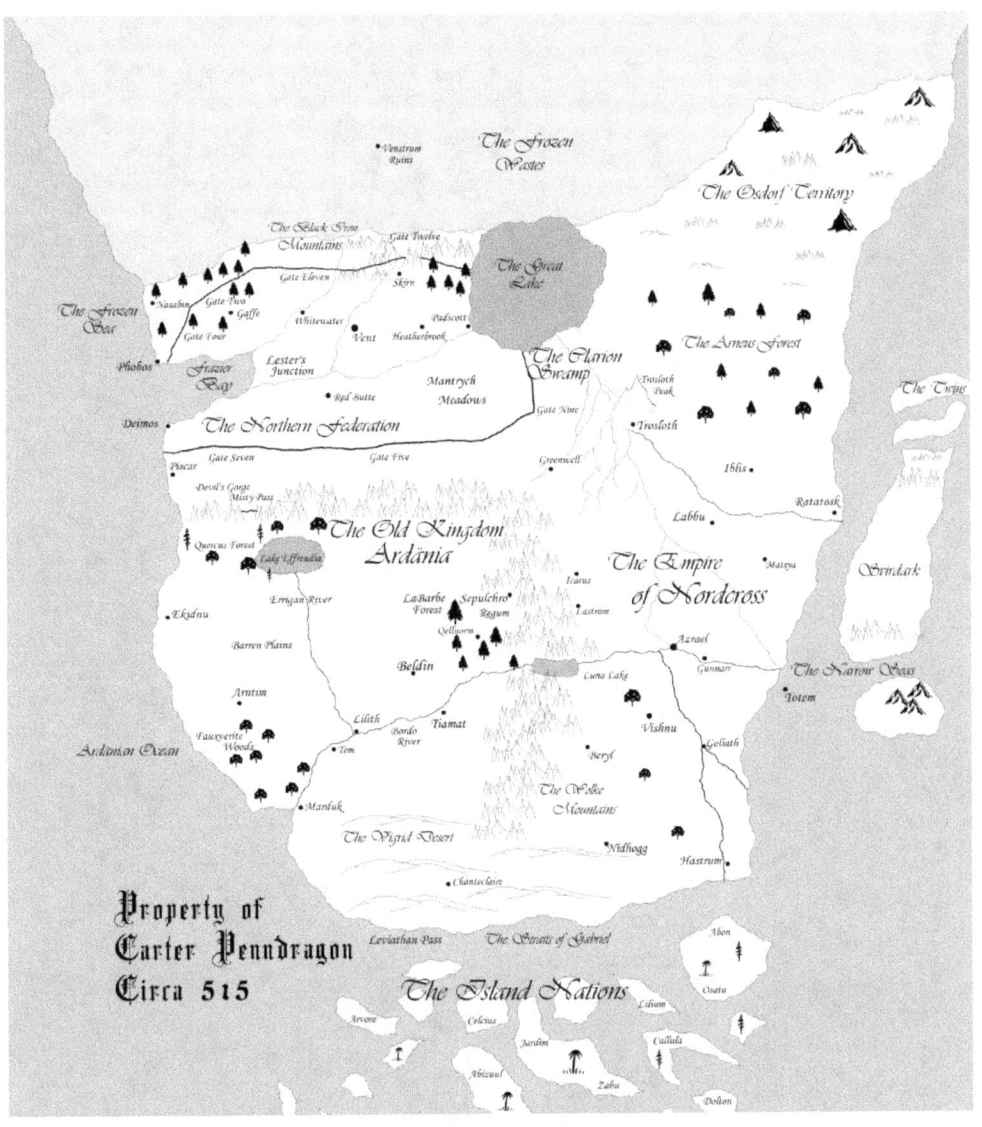

The Frozen Wastes

Venatrum Ruins

The Osdorf Territory

The Black Pyre Mountains
Gate Twelve
Gate Eleven
Skirn
The Great Lake

The Frozen Sea

Nasahn
Gate Two
Gaffe
Gate Four
Phobos
Whitewater
Vent
Heatherbrook
Padscott

The Amens Forest

The Twins

Frazier Bay
Lester's Junction
Red Butte
Mantych Meadows
The Clarion Swamp
Trisloth Peak
Trisloth

Deimos
The Northern Federation
Gate Nine
Greenwell
Ibfis

Piscar
Gate Seven
Gate Five
Labbu
Ratatosk

Devil's Gorge
Misty Pass
Quercus Forest
Lake Uffendia
The Old Kingdom Ardänia
The Empire of Nordcross
Matzya
Svindak

Ekianu
Ernijan River
LaBarbe Forest
Sepulchro
Regum
Icarus
Lastrom
Azrael
Gunnar

Barren Plains
Qelligorn
The Narrow Seas

Beldin
Cuna Lake
Totem

Arutim
Lilith
Tiamat
Vishnu
Goliath

Fauxyette Woods
Bordo River
Tem
Beryl

Marduk
The Solee Mountains
Nidhogg
Hastrum

The Vigrid Desert

Chanteclaire

Property of
Carter Penndragon
Circa 515

Leviathan Pass
The Straits of Gabriel
Abon

The Island Nations

Arvore
Celcius
Jardim
Abizuul
Zabu
Lihian
Osatu
Callula
Dolton

Ardanian Ocean

To see more maps of Cygnus, visit Carter's Archives at
www.cartersarchives.tumblr.com

# Old Language Glossary

**Ahan:** Sense

**Anarr:** To fall

**Anlig:** Nothing

**Anlön:** Death

**Anlönmömig brotro:** Ghost story

**Anmäch:** Barrier

**Anna:** But

**Anray:** To forget

**Anray'n:** Moron

**Anręxlig:** Silly thing (insult)

**Anręxmömig:** Silly person (insult)

**Antęza:** To let go

**Antzę:** To fail

**Brotro:** Long story

**D'sävv:** Forever/permanent

**Daz/d':** Many/all

**Dra:** To eat or drink

**Dran:** Glutton/drunk (slang for topsider)

**Kallö:** To heal

**Kas:** To dream

**Kas'n:** Dream

**Kasmömig:** Dreamer

**Kasprön:** Harbinger of dreams

**Kìtanarr:** The Sinking of Ardan

**Kìtlön:** Old life (before Ardan sank)

**Kìtsävv:** Yesterday

**Kìttęza:** Remember

**Klynlön:** Newbirth

**Klynmig:** Boy

**Klynmö:** Girl

**Klyntar:** Little moon (title)

**Lamäch:** Marriage

**Lamömig:** Loved one

**Lamig:** Boyfriend

**Lamö:** Girlfriend

**Lödran:** Healing tonic

**Mig:** Man

**Raysnít'n:** Training

**Ręxlamig:** Husband

**Ręxlig:** Important thing

**Ręxoo:** Destiny

**Ręxpol:** Topside

**Ręxsnít'n:** Battle

**Ręxträg:** Castle

**Röm:** Happy

**Römmömig:** Friend

**Rù:** *Indicates second person*

**Sintar:** Middle moon (title)

**Snít'n:** Fight

**So'o:** Honest

**Sù:** *Indicates first person*

**Taraha:** To use magic

**Tìksävv:** Tomorrow

**Träg:** Home

**Tur:** To be

**Tzęprön:** Harbinger of ends

**Xùn:** *Indicates conditional*

**Yamömig:** Who

**Yid art:** Old fart (insult)

**Yidmömig:** Elder

**Yidtar:** Big moon (title)

**Yunträg:** Lost

**Z'aha:** To see

**Zo:** To control

*"When the die is cast,*

*Forget the past."*

# *BREAKING NEWS*

**Mucca 22nd, 508**

Today is a grim day for our empire. Nordcross has officially declared war on our western neighbors for the assassination of Emperor Erranko's wife Karissa two years ago.

Recent evidence points to a man named Jaspar as the empress' killer, though the dilapidated Kingdom of Ardänia refuses to turn the criminal in. A hefty bounty has been issued for him—alive.

Let us all hope for a quick and bloodless end to this manhunt.

**Corvo 31st, 508**

Leading his royal escort, Emperor Erranko apprehended his wife's murderer himself. The following night, however, the insidious Jaspar orchestrated an escape and fled somewhere in the Wolke Mountains. The bounty on this assassin's head has tripled.

Commander Rios has advised that all travel near or through the mountains should be postponed until further notice.

**Aquila 17th, 510**

A rebel faction from Ardänia led a two-pronged attack in the Northern Federation last week. The damage was devastating—both Trosloth and Mantrych were demolished, their citizens were slaughtered, and many of the Gate Cities were destroyed.

"Everyone I know was killed and my house was burned to the ground," says one survivor. "We had no idea that Mantrych was harboring terrorists."

The rebel group left Mantrych without a trace, but current intelligence suggests that the faction is led by a woman with dark green hair who uses a longbow. Her cohorts are a man of large build with bright red hair and a teenage boy who has black hair and wields a staff.

"It is truly a sad day for the North," Emperor Erranko announced earlier regarding the attack. "Rest assured that Nordcross will not forget its ally in these dark times."

Rumors that the infamous Jaspar was involved with this tragedy have been confirmed by several anonymous sources within the Nordcross Intelligence Bureau. These sources have also indicated that the criminal is currently en route from the Northern Federation back to Ardänia.

Should anybody receive information about the three terrorists or Jaspar, please contact the proper authorities. USE EXTREME CAUTION! They are armed and dangerous.

## TERROR IN THE NEW FRONTIER
### Erranko 1st, 510

The terrorists have attacked again. A small mining town in Nordcross' new Western Frontier was attacked just days ago. Qellnorm, a town consisting of coal miners and a random assortment of shops, was raided by the three war criminals that were last seen in the Northern Federation.

"People were dropping left and right. It was awful," says one man who watched his family die in the bandits' onslaught. "They didn't give any warning! They just attacked and killed, then kept killing. Anyone who thinks this is some kind of joke shouldn't. They ARE serious!"

Experts have agreed that this will create economic hardships in the surrounding areas, hindering Nordcross' abilities to restore the basic systems in its Western Frontier.

"Qellnorm was a mining town, and as such it was the main provider of raw materials in the area," Commander Rhett told us. "Nordcross will now have to import basics like coal and steel until the mine can be brought back online. This will cost us more than coin; the rehabilitation of the new territories may now take years longer than originally expected.

"I want to stress, however," Commander Rhett continued, "that the citizens of the Western Frontier have proven cooperative and are thankful for the opportunities that we have provided them. These attacks are due only to the actions of a fringe element, but Nordcross will always prevail."

Again, if anyone has any information, this reporter urges you to contact the authorities.

**Erranko 9th, 510**

The rebel leader and notorious murderer Jaspar has been captured by Nordcross officials and is pending a trial before sentencing. Details are limited as this is a high-profile case, but very credible sources have informed us of this much. The end of the war is near!

## *Terrorists Strike Again!*

**Erranko 12th, 510**

Things have taken a turn for the worse as another town in the Western Frontier has been assaulted by the terrorists. Beldin, the site of a police training camp, was raided by the rebels without warning.

"They came under the cover of night and murdered our empire's finest young warriors. The fact that the rebels are willing to attack civilians and other noncombatants is despicable," Officer Drazin explained, visibly shaken.

A checklist of safety protocols is printed on the reverse side of this sheet, and Emperor Erranko urges everybody to review these precautions.

**Drago 30th, 510**

More details have been released concerning the destruction of one of Nordcross' most vital trade routes. In an effort to rescue their leader, the Ardänian rebels caused a landslide that buried the emperor's escort and demolished much of Leviathan Pass' road.

Shortly after capturing Jaspar in Arntim last month, Emperor Erranko's caravan was ambushed at Leviathan Pass. According to a statement by a member of the Nordcross Intelligence Bureau, "The royal guards rescued our emperor, but many of his fellow travelers did not share his luck."

It took several weeks for Nordcross ships to comb through the wreckage below the pass, but between the bodies recovered and the eye-witness account of our emperor, an accurate report was manufactured. Meyral, Maxine, and Alberto—the rebels who allegedly led the attacks on Qellnorm and Beldin—were among the casualties listed as a result of the attack.

Although much of the Remnant faction has been disbanded through the tireless efforts of the Nordcross military, Jaspar's body was never discovered. It is possible that the rebel leader survived the attack and is still at large.

The NIB is currently researching new routes into the Western Frontier as an alternate to Leviathan Pass, though currently the Vigrid Desert is the most popular option.

### Maiale 22nd, 511

Emperor Erranko announced that he has proposed to his Commander-in-Chief, Sera. The date has been set for this coming spring. Keep your fingers crossed that the wedding will be open to the public!

## *Search Called Off, War Is Over!*

### Corvo 22nd, 511

A conference was held in Lilith regarding the ongoing search for casualties at Leviathan Pass. Due to inclement weather, NIB officials have called off the investigation. One topic brought to the table was whether or not the notorious war criminal Jaspar survived. The conference attendees unanimously agreed that, even though his body was not among those recovered, Jaspar did not survive. As a result, the war has officially ended.

I believe I speak for all of Nordcross when I say thank you to our brave soldiers, and my condolences go out to the families of those who didn't make it home.

### Aquila 13th, 513

Emperor Erranko and Empress Sera have announced that they will be adopting a child from Svirdark. The child's name, Calla, was the only identifying information released in the announcement.

Svirdark is a large island off of the eastern coast of Nordcross, colonized nearly twenty years ago after the Tandem Wars. When Emperor Erranko names Calla as heiress to the empire, it will be the first honorable recognition the colony has ever received. Officials have yet to comment as to how this might affect Svirdark's future political relations.

The emperor says that he is "overjoyed that the child will be raised without having to know war."

# Death in the Vigrid Desert

**Aquila 23rd, 514**

Another trade caravan has disappeared in the desert, making a total of six in the last two years. But even when faced with the threat of death, these Nordcross merchants never lose hope.

"If everyone else is dead, it means more money for us!" one exuberant trader told this reporter. "All we have to do is make it through the desert alive."

Rumors have recounted the existence of numerous monsters and villains, each less likely than the last. However, several eyewitness accounts all describe a cloaked bandit, one who may have a connection to the disappearances.

**Erranko 7th, 516**

Yet another trade caravan has fallen victim to the fury of the desert, thanks to one criminal. Officials have confirmed that there is a single man responsible for the disappearances, and a reward has been offered for his capture.

Little is known about the outlaw, and descriptions have ranged from "seven-foot-tall menace" to a "blue dwarf that can turn invisible at will."

Whoever he is, this reporter urges every trader to be on the defensive when traveling.

**Ruolo 21st, 518**

The Blue Bandit is now being described as a man in his early twenties with black hair and blue eyes. He wears a black cloak and has tattoos that cover his right side.

If you have information that leads to an arrest, the reward is now 100,000 pieces of gold. Turning him in DEAD will earn you zero—he is worth nothing to the empire that way.

**Corvo 2nd, 518**

Northern and Nordcross officials revealed yesterday that a secret treaty had been signed between the two countries mere weeks before the terrorist attack on the Northern Federation in 510.

Newly appointed Lieutenant Drazin commented, "When Nordcross caught wind that the war criminals were hiding in Mantrych and Trosloth, we immediately sent reinforcements to aid our new ally. Unfortunately, everything was already in flames by the time we arrived. The citizens were beyond help."

Drazin was recently promoted for his work in advancing the Rail Project.

# CHAPTER ONE: SOLITUDE

Lars watched as a man in an old, dirty cloak pulled out another newspaper clipping and stared at it. He'd been at it since the bar had opened. He would pull article after article out of that ratty coat, read each crumpled piece once or twice, then shove them back in frustration.

*Have I seen this guy in here before?*

Lars dismissed the thought quickly. After getting stuck out in the desert, he'd seen hundreds of caravans come through. It had become difficult to tell who was hitchhiking and who was a veteran merchant, so he'd stopped caring. He reached down, grabbed a dirty glass, and began wiping it, lost in his thoughts.

*This shitty tent could never pass for a real tavern. I would know! I used to have one of the best in all the Northern Federation. Wood paneling on the walls, a solid mahogany bar stocked with exotic drinks from as far south as anyone's been...even the rugs were Old Kingdom silk! And the chandeliers, oh, how I miss them.*

"Barkeep," Lars' old friend slurred, "gimme a pint of your finest."

"I could be selling you watered down piss and you wouldn't know the difference," Lars muttered. He filled the glass he'd been cleaning and passed it to his favorite drunk.

*I guess I still have Karloff. I'll probably always be stuck with that stinkin' drunk. How a halfwit lawyer makes any money out in these sands, I have no idea, but he followed me. Shit, he'll probably outlive me and be the only one at my grave. That kinda gives me chills.*

As the bartender reached for another glass and continued to ponder his future, his eyes landed on his only employee. She had long, copper hair that was slung over one shoulder, trailing just above her breasts.

*Her "money makers," she calls them. Remember that time we were snowed in?* Lars grinned to himself as the memory surfaced. *'The closer they are to fumbling out, the more I make in tips,' she'd said. All I know is tonight is gonna be a good night for her coinpurse.*

Her shirt was low in the back, too, and the ends of a tattoo were just visible between her shoulder blades—Lars knew from experience that it was a very intricate dreamcatcher.

*I guess if I'm lucky, Karloff might not be the only one at my grave. It was her idea to move out here to this hell. Chanteclaire...what a pretty name for such a shitty place. Although when we first arrived, it wasn't much more than an old temple and some crumbling huts. This town has tripled in size since then, but it's still too hot and sandy for my taste. Jasmin is all that makes this wretched place sufferable...I could die happy in that woman's arms.*

The cloaked man rapped his knuckles on the bar and Lars was pulled from his musings. He poured two fingers of whiskey into the second glass and slid it down the counter. The man in rags caught it with his left hand.

*This guy is quickly replacing Karloff as my best customer. He's already on his second bottle today,* and *he paid for three in advance...something Karloff's never done. Hell, if I really wanted to retire, I could just call in that old drunk's debt.*

"Hey, Lars, did ya hear that those Northern ber'crats knew we was gonna be invaded?"

"Karloff, don't be a jackass. They didn't know anything about it."

Karloff let out a hiccup and waved his hand in front of Lars. "Ya really t'ink three men and a woman could lay waste to two cities and all the Gates in one week? C'mon..."

"I heard there was a fourth man," a merchant called out from the nearest table.

"Right," Karloff wagged a finger, "but tha's still only five people."

Lars sighed and grabbed another glass. He knew enough to ignore drunks when they started babbling, especially Karloff and his half-baked conspiracy theories.

"Well, some of the Gates were caught up in the Paper Riots, you know..." a salt trader added as Lars looked back up.

"Don't matter, it was all a ruse." Karloff leaned forward, and Lars could smell the usual aroma of booze and smoke clinging to his friend. "We're out in this blasted desert," he pointed around erratically, "in a damn sandstorm 'cause those damn ber'crats hired some damn merc'naries to take care o' them damn Gates!"

"My sister married a guy who kept talkin' about how corrupt he thought the government was," the salt trader said slowly. "It got her killed. Toward the end, they were talking about conspiracies and other crazy ideas…just like you."

"So wha' ya gonna do about it?" Karloff asked with a raised eyebrow.

Lars shook his head irritably. "Karloff, you know I don't tolerate fighting in my bar. Anyone who has a problem with that can leave now."

The merchant and a couple others from his table stood up and slowly walked outside. He turned as he pulled the flap aside and said, "We'll be waiting for you."

Just before the tent closed, an old man bumped his way past the angry traders. A gust of wind and a fresh sheet of sand entered with him.

"Oh yea?" Karloff shouted as he got up and made to follow them.

Lars reached forward, grabbed the back of Karloff's dirty tunic, and pulled him back into his seat. "Sit down," he said gruffly, "and have one on the house."

Karloff looked at him and Lars could tell he had more to say. The drunk opened his mouth, but instead of ranting, he filled it with beer. Lars scoffed and looked back at the tent flap. The old man still stood at the entrance, slowly looking around the bar.

*Definitely a new guy…*

The old man wore dress pants and his shirt was clean. His plaid vest was red and purple, but his shoes were an awful shade of indigo. Lars watched the new customer pull out a handkerchief, spit into it, then look inside the used strip of cloth. He replaced it in his pocket and walked toward the bar.

Karloff stirred, but before he could spout out any more rants, the cloaked man rapped on the counter. Lars was more than grateful to have an excuse to walk away from his old friend.

*I'd love to sneak a peek at who the hell my new best customer is…*

Lars purposely undershot the drink so that the man would have to reach for it, then waited and watched as the cloaked man stretched out his arm for the glass. His entire right hand was covered in thick, blackened scar tissue. Lars had seen some things back at Gate Five, like a man who had somehow survived being burned at the stake…but these scars were different.

Lines of cobalt shone through the torn flesh around his joints and knuckles. The scars on the back of his hand made a design like a swirl, and more fissures disappeared under his sleeve. The deepest of these cuts flashed more of that luminous blue. Lars turned away when he realized he was gawking.

The man let out a slight chuckle. For the first time that day, he raised his glass high enough that he had to lift his chin from his chest. His hood and hair fell back, revealing a horribly scarred face that perfectly matched his hand.

Three burn-like slashes traveled from under the collar of his cloak and up the back of his neck. They each took out chunks of greasy hair and parts of his ear as they continued around his temple and up his face. The scars ended just above his right eye.

Lars shuddered and continued to stare.

The eye itself was solid white, with no pupil or iris to speak of. It was ringed by more of that burnt scar tissue, and its eyelid was completely missing. His staring, exposed eyeball made his features seem too large for a normal man's skull.

"…and so, it's really all connected. Leviathan Pass, the Gates, and why us merchants gotta roam the desert now."

"That's brilliant, Karloff," Lars said in a bit of a daze.

When the bartender managed to steady himself, the man gave a slight scoff and pulled his hood back up. Then he reached out his gnarled hand and knocked on the bar, but the noise it made didn't sound quite right.

Lars' eyes never left the man as he poured him another double. He spilled more booze onto the countertop than into the glass. Finally Lars slid him the drink, but it stopped short again. He groaned and readied himself for another look at the horror before him.

*Shit, get a hold of yourself. You've seen worse…*

The dirty man grunted and reached out with his right hand, deliberately shaking the sleeve back to give Lars a better look at his arm.

*Maybe he's a soldier here to escort the convoys. Nordcross kept promising to send some.* He began to feel a little better. *Hell, I bet he's either undercover or off duty…even so, something about this guy makes me a bit uneasy. And it's not just the scars or his crazy eye.*

4

"Excuse me, barkeep."

Lars gratefully pulled himself away and addressed the old geezer who'd just entered. "What do you want?" he asked.

"Name's Guillaume. I'm a miller by trade." Guillaume reached out his hand, but Lars didn't take it.

"Miller? Does it look like anything grows around here?"

"No, I guess not…" Guillaume trailed off. After a moment of silence, he added, "May I please have a sherry?"

Lars reached under the bar for a dusty bottle and a glass. "That'll be two pieces."

"Would you take a small diamond in trade?" the old man asked as he fished a velvet pouch out of his vest.

"We only deal in gold out here," Lars said. "If I started bartering, I'd be up to my ass in goats and salt by the end of the week…so no."

"I get that a lot," Guillaume said with a frown. He fished two gold coins out of his coinpurse and handed them over.

Lars bit one to make sure it was real as his new customer rambled on about some swamp, a mine, and how Nordcrossers don't appreciate fine jewels. He ignored most of the monologue and poured the man his sherry.

Guillaume took a sip before glancing around the bar appreciatively. "This is a lovely place," he mused.

"It's just a tent," Lars shot back.

"Well," the old man continued, "the town is quaint…"

"No, it isn't! The only reason anyone gives two squirts of piss about this burnt piece of land is the well."

"I guess water would be worth more than gold around here."

There was a long pause, and Lars got the feeling that the old man was thinking hard.

*He wouldn't be the first to try to control that well. No quicker way to wind up dead out in the desert. Using free water to dilute booze, then selling it to parched merchants? Now that's legitimate business.*

Guillaume took a longer drink this time, and the look on his face told Lars that he hadn't been in the desert long enough to forget how sherry should taste. Guillaume swallowed hard and set his glass a little farther away than someone who intended to finish their drink would. "That's why I'm traveling out to the Western Frontier," he

5

continued. "I hear there's all kinds of work out there, and a man can make himself a fortune if he's smart."

The dirty man slammed his fist on the bar and Lars walked away to pour another drink, thankful to leave the newest yahoo in a long line of yahoos still to come. Lars turned to Karloff as he filled a glass with whiskey, but the drunk had already, much to Lars' dismay, slid his way down the bar. He sat next to the cloaked man with his back to Lars.

"See, way I heard it…" Karloff paused with a dazed look on his face until a hiccup brought his mind back into focus. "My uncle, see he's one o' them senators, he said Nordcross offered five times what them terr'ists' bounties were to be split 'tween the ber'crats."

The cloaked man stayed perfectly still and Guillaume mimicked him. The three of them were each listening to what the drunk had to say, and Lars guessed that they each had a different reason. All he wanted was to keep his friend from getting a beating…again.

"Lars, m'boy," another hiccup took Karloff by surprise as he turned back to the bar, "ya mind…uh…wazzit…pourin' me another drinky poo?" Karloff's eyes were now set in completely opposite directions and the reddish blotches on his cheeks had spread to his entire face.

"Dammit, Karloff, you've had enough! I'm cutting you off before—"

"Lars, 'lax…I'm fine, ya dig?" The drunk mimed punching, but he fell over in the process. "Jess' like that," he said from his spot on the sandy ground.

"You dolt, you're gonna hit one of these support beams, and then the whole damn tent is gonna come down!" Lars shouted.

Guillaume offered Karloff a hand, and with the old man's help, the drunk clumsily climbed his way back to a standing position and took a seat.

"T'anks, mister."

"Don't mention it. You said your uncle is from the North?" Guillaume asked. "I'm from the North too. What's his name? Maybe I knew him."

Lars saw a greedy twinkle find its way to the old man's eyes, but Karloff didn't notice. He was too busy finishing the abandoned sherry for his new friend.

"His name is Irgoth of Skirn, Order of the Crow," Karloff said as he smacked his lips noisily, "ya heard of 'im?"

Guillaume only smiled and shook his head.

Karloff nodded stupidly and looked back at the dirty man a few stools away. "The hell's your problem?" Another hiccup found its way out of his mouth. "You ain't said a word. I'm sure you got somethin' to say 'bout those terr'ists and…and all the shady shit…"

The man finished his drink as Karloff left Guillaume and stumbled back down the bar, smoothing out his frazzled mustache as he went. Lars made a motion to stop him, but Karloff wasn't paying attention. The drunk's eyes somehow focused enough to read the words that the man had been carving into the wood with his fingernails:

*Their numbers are few,*
*And stained in sin.*

"This feller's a weird one!" Karloff shouted as he read over the scarred man's shoulder. "Oughtta kick his ass out into the sandstorm, thass what I say." He slipped a little as he stepped back and was just able to grab the bar before he fell over again. It took a second for him to recover, and after he smoothed his coat, he stumbled back toward Guillaume and continued like nothing had happened. "Boy, as soon as I go see m'uncle, he's gonna gimme a buncha the money Nordcross gave 'im, I tell ya what…"

A violent twitch from the scarred guy told Lars all he needed to know about his feelings toward Nordcross. For once, the bartender was thankful that Karloff was bothering more than just one customer. He scoffed and reached for the last of his dirty glasses when Jasmin approached the bar. She stood next to Guillaume, drawing Lars' and Karloff's attention. Her face was twisted in a look of disgust as the old man next to her blew his nose and stared at the snot in his cloth.

"Well hello, my dear." Guillaume gave her a friendly nod as he shoved his handkerchief back in his pocket.

"Takin' a break, Jasmin?" Karloff slurred. He put a hand on her shoulder to steady himself as he tried to look her in the eyes.

"Screw off, Karl. You're the last person I want to deal with right now." She gave the drunk a look like she'd just tasted something rotten, then turned to Lars. "Hey barkeep, table four wants three pints

7

of our worst."

Her sour face gave way to a flirtatious smirk and Lars laughed. It was impossible for him not to when she stared at him like that.

"Y'oughtta ditch this loser," Karloff jabbed his thumb at Lars, "and go home with me. I'll show you...a good time..." At this he began thrusting his hips back and forth in the most unbalanced and vulgar style that Lars had ever seen in his thirty years of bartending.

Jasmin laughed first, then Lars, but before Guillaume could join in, a glass burst against a pole above their heads. They all turned to the cloaked man standing next to his stool. He sat down, then slowly and deliberately knocked on the bar for another shot.

"Who th'ell do ya t'ink y'are?" Karloff half stumbled and half pushed the man, who stood back up with a fluid grace that Lars admired.

*Two bottles of whiskey and he didn't even wobble!*

Karloff reached out a hand—to hit the guy or to steady himself, Lars wasn't sure—but in a flash the man's badly scarred fist collided with the drunk's face and sent him into a support beam. A section of the tent collapsed instantly, and those who weren't trapped under the thick canvas ran out from the bar-tent screaming.

"Ah, dammit Karloff, how many times do I have to tell your sorry ass? NO FIGHTING!" Lars bellowed as the screams drowned his voice out. "Shit!" he said under his breath as he grabbed the short stick that he kept under the counter. He jumped over to break up the fight and protect Karloff.

As Lars cursed his bad luck, the cloaked man kicked his stool over and flipped it upside down. He tore one of its legs off with ease.

"Now see here, that's totally unnecessary," Lars reasoned as loudly as he could without yelling. "He's drunk and didn't mean nothin' by it! Lemme get him to bed, don't go breakin' my stools—"

Lars gasped as the man turned his head toward him. The mangled eye shone bright blue. The bartender froze until Jasmin pulled him away. They ran out into the sandstorm with the others as more of the tent collapsed behind them. The sound of shattering glass followed, and the bar's canvas caught fire seconds later.

Inside they could hear the sounds of wood hitting flesh and Karloff screaming. Lars made as if to go back, but Jasmin grabbed his wrist.

"You always said he'd die in a bar fight someday," she said, leading him away.

Lars turned from the pile of burning canvas and his friend's cries. He followed Jasmin into the darkness. It was Chanteclaire, after all; they were in the middle of nowhere. No help would come. The best Lars could hope for was a quick death for Karloff and the fire to finish off his attacker.

\* \* \*

Wind…not like a cool breeze. Hot, blistering, desert wind. The kind that blinds men and peels their skin off. This was a wind that belonged in a desert, a wind that could only bring suffering.

He woke up in the middle of a sandy hell that people called a desert, not knowing who he was, where he was going, or how he had gotten there. He endured the sweltering heat until nightfall, when the sands became too cold to bear. With no shelter and no direction, he continued to wander sleeplessly for days until the weather took its toll and he finally collapsed.

Three nights after he had first awakened, a vulture landed on his corpse, preparing for a meal of rotted flesh. It pecked at the tough scar tissue and the body gave a start. An arm shot up and a hand closed around the bird's throat. When the young man had finished repaying the vulture for waking him up, he started to walk again.

Stars dotted the still, moonless sky that night, and a soft melody played in the boy's head. As the music grew stronger, he began to walk with a little more purpose, all the while admiring the beauty above. As dawn approached, he found himself in front of a cave.

Inside he found a cart piled high with boxes, and leaning up against a broken wheel was a skeleton in a black, tattered cloak. Without a second thought toward disturbing the dead, the boy stole the cloak off the body, which crumbled to dust in response. Then he rummaged through the boxes, scavenging any bits of food that had survived since the merchant's death.

The last box he checked contained a bottle of whiskey, and as he hid from the burning rays of the sun, he made good use of it. In his drunken stupor, he had dreams of green fire, blue lightning, and death. But those were little more than rushed blurs. One dream dominated the rest, a vision so vivid that it was all he focused on for days afterward, trying to decipher any meaning behind it.

He dreamt he was standing in the middle of a land more ruined than the desert. The ground had dried and cracked, forming large, geometric patterns. Everything was covered in a thin layer of whitish dust that stung his eyes and burned his throat. The sky above him was deep red, and the sun shone a dull shade of gold. The only thing that broke the monotony of the desecrated landscape was a lone tree sitting atop a small hill in the distance.

The tree's bark was almost white and had begun to peel back. Its roots were shriveled and dry, and some poked out of the broken ground like overgrown maggots. There were no leaves, no critters around it, not even as much as a single insect crawling along its withered frame.

The nearer he got to the tree, the harder the hot wind blew against him. He screamed, but no sound came out. Time stretched on until the vision shattered like glass. When he woke the next day, he knew his name.

Meyral.

With that and no other memory to accompany it, Meyral spent his time searching for his past. He would join the caravans that traversed the desert, always trying to run into someone that might recognize him. More often than not, all he found were greedy, desperate merchants and castaways.

The only glimmer of hope in his dark and lonely life was the newspapers that he would come across. They were usually weeks or months out of date, but he would read them obsessively. Without knowing why, he kept the articles that had to do with the ongoing war, the Northern Senate, and the emperor.

He also gathered information from the drunken ramblings of old men in bars or around campfires. They would tell the usual tall tales that old men do, but sometimes others would recount more recent stories of the war. Stories tainted with pain and truth.

It was during this time that Meyral first noticed the hallucinations that he could only see with his right eye. Eventually he realized that these visions were the truths behind the stories, histories of places he'd never heard of, and thoughts of people he'd never seen.

Over time, bits and pieces of his memory came back to him, mostly in his dreams. He would recognize some of the people, but others were like names on the tip of his tongue that he couldn't quite spit out. He often woke up frustrated and screaming, terrifying the vultures that tended to roost near him.

When the caravans reached the grasslands, Meyral would abandon them. He didn't know why, but he resented and feared what lay beyond the borders of the Vigrid Desert. Only twice did he try to leave, but with every step he took that strange melody returned louder than he could stand. His body shook until he could no longer stand straight. So, for almost eight years, Meyral wandered the shifting sands alone, stuck in his own personal hell by a force he couldn't fight.

In those eight years, the visions he saw through his dreams languished. They were never as clear as they'd been in the beginning. It seemed that with every memory that Meyral recovered, his eye's visions became more faded. He remembered his father, his childhood, and his friends. He remembered everything until the night he stood under an ash tree in his backyard, with Nordcross making good on their threat to invade. Then there was nothing but blackness until he woke in the middle of the desert, nude and scarred.

* * *

The man in the tattered cloak walked calmly past the corpses that lined the sandy ground before him. He could still hear the screams of the travelers that weren't fast enough to escape his wrath. As their cries echoed back to him, his face split open with a twisted grin.

The darkness above seemed to envelop him and his body shuddered. The bright blue light shining from his eye dimmed until it returned to its white hue.

*What happened here? Where did the bar go?*

Meyral backed up and tripped over something. It was a scruffy man, who, even over the stench of fresh blood hanging in the air, smelled like an open bottle. The corpse stared back at him from the ground with cold, accusing eyes. Meyral yelled as he crawled backward, dragging himself through the sand. When he finally stopped, he turned his sights to the dead bodies scattered all around him.

"By the moons," he said out loud, "did I…no…" Meyral stood slowly. "Did I do this?" He looked down at his bloodstained hands. Without warning, he let out a horrific roar and ran into the night, running from the darkness that haunted him.

11

# CHAPTER TWO: SCARS

While Karloff ranted in the bar, Meyral's eye started to act up again after a year of nothing. He knew the drunk was telling the truth. He knew that the Northern Federation was headed by a group of greedy, old men who sold out their own nation for a few gold pieces. Meyral could even see their faces, some silently laughing, some crying, some pale and shaken. He also knew that, for reasons as mysterious to him as his past, he hated them for it with every ounce of his being. That hate fed and sustained him.

Meyral hadn't stopped once since he had left Chanteclaire. He managed to make it to the port city of Marduk in three days, a journey known to take four by buffalo. His stride was driven by a vengeance that he didn't understand, and even as the towers of Marduk appeared on the horizon, he allowed it to continue pushing him.

It wasn't until he reached the edge of a small wood growing near the eastern gates that an intense feeling of vertigo overtook him and he dropped to his knees. For a moment he could hear the melody he feared so much, but then it disappeared. His sight blurred as his right eye started up again. He closed his good eye and the vision cleared a bit. He could see soldiers in full armor marching into the city while women, children, and old men fled into the night. The vision faded and Meyral stood, pulling his cloak tightly around his body.

Below him a long line had already formed in the morning light, but Meyral wasn't worried. People always got out of his way. He flipped up his hood like he had done so many times before, concealing his identity as a precaution.

Meyral looked up at the banners that flew over the ramparts as he took his place at the end of the line. The flags were deep plum, and as they flapped in the breeze, he noticed a golden snapping turtle in the center of each. He recognized the Nordcross insignia from goods he had seen coming from the east, but seeing it outside of the desert disturbed him.

A short, plump woman in front of him admired a turtle the size of three buffalo stacked up like a pyramid.

"I see you've met Corsair," an old man said as he stepped out from the turtle's shadow. "I'll bet you're wondering what it takes to ride a beast like this."

The woman laughed and nodded. "What gave me away? I haven't seen one of these in ages…"

"Corsair and I, we go way back." The geezer smiled and knocked on his beast's shell, which sounded unnaturally hollow. "I tell ya, there's nothin' a mammoth tortoise can't walk over. Slow, but powerful."

"I believe it," she said. "Tell me, have you ever been to Marduk before?"

The old man seemed surprised that the woman wanted to make small talk, but he didn't let it stop him from talking back. "Yes I have, little lady. In fact, I used to visit this place back when they still called it Drum. It was the first major city to lose its Ardänian name."

The woman nodded along politely as she stifled a yawn.

"It's here that the mighty Errigan River flows out into the sea. You know, this whole place used to be just one pier built by a couple of brothers. Over the years, though, it's grown into what you see today—the most important port in Nordcross' Western Frontier. Goods from inland travel downriver and stop here to be transferred to seagoing vessels, and the other way around."

"If it was such an important piece of the Old Kingdom, then why didn't Nordcross tear it down like the rest of the cities?" the woman asked with a curious look toward the front of the line.

"Yes, well, that's because to this day it's one of the busiest ports in all the nations—north, south, east or west! Tearing it down would have crippled the rebuilding effort, so they officially changed Drum's name to Marduk."

"What do you have in the cart?" she asked.

A waxed and polished wagon was harnessed to the tortoise's back with brass screws. The carriage was piled high with cargo that looked lumpy under the sheet that covered it.

"Cabbages!" the old man shouted. He turned away to check a few of his ropes. "Gonna take these goods to the engineers and architects rebuilding Bonthon—sorry, I mean Lilith. That place is a gold mine, and I want to get in on the ground floor, ya know?"

"An honest merchant heading north," she mused.

"As honest as they come!"

14

"There's a lot of room in that wagon of yours," the woman said. "You don't have anyone traveling with you? A wife or a daughter, perhaps?"

"Wife died," the merchant grunted as he checked the last of his ropes' knots. "Few years back now, come to think of it."

"That's too bad," she replied, although her face betrayed a hint of excitement.

"It's not so tragic," he continued as the woman's face sagged. "You get used to the lonely road after a few years. But—"

When the old man turned back, the woman was gone. She had moved on to the group of people on Corsair's other side. The scrawny old man jeered as Meyral's eye showed him a new vision—he was hiding in a cart of cabbages with Alberto. A younger, unblemished Meyral peered through a knot in the wood as Maxine talked to a man in armor.

*This old man is going to be my ticket to the North.*

"Excuse me, sir?" Meyral's voice had become a raspy, gravelly version of the boyish one he once used. "I couldn't help but overhear you saying that you're heading inland. I'm going the same way, and maybe we can help each other out. I can do whatever manual labor you need. All I would ask in exchange is a trip north."

The cabbage trader eyed him for a long minute before speaking. "You seem strong enough, but Corsair and I can handle it ourselves. I'm not as old as I look."

"I don't doubt that," Meyral said, though he thought the man was every bit as old as he looked. "You said you're going to Lilith? It might look better if you have an assistant. Everyone knows that only successful traders can afford employees."

The old man scratched his short beard. "What do you know about trading?"

"I spent a few years running with caravans through the Vigrid," Meyral answered. "I didn't say much, but I heard plenty, sir."

"Stop sir-ing me," the old man grumbled. "Why are you hiding your face? Are you some kind of outlaw? I don't want any trouble."

"No."

*Not that I know of...*

"I have a birth defect that has rendered me hideous." Meyral pulled back his hood an inch, revealing only his right eye.

The old man reacted like all the others before him had.

"I'm...I'm so sorry." There was a long pause, and then the merchant waved it off. "You're hired. Your first task is to keep Corsair company while I pee."

"You got it, boss."

"Boss nothin', name's Ordell. And you are?"

"Just call me 'boy,' if you don't mind."

"Okay, *boy*, watch the cart!" Ordell yelled back as he ran into the bushes.

Meyral waited nearly twenty minutes for the old man to return. He watched as a soldier with a snapping turtle on his purple breastplate asked the plump woman from before for her papers. She started crying and pleading with the guard, whose captain stood behind him.

"...you can't get in without a travel permit, lady," the soldier explained.

"I left it with my sick mother, she—"

The guard pushed the woman aside. When he turned his back, she darted forward and was immediately run through by the captain's broadsword. There was a look of shock on the woman's face as blood began to pour down her dress.

"Let that be a lesson to you all," the captain addressed the crowd with a booming voice as the woman collapsed to the ground. "There *will* be order here!" He gestured toward the corpse and a pair of young men dragged it away.

*She was trying to use Ordell's travel permits...wait, I don't have a permit. Does he have one for me?* Meyral started to panic. *Does he have* any *papers? Where is that old son of a bitch?*

Before long, Meyral was next in line and Ordell was still nowhere to be found. The nearest guard motioned for the next person to step forward. Meyral looked around, hoping that someone would take his place. Nobody did.

"You!" the soldier shouted as he grabbed his spear from its spot in the soft ground. "Don't make me say it again."

"I'm trying, but the turtle..." Meyral muttered as he feebly tugged on Corsair's shell.

He felt his body tense up just as Ordell appeared at his side. The old man placed a callused hand on Meyral's shoulder and he smiled carelessly.

"It's a tortoise, actually," Ordell explained as he walked toward Corsair. "A lot of people don't quite understand the difference. See, a turtle lives most of its life in or near water. They have fins or the like, and they're good at holding their breath." The old man stepped behind the tortoise, ducking around like he was looking for something. "But Corsair here, he's a tortoise." Ordell's face lit up. He reached into his cart, and when he turned back around, he had a sack of gold in his hand.

The captain of the guard pushed past the other soldiers. "Is there a problem here?" he demanded.

Ordell winked at Meyral and walked slowly toward the captain. Meyral didn't know if the old man had seen the example that the captain had just given, so he tried to grab Ordell's attention. The cabbage trader strolled past him calmly while fiddling with the bag in his hands.

"A tortoise is set up to live in arid regions. Built to store water and walk on sand. Hell, Corsair here will pretty much walk over anything."

The captain fingered the hilt of his holstered sword and glared at Ordell, who didn't seem to notice.

"But from a strictly biological perspective," Ordell said as he wagged a finger, "all tortoises are kinda turtle-like, so I guess my associate was right to a point. But not all turtles are tortoises…well, here are my permits." He finally reached the captain and handed him a blank scroll with a couple pieces of gold tucked inside.

"This all looks in order," the captain announced as he slid the gold into his coinpurse. "Now get this antiquated beast away from my gate. You're blocking trade!"

Ordell leaned toward Meyral and whispered, "Gold talks, boy, remember that."

"Dammit, where were you?" Meyral asked quietly.

"When you hit my age, boy, you'll understand. The simplest of things become tirelessly difficult…" Ordell sniffed once and added, "Let's find you a bath. Come along, Corsair."

When they reached the other side of the walls, Meyral started to relax. Marduk impressed Meyral greatly, which wasn't hard, considering that he'd been traveling through a desert for almost a decade.

The buildings were all round, and some were as tall as the surrounding trees. All the walls were white plaster or stone, and the domed roofs were made of copper, which had developed a green patina from the salty air. The smell of grilled fish filled the streets, which was a much needed improvement after the stench that always followed the caravans and their drunken traders.

It didn't take long for the bustling people to overwhelm Meyral. He stopped under the shade of one of the many trees that grew along the cobblestone streets and simply stared.

"Yes, yes, take it all in, boy," Ordell said as he doubled back for him. "Now let's go!" The old man led Meyral around a corner, and suddenly they were standing at the mouth of the Errigan River. "I know a place on the other side of the harbor where they have hot food, good beer, and soft beds for cheap. Don't dawdle, or we'll leave you behind."

By the time Meyral looked up from the water, his companions had already reached one of the many bridges spanning the bay. Corsair was clearly much faster than he looked. Meyral caught up halfway across the bridge, but he stopped again to watch a tall ship pass beneath them. When he looked over the other side to watch it go, he got a view of the entire bay.

Docks lined the shores, and a myriad of different types and styles of boats bobbed in the water. Rafts, barges, rowboats, and ships floated with the hypnotic rhythm of a pendulum. Banners with all sorts of emblems blew in the breeze, and Meyral stared at the beautiful chaos as the boats navigated the waterway below him.

"Look at it later boy, we need to get a room before they all fill up for the night!"

Ordell had to practically drag Meyral through the streets. When the old man finally came to a stop, they were in front of a row of storehouses. A boy no older than ten waited nearby, and after Ordell handed him a piece of gold, the kid led Corsair away.

"Yes, sir. Home away from home!" Ordell announced.

Meyral realized that he was referring to the dilapidated, three-story building that looked like someone had unceremoniously shoved it between two of the storehouses. A sign read "The Drowning Gopher" in bronze letters.

"You're going to like this place," Ordell said with a wink. When he opened the door to the inn, a cloud of smoke wafted out from the dark interior. "It's a home to freaks of all kinds, so nobody will care about your little problem." Ordell pointed to his face before disappearing into the building.

Seconds later, Meyral thought he was on another planet.

*He wasn't kidding...these people really are freaks.*

There was a man with one arm, a woman who was twice as tall as Meyral, and another woman who was covered from head to toe with hair, all sharing a booth and laughing loudly. A set of twins smoked from a hookah at the next table, and when Meyral looked closer, he realized that they shared one body from their waist down. On the dance floor, two men covered in elaborate tattoos and strange piercings kissed vigorously. When they caught him staring, one of the men stuck out his forked tongue.

He turned to leave, but Ordell tapped him on his shoulder. "It might take some getting used to, but it's the cheapest place in the whole city. And why are you still wearing that cloak? The ass of a buffalo in heat would be cold compared to this!"

Meyral slowly lowered his hood, expecting the gasps and the finger pointing that he had become so used to, but nobody seemed to even notice him.

*Great. The one place I fit in, and it turns out to be a haven for outcasts.*

"Our room is downstairs," Ordell said as he held up a key.

Meyral looked behind the old man and saw a woman the size of a buffalo standing behind a thick, wooden counter. A furry tail swished back and forth between her and the wall, which was littered with empty hooks. Three of these still had keys hanging from them, each with a different number etched into it. Several seconds passed before Meyral realized that the tail belonged to the woman—and judging by the glare she gave him, he figured it'd be better not to ask.

He turned and followed Ordell toward a dimly lit hallway. They stepped down a small flight of stairs, and after passing a few closed doors and dusty paintings, they reached an open room.

"My lucky number," Ordell said with a toothy grin as he pointed at the bronze "13" tacked to the broken door.

When Meyral stepped inside, he was less than impressed. The furniture was dingy at best, with only one small bed and a low dresser. A damaged door leaned against a wall several feet away from the room it once shielded, which was now permanently left open.

"It's not much, but it's safe enough. The bathroom is in there," Ordell said, pointing to the open doorway. "And you can sleep on that...couch." Using his other hand, he pointed to a pile of old, moth-eaten cushions in a corner. "I'll be at the bar if you need me, and hopefully I won't be alone. I've had my eye on Daisy since before my wife passed, but I would never…only now…you understand, right?"

Meyral raised an eyebrow and Ordell stared back at him eagerly. "Who?" Meyral finally asked.

"The owner! You know, the blonde with the big, beautiful, brown eyes…dammit, the woman with the tail!"

He nodded slowly as he recalled the hefty woman.

"Well, the tail doesn't bother me," Ordell continued. "I like 'em big, too, if you know what I mean." Meyral didn't know, and he wasn't going to ask. "Anyway, don't stay out too late. Those river boats don't wait for anyone, and neither do I."

Ordell left the room, and Meyral was once again alone. As he looked around, he spotted a newspaper that had been left on the dresser. He picked it up, amazed to see that it was only a few days old.

Meyral read every page twice, but the only article that even remotely interested him gave a detailed account of the Blue Bandit's latest trail of carnage through the desert. He ripped out the page and shoved it into a half-filled pocket. For a moment he hesitated, and then he undressed and headed toward the bath.

A cracked, wall-length mirror sat across from the tub. Meyral glanced at his reflection and realized it was the first time he had seen it since he'd woken up. He held out his right arm and inspected it—he'd seen his hand plenty of times, but now he could watch the entirety of the cobalt lines wax and wane as he flexed. Four blue lines twisted through the blackened flesh of his forearm and ended just below his elbow. They tapered off the higher they got, until they looked as if they were painted on, but Meyral knew better. Whatever had happened to him had become a part of him.

Meyral turned and looked at his elbow for the first time. Seven lines radiated out to form a perfect circle as he held his arm straight. When he pulled the skin tight, the cobalt from underneath showed through his skin with such intensity that Meyral wondered whether it was part of his skin, muscle, or bone.

He rotated his arm and got a good look at the flat swirl that started on the inside of his upper arm, then moved to his shoulder and disappeared under his shirt. Meyral pulled his grimy shirt, a once-white tunic that he had won in a knife fight, over his head and stared. His eyes narrowed as he studied the lines spiraling around themselves down his torso.

The toned muscle of Meyral's abs had been left alone by whatever burned him. His chest wasn't as lucky. His right nipple was missing, and more of those blue scars circled the side of his chest. They ran down his ribs and trailed around to his shoulder blade in nearly perfect symmetry.

Five cuts, like a large, fiery hand had raked his lower back, ran from his spine outward and then down his flank. He pulled off his black pants, which had never fit him right, and followed the lines. He was still surprised that they simply stopped at the bottom of his hip.

Meyral touched his shoulder with his left hand, then ran it down along his side. He made a fist with his scarred hand and held it up. His arm trembled as his fingers barely touched his palm. The cobalt on his knuckles gave off a slight glow as his muscles began to flex. He clenched harder and completed the fist. The lines up his arm were now glowing, and Meyral almost snarled as he pulled back and punched the mirror. Shards of glass dropped to the floor and he inspected his knuckles.

For almost a whole minute, he stared intently at his flesh. Other than the scars, his skin was undamaged. None of the glass had cut him. He opened the faucet and began filling the tub.

*Lucky shot, I guess.*

* * *

"Get those cabbages onboard, boy," Ordell said as he led Corsair up a separate loading ramp for livestock. "I know you don't like boats," he added as he patted his companion's shell, "but it's either this, or you'll have to run."

The tortoise didn't move any faster, and Meyral got the feeling that it didn't understand anything Ordell said to it. He eyed the ramp warily as it began to bend under the tortoise's weight. Despite its size, it boarded without any significant problems and Meyral disappeared below deck to tie down the cart. As he secured the last of the boxes, Ordell approached him.

"Well, Daisy liked what she saw last night," he said with a sigh, "but unfortunately Little Ordell wasn't working…again. Remember what I said about being old? Well, at least it's not all bad. There are plenty of ways to catch a skalecat, if you know what I mean."

Meyral gave his new boss a weak nod and tied off his last line.

"Saw the mirror this morning," Ordell continued. "If I had to guess, I'd say someone punched it." He waited, but Meyral refused to speak. "I know what it's like to be alone—"

A cabbage fell from a box on top and interrupted Ordell. Meyral bent to pick it up.

"I come from a place not far from here," the old man continued. "When I was just a lad, though, my mom moved us to the North. I never knew my pop, so she raised me and my brothers on her own." Ordell stopped, waiting for a reaction, but Meyral focused only on testing his knots. "Look, I don't mean to tell you what to do, but it might help you to…well, to have a friend." He held out his hand.

"No thanks," Meyral replied with a scowl. He saw a flicker of hurt cross Ordell's face before the old man turned away.

"Yea, it's probably better that way, y'know. Business and pleasure, they never mix." Ordell adjusted the crotch of his patched pants and coughed. "No matter, I'll be in the cabin. Oh, and if you find any rotten cabbages, you can feed them to Corsair. He loves 'em."

After that conversation, Meyral tried to stay quiet and out of the way for the rest of the voyage. Unfortunately, it was impossible to avoid Ordell completely.

The old man would find him and talk at him about the most random things while Meyral performed odd jobs. He would go on about the pros and cons of buying and selling during different seasons, the benefits of the barter system, how cabbage was the best vegetable for you, and even lectured him once on the eighteen or so names the North had for snow.

When Ordell finally left him alone, Meyral's only solace was pulling out his newspaper clippings and poring over them.

* * *

"Did I ever tell you about my first trip out of the North?"

The old man didn't wait for Meyral to respond. In the last few days, he had gotten used to having one-way conversations.

"It must'a been ten years ago, I think. I was just coming out of the Wall when I came across this big, redheaded son of a bitch hollering about how his wife was dying. So, me being the nice guy that

I am, I stopped to see if I could help. Next thing I know I'm back in Gate Five with a massive headache and twice as much gold as when I'd left!"

Ordell let out a hearty laugh and slapped Meyral on the back. Once he realized that his cloaked friend was still silent, he risked a glance at him. From under Meyral's hood he could swear he saw a faint blue glow. Ordell rubbed his eyes with the backs of his thumbs, and when he refocused, the glow was gone.

"I must be getting old," he muttered. "Here, boy, I got you this." Ordell handed Meyral a leather fold with what looked like a bit of bone used to hold it together. "I always see you reading those newspapers, so—"

"I told you, I don't need a friend," Meyral growled.

Ordell narrowed his eyes and tossed the fold at him. "Right, you don't need a friend like I don't need Little Ordell to start working again! You spoiled little…" The old man continued to mumble as he walked away and turned the corner.

* * *

The next morning, Meyral stood on the deck of the riverboat and watched the doxyls out front pull them forward. The dozen or so colorful river-dwellers made mewling noises as they frolicked in the water.

Meyral liked being up top in the early hours of the day. Nobody was around, so he could let his hood down and enjoy the breeze without all the whispering. Meyral pulled out several of his newspaper clippings, read each one twice, then put them away in the fold.

"Boy, Corsair could use a little delousing if you're looking for something to do," Ordell said quietly. He had once again crept up behind Meyral.

"Sorry, I was just lost in thought…trying to remember something about this river." Meyral shook his head slightly. "You really aren't gonna leave me alone, are you, old man?"

"I only worry for the safety of my employees is all," Ordell said with a shrug and a wry smile. "Besides, maybe I could help? I've been up and down this river about a million times, so there isn't much I don't know. Tell me a bit."

"A statue of a knight with one arm and the name Prince Pete is all I've got," Meyral muttered.

Ordell pierced Meyral with a peculiar gaze. "That sounds like complete nonsense to me," he finally said.

"I know."

"Well cheer up, boy," Ordell said with a wide smile. "We should be at the settlement soon. There'll be plenty of work for you to keep your mind busy!"

Meyral grunted. The old man snickered and walked away.

"Prince Pete," Ordell turned around and wagged his finger at his assistant, "that's a good one."

\* \* \*

They reached Lilith as the fifth day came to an end, and Meyral vaguely recognized the scenery. His mind cramped as a memory of Bonthon's docks invaded his head and he realized where they were. In the twilight, Meyral could just make out what was left of the old Ardänian capital: nothing. The ground had been leveled, leaving the place little more than a pier and several large piles of raw materials.

"Would you look at that?" Ordell let out a low whistle and pointed to the unfinished outer wall as workers carried stones toward it. "Someone must have big plans for this place. Bonthon was only half this size!" The old man clapped his hands together and shrugged. "Well, no rest for the weary. Let's get those cabbages off this boat and into their bellies."

Ordell headed toward a handful of purple tents with a large yurt at its center, leaving Meyral to do all the work. As he tugged at Corsair, he noticed that the tents each had snapping turtles embroidered on their sides, and they were scattered around in a sight that Meyral had become familiar with during his years in the desert. A tent city had been erected where the two rivers met.

Meyral unloaded the cargo and rode Corsair toward the merchants' tents, relieved that there were no soldiers in sight. At the back of the makeshift town, a large, two-story house still stood. It looked old and forlorn against the backdrop of the newly constructed section of wall, but there was a candle burning in the upper bedroom. Meyral knew it was still being used, despite it being the only thing around that hadn't been made by Nordcross.

Ordell returned and announced his arrival with a laugh. "Corsair must like you. He hasn't let anyone ride him in ages...including me." The old man turned away, chuckling and grumbling about overgrown lizards. Then he pointed to an unused patch of land. "Set up shop there, use the cart as a stand. And that bundle of stuff there is gonna become our home until we unload these cabbages. Corsair can take care of himself while I go find the mayor of this dump." He emphasized "mayor" by pointing to the large house in the back.

Meyral nodded and got to work setting up.

Ordell walked to the tortoise's head and jabbed a finger toward the giant beast. "I don't want a repeat of Tiamat, so if you see any scalekats, leave them alone! Got it?"

Minutes after Ordell left, Meyral had the tent up and the shop running. He was already selling cabbages when he spotted his employer walking across the camp with another man in tow. A great mess of facial hair covered his otherwise handsome face, and he kept nervously spinning a bulky watch on his wrist. When he came closer, Meyral noticed that he wore a Nordcross officer's uniform that seemed to fit him about as well as a dress would fit Ordell. As he studied the man, his vision blurred.

With his good eye, he continued to see reality, but in his right eye he saw a woman with blonde hair walking behind the guy he assumed was the mayor. She would have been gorgeous, except for the hungry grin on her face and the pointed teeth that twisted her into something monstrous.

"Boy, this is Lieutenant Drazin. Since Mayor Nancy is away, he's in charge, and he has more than generously offered to help us," Ordell explained, wringing his hands together. "I don't want to hold you back from finishing your tour, I'm sure you have very pressing matters to return to in..."

"It's no bother," Drazin said merrily, "I visited Marduk earlier this month, and I don't leave for Arntim until the end of the week. Then at the end of the month I leave again for Tiamat. I've been charged with keeping an eye on the overall progress of the Western Frontier. It's amazing how a kingdom could have survived without even the most basic sewage system."

The interim mayor started to drone on about something that Meyral was sure even Ordell didn't understand, but the old man nodded along nevertheless. Meyral had stopped paying attention altogether, though. As soon as the name "Drazin" had left Ordell's mouth, another figure had materialized next to the woman. He was tall and didn't sport a beard, but he and Drazin shared the same face. The man was everything the blonde woman wasn't—he had kind eyes that made Meyral feel at peace. In his arms, he held a small child with a tuft of blond hair.

It was the first time Meyral's eye had given him conflicting information.

"Boy, did you hear Lieutenant Drazin?" Ordell asked with an anxious glance back at the Nordcross officer. "He's trying to welcome us."

"Sorry, I…sorry."

Drazin eyed Meyral a bit, as did his two phantom companions. Ordell gestured for the lieutenant to proceed.

"Right, as I was saying," Drazin said with a slight bow. "Welcome to Lilith."

"Lilith? No, I thought this place was called Bonthon…" Meyral mumbled.

Ordell coughed nervously. "Excuse my assistant, sir. He's not all there, you know," the old trader said as he rapped lightly on his own head.

"It's no problem," Drazin said with a smile. "It certainly was called Bonthon," he explained, "but Nordcross believes that as long as Ardänian names still hold, so will the spirit of Ardänia." He sighed lightly. "Doesn't matter if we're improving their lives or giving them new opportunities. Pride is a hell of a thing."

"Then why not change the names of Arntim and Tem?" Meyral growled, not even aware of why he was angry.

Ordell opened his mouth to scold him, but Drazin held up his hand. "Arntim and Tem have more…proper histories than Bonthon," the lieutenant answered. "It's just a way to appease the masses. We try to maintain their history while providing an integrated future."

Meyral had no idea what he was doing, but suddenly he felt intense hatred for the squat, hairy man in front of him. "So that's why they burned Tem to the ground, right? To *maintain* it?"

*Did they burn down Tem?* he wondered quickly. *Did I know that? I must have read about it or heard it somewhere.* A surge of emotions flowed through him as a list of names formed in his head.

"And what about Westmore? Berrywillow?"

The names stopped as Meyral saw the man with the child smiling silently at his questions.

"You can't make an omelet without breaking a few eggs!" the old man interrupted, glaring at Meyral.

"You seem to know a lot about Ardänian history, Mister...I don't believe I got the pleasure of your name," Drazin said curiously. He extended his right hand.

A gleam of excitement shone in the phantom woman's bright eyes. Green flames erupted around her and licked at her skin.

Meyral handed the lieutenant a cabbage with his left hand. "Only two gold pieces for a delicious and nutritious head of cabbage...sir."

As he recited the sales pitch Ordell had him memorize, his vision cleared. All that stood in front of him was the lieutenant eyeing him strangely.

"We would never charge you, sir, take as many cabbages as you like," Ordell intervened before Meyral could say anything else. He shot his assistant a shifty look as he led Drazin away. "In any case, let's wrap this up and get those permits, hmm? You said you also manage Tiamat and Arntim...that's fascinating. How are the food stores there?"

The two men walked away, still discussing business.

*  *  *

During the rest of his time in Lilith, Meyral kept mostly to himself. He ran the cabbage trade while Ordell schmoozed and greased palms with the other merchants. Drazin made his rounds once a day, and Meyral got the feeling that he knew more than he was letting on. Before long, the lieutenant left for Arntim and Meyral ran out of cabbages. When Ordell finally showed up that night, he had a bottle of whiskey in his hand and looked like he was already drunk.

"Tonight we celebrate, m'boy!"

"Why?" Meyral croaked as he continued to polish Corsair's shell.

"Put that down and come here," Ordell said with a wave. The tortoise let out a low rumble and Ordell replied, "Oh hush, you." He took a swig from his bottle and handed it to Meyral. "Lieutenant

Drazin gave me a huge advance before he left. He wants me to bring more produce to Lilith! I'm rich—we're rich!"

Ordell shoved a large sack of gold into his employee's free hand. Meyral stared at it for a moment and set it on the ground.

"The deal was for passage only," he explained. "I don't need this."

"Don't be a fool, you did most of the work. It's yours, you've earned it," Ordell said. He noticed the distant look on Meyral's face and asked, "You still plan on going through with it then? Leavin' on some great adventure to discover yourself and whatnot?"

"Take my share and get me a boat," Meyral snapped.

"Phooey!" Ordell waved both his hands at Meyral dismissively. "Alright, alright," he said after a moment. "I can send you as far east as the Nordcross border, or as far north as Lake Effreudia…though I hate to see you go. I mean, what's so wrong with the life of a trader? Gold…booze…women! You could have it all, right here! Well, maybe not here, but you catch my meaning."

"There will be others to shine your tortoise's shell and stack your damn cabbages," Meyral growled.

"I know, but how will I find someone with your cheery disposition?" Ordell winked. "Besides, Corsair likes you. And he's not the only one."

Meyral stared up at the night sky silently.

"I know, I know, you have to go," the old man said. "I wish you a safe journey then. But tonight, we drink." Ordell snatched the bottle back and took a swig.

# CHAPTER THREE: MASSACRE

Ordell kept his promise, and he'd gotten Meyral passage aboard what he assumed was the cheapest boat the old man could find. On the first day of his journey, Meyral found a sack of gold that Ordell must have slipped into his cloak while they were drinking. He cursed the trader's name only half seriously, and a week later, Meyral found himself on the shores of Lake Effreudia at dusk.

Standing knee deep in the water, he watched the talkative captain wave. The man never shut up, but he didn't ask many questions, which suited Meyral just fine.

When the boat was out of sight, Meyral turned to walk the rest of the way to shore, but a toppled parapet caught his attention and he had the strangest feeling of déjà vu. He pulled out his fold of newspaper clippings, but he put it away before he even opened it.

*This lake seems so familiar…but I know I haven't read about it.*

Meyral turned around and gazed into the Quercus Forest. A chill ran down his spine, but no memory came with it, so he continued toward the dark trees anyway. As he slipped into the shadow of the canopy, he heard two voices speaking in hushed tones. He pressed himself against a tree, waiting for them to pass, but they only came closer.

"We need food," he heard one voice say.

"Yes, sir," the other answered.

Two tall, lean men stepped out into the dimming daylight and made their way toward the lake. Both had dark skin, but one man was bald and the other's head was decorated with short, purple spikes. The bald man wore a grey tunic, thick pants, and heavy, black boots. His only other possession was a thin, partially rusted sword that he carried without a sheath. His companion had only a pair of burlap pants and a canteen around his neck.

"Would you like fish, sir?" the shirtless one asked.

"Mahama. Fish, yes," the other said. Suddenly he stopped and added, "Bezta." He turned and stared right toward Meyral.

*Can he see me through the shadow?*

"What is it, Kitsune?" the man with spiked hair asked.

"There is man there," Kitsune grunted. He pushed the shirtless man back and raised his sword. "Only evil hides in dark place," he called out. "I no wish to kill. Walk into light!"

Meyral stepped forward from his place against the tree. He slowly approached until he joined the other two in the light. Then he stopped, slid his hood back, and waited for their reaction.

Kitsune shouted and began chanting something in gibberish. He held his sword in a defensive position and backed up, his wild eyes trained on Meyral.

The other man calmly walked between the newcomer and his babbling companion. "There is a deep pool of hatred in this man's heart," he said quietly, "but it is not for us, sir. He does not wish to harm us."

Kitsune hesitated, then stabbed his blade into the ground, but he didn't relax. He continued to watch Meyral warily, his deep, dark eyes flickering between him and the darkness of the forest.

The shirtless man gave a slight bow. "Hello, sir," he said. "This is Kitsune. He only knows some Commonspeak, as he is a Svirdarker. I am Lee."

Kitsune nodded along, though Meyral wasn't sure if he understood what his friend had just said.

"Mey-x...Max. I'm Max."

Now that Meyral had gotten closer to them, he could see their faces more clearly. Lee looked slightly older than Meyral, and his deep, purple eyes matched the spiky hair on his head. Kitsune's irises were as black as his pupils, and his eyelids were slightly slanted. His skin was a few shades lighter than ink, making Lee's olive skin look pale in comparison. Lee didn't have as thick of a build as Kitsune, though both men looked like they were made of pure muscle.

"Misty Pass," Kitsune grunted with a nod to the northwest. "Dama do dama to nao nin."

"Right," Meyral said slowly. "Me too."

The three men stood silently for a moment. Then Lee bowed again and started collecting nearby twigs. Kitsune knelt down and gathered some leaves in a pile.

Meyral looked back to Lee, who held an armful of thin sticks. He noticed a dark mark on the top of Lee's right foot, and as he stared, he rubbed a hand over his own scarred face.

"It is my mark, sir," he said, answering the question Meyral never intended to ask. Even while gathering kindling, Lee was aware of Meyral's gaze. "In the Island Nations, we slaves are branded on our feet."

"Does that mean," Meyral lowered his voice and leaned close, "this guy is your master?"

Kitsune, ignoring his companions, piled the leaves around his sword, which was still stuck in the soft ground. He pulled a hunk of flint from his pocket and kneeled, then dragged it across his blade. A few sparks fell and lit the leaves, and as a thin trail of smoke rose, he threw a stick onto the embers.

"No, sir," Lee said as a meek smile formed on his tan face. "I was freed by a man as fierce as a hurricane, yet as gentle as the midnight breeze."

"A freed slave, huh?" Meyral muttered. Ghostly music began to play in his head, and he wondered how long he would have to continue being a slave to his demented past.

* * *

That night, as the three men lay silently around the crackling fire, Meyral drifted to sleep. He suddenly found himself in a dark room, and the same moonlight he fell asleep under streamed in through a wall of windows.

*The light here is too...real. But that doesn't make sense.*

As he studied the light in the window, he realized that Lake Effreudia sat right outside, only now it was ringed with buildings and gardens.

"The Great Moon Temple," he muttered as a story his father once told him about the Priesthood echoed in his head.

He turned and noticed that he was surrounded by beds. The room was organized neatly into three rows of five beds, and in each one slept a young woman. He walked around them, careful not to make a sound, but he stopped when he realized that they were all sleeping the same way—on their backs, hands crossed over their chests, and their breathing synchronized.

He stared down at the woman nearest to him. Her long, black hair fanned out across her pillow, except for a few strands that crossed her peaceful face. Meyral felt an overwhelming urge to brush the errant hair back, but when he reached out with his right hand, he immediately pulled it back.

The blackened skin was gone; the scars had somehow smoothed and healed. The sensations and feelings he once knew came back to his fingertips, and he reached up to touch his eye with his right hand. It was once again protected by a lid, and the skin around it was unbroken. Meyral was whole.

As his awe continued, he faintly heard the dormitory door creak open. By the time he looked up, a mob of men had poured into the room and taken up positions by the beds. The man that stopped at the bed across from Meyral was young, terrified, and looked as if he was suffering from some sort of pox. He nervously pulled a silver dagger from the sheath at his hip.

The room grew cold as a man seemingly made of shadow entered the doorway and raised his arm. The young man across from Meyral raised his blade and cut deeply into his palm. Blood ran down his forearm as he lifted his injured hand and wiped it across his brow. He chanted under his breath, and though his voice shook slightly, his bloody face showed no remorse. The air took on an acidic flavor as the rest of the mob followed suit, some cutting their hands and others slicing into their wrists. Together their chants coalesced into a single, pulsing rhythm, and Meyral could feel the hairs on his neck stiffen as dark magic filled the chamber.

"Wake up!" Meyral shouted. He reached out his newly healed hand to shake the sleeping brunette, and to his surprise, her eyes shot open. The two of them stared at each other, and Meyral's jaw fell as he realized that her blue eyes were almost identical to his father's and his own.

In his peripheral, Meyral saw the shadow man lower his arm. Fifteen silver blades stabbed down, but not into their intended victims. Instead the daggers pierced the chests of their owners and identical wounds appeared on the sleeping women. Some convulsed violently while others simply sputtered as they choked on their own blood. Only one had missed its mark; Meyral had tackled the young man before he could finish his ritual. He wrestled the blade away from him as fourteen women died and silence enveloped the chamber.

The priestess rolled out of her bed and grabbed her attacker's abandoned dagger. She stood and cut through Meyral like he wasn't there, and as he spun around, he watched her slice the intruder from his shoulder to his navel. The shadow man took notice and stepped forward, calling out to his dying accomplices.

"Kill the moon witch!" the shadow man yelled.

"Run!" Meyral shouted.

The woman didn't make any acknowledgement that she had heard him. She spun around and pulled a second blade from nowhere, this one made of quartz. A large man with a splintered pitchfork stepped into the doorway and blocked her exit. Undaunted, she dropped the silver dagger and jumped toward him. She grabbed his face with her free hand, and as she leapt off of his chest, his face crumbled into sand and his head followed shortly after. His body collapsed to the ground and he dissolved into a pile of dirt.

The few intruders that still stood, slowly bleeding out, gave her a wide berth as she passed. She paused at the door and pointed her quartz sword toward them, then did a double take when she looked directly at Meyral. She shook her head and disappeared down the hall.

"What are you afraid of?" the shadow bellowed, though his voice now came from somewhere outside of the room. "If she gets away, this will all be for naught! Your lives are already forfeit!"

Meyral bolted through the door and past the mob, searching for the shadow man. The hall outside curved and seemed to go on forever. The right side of the walls were lined with glassless windows that looked out onto Lake Effreudia, and as he sprinted past the endless doors on his left, shouts and cries echoed around him. In one room, he watched as ten men performed the same ritual from before to kill one man who hid behind a thick shield of granite. In another, children were being rounded up at knifepoint.

He caught up to the woman from before and watched as her white robe billowed behind her. Nobody in the labyrinth of halls and rooms wore flowing robes like her, but there were plenty of men like the ones in the dormitory. Three of them barred her path and she slowed to a walk. As she approached them, they dropped their weapons and clawed at their throats. They quickly fell to their knees and their eyes rolled back into their heads. When she passed, sand flowed from their mouths and they collapsed.

A shrill scream came from an open door on their left and the woman stopped. Inside, four men closed in on a small girl in white robes.

"Andrasté, help!" the child sobbed. Dark red flames engulfed her hands, but as she slipped into hysterics, her magic disappeared.

Andrasté raised her hands and the men sank into the stone floor up to their knees.

"Murderers," she hissed. "And children, no less?"

"This magic," one man cried. "You're all abominations! We're *saving* this child from your corruption! We are ready to die!"

One of the stone tiles beneath Andrasté burst, and the debris hovered just above the ground. She raised her right hand and the broken stones floated upward. She made a few simple movements with her fingers, and then the pebbles shot forward at an incredible speed.

"That's what they want!" Meyral shouted frantically.

The floating stones immediately stopped, just dimpling their targets' skin. Andrasté turned and looked right through Meyral, but it only lasted a moment. The little girl resumed her cries for help as the attackers turned their blades back on themselves. Before the sacrifice could be completed, Andrasté brought her hands down swiftly and the men sank into the floor up to their necks. They shouted curses, but Andrasté ignored them as she offered the frightened girl her hand.

"Thank Effreudia," the little girl cried. She wiped her tears from her cheeks and took a deep breath. "I couldn't sleep, and these men came into my room, and then they chased me down the hall and you saved me and thank you, thank you—"

"Rydia," Andrasté commanded coldly, "remember your place, Fledgling. We must leave."

"Yes, Sister Andrasté."

Meyral heard heavy footfalls behind him, and when he spun around, he found the shadow man approaching. With a quick glance to the two priestesses, he ran down the hall. "Come on!" he shouted to distract the monster. "Come after me, coward!"

The darkness split into two entities—one was pure shadow, but the other was a hulking man entirely covered in black cloth. His red eyes and heavy flail turned toward the open door, but the shadow continued after Meyral.

Smoke began to fill the halls and blot out the moons as the temple caught fire. The shadow disappeared in the smoke and Meyral turned back to the door, where the leader of the revolt threatened the two priestesses.

"Dammit," Meyral muttered. He sprinted and shoved the man in black aside, clearing the doorway. "Run!" he shouted to the others.

Rydia turned pale, but Andrasté nodded. She grabbed the fledgling's hand and dragged her from the room as their attacker swatted toward Meyral, but his hand passed right through him. Meyral grabbed him and pulled him into the room, then shut the door. The man shouted and banged on the heavy door, but it wouldn't budge. Meyral concentrated, pressed against the door, then passed right through it. When he turned, Andrasté was out of breath and the door had become part of the wall.

"Andrasté, this way!" a man's voice yelled from down the hall.

Meyral turned and found a pale, grey-haired man in front of the flames. His hands were spread out in front of him, and the tongues of fire that reached forward bent harmlessly away. At his side, a tall man with bright blue hair mimicked him.

"Jude, Pilot," Rydia cried with a sigh of relief, "you're alive!"

"Are there any others, Jude?" Andrasté asked the grey-haired man.

"I checked the men's dormitories and the upper halls..." Jude shook his head sadly as the flames died and he lowered his arms. "I didn't find any survivors other than Pilot. How did you two escape?"

A concerned look crossed Andrasté's face as she looked toward Meyral. "I woke up and caught my attacker by surprise," she said quietly. "How did they get through our enchantments?"

Pilot shook his head. "I don't know. Looks like blood magic, though..."

Then Meyral saw it. Although his skin didn't glow and his eye was back to normal, his mind was torn to yet another place and time. The sun set, partially blinding Meyral, and all he could see was someone in white robes stabbing a sentry in the back. The main gate opened and the shadow man entered the campus moments later.

The vision faded as he once again sensed the shadow closing in on him. He turned away from the traitor to warn the woman. "It was him," Meyral whispered in her ear. "He has a knife, he let them in!"

Andrasté turned her head slightly, as if she heard something, and she turned back to the two priests. "The intruders each had a silver blade," she explained. "Jude, Pilot, may I see your hands?"

"Why?" Jude asked. His voice was steady, but the sudden sweat on his brow didn't go unnoticed.

"Your hands. Now," Andrasté demanded. "This is an order from your superior. Comply, or I will be forced to take action."

Suddenly Pilot lunged forward and a strong gust of warm wind blew Andrasté and Meyral back. Before the priestess could recover, Pilot stood panting over Rydia's incinerated corpse. Andrasté's eyes widened as they lit on the silver dagger clutched in her Fledgling's hands.

"We need to—"

Andrasté's voice caught in her throat as she looked back to Jude. The shadow man stepped out from an adjacent room and smashed the head of his flail against the side of Jude's chest.

"Go..." the priest managed as he dropped to his knees. "Go!"

The roof started to collapse all around them and Jude raised his hands. The rubble slowed, but he was too weak to stop it. Andrasté blasted a nearby door and sprinted through the room with Pilot behind her. She blew a hole in the wall and dove outside, and Meyral followed until they were at the edge of the Quercus Forest.

As they both looked back on the Great Moon Temple, one of its parapets crumbled from the heat of the flames at its base and fell over. Its tip pointed toward where they stood, and as Meyral turned back to Andrasté and Pilot, the mountains rushed forward and the lake disappeared.

They stood on a plateau in the middle of two mountains. They faced the rising sun and Andrasté fell to her knees. Pilot rushed to her side, but they both slowly began to fade, and despite Meyral's shouts, they disappeared.

Meyral stood still for a moment. Then a raspy cough behind him struck icy terror into his heart and he spun around. A rope bridge that spanned the ravine swayed ominously, but it was the shadow in front of it that froze Meyral's insides. The darkness started to fade, and a corpse walked forward from the shroud. Its skin was completely blackened and shriveled, and each of its eyes was solid white. Strings of dirty, black hair hung down in front of its scorched face. As the thing stumbled forward, it reached out one of its gnarled hands.

"Who are you?" Meyral asked, his voice shaky with fear.

"Do you really need to ask?" his own deep, raspy voice echoed back to him.

Meyral stood, paralyzed. Waves of demented pain and hunger rolled off of the apparition and a phrase surfaced in his mind.

*The monster inside my head,*
*The It that wants me dead,*
*It fills me with dread.*

*"MEYRAL!"* the thing yelled.

The two lunged at each other and began to wrestle, but the corpse quickly broke away. Meyral felt a sharp pain in his shoulder and…

…he woke up. He was face to face with Kitsune, both of them out of breath. The Svirdarker had his sword in hand, but its tip had broken off. Meyral noticed a tear in his cloak, between his shoulder and his elbow, but the blackened skin underneath didn't have the slightest scratch.

Kitsune had a cut under his left eye and he gibbered away in his native tongue. Meyral watched his animated body language. The man was furious, but he seemed scared to get too close to Meyral. He repeatedly gestured toward Meyral's arm where the cloak had ripped, and he seemed more transfixed on that rather than his own injuries.

"Indama, shama…" Kitsune muttered when he finally calmed down. "Demon, how is your arm not severed?"

As the faint sound of creatures rustling in the underbrush of the forest reached them, Meyral opened his cloak. "These scars run too deep," he muttered as the other two men fell silent.

He spread his arms and let the cloak slip off of his body. When he was sure the others weren't going to attack him, he removed his shirt as well. When the moonlight bathed his skin, his scars began to glow. The humid air took on a blue tint around him and both travelers gasped.

"They won't let me die," Meyral announced solemnly as he lowered his arms. "A demon, you called me?" he muttered. "No. No, 'demon' does not do me justice."

He pulled his shirt and cloak back on and strolled silently past the two stunned travelers. As he walked toward the forest, he heard one of the others move.

"Jaspar is alive, sir," Lee called out.

"How do you…?" Meyral stopped. He turned and stared at the man's face, which had grown surprisingly pale.

"Just now, when you were so filled with pain," Lee continued. "It was the same with him, only his pain he felt for others…but you look like him, sir. Like the man who freed me."

Meyral flipped his hood over his face with a sour laugh. "He looked like me, did he?"

"I see him in your eyes...eye."

Meyral took one step toward the freed slave, but when Kitsune stepped between them, he stopped. "Where is he then? Where is my father?" he demanded.

"I am sorry," Lee said as he shook his head. "I do not know."

*Is he telling the truth? Moons damn this eye...it shows me things I don't want to know when I don't want to see them, and now it shows me nothing.*

He looked from the fear on Lee's face to the sword in Kitsune's hands and left without another word. Meyral pointed himself in the direction of the toppled parapet to find the plateau from his dreams.

\* \* \*

Around midday, he reached a wall of cliffs that stretched for a mile on each side of him. Meyral climbed a nearby boulder, then two more, and he found a small ledge barely large enough to stand on. He shimmied his way across the pebbled walls until the path finally widened.

When he had enough room to stand comfortably, he rested his hands on his knees and took deep breaths. His arm wasn't as strong or as flexible as it used to be, and that short climb was enough to wind him.

A falcon screeched overhead and he straightened up. He tightened his cloak around him and continued through the mountains until he reached a rope bridge at the end of a plateau. Once again his eye showed him nothing. He crossed to the other side, hoping that the frayed rope would hold, and then he headed north again.

\* \* \*

The trip down the northern side of the Wolke Mountains was uneventful, and Meyral found himself in knee-high grass before the sun went down. The foothills of the Wolke were painted in shades of browns and silvers. Meyral knew he'd been there before, but now he was alone and driven by anger, rather than fear.

He looked out at the Wall and the many banners that lined its perimeter. The blue flags with ravens perched on crescent moons were joined by plum banners bearing snapping turtles. He cursed the North as he turned right, but he could feel something pulling him south. A faint, blue light pulsed far off in the distance, but he could only see it with his scarred eye. He turned back and resumed his trek.

Soon Meyral stood outside of Gate Five. A feeling of dread filled him as he stared at the dark clouds beyond the Wall and wondered if he'd be able to get through. Two dozen guards in plum armor kept watch over the mess of people trying to enter. Traders with their carts piled high, wayward citizens trying to get back home, and whole families of refugees looking for a fresh start were all being turned away left and right.

One by one, as the rejects gave up on trying to force or coerce their way in, they began setting up camp on the south side of the Wall. With the fort on one side and the tents on the other, the Gate City took on a whole new aura.

Meyral pushed to the front of the line, allowing his face to show more than usual to scare people out of his way. As he approached the guards, he shook his bag of gold to catch the captain's attention. When the lead guard approached him, Meyral handed him a blank scroll with most of his coin rolled up inside. The captain slipped them into his purse and waved Meyral on.

*Gold talks!*

# CHAPTER FOUR: ICE

Meyral walked through the fort and into the blackened remains of the Gate City.

*I guess the North is a little slow on cleaning up their messes.*

All of the buildings around him were in a deep state of decay. He quickly walked down the main street and rounded a corner. His vision started to blur, so he closed his left eye until he saw the demolished building in front of him spring to life again.

Images of a tavern floated to him, and he saw Alberto at the bar with a beautiful, purple-haired woman who carried a large axe on her back. Maxine sat at a booth with a sad old man, and his younger self gambled with some shady men. Reaver played a mandolin on the stage, collecting tips.

He stayed where he was for a moment, lost in the memory, relishing in the nostalgia that washed over him like a warm, comforting wave. Then the vision faded.

*A different time, a different place. Nothing more than a cemetery...*

A loud noise came from the alley between the tavern and what was left of its two-story neighbor, and Meyral reached into his cloak. A couple ran out from between the buildings' carcasses, holding hands and laughing. They were filthy with dirt and soot, and in the man's right hand he held an old, dirty bottle that he must have scavenged from the wreckage.

Meyral released the handle of his knife and continued to walk on, not caring to avoid the piles of ash in his way. As he was leaving, he noticed a single, unmoving goat standing back at what used to be the tavern. Meyral studied it for a minute, until a cold wind stirred up a smokescreen of ash. He pulled his cloak closer around him and headed north.

\* \* \*

Meyral had been stuck in a blizzard so intense that it left him wandering in confusion throughout the Northern Federation for an entire week. He had no idea how people in that frozen land were even able to survive, and more than once he'd wished for the scorching heat of the Vigrid Desert.

Everywhere he looked, he could only see a blinding, identical white blur, but when he closed his left eye, he could see a faint blue pulse in the south. It was the only thing keeping him from getting completely lost, but the cold was winning. He could feel it deep in his bones, an icy fist taking hold inside of him. He knew he had to abandon his search for the only place he remembered. Mantrych would have to wait until the storm broke.

He set up camp between two large boulders on top of a hill. Using them as a shield against most of the biting wind, he was able to start a small fire and drift into a disturbed sleep. Every couple of hours, he would wake up shivering. He thought he could hear his name being called from out in the storm. At one point during the night, he got up and took a few steps out into the blizzard. He couldn't hear anything outside of his cave except for the howling wind. As he walked back to his ratty cloak and smoldering embers, he heard a familiar voice call to him.

"Son, I think you dropped this."

Meyral looked up and saw a man he didn't recognize place a log on the fire, which roared back to life and heated up the small cave.

"Do I know you?" Meyral yelled over the screaming wind.

The owner of the voice was young—he had bronze skin and a wide smile. His brown, curly hair draped down to his shoulders, and he chuckled as he bent over. The man pulled a small, leather-bound book from beneath a rock and tossed it to Meyral, who caught it on instinct.

"Go on," the young man urged. He spoke quietly, yet somehow Meyral could still hear him over the storm. "Open it."

The voice sent something crashing in his mind, but as he tried to focus on whatever memory was teasing him, it evaporated into nothingness. Meyral looked down at the book with confusion on his face.

"What is this?" he asked.

The book became hot in Meyral's hands and he dropped it onto the frozen ground. It flew open as it landed on its spine. The pages flapped in the frenzied wind, then calmed and started to turn on their own, as if some invisible hand was slowly flipping through them. He started to see things—with both eyes.

He watched his kid self running away from Berrywillow, clutching a staff with a sapphire on the end and an inscription down its shaft. Then he was riding a barge upriver with Alberto and Maxine. They disembarked and ran north, where they were joined by Reaver. They traveled through the mountains, past the Wall, and eventually they reached a town—Mantrych.

A lone figure stood out against the purplish mist that clouded his mind. A beautiful woman with blonde hair that ran down her back in a solid plait stood before him, draped in a crimson robe that had black ribbons of silk trailing up and down its sleeves. Her red eyes seemed to look directly into Meyral's soul, but they were full of kindness.

*Taryn...her name is Taryn, and there's more...but why can't I see it?*

The book closed and the other man was gone. Meyral walked slowly back to his bedroll as the storm raged on. All he could think about was what or who it was still lingering on the edge of his consciousness.

* * *

The blizzard lifted the next morning. Meyral opened his eyes and groaned as the sunlight reached him. His head was pounding and the dream was still swirling around in the back of his mind. He shifted onto his side and felt something at the foot of his bedroll. When he reached for it, he found a leather-bound book.

Fear racked his body and he threw the tome out into the new snow. He stared at the book for a long time, trying to remember how it had gotten into his bed. Clips of the previous night and his encounter with the mysterious young man returned to him.

He finally left his shelter and grabbed the book as he went. He surveyed the landscape as a light snow fell through the weak daylight. There was a withered grove that grew near the bottom of the hill, but the trees were so covered in snow that it was impossible to know what kind they were.

Down the hill and a few feet away from his camp, he saw

something odd in the fresh powder. He walked over to the object and reached down.

Meyral grabbed a fistful of snow-covered hair and froze for a second. He started to dig feverishly and, with fingers red and numb, he pulled a body from the powder. He dragged it back to his camp as his eye started acting up again.

He closed his left eye and saw blackness. The blackness slowly transformed into two women, one with green hair and the other with auburn—the latter was the same woman he had just rescued.

They were lying under the shade of an almond tree, talking passionately in hushed tones.

*"My father died when I was very young, you know. He left me and went off to battle a bandit uprising from the Black Iron Mountains."*

*"I don't want to talk about it, Rubi."*

*"I didn't talk to anyone about it at first either. For years, I was too brokenhearted, too sad and miserable...but eventually, Taryn helped me realize that living in the past is not living at all. We have to move on."*

*"I..."*

*"Maxine, please. I'm here for you. I know what it's like."*

*"He...he left us to become a thug, nothing as grand as a soldier like your dad...just a thief."*

*"It makes no difference. He was your father, and you didn't have a choice in the matter."*

Tears streamed down Maxine's face.

*"I was never able to be a kid. I missed out on my childhood because Mother fell ill and I had to become the parent. I didn't have Taryn to raise me or to help me."*

*"Neither did I! Taryn didn't show up until a few years ago. But when she did, she helped me see what I still had in this life, even without my dad. You, Maxine, have more than I ever did. You have Bert and Meyral and me."*

Maxine's violet eyes met Rubi's orange ones as she finally looked up.

*"Take control of your destiny, Maxi, or forever be pushed around by it..."*

The vision finally broke. Meyral looked down into the face of the woman named Rubi. She was breathing, but barely. He wrapped her in his cloak and stoked the dying fire.

* * *

About midday, Rubi stirred and opened her eyes. Meyral dropped the firewood he was carrying and made his way toward her.

"You're alive," he said. He couldn't tell if he was surprised or disappointed.

Rubi's eyes flew open and she backed herself against one of the boulders. She pulled a knife from her boot and pointed it toward him. "Who the hell are you?" she shouted, her teeth chattering.

"The guy who saved you, now come back to the fire before you freeze again." Meyral sat down with his left side facing her, a habit he had learned back in the desert.

"Meyral? Is that you? You're alive!" She crawled over and held his face in her hands. "What happened to you?" Rubi asked softly. She ran her fingers over what was left of Meyral's ear.

"I don't remember what happened. I don't remember much of anything, but I do remember you...kind of. I know your name is Rubi, and that you knew Maxine, Alberto and me...but I don't know how."

"We all met in Mantrych—"

"That's where I'm headed," Meyral interrupted eagerly. "Do you know where it is?"

There was a long pause. Rubi looked at the right side of Meyral's face, then her eyes trailed to the orchard at the bottom of the hill. "You're here," she whispered.

Meyral looked around.

*The orchards...is this all that's left?*

"Help me remember," he asked.

She nodded. "The three of you arrived one night with a message for Taryn—"

"The beautiful woman with red eyes?"

"The Taryn we knew was very old." Rubi fixed him with an odd look. "The next day, you started to train under her with Tyler and me. A year and a half later you left for war and...and I never saw you again."

"Until today," he corrected her.

"Yes! Sorry...I'm still a little dazed." She shivered.

Meyral reached to put his arm around her and she looked at

45

him with questioning eyes.

"Body heat…it's the best way to warm up," he explained.

She nodded slowly. He threw his cloak over both of them and held her close to his scarred chest. He felt Rubi reach across his torso, but when her hand found his blackened skin, it retreated and came to rest between them.

"About a week later," she started, "we were attacked. Taryn and I managed to escape."

As Rubi continued to recall her story, Meyral's eye activated. He could see the events unfold as clearly as if he had been there.

"I was on gate duty when…"

Rubi was standing by the guard hut when smoke started to rise from the edge of town.

*"What the hell is that?"* Markus asked as he stepped out of the hut. *"That looks like it's in the direction of Taryn's. Rubi, you…"*

By the time the old guard had noticed Rubi was gone, she was already running toward her master's house.

When she arrived at Taryn's, she found the orchard already in flames. A squad of soldiers stood in front of the house, their spears at the ready and their backs to her. She drew her swords and proceeded with caution, but bodies began to fly through the air before Rubi had a chance to attack.

Taryn stood in the center of the destruction with a scimitar of ice in her hand and a stack of bodies already at her feet. Before the soldiers could regroup, Rubi attacked from behind, and together the two women easily cut down what remained of the troops.

Rubi disposed of body after body until her sword met ice. She came out of her trance and realized that she was face to face with her old teacher and they were surrounded by death.

*"What's happening, Lady Taryn?"*

Instead of answering, the old woman turned and dropped her weapon, which turned to water as soon as it hit the ground. Before she could ask again, Taryn ran into the house. Rubi followed as the warning bell began ringing from the town gate.

"The one thing I loved with all my heart, Mantrych, was under attack and burning in the night."

Meyral realized that he had been drifting through both worlds,

46

and he allowed himself to get taken back into the past, enjoying the lucid imagery that no words could match.

Rubi heard voices coming from outside, so she abandoned her search for Taryn. Drawing her blades, she ran through the front door, but she found nothing. As she re-entered the house, Taryn burst through the second-story window, followed closely by a man in black.

They both hit the ground at the same time and rolled into defensive positions. The man wielded dual swords, similar to Rubi's. Taryn held something in a long sheath, which peeled back just far enough to reveal a glowing sapphire.

Meyral felt his blood run cold.

*"Looking for this?"* Taryn panted. A bruise had already formed on her cheek and blood trickled from her forehead, yet the look on her face was pure ecstasy.

Rubi stepped forward, but with a gesture of her hand, Taryn commanded her student to stand down. Both women's eyes remained on the assassin.

*"Cowards! Attacking civilians without warning!"* Tyler screamed as he tackled the man in black from the side. He knocked the swords out of his hands as the two of them wrestled on the ground. *"Run! Taryn, take Rubi and run! I'll hold them off!"*

Without hesitation, Taryn grabbed Rubi and ran into the burning orchard. The assassin broke apart from their savior, but Tyler didn't let him pursue the others. He drew his greatsword and blocked his opponent's advance.

*"Where are you going, coward? Afraid to fight a man?"*

The assassin eyed his two swords at Tyler's feet. Tyler kicked them back toward their owner.

*"I don't fight unarmed men,"* he snarled.

The man in black reached down for his swords carefully. As soon as his hand closed around the first handle, Tyler attacked. The assassin parried his hits effortlessly, but that didn't slow the relentless assault.

"I notched an arrow as the man in black used one of his swords to knock Tyler's weapon away...he used the other to cut the back of his ankle. His scream was the worst thing I think I've ever heard.

"I shot, but the bastard batted the arrow out of the air without even flinching. He started to walk toward the orchard. Tyler tried to stand, but he only fell back down. I wanted to go back, to help him…"

Tears rolled down Rubi's face. She took a second to compose herself before continuing.

"I tried to rejoin the battle, but as soon as I stepped forward, I felt a pinch on my cheek. I reached up and touched my face…and I was bleeding. Taryn tackled me to the ground, and all of a sudden, the air was filled with throwing knives that came from nowhere. She told me to run…and so I did…"

Meyral could see Rubi and Taryn running through the meadows that surrounded the burning town.

*"We need to head south. I have to go to Ardänia,"* Taryn said matter-of-factly.

*"Fine, anywhere but here!"*

They changed directions and ran with renewed vigor. Meyral stayed behind, watching the women flee, and a new presence stepped out into the moonlight.

A man in black with hundreds of blades strapped to his body joined the other one with dual swords. Blood seeped into the rags around the first assassin's face as he rubbed a particularly large gash that Tyler had given him. The second one bent down and ran a hand over the disturbed dirt where Taryn and Rubi had just stood.

*"Come back, you coward!"* Tyler's voice called out from behind them. *"Fight me like a man! Come back, damn it…"* Tears clogged the boy's throat and his cries dwindled.

The assassins nodded to each other, and the one with the swords drew his weapons. He walked back in the direction of the hysterical shouting while the other sniffed the ground twice and headed south.

"…and we could see the Nordcross army from the hills. It was one of the most awful moments in my life, seeing those murdering bastards and not being able to do a thing about it.

"Taryn never stopped. She didn't allow us a single moment to mourn. She led the way like she knew exactly where she was going, and I followed."

48

Meyral saw a tiny meadow in the belly of a valley bathed in moonlight. Taryn sprinted through the knee-deep field of white-tipped flowers. His old teacher's silver hair billowed behind her as she slowed from a run to a cautious walk. Rubi arrived moments later, red-faced and out of breath. The young woman stopped running and doubled over.

*"Rubi,"* Taryn said breathlessly, *"you have to go back."*

*"But—"*

Before the redhead could finish, a bright pillar of emerald fire burst from the ground. It dissipated into a shower of ash, and a blonde woman stepped out from the smokescreen with a man in black behind her. Blood ran down the assassin's face as he stepped out from the sorceress' shadow with a snarl. He drew his swords from the scabbards that crisscrossed over his back.

*"What do we do, Lady Taryn?"* Rubi asked as she drew her own swords.

*"I already told you, Rubi, run! I'll take care of Sera!"* Taryn yelled.

Sera stared at Rubi for a tense moment and turned back to Taryn. *"A girl this time, how very interesting!"* she said while eyeing the staff sheathed on Taryn's back. Long, thin blades were strapped to Sera's right hand along her fingers, and they made an awful, metal-on-metal screech as she clacked them together.

Meyral could see the fire burning in Rubi's eyes, her desire to avenge Tyler's death, to stay by Taryn's side. Rubi froze, trying to decide whether to ignore her teacher or flee like she was told to.

Taryn pulled the staff around and stepped forward. She started to speak in a language Meyral didn't understand, although he knew he'd heard it before. Sera responded with the same manner of speech and the blood drained from Rubi's face. The redhead sheathed her blades and backed up before running away, all bloodlust gone from her body. Only Meyral noticed the shadow following her as she escaped.

The assassin lunged forward and grabbed for the staff, but Taryn danced out of his reach without breaking her chant. The orb at the staff's tip began to glow and a bright aura surrounded the two women. The fear on both of their faces was undeniable.

*"You have no idea what you're doing!"* Taryn shouted, finally breaking her concentration.

The assassin attacked suddenly, but he was left suspended in midair. Time stood still for a moment.

*"I know exactly what I'm doing,"* Sera replied with a grin.

Suddenly Meyral was left alone in the meadow, amid a small circle of trampled flowers. He spun in a circle once, twice, and on the third time, a bright light flashed from the south.

Meyral found himself frustrated as he returned to the present. He wanted to know more about the ensuing battle, but Rubi hadn't been there to watch and her story pressed on.

"I ran until I was up to my waist in rye grass. I could barely feel my legs. My home was gone and I'd lost Taryn...I felt like I was a kid again, when the man from the militia came and told me my father had died in battle.

"I thought about trying to find you...maybe you made it back to Mantrych, or maybe I could find you in Trosloth. But then I saw it..."

Meyral stood in the shadow of a small mountain. It took him a few seconds to realize that Rubi had collapsed into a ball at its base and was crying. Suddenly she leapt up with a fearful amount of ferocity. Before Meyral had time to process anything, Rubi notched an arrow and let it fly.

He followed the arrow's trajectory into the top of a lone tree. It made the swish of passing through leaves, but the expected thump it should have made when it met a branch never came. A man in black leapt down from his spot high in the tree. He held Rubi's arrow in his left hand and a trio of knives in his right.

She pulled another arrow, but the assassin didn't make a move. He stood completely still, waiting. Meyral felt himself growing anxious as he waited for Rubi to fire. When he began to wonder if the vision had simply stopped, she let it fly. Before it landed, she shot another arrow and sprinted away, not bothering to watch where her missiles landed.

"...a Tracker. That's why I couldn't come back. I would have led him right to you. So I became Jewel of Nasabin, and after a while, I couldn't sense him anymore. Nobody questioned my identity and I didn't question my good luck. So I spent years learning to become someone new…to act impartial to news of the war…to not cry when I heard that you, Maxine, and Alberto had all died. It's been awful."

"Then why are you out here?" Meyral asked as his eye's vision faded. "Isn't Nasabin on the other side of the Federation?"

"I…" Rubi's cheeks flushed with color. "I had a dream. You were in it. You as I remembered you—a boy, like when we first met. It was so vivid. A man showed me a map and I knew where to go. I can't explain it, but it was impossible to ignore. I left town without a word. But that blizzard rolled in and I passed out, and then…you found me."

When Meyral's eye died down, he looked at the redhead. "The man in your dream," he said, "did he have dark, curly hair?"

Rubi seemed to be studying his face, as if looking for something that was no longer there. "I couldn't tell," she said after a moment. "Everything was murky, like I was underwater, but the map was so clear…it seemed so real."

Meyral brushed a lock of Rubi's hair behind her ear as his body relaxed. A soft, warm hand slowly moved across his chest, and deft fingers found the border where his skin ended and his scars began.

Rubi's eyes followed her hand as she lightly trailed her fingers over Meyral's torso and down his stomach. She stopped just above his navel and her hand hovered a moment. Then she wrapped her arms around Meyral's body and put her head on his chest. She fell asleep, and before long, Meyral followed.

* * *

Early the next morning, Rubi found herself underneath several blankets. She could just make out Meyral shivering under the one he kept for himself in the low light of the largest moon. Rubi rose to her feet and covered Meyral with a few of her own blankets before restarting the fire.

Meyral rolled over in his newly discovered comfort and a leather fold fell out of one of his pockets. Rubi picked it up and watched him for a moment, waiting for him to awaken. When he didn't budge, she carefully opened the fold and found hundreds of newspaper clippings. Once the fire burned strong enough for her to see, she started to read.

When Meyral finally woke, Rubi stood over him with

accusation in her eyes. "These things," she said as she held the fold up in the light. "Terrorism...the Blue Bandit...are you...did you...?"

"No," Meyral responded groggily. "Rather, I don't actually know..." He got to his feet and his eyes widened. "But...but you do. You said I lived with you, trained with you for almost two years. Tell me, did I do this? Could I? What about Alberto or Maxine?"

Rubi sat down as tears filled her eyes. The desperation in Meyral's voice was enough to break her heart.

"I need to know, Rubi," he pleaded. "More people might get hurt—innocent people."

She thought back to a conversation she had with Tyler. *"There's a war going on just to the south of us..."* he'd said. *"For all we know, they're planning to drag us in. Are you willing to risk it?"*

*But he wasn't serious,* she thought. *He didn't know what he was talking about...he was just being dramatic, just letting his love for me cloud his judgment. Meyral would never...at least, I know Maxine wouldn't have...*

She looked back to Meyral, still sitting by the fire and waiting for her to answer. Rubi made up her mind and locked eyes with her silent companion. "If all the stuff in there is buffalo dung, then why would you keep it?" she asked.

"I think it's...proof of how the Northern Federation was, and still is, working with Nordcross, to...to..." he trailed off. His fists clenched and he sighed.

"You're saying you believe the story that the senators sold us out?"

"Damn straight."

"Meyral, where are you going?" she asked, finally getting to the question that she'd been dreading all along. "I mean, after all these years, why are you here?"

"That's the same question I've been asking myself all along," he answered gruffly. "And for whatever reason, I've never had an answer. But now I know at least one thing—those Nordcross bastards and their Northern allies are responsible for whatever happened to me."

Rubi gasped as Meyral's wrecked eye flashed blue. The once happy and overly exuberant kid looked at Rubi with his good eye, and she saw the answer there before he said it.

"Revenge." The word hung in the air like a heavy, dirty bubble.

"I will have my revenge on Nordcross and anyone who helped them. I intend to hunt down every member of the Northern Senate that sold out their own country…and kill them. I will have my justice. I will have my answers."

As Meyral spoke, Rubi felt something shift inside her. She was tired of running, tired of mourning lives she had lost. She was ready to live again. "I'm going with you," she said suddenly. She looked at Meyral with her orange, steely eyes, daring him to stop her. "They took everything from me, too. And now that you're back, I…I can't just sit idly by and let it happen again."

# CHAPTER FIVE: BLOOD

Harold took a long look in the mirror. He had looked in plenty of them over the course of his career—to comb his hair, to trim his mustache, or to pluck his eyebrows—but this was the first in a long time that he really looked. He noticed the extra wrinkles that had developed, the bags under his bloodshot eyes, and the streaks of grey in his hair and beard.

His hair, no longer shiny and kempt, had become a stringy mess that hung down his back in a thick ponytail. His beard that he had once taken so much pride in had become little more than a fuzzy bush that sat on the front of his face and chest.

It had been months since he'd done anything that would equate to some semblance of a normal life. He no longer went to the markets or vacationed in the bathhouses of Gaffe, and on top of his work, he had to deal with his awful wife.

Harold had spent the last two weeks holed up in his office, avoiding the trek from work back home. It wasn't the once-in-a-lifetime blizzard whose snow had shut down most of the Northern Federation that scared him. No, it was going home to that bitch that bothered him. Lately she'd taken to nagging him even for the things that he couldn't control. The latest, of course, was the weather.

*If I wanted to hear her opinion on something, I'd have already said it for her.*

If he hadn't been married to her for thirty-seven years, he would have probably had her killed. But he was an old man, and he didn't have the heart to pretend like he cared for her at her funeral, or the energy to go out and pick up a new woman. Instead, he decided to live out the rest of his days in a cowardly game of hide-and-seek.

He left the mirror with a sigh and headed for the assembly hall. Almost twenty years before, he had first entered the tall oak doors, just as he was doing now, in the middle of a line of old men dressed in identical blue-and-gold robes.

*Nothing has changed. I doubt anything ever will.*

The hall was a large semicircle with stairs running down the center. Three horseshoe-shaped tables, each on a level lower than the last, sat staggered on either side of the stairs, and a podium stood at the bottom. Behind that, a stained-glass window depicting the traditional Raven and Moons stretched from wall to wall and floor to ceiling. On the curved walls surrounding the window, corkboards with dozens of large maps and charts tacked to them overlooked the chamber. The corkboards ended just short of the double doors, through which the old men shuffled forward to take their seats.

Each table sat thirteen men, and each seat's position directly related to the rank of the man sitting in it. The stairs didn't divide the tables evenly, forcing the rows to alternate between six and seven seats per side.

*I hate these tables,* Harold thought. *And this asymmetrical, bullshit zigzag pattern. The ranks don't even fit properly.*

The senate was divided into six orders—twelve robins, ten starlings, eight crows, six herons, three ravens, and the owl. The latter was the title given to the elder, and his closest advisors were the three belonging to the Order of the Raven. Robins were the newest members of the senate, although the last time the Twelfth Robin had been inaugurated was over five years before. A new senator was only recruited when another died, in which case each person below the deceased was promoted one rank. Harold was still only the Sixth Starling.

Elder Jarno entered last, accompanied by a man and a woman, both in black-on-black suits. Harold had seen a lot of things, but he'd never seen a couple so young dressed in anything quite that lavish. They certainly made their silver-haired elder in his deep blue robes look ridiculous…which made Harold very happy.

Jarno took his position behind the podium on the lowest level and his guests sat on either side of him. Harold remembered how, over eight years ago, that crazy blonde bitch had followed Jarno in and sat at his right side. She called herself Sera, but Harold was more transfixed on her full lips and the way her dress stretched across her chest than what was coming out of her mouth.

She mentioned something about terrorists from the south and a treaty, but she didn't get a reaction until she informed the senate that they would be handsomely rewarded for their cooperation. All of a sudden, she had their undivided attention and, in only a matter of minutes, their consent.

The only thing Jarno and his cronies wanted to talk about after that was war. The treaty was a secret at first—a few Nordcross Information Officers in plainclothes looked for the fugitives—but before long, the whole thing boiled over into the streets and cities were burning.

A town in the southern part of the Northern Plains had been burnt to the ground and a Clarion outpost was torn down within a day of each other. Nobody could explain how four people—or five, depending on whose reports were being read—could cause so much destruction in two places in such a small space of time.

Then there were the Paper Riots that decimated the Gate Cities. Maybe if the senate had paid a little more attention to their own people instead of chasing shadows, they could have seen that insanity coming. But then again, it all seemed a little too coincidental that a series of riots over a few maps happened the same week as the terrorists' reign of destruction...

All the senate did to protect their country was comply with Sera's demands, though. Harold, along with a few others in the lower orders, refused to be a part of the pact, and they were therefore not given any part of the reward. Something his wife had pointed out every day since.

But years had passed, seasons were changing, and rumors of battle had restarted. Nordcross was becoming restless. Tension filled the air. At the last meeting, the Suits had appeared, calling themselves Will and Farah. They claimed to be Nordcross Information Officers, and Will droned on and on about their beloved phantoms. Farah seemed as bored as Harold felt, but so long as they kept mentioning gold, they had every senator's attention.

Harold had no doubt that this meeting would be about another imminent threat that would never quite come to fruition. In the end, Jarno and his cohorts would come to some inconclusive verdict, involving a necessity for more information and resources to be turned over to the Nordcross Empire.

Harold looked over at Farah as she yawned again, not even bothering to cover her mouth. She noticed him looking at her and she looked back, staring at Harold with her strange eyes—one blue and one bright green.

*She's certainly nice to look at. I wish she would do the talking. I mean, I could listen to a lecture on the life cycles of ice beetles as long as it came out of her cute mouth.*

Harold sighed as Jarno...

*That old bastard, why doesn't he just die? Nothing but a waste of flesh and bones!*

...cleared his throat from behind the podium and called the session to order. Thirty-nine old men, with Jarno bringing the count to forty, sat down. Harold fixed his eyes slightly above the elder, just as he had done at every meeting, to pretend that he was paying attention.

"My brethren," the elder croaked from the front of the semicircular room, "we are in the midst of yet another terrorist threat."

A few dry chuckles echoed from the back of the room.

"This time it is a real threat," Will stood and announced, his slick voice undercutting all the murmurs. "It's not something that we have put into motion ourselves."

"The Blue Bandit is heading north," Jarno added, ending the chatter behind Harold.

The temperature in the room seemed to drop to zero within a matter of seconds. Farah yawned again and stared up at the ceiling.

"Sir," one man piped up, "how do we even know that our information is accurate?"

"We need to cut ties with Nordcross!" a second voice rang out.

"Enough!" Will shouted.

The second man shut his mouth like a bug had flown down his throat.

Jarno raised his ancient, withered arms until the chamber quieted down. "Now, the reason this meeting has come to order is obvious: how do we deal with this threat? Our Wall is designed to keep out armies, not individual psychopaths."

The man sitting directly in front of Harold, who he'd come to know as First Crow Irgoth, stood. "Station archers in each of the demolished Gate Cities and kill the bastard!"

A few weak hoorahs and whoops rose up, mostly near the back of the room, but they were quelled after a quick wave of Jarno's hand.

"We have considered our options," Will explained, "and we have come up with three possible scenarios. The first of which—"

At that moment, the oak doors were thrown open and a swirl of snow blew in, turning the brown tile at the entrance blinding white. Every ancient head turned in the direction of the doors, and every pair of tired, yellowed eyes landed on a dirty man in a tattered cloak. The intruder clutched a Northern-style katana in his scarred hand, which seemed to be glowing blue in spots. Harold rubbed his eyes as the man dragged the blade along the tile.

The doors slammed shut behind him, blocking the view of their now lifeless guards. The man in rags walked slowly down the stairs, making his way toward the lowest level of the chamber. Irgoth stood from his seat with a look of outrage.

"What is the meaning of—"

The man cut off his head with one swift motion. Irgoth's body sat down as if he'd suddenly given up on his objection, but his head rolled down the center aisle. It came to a stop in front of Jarno, who cowered behind his podium. Will straightened his suit and stepped forward, but Farah only rolled her eyes and crossed her arms.

The man paused for a moment and a blue light came from under his hood. He pointed at Will with the katana, Irgoth's blood dripping from the end. "You were at the bar," he said with a gravelly voice. "You spoke with Maxine. What did you say to her?"

"And who might you be?" Will asked calmly.

"I'm asking the questions here," the man snarled.

The Suits were the only ones near him that didn't flinch.

"I assure you," Will continued slowly, "I have no idea what you're talking about. Now, would you please answer my question?"

"I'm surprised. I thought you'd recognize me..." The man in the cloak pulled back his hood. "I'm the Demon of the Desert. Nordcross' worst nightmare. The Blue Bandit."

Will smirked as the monster made his way down to the elder. The senators around Harold breathed heavily, and he could smell the acrid stench of fear. The scarred man shoved Jarno into Will's vacant seat and he stepped behind the lectern. He chuckled, a sickly sound that sent a series of chills down Harold's back.

"You are all greedy, selfish, treasonous bastards," the man announced as he addressed the senate. "You sold out your own country and your own people for a few bags of gold."

"I didn't want to!" someone yelled. "He made us do it!"

"*He made us do it!*" the Blue Bandit mimicked. "The truth is that some of you, indeed, did nothing."

Harold heard sighs erupt around him, but he didn't let his guard down. As he expected, the psycho didn't look pleased.

"But, you did nothing—nothing to stop it. You just...let it

happen." The man tossed a leather fold out of his cloak and old newspaper clippings scattered around the podium.

Farah snatched an article that fluttered in front of her face, glanced at it, then tossed it aside.

"One hundred and thirty-nine newspaper articles, some of which include interviews with members of the Northern Senate, and yet not one denounces Nordcross. Not a single one mentions that Nordcross started this meaningless war, that the supposed 'terrorists' are nothing more than scapegoats…"

"T—terrorists?" Jarno stuttered.

It was the first time that Harold had seen the elder rendered speechless. He began to truly fear for his life, although the Suits seemed almost amused.

"…that they were framed by Nordcross and the Northern Federation so that your *elder* could line his purse!" The Blue Bandit slammed his fists on the podium and a low growl escaped his throat. "If you are not part of the solution, you must be part of the problem!"

Harold's blood ran cold and nobody in the chamber moved. The man slowly made his way around the lectern. The stained glass behind him lit up as the sun began to set, casting him in a demonic glow.

The Blue Bandit reached down and lifted Jarno up by his neck. "This," he said as he tightened his grip, "is for Mantrych!"

Elder Jarno's eyes bulged from his head as he was lifted off the ground. The man shoved the elder against the corkboard across from Harold. He stabbed Jarno right through the chest and pinned him to the wall with the katana. The elder struggled to free himself. He shredded his hands on the blade and soaked the corkboard in his blood. A weak sigh escaped his mouth as his hands finally dropped.

The Blue Bandit turned around to face the rest of the room. Five of the younger senators were already stumbling over each other to try to get to the doors. When they opened them, a young redhead was waiting with two straight swords. She swiped at the fleeing men and their blood pooled on the tiled entrance, melting the snow and turning the slush bright scarlet.

"Fly free, little sparrows," she whispered almost like a prayer.

Harold dove under his table while everybody was focused on the wannabe escapees. The psycho began to whistle a tune from the front of the hall, and then a body fell to the floor. Harold guessed that

60

the sword was no longer pinning Jarno to the wall, and by the screams that drowned out the tune, he knew that the monster had started what he came to do.

Pandemonium filled the chamber, and the whistling was punctuated by bodies thumping against the ground. Before long, the screams died out and the few remaining senators either cried themselves into hysterics or pleaded for their lives.

One by one, the chamber became quieter as the whistling continued without a break. Harold remained completely still under his table, petrified. A head stared back at him from a formerly occupied chair. It was so badly mutilated that he was unable to identify who it had belonged to. Blood started to flow by him from the level above, and a puddle of gore formed right in front of his face. Harold mustered all of his remaining strength to not scream or cry or vomit.

A pair of thick boots appeared in his row and the whistling stopped. Harold heard more footsteps walking down the hall.

"Thirty-eight," a woman's voice called out.

Harold understood. The bastards were keeping count, and they knew there were two more still alive. He didn't dare look, but he wondered why the Suits weren't fighting back.

"What about them?" the woman continued. "They are Nordcrossers, after all."

"I'm not here for those two," the demon responded.

The other survivor yelled and emerged from his hiding spot about ten seats away. From where Harold cowered, he saw a man covered in blood sprint down the rows, throwing chairs behind him as he went. More manic laughter echoed as the owner of the boots walked calmly back to the center stair.

"Help me!" the bloody senator yelled. "You have to help me, you're with the NIB!" He hopped across the middle table and landed onto the bottom one. He slipped on the surface and scattered a myriad of freshly removed limbs as he fell.

Harold risked a peek from under the table. The other remaining bureaucrat reached Farah, who remained seated, and collapsed into a ball at her feet.

"Please," he begged her, "please help me…"

Farah yawned and looked away.

"Here," Will interrupted as he pushed his chair toward the senator. "Use mine."

"Your...your chair?" the senator murmured. "No, help me! Please! Don't you know who I am?"

"Nathaniel Torr, Order of the Heron," Will answered plainly. "You own most of the property rights of the Black Iron Mountains, including the mines. You're a very wealthy man, but gold won't help you here."

"He won't stop with me," Nathaniel panted. "He'll kill you, too. We're stronger together, if you would just—"

"Do you see a weapon on me?" Will asked. He held his arms out and turned slowly around, but there wasn't so much as a crease in his suit. "Do you really think your guards would have let me in armed?"

The whistling restarted and Harold knew that the crazed lunatic was closing in on Nathaniel. In desperation, the senator took his only option to escape. He grabbed the chair that had been offered to him and slammed it against one of the windows. The chair bounced back and hit him in the face. Nathaniel fell to the floor, clutched his broken nose, and cried like a child. The whistling stopped.

"Here, let me help." The Blue Bandit kicked Jarno's podium through the window. The stained glass shattered and formed a gaping hole just beneath the lowest of the moons. He took a few steps back and gestured to the senator. "Proceed."

Nathaniel, still sobbing, didn't move. The man in the tattered cloak picked him up by the shoulders with a grunt and hurled him through the open window. The senator screamed the whole way down, until Harold heard him splatter on the frozen ground eight floors below.

"I do admire your work," Will said from his spot where the lectern had been. "What do you think, Farah?"

"Seems out of control to me," Farah replied. "A bit too sophomoric for my taste."

As the two taunted the Blue Bandit, Harold poked his head over the table to risk a better look. The man took one step toward the Suits and raised his blade.

"You said you weren't here for us, remember?" Will snarled.

"I'm a 'terrorist', remember?"

There was no denying it now—the self-proclaimed Blue Bandit was definitely glowing. Harold didn't understand why the others weren't worried. Suddenly the cloaked man attacked, but Will sidestepped him easily, and a second later he had a tonfa in his hand. Farah stood and drew her own baton so quickly that Harold hadn't even seen her reach for it. Together the Suits were like a horde of angry bees, constantly barraging the Blue Bandit without giving him a chance to strike. Their batons made contact several times, and for a split second Harold allowed himself to believe they might win.

The monster continued on unfazed, regardless of how many times they hit him or where. Harold got the feeling that they were playing with fire, like poking a rabid boarhound with a stick, and he just hoped he wasn't around when the Blue Bandit finally snapped. He heard light footsteps to his left on the stairs, and he quickly devised a plan to sneak out the back while the others were fighting.

"Guard the door," the terrorist's gruff voice called out in between grunts. "There's still one left. If we let him get away, this was all for nothing."

The footsteps from before headed back to the entrance just as the man caught Will by the arm. He spun and parried Farah, knocking her into a back flip. Harold thought she was going to land on her face, but at the last second, she managed to land on all fours with an unnatural hiss.

"It seems we have overstayed our welcome," Will said with a grimace.

"Yea, I'm exhausted," Farah sneered as she got to her feet. "We're out of his league anyway. We're only wasting our time."

As the Blue Bandit turned toward Farah, Will lunged forward and lassoed a rope around the terrorist's waist. He grabbed Farah and leapt out of the hole in the stained-glass window, still holding the rope. The Blue Bandit was forced forward, and he slipped on the blood and gore on his way to the window. He dropped his blade as he braced himself against the broken glass.

Harold watched as blood ran down the monster's good arm, but not a drop could be found on the blackened one. Then the glass began to crack all around him, creating a design like a spider web. Harold prayed to every god he could think of that the window would shatter and take them all down to the deepest of hells. The rope went slack, and with a roar, the Blue Bandit stepped back and grabbed his abandoned blade.

"Are you alright?" his female companion called out from the door.

"Thirty-nine," the man growled back as he cut the rope around his waist.

Harold became vaguely aware that warmth had begun to spread between his thighs. He involuntarily let out a whimper, then clasped a hand over his mouth. Two pairs of boots appeared next to his chair in an instant. He felt a strong arm pull him to his feet and found himself face to face with a monster.

One eye was as white as the snow outside, and it was surrounded by a circle of burnt flesh. Harold opened his mouth to scream, but only a high-pitched whistle came out. He didn't realize it was him making the noise until the woman slapped him and it stopped.

"Harold Prescott, Sixth Starling?" the monster asked as his glowing veins of cobalt dimmed. His good eye was fixed on the nametag pinned to the front of Harold's bloody, piss-soaked robes.

"Y-yes," the senator answered.

The two murderers exchanged looks. "You're not going to beg for your life?" the man asked warily. He fixed Harold with that creepy, one-eyed stare.

"What would be the point in that?" Harold asked.

"Impressive," the woman said as she stepped forward and looked into his face. "Tell me, Harold, what should we do with you?"

"All the things you said today are true. I knew about the corruption, I knew that innocents would die. But I did nothing. Even now, when you killed my colleagues and friends, I hid under my desk and pissed myself. Hell, I'm even afraid of my bitch wife. I'm a weak, cowardly man, and I deserve worse than most." He braced himself and waited for the end.

The one-eyed killer held the katana up for a moment, then wiped the blade on Harold's robes. Harold's eyes widened.

"Do you know where I got this sword?" the Blue Bandit growled.

"No doubt you killed our guards and stole it," Harold answered.

"Do you know why your guards use katanas?" the woman asked.

"It was the choice sword of the first elder, who united the people of the North under one banner."

"What was this elder's name?" she continued.

Harold's fear began to dissipate. He didn't understand the

strange line of questions, but he was just happy his head was still attached to his body.

"His name was Harold," he answered. "I was named for his deeds."

"Do you know what happened during Elder Harold's first battle?"

"He and a small squad of heroes drove out the Tribes of the Monolith. Most of our legends stem from—"

"Wrong!" the auburn-haired beauty yelled, making Harold flinch. "When the man that would go on to unite the North was given his first squad of soldiers to command, he led them right into a trap. That's what happens when the aristocrats are deluded enough to think that ordering around an army is as simple as contracting a new milkmaid. All of his men were killed, and he was held for ransom. But you never heard that part, did you?"

"N-no," Harold whimpered.

"The thing about great men is that they weren't always great," the woman said, shifting her weight. "The first elder had to start somewhere."

"Do you know why we're here?" the cloaked man asked, his gravelly voice bringing Harold back to the edge of fear.

"Vengeance?" the old senator answered quickly.

They both nodded.

"But, but wait!" Harold cried. "You saw them, the Suits! They're part of the Nordcross Intelligence Bureau, the NIB. If you kill all the senators, what do you think will happen? Who do you think will take charge? Don't let your vengeance destroy this country."

The woman nodded slowly. "He's right, you know," she told her partner. "Nordcross would use it as a chance to restart the war and fill the senate with their own puppets. We'd be doing them a favor."

"Yes, yes!" Harold added. "At least with the old senate there were people like me who refused to cooperate with their corruption…"

"Then I have a question for you," the redhead said. "Will you be able to take the initiative to rebuild this nation, to live up to the honor of your namesake?"

Harold looked at his captors. He didn't really have a choice in the matter if he wanted to live.

"I will," he murmured.

The Blue Bandit swung his sword at Harold's head—it was so

fast that the old man didn't have time to react. The blade came within an inch of Harold's face, and he felt blood trickle down his neck. The monster pinned the freshly removed chunk of the old man's ear onto the table in front of him.

"Just to give you a permanent reminder of why you're doing what you're doing," the monster said. As he hesitated, Harold saw a human emotion flit across his burnt face. "Don't believe what Nordcross tells you. I didn't die at Leviathan Pass...though plenty of others did."

Harold's mind whirred and he finally understood what he meant. "You...you're Meyral of Berrywillow."

The monster nodded slowly and turned around. "Don't make me come back here. There are things worse than death."

"We will be watching you," the redhead threatened.
The two of them strolled out of the hall with the air of just having taught a room full of children an important lesson. Harold was left alone, surrounded by what used to be the Northern Senate. He took a deep breath and pulled the katana from the table.

# CHAPTER SIX: REGRET

Rhett poured milk into a chipped mug. Nightmares had been plaguing him for the last week. He tilted his head back and poured the drink into his mouth. As the milk ran down his throat, he thought back to when the nightmares started and immediately hated himself for it.

*Why couldn't I have just kept my damned mouth shut?*

He stared into the mug, his transparent reflection staring back at him from the thin layer of remaining milk, and he remembered it with awful clarity. He had walked into the circular room underneath Azrael. In front of the Black Throne...in front of her.

*"Your Ladyship, the Northern Senate has been slaughtered, except for—"*

*"The senate!? By whom?"*

Rhett knew she was in a bad mood, but he couldn't help himself. He knew he couldn't trust her from the moment she had started drafting him and his old comrades.

*"We aren't sure, but rumors have indicated that it was the Blue Bandit and an accomplice."*

*"And?"*

Since he'd been given the position of commander, it was always the same thing with that bitch. She kept issuing him one impossible task after another. Each time, she wanted more, and when he couldn't deliver, he was the one to blame. He was supposed to be High Commander—he was supposed to be leading the royal guard, not playing lapdog for that siren.

*"...and that's all that we have. But we have a team trailing them as we speak."*

*"FOOL! You think that your men will be able to take him on? How am I supposed to trust your men to do something that you cannot?"*

And that's when it happened, when his mouth outran his mind.

*"How am I supposed to trust you when you won't tell us what we're looking for?"*

That look...he still felt the fire in her eyes chewing on his soul.

He set the mug down and looked out of his window. The park across the street from his villa had become a breeding ground for hoodlums. They were just kids, though. Just spoiled, bored kids. He knew some of them from around the neighborhood.

Rhett stood where he was, in the middle of his kitchen, watching the punks run amok. In that moment, he felt a strong urge to go join them. For a small, infinitesimal second, he considered leaving his entire life behind and starting anew.

The thought was enticing, seductive, and he knew that all it would take was a couple steps out of that door. As he contemplated his escape to a different life, he failed to notice the pair of black, red-rimmed eyes watching him, just like he watched the thugs outside.

"Well, that's never going to happen. Maybe I could become a traveling merchant…like everyone else these days." He yawned and wiped his eyes as he made his way back into his room. "I'm sure I'd have made more in that business than anything that crazy bitch has to offer…"

Rhett lay back down and sighed as his head hit the pillow. He pulled his wife's pillow to his chest and hugged it. He had sent her and their two sons out of the country, but only until things settled down. Her scent filled his nostrils as he hugged the pillow and closed his eyes, waiting for sleep to take him once more, hoping that the nightmares would stop.

Then Rhett's eyes flew open as his mouth filled with foam.

*Poison?*

He finally noticed the other person in his bedroom as his body started to convulse. It was then that he understood what was happening. He'd heard rumors that someone had been harvesting some of the more lethal blooms from Erranko's garden. Rhett had even cleaned up after a murderer that had used one such poisonous flower. On Sera's orders.

*I've had this coming for a long time.*

Rhett's body gave another spasm as his limbs quickly turned black, necrotizing. Seconds turned into days and minutes turned into lifetimes. Excruciating pain crippled his mind, but it was nothing compared to the guilt that had plagued him for so long.

*Ever since I gave that thing to Drazin, I knew this day would come…*

\* \* \*

Alberto had been having the same dream for almost a decade—Chloe and the family that he could have had with her, an assassin, his father leaving, his mother dying...and then Maxine. Almost every night, he saw their deaths playing in his head on some horrible, infinite loop. He learned to ignore it, but some days it would still affect him.

It often brought to surface memories of Leviathan Pass...old memories of the night that his entire life, like that small ledge, fell apart. He had no home, he had no family. He'd just murdered his own sister and his best friend had exploded in a rain of fire. All he had was Aldomein, and she was looking to him for direction.

He had decided to continue to Arntim, as if the devastating battle had never happened. As he made his way back into Ardänia, he ran into refugees—some Ardänian, some Nordcross, and others with no affiliations. Regardless of where they were from, they were all looking for someone to blame for their hardships, and Alberto was convenient.

When he finally made it to the pile of ash and rubble that had once been the center of Ardänian education, he noticed a sizeable group of people around him, watching and waiting for his next move.

He climbed a heap of demolished wood and addressed the crowd. "I know some of you hate me. I know all of you blame me..."

*By the moons, even I blame me...*

"You have no homes," Alberto continued. "You've lost your families. Everything you once knew and loved has been laid to waste."

He caught the gaze of a dark-eyed woman in the crowd. Her hair was matted and she was covered in dirt and filth, as if she'd been sleeping outside for ages.

"But your story isn't unique. It's all of ours." Alberto looked around at the haggard faces in the crowd, each one filled with despair, fear, and loathing. "Nordcross. They take, they kill, and they destroy. And for what? What did we do to deserve this?"

There were a couple of shouts and a few nods.

"But we can rebuild. We can restart. Today, we can choose to begin a new life, because choice is something they can never take away!"

The crowd actually cheered as he climbed down from the heap. Even Aldomein had tears in her eyes.

A large bonfire was built from the piles of damaged wood. Food was scavenged, drink was shared, and soon Alberto and his followers were celebrating the rebirth of Arntim.

\* \* \*

Late into the night, a stone flew by Alberto's head and landed in the fire, but the assailant ran off into the darkness before anyone could react.

"Damned fools…" the man nearest to Alberto muttered. He had a small goatee and grey hair that was slicked back with oil. His eyes were trained on the burning stone, and as soon as Alberto looked up, he grinned. "The name's Valdis."

Alberto shook the hand presented to him.

"You know, they'll always need someone to blame. And unless we get things organized, that's only going to repeat itself. Next time, though, it might just be a boulder that's crushing you."

Alberto turned to Valdis. He momentarily considered urging him to shut up, but the slick man continued before Alberto could say anything.

"I mean, people can't live without order, you know? We need to create some kind of governing body to help and guide these people…to keep them safe."

"You talk too much. I don't like it," Alberto retorted. "Get to the point."

"We need a leader."

Alberto laughed and looked to Aldomein. She stood behind Valdis, staring at the back of his head with a glare etched into her face that almost made Alberto cringe.

Oblivious to Aldomein's opposition, Valdis stood to emphasize his point. "Without direction, we will soon devolve into chaos! Without law and order, we will be no better off than a pack of stray dogs. We need leadership!"

Aldomein scoffed when Valdis finished his quick and emphatic speech.

"I suppose you should lead us?" an old woman nearby yelled.

"I say we put it to a vote. Let the people decide." Valdis turned to Alberto and spoke loud enough for everybody to hear, "Choice, right?"

Alberto didn't have to look around to know that almost everyone there was listening.

"...and I would like to nominate you, Alberto."

Immediately people began shouting. The clamor sounded furious, but one thing was certain. They were choosing him.

"The last thing you want is Nordcross' most hated enemy as your leader," Alberto explained as he vehemently shook his head.

"You're very right," Valdis said as if the thought had just occurred to him. "Well, while we're on the subject, might I suggest something?"

The roars of the crowd died down. When Alberto realized they were waiting on him, he looked at Valdis and nodded.

"I believe you ought to change your name. Perhaps your appearance, as well. You're a rather...discernible person, even at a distance. We can't risk you being spotted, what with Nordcross' wanted posters still scattered throughout the land."

Many people bobbed their heads in approval and Alberto could already see what was coming. In the end, the people chose Valdis as their governor. He set up a small council out of his runner-ups, and they quickly appointed Aldomein as Arntim's Sergeant-at-Arms. Alberto felt uneasy about the new governor, but he had to admit, the guy had some good ideas.

At Valdis' suggestion, Alberto had dyed his hair black and changed his name to Russell. He acted as Aldomein's chief advisor.

Only a few months later, an engineer and a small squad of soldier-workers bearing the Nordcross insignia arrived to help rebuild. Even though everyone was there because of the misdeeds of Nordcross and had cheered for their demise not long before, not a single person lifted a finger in protest. Valdis welcomed them with open arms.

When Alberto found out that Valdis had been friendly with Nordcross the whole time, he wanted to hunt him down and rip him apart. Aldomein managed to convince him that it was unnecessary— she told him to wait it out, to not bring any attention to himself. Grudgingly, the redhead agreed. But when Valdis announced that Nordcross planned on renaming Arntim, Alberto couldn't hold back any longer.

\* \* \*

Alberto had faced armies without a second thought, but as he stood in front of the seven-man council, he wanted nothing more than to crawl into the nearest hole and hide.

"Russell," one man called out with surprise in his eyes, "it's been too long. We haven't seen you near the council in ages. To what do we owe the pleasure?"

Alberto scratched his head and took a step back, but Aldomein gently laid her hand on his shoulder and he steadied himself. "It's bad enough that we have accepted Nordcross' help," he said, "but now we're told the cost is our name? Our history? Our *identity?*" As Alberto spoke, the words began to come much more easily. He looked the councilmen in the eyes and continued. "By the moons, we aren't just going to roll over and die...and I know damn well I won't!"

"Is that a threat?" a younger councilman asked.

"I assure you," Valdis cut in from his spot in the center of the council's table, "this is all for the best."

Alberto could still see the single bead of sweat forming at Valdis' temple, just below his hairline. His slightly wrinkled fingers were intertwined and his breathing was steady, but Alberto couldn't take his eyes off of that droplet hanging on for dear life, ready to fall at any moment.

"Look," Aldomein cut in, "this town means almost nothing to Nordcross. It doesn't export anything. There's nothing of value here and it's not even a great location—which are all the reasons they took Drum, Sweetwater, and Bonthon."

"Right," Alberto agreed, "the only reason these people came back to Arntim was because it was somewhere they could feel at home. You're talking about taking all of that away."

"We have done nothing of the sort," Valdis said. He slammed his palm on the table for emphasis. "Nordcross is an empire that has stood solidly for a great many centuries. Ardänia is decrepit and falling apart. Our lives will be greatly improved if we all just fall in line and adopt a new way of life, a new history."

"Councilman Valdis," Aldomein continued, "may we speak in private?"

Valdis reluctantly nodded and left the protection of the council's stout table. He joined Aldomein and Alberto, and together they proceeded to an adjacent room much less grand than the last.

"You know Drum's current mayor is an old duke, right?"

Aldomein asked at just above a whisper. "Sweetwater is run by a retired admiral, and Bonthon is in the hands of the man that delivered it to Nordcross without any blood being spilled."

"Is there a point to this?" Valdis asked as the sweat on his brow grew.

"Only that your credentials aren't as…impressive as those of your colleagues." Valdis puffed up like a pissed-off rooster, but Aldomein talked over him. "Do you have a direct order to change Arntim's name? After all," she smirked, "'Nordcross is an empire that has stood solidly for a great many centuries.' And you know they don't handle their business simply by word of mouth, especially with a nobody like you." Aldomein rested her hands on her hips and stared down at Valdis.

Alberto towered over the grey-haired councilman. "But if you allow us to keep the name, I can forget all of this. Hell, I'll even stand by you if Nordcross decides to make a replacement." Then he patted Valdis on the back and whispered in his ear, "And you might be thinking it'd be in your interest to simply betray us in favor of Nordcross, but I promise you this: if a fight comes, I will make it my final act to see you dead before the dust settles."

Before Valdis could retort, Alberto and Aldomein strode back into the other room. Alberto looked back and saw Valdis take a moment to smooth his shirt and put on a smile before he returned to his seat.

"Without its schools and libraries," Valdis announced, "this town has already lost so much. We're talking about more than just buildings and people here…we're talking about homes and families. So, until further notice, the proud city of Arntim will remain…Arntim."

\* \* \*

Not long after, Aldomein and Alberto set up a farm on the edge of town, but Aldomein retained her position as Sergeant-at-Arms to keep watch on Valdis. As it turned out, he was more than competent when it came to governing.

In only four years, Arntim was rebuilt. On top of the name, they managed to retain most of its former Ardänian layout, but Arntim took on a powerful Nordcross element. The Argentum Academy and its Thalamus Library were excluded from the designs—per Nordcross orders, copies of which Valdis made sure to keep. Those two establishments would never see the light of day again. The spaces they once occupied became reserved for an open park. Alberto figured it could have been worse.

But now Alberto's head was pounding…or was it? He sat up and scratched his ass. Then he heard it again. Someone was knocking on his door. He wiped the sleep from his eyes and whispered his lover's name. When she didn't answer, he reached over and felt the cold spot where she should have been lying.

Groaning, he made his way out of the room and listened for the sounds of weapons. Caution had become a habit with Alberto, and despite the eight or so years of peace, he always felt a bit on edge. Another impatient bout of knocking reached his ears, and when he made it to the door, he threw it open.

Still half asleep, it took Alberto a few moments to realize that there was a man in front of him. His head reached Alberto's chest and he had a bulky watch on one wrist that he kept nervously spinning. The beard around his chin was dark brown and wiry, as unkempt as always. It was Drazin, Nordcross' head civil engineer, standing before him.

Alberto was mildly surprised. Last he'd heard, Drazin was supposed to be traveling along the Errigan River and visiting the settlements on its shores. He made it a point to visit every town in the Western Frontier once a season, and he had already visited Arntim.

"Sorry to wake you, sir, but I was wondering if I might…" Drazin looked from side to side, as if expecting someone to be hiding inside. "I might be able to come in. I have something important to talk to you about."

"I don't know. I have a lot of work to do." Alberto narrowed his eyes. "These goats don't just feed themselves, you know?"

Only once had Drazin actually approached Alberto personally. It was at a bonfire, a celebration for when they had finished constructing the last building. The booze had run like water that night, though Alberto hadn't partaken in the festivities. Drazin had eyed Alberto like he knew him from somewhere, but he left him alone. A few hours later, he had come back and asked if they'd gone to the university together. Alberto only laughed and asked what the weird machine on his wrist was.

"Please, sir, it will only take a moment," Drazin said. He seemed even more nervous than he had during that bonfire.

Alberto stepped to the side to let the portly man in. "I've got milk if you'd like a glass. Goat milk, that is."

"Don't mind if I do," Drazin muttered. "Thank you."

He followed Alberto into the kitchen, where the big man grabbed a container from the counter. He pulled out a dirty mug for himself and a fresh glass for his visitor. He filled both cups and drained his instantly before wiping his chin with his sleeve. Drazin retrieved a small vial from his coat and pulled out its stopper, still staring at his milk.

"What the hell are you doing?" Alberto asked.

Drazin added a few drops of green liquid that turned the milk yellow. He sighed and looked back up at Alberto.

"I mean no offense, but one can never be too careful in these times," the lieutenant apologized. His voice had lost its skittishness. "I don't want to waste your time, so I'll get right to the point. I have reason to believe that my life is in danger. But more than that, I believe that this entire continent is in danger."

"The hell does that have to do with me?" Alberto blurted out.

"We both know your real name is not Russell, Al—"

Before Drazin could even flinch, one of Alberto's meaty forearms slammed against his neck and pinned him to the wall. His glass shattered on the floor, splashing yellowed milk all over the kitchen.

"What the hell do you want, Nordcross scum? Who else knows? Did Valdis send you?" Alberto whispered, their faces almost touching.

"Stop…please…let me explain!" Drazin managed as his air supply was cut off.

Alberto let him drop and he took a step back, still ready to snap his neck if he made any sudden movements.

"I was promoted—sorry, promoted is the wrong word. More like *forced* to become High Commander when my superior officer died. Their reasoning was that I had been doing so well as Senior Engineer…" Drazin stopped, aware that he was rambling. "I believe you met Commander Rios?"

Alberto stood completely still, but Drazin continued as if he'd acknowledged him.

"Well, after he failed in battle, he was replaced by Rhett, and then—"

"So you're here to kill me? To finish the job?" Alberto asked as he pinned Drazin against the wall by his neck again.

"He's not here to kill you, Bert. He's here to compromise— aren't you, little man?" a voice spoke out from behind Alberto, and Drazin tried to wiggle his way around to see who it was. A tan woman with purple hair stepped out of the shadows and stared intently into Drazin's face. "Treason is a very serious crime, *Commander*." The spite in her voice was like poison.

"I won't be a commander for long!" Drazin shouted back. "I came here because Alberto might be our only hope."

Silence ensued, and Drazin let it continue.

"What do you mean?" Alberto asked slowly as he set the former engineer down.

"I mean just that. The only people who openly opposed Nordcross and survived for more than a month were you and the other Remnants. Sera claims that you all died at Leviathan Pass, but I've always been skeptical about that. I've never trusted her, but I never had any proof."

At this, Aldomein's eyes widened.

The short man continued. "My higher-ups have a habit of dying. The most recent was Rhett, who was killed in his sleep after questioning Sera. His death was ruled an accident, the result of part of his roof collapsing."

"Yea, political assassinations being covered up, what a surprise," Aldomein said nonchalantly. She ran her hands down her tight, red dress that barely reached her knees, and then she tugged at its hem.

"What does that have to do with us?" Alberto asked as his fists closed.

"You know how peaceful it's been?" Drazin responded. "Nothing has happened. The war was called off years ago."

Alberto gave a small shrug of agreement.

"Think about it! Who assassinates high-ranking officials in times of peace when there's no room or motive for political gain? Sera is still fighting a war! She still has a hold on Nordcross troops, and she uses us like we're in the middle of a heated battle."

"So what?" Aldomein snapped. Alberto caught her

absentmindedly fingering the hem of her dress. "She's abusing her power so you betray your own empire? They have bounties on the heads of people like you." She eyed Drazin hungrily.

"It's more than that. Erranko started the war to find and kill Jaspar, right? I know there was a bounty hunter at Leviathan Pass who helped Jaspar escape. I have a hunch that Sera was the one who contracted the mercenary. I ask you, why would you steal what you already have, only to let it go?

"The emperor's wife died over a decade ago, and he should have mourned and moved on, especially given that he has remarried and started a family. Even if his captive had disappeared, it shouldn't take this long. My theory..." Drazin was spinning his watch around his wrist so quickly that Alberto was surprised his arm hair wasn't burning off. "...is that Sera is keeping the wound open to prolong the war."

"Why would she do that?" Alberto asked. "I know she's crazy, but that's just evil!"

"I don't know why," Drazin answered. "Maybe she likes being in control? Maybe she likes causing pain and wreaking havoc? I don't care. But I know it's not good, and I want your help to stop it."

"Nothing good comes of war," Alberto said. He started to shake his head slowly. "What if I refuse to fight?"

"The war will continue even if you don't fight, but the only way it can end is if Sera dies. I'm certain of that much. And you might be the only one who can make that happen."

Alberto clenched his teeth and his hands began to shake. "Get out!" he shouted.

"Pardon?"

"OUT!"

Alberto grabbed the man by his shoulders. He lifted him, less gently than he intended, and set him on the front porch. Drazin turned back, sputtering, but the door had already been shut in his face. He sighed and looked around, making sure nobody was close enough to have overheard. The last thing he needed was Sera to find out he was plotting against Nordcross.

Again.

\* \* \*

Aldomein listened without moving as Alberto stormed about in the kitchen. She knew his anger and understood that he needed to be left alone for a few moments.

*Seven...eight...nine...*

She kept count in her head as he opened and shut each cabinet in order. He didn't always go to the kitchen, but it seemed to be his usual spot.

*Fourteen...fifteen...one...*

Her counting restarted as he reached the last cabinet, paused, and returned to the first. Occasionally he would shuffle the contents of the cupboards, but she knew that all he was doing was blowing off steam.

*Five...six...seven...*

"Never again, Aldomein, I won't do it," he finally called out as he slammed the pantry door twice in a row. "I've already caused too much pain and suffering. I can't go back to that place..."

"What place?" she asked as she leaned in the doorway.

"The place where people die," he muttered.

"You should sleep on it," Aldomein said quietly. "I think it would really help you with...well, it might help you."

Alberto turned to the stove and pulled a skillet off of the rack above it.

"I love watching you cook," she whispered in his ear as she wrapped her arms around his thick torso.

Alberto's head rocked back and he looked at her as if he didn't recognize her, the woman he'd shared a bed with for almost a decade. She pulled away quickly and he cursed under his breath.

"By the moons, you're so quiet when you walk," he said breathlessly.

"Look, Bert, I know what it's like to..." Aldomein paused and bit her lip. "I still have trouble with free will, you know. I can't make decisions on my own." She rubbed her weapon, which she still carried around with her at all times. "Contracts, bounties, missions...they're just orders that I carry out because I don't know any different. Why do you think I followed you?"

Alberto glanced down at her right foot. A colorful tattoo of a tiger lily on the end of a chain covered up her slave brand. He was the only other person that knew, deep in the heart of the ink, in the center of the flower, her skin was still scarred. Her mark was eternal.

"You were there, Aldomein. You saw the destruction."

"I know. I know what I saw. But I also know you, Bert. If you can help end this, then you will. You can't go on pretending it's any other way."

Alberto made to leave the kitchen, but Aldomein blocked him with her weapon.

"One more thing," she said as she pulled a piece of paper from her cleavage. "Drazin dropped this as you…showed him out." She opened the flyer and scanned it. "It's a contract for the Blue Bandit. I'm guessing that's what he came here to give you."

"You picked his pocket?"

Alberto and Aldomein locked eyes. They both knew what was coming. Any mention of their old lives always seemed to put her in the mood for something more physical, but Alberto acted first this time. He charged, but Aldomein was too quick. She shoved him against the wall and pinned his neck against it with her axe.

Alberto struggled, huffing like a bull. Aldomein pressed against him with more pressure, turning his heavy panting into hisses. She felt him growing and she stepped back. Alberto stalked toward her and stopped a few inches from her face.

"You still say her name in your sleep, you know," she whispered huskily.

Alberto's head snapped back like he'd been slapped. "I'm sorry."

Aldomein leaned in and bit his lower lip. She covered his soft lips with her hungry mouth, and Alberto rested his strong hands on her hips. Then Aldomein pushed him away so suddenly that his mouth was still open and his tongue was still lolling out. She turned and her wavy, purple hair, pulled back into a high ponytail, hit Alberto in the face. The smell of juniper forced its way into his nostrils and he found himself uncontrollably aroused.

With a flurry of cartwheels, Aldomein made it back into the dining room by the time Alberto turned around. He eyed her like a thirsty man might stare at an oasis, and she set her axe down and stepped away.

Alberto rushed forward. Aldomein watched him dip down, lift her up by her smooth thighs, and slam her onto the sturdy table next to her axe. She sat up with her long, tan legs spread lewdly. Alberto filled the void between her thighs and held her tight against his body.

Aldomein began to pant. She writhed under him as he bit her neck and shoulders. In one quick motion, Aldomein wrapped her legs around her lover's thick torso. She could feel Alberto fumbling with the laces at the back of her dress and she smiled to herself.

"Tear it off," she breathed into Alberto's ear.

He rested his hands on her shoulders for only an instant before he tore the dress from her body. Her exposed breasts glistened with sweat as she watched Alberto's emerald eyes scan her toned body. He covered every inch with his lustful gaze, until Aldomein reached up and slowly began unbuttoning his shirt. She pulled it up and over his head, then ran her hands down his body.

His muscle had waned a bit in the eight years of peace, but Aldomein loved him just the same. Her deft hands enjoyed every rounded edge of him, until they reached his navel and finally the top of his pants. She quickly untied them and Alberto stepped away from her.

He tugged, freeing his growing bulge, and Aldomein automatically flipped onto her stomach. There was a touch of pain in her heart as she acknowledged once again that this was the only way she could make love. She'd contemplated telling Alberto why, to explain to him the countless atrocities that had been perpetrated against her body and their scarring effects on her soul. But she could never find the right time…and this certainly wasn't it.

Alberto suddenly pinned her down with his thighs and entered her. Aldomein cried out with pleasure as Alberto built up to a steady pace. The purple-haired hunter hooked her smooth, dark legs behind Alberto's knees as she moaned, inviting her lover to lean in and make as much contact as possible.

Alberto put more of his weight on her and breathed heavily in her ear. Their love became strong and animalistic. He pressed his forearm against the nape of Aldomein's neck and sped up while his name escaped her lips like an angry curse.

She could feel the crescendo rising in her lover, one that matched her own. At the last moment Aldomein bucked the bewildered redhead off and kicked him away.

Momentarily stunned, caught between confusion and frustration, Alberto stood there as his nubile goddess grinned mischievously and walked away. She sauntered down the hall, knowing that her backside was Alberto's weakness, and she used all of her womanly wiles to torture him as she went. At the door to their room, she turned back and beckoned him with a finger and a smirk.

\* \* \*

That night Aldomein slept quietly while Alberto tossed and turned, plagued by strange dreams.

He dreamed of a man sitting in a chair on the moon and playing a guitar. Something in the back of his mind seemed to call out to him, a memory from long ago, but it was too distant to reach. The music was soft and low, and it filled Alberto with a sad nostalgia.

"Why am I here?" he asked.

The man only nodded to an orb floating behind him. As Alberto turned, the ball began to grow. It unfolded and transformed into a string of images.

It showed him the past, things that Alberto remembered and guessed. How Nordcross had initially invaded, how the North had betrayed their own people, how relentless the troops had been in slaughtering innocent civilians. It showed him his futures, his hopes, his fears. Families that could have been and children from the woman he once loved. He saw those families taken away, along with the families of others.

Most importantly, though, it showed him the things that Nordcross was doing in the present. He knew, deep down, that he hated it, that he couldn't allow it to continue.

He felt like he'd been watching for days before the blond man finally stopped. The music continued as the images disappeared, and Alberto didn't seem to have much choice. He felt something click in his head, like an arrow finding its mark.

"Fine, I get it. I'll fight. Are you all happy now?"

He could have sworn he saw a smirk appear on the man's face before the dream broke apart and Alberto woke with a jolt. He wasted no time gathering his things. As he reached for the door, something in the back of the closet caught his eye. A small blade reflected a sliver of moonlight back at him. He pulled it from its hiding place and gazed at it.

The hilt was worn and the red symbol at its base was blotchy. The metal still had a thin coating of old and dried blood—his blood. He pricked his finger with the tip, remembering how it had once been stabbed into his forearm. Then he remembered Maxine falling into the ocean for the umpteenth time.

He didn't quite understand why he did it, but he shoved the dagger into his rucksack and left without saying a word. He knew that Aldomein would understand.

*The Blue Bandit...this ought to be interesting.*

# CHAPTER SEVEN: ANGER

It was a long walk to Marduk, but it was the closest major city that still functioned, and Alberto needed information. The Blue Bandit was rumored to be in the Vigrid Desert, and the port was in that direction anyway…but so was Westmore. He hadn't been to the Fauxverite Woods in ages, but he still knew how to navigate them. He marched stolidly, ignoring the old paths he once walked, and only stared forward. Alberto couldn't bear to search for his hometown's ruins.

When he reached the western gates of Marduk, he walked to the front of the line and presented the nearest guard with his official government travel pass. Valdis had given him the permit when he had taken up his position with Aldomein. Alberto suspected that Nordcross could use the permit to track him, but he didn't care.

*Let them find me.*

Alberto walked straight into the first tavern he saw. He had learned long ago that a bar was the best place to get good information, especially on wanted criminals. After all, he'd been one.

When he entered, a group of men were already talking about the Blue Bandit. Alberto smiled at his luck and sat at the closest table he could find. When the server reached him, he ordered a beer.

"The thing is a monster, I tell ya!" the oldest man said. He gestured wildly and spilled a good portion of his drink on the floor.

"Now where did you hear a dumb thing like that? It's just a bunch of jackasses, y'know, same as always, and then they lump 'em together and pin it on a single thing," a second man slurred.

"I was there, in Chanteclaire," the first man said. "I saw it with my own two eyes. It's a demon!"

"What kind of monster could destroy a caravan in the desert one day and then show up a month later and slaughter the whole Northern Senate?" the third man asked with exasperation. "Who d'ya know that could go n' do a thing like tha', eh?"

"A month?" the first man asked as he looked into his mug, wondering where all his beer had gone.

"That's what I heard too…" the second man added. "I guess maybe he's some kinda…devil or summin'."

Alberto stopped listening and waved the server back over. "Is the Blue Bandit really the one who murdered the senate?" he asked.

"Yea, and I'm from Yidtar. He's just a fairy tale, a damned scapegoat. No bounty hunter that's worth a damn is gonna go north lookin' for that asshole, it'd be a waste of time."

The server went back to wiping tables and ignored Alberto's skeptical gaze.

*Of course nobody's looking for him up there…that's all the way on the other side of the continent. Back to Mantrych…back to Chloe.*

\* \* \*

That night, while Alberto slept on a boat heading upriver, the blond man came to him again. He was playing his guitar, strumming the same melody as before. Seven orbs surrounded him this time, each of which shone a different hue of green. The sphere directly in front of him rose up and spread across the sky.

He found himself back in Mantrych, behind Number Twenty-Eight, where he'd spent so much time during those happy days. Footsteps on the wet grass led toward a tree, and he followed the trail to his sister. Her forest-green hair was barely visible through the branches of the weeping willow. A woman shrouded from head to toe in a violet garb listened to his sister.

"…tell her to give me more time," Maxine murmured quickly. "I haven't heard a thing about Jaspar, but she knows where we are. Obviously."

"That's not what she wants to hear. Either tell me where Jaspar is or hand over the staff," the shrouded woman demanded.

"I…I can't do that. I'm not stealing the staff for you."

"Too bad," the mercenary said. "Sera isn't going to be happy. You do know what'll happen if you refuse to cooperate?"

Maxine bit her lip. The wind blew through the branches and brushed the shrouded woman's veil aside. Alberto caught a glimpse of her face, and he wasn't at all surprised to recognize those green eyes with streaks of gold in them. Aldomein already told him that she had been contracted to relay Maxine's information straight to Nordcross.

84

"I'm done," Maxine said. "Jaspar isn't coming back, and the staff is safely locked away."

She walked back to the house and Aldomein jumped up into the branches. A cat slinked out from behind the tree and sniffed the spot where Maxine had just been standing. Moments later, Chloe emerged from the back door and followed the footsteps to the base of the tree.

Tears filled Alberto's eyes as he ran to his lost love. He opened his arms and wrapped Chloe in a crushing embrace, but all he found when he opened his eyes was a heavy mist surrounding him. Chloe continued walking to the tree just as she had almost a decade before as Alberto watched on like a ghost.

"I already knew Aldomein was part of it, you shit," he cried out to the man on the moon. A fat tear rolled down Alberto's cheek, but he didn't notice. "Why are you showing me these horrible things? How in the moons does this even help? It's in the past, I can't stop it. I can't do a damned thing about it. I can't even forget it…"

The vision dissipated as Alberto rounded on the man and his guitar, that haunting melody refusing to cease.

"I was there, dammit, I lived this…don't you get it? Reliving these things is torture! Do I have a choice in whether or not I watch this shit? Do you even care?"

Alberto heard the sound of another orb shattering, and suddenly he was standing in a bedroom. The only furnishings were a bed, a dresser, and a tall mirror, against which Maxine's bow and quiver leaned. A large window looked out on the backyard across from the door, and a magpie swooped in and landed on the windowsill. It warbled for a moment, then ruffled its feathers and relaxed, all the while staring at Alberto.

A moment later, the door opened behind him and his sister stormed in, her dewy boots held in her hands. She grabbed a bag from under her bed and filled it with the contents of her dresser. As she picked her weapons up, the magpie dove from the window and flew away.

Maxine set her belongings on the bed and looked around the room. Her reflection caught her eye and she paused. Several ribbons hung from the corner of the mirror. Maxine reached out and held them in her palm. She stared at the colored strips of fabric for a long time. Alberto knew, despite his sister always reminding him of what little attention he paid, that each of those ribbons held a special meaning to her.

Maxine chewed her bottom lip until it bled. She let go of the ribbons, pulled on her cream-colored dress and her Ardänian shirt, then fit a wide belt around her waist. She turned back to the mirror and pulled one of the ribbons down to tie her hair back into a ponytail. Alberto recognized the black silk, worn and tattered with age. It was the ribbon he had bought her after their first harvest without their dad.

"Why, Maxi?" he asked softly, trying to reach out to her. "Why did you betray us...why did you betray me?"

Maxine didn't answer. Instead she hoisted her pack and grabbed her bow, then sneaked downstairs. She paused at the last step and looked toward the dining room. Her eyes landed on the hulking form of her sleeping brother and Chloe wrapped in his arms.

"Goodbye, Bert," Maxine whispered. She reached for the door and slinked outside.

Alberto reached out, but the world spun and the colors blurred. When everything reset, Alberto found himself on the wrong side of the town's southern gate, where they had first entered Mantrych. Before long, a slim shadow jumped down beside him, and Alberto didn't need any light to know it was his sister.

"I too enjoy a moonlit stroll every now and again," a familiar voice called out.

Alberto and his sister jumped as Reaver leaned out of the shadows. The master thief was smoking one of his thin cigars and he took a long drag. The light from the tip lit the left side of his face. He wore a concerned look, one that looked so unfamiliar on their usually jovial guide. Reaver blew out a cloud of smoke that lingered in the air.

"...although when I do go on these walks," he continued as the smoke disappeared with his apparent unease, "I tend to use the big hole in the wall called a gate." He stepped out into the light with a smirk. "Unless, of course, I have more unsavory plans on my mind."

"How did you know where to find me?" Maxine asked with narrowed eyes.

"I'm a thief," Reaver scoffed, "that is one of my many talents. But as much as I love talking about me, let's not change the subject."

"I'm leaving," Maxine said quietly. "Please, don't try to stop me."

Reaver only continued puffing on his cigarette. He stared and stared, and Maxine's fidgeting only got worse. Alberto could practically feel her anxiety.

"I...I don't belong here," she finally murmured. "I never did."

"Oh? The big redhead, Jaspar's son, the old hag taking care of my staff...they think this too?" Reaver asked as he dropped the cigar and stomped on it.

"They're better off without me." She turned and took a few steps forward, then looked over her shoulder. "Everyone is. Trust me."

Reaver rubbed a rough hand over his scruffy chin. "What makes you say that?" he asked.

Maxine stopped, but she stayed silent.

"A game of guesses, then," the thief continued. "A silly man might assume that this has something to do with an impetuous kiss." Maxine scoffed and Reaver quickly amended, "But I am not a silly man. No, I think this has more to do with a certain young lady named for a jewel that shines with the same fire as her mane. Or maybe," the thief gave a sideways grin, "something you saw in a tree, perhaps a purple-haired shadow? The night can play such strange tricks on these old eyes of mine."

"I can explain—" Maxine stammered.

Reaver held up a hand and closed his eyes. "Please. I neither need nor want it."

Maxine closed her mouth and shifted her pack.

"The less I know, the more I don't have to tell," Reaver continued. "But do explain how running away has solved anything...ever."

"I'm not running," Maxine snapped. "I've made...certain agreements. I can't go back on my word or people will die, but I can't betray my family, my friends..."

"Like Rubi?" the thief prodded softly.

"Yes," Maxine answered solemnly. "If I don't leave, someone I care about will get hurt. If I go..."

"The burden is always yours to bear, isn't it?"

Tears rolled down Maxine's face. "Damn you, Reaver."

"Tell me," he said, his tone regaining its usual, upbeat rhythm, "before you made these *agreements*, were Meyral and Alberto safe? If you disappear in the middle of the night, will their pursuers just give up? Do you suppose they'll just say, 'Well, we lost Maxine. I guess it's time for a spot of tea before we make our next move.' Is that what you're imagining?" Reaver raised his eyebrows and waited.

"That would be..." Maxine bit her lip and looked at the ground. "No, of course not."

"So if Nordcross attacks here, and you're gone...?"

"Who said anything about Nordcross?" Maxine asked quickly.

"Deflecting," Reaver said in a singsong voice.

Maxine shrugged. "There would be one less bow to protect them."

"You're more than just a bow, Maxine. Imagine, just for a moment, that you did leave. Then, while you're away, something happens—maybe they come looking for you, or someone comes looking for them—and then they're gone forever."

Tears shimmered in Maxine's violet eyes.

"You would carry that with you the rest of your life," the rogue continued. "A pile of rocks like that sitting on your conscience...now *that* would be a burden to bear." Reaver stepped closer. "One more question, Maxine. When you look at yourself in the mirror, what do you see?"

Maxine let out a soft grunt as she looked up to the moons, as if the floating orbs might give her an answer. After several tries, Maxine's face sagged. "I see a coward," she managed.

"What would you like to see?"

She looked up into Reaver's orange-and-black eyes and took a deep breath. "Someone who fights for what they want."

"Then become that someone. Fight...and win. A martyr is useless in these times."

"I hate it when you're right," she muttered.

Reaver clapped a hand on Maxine's shoulder and the vision exploded in an array of bright colors. A nostalgic melody filled the air, and Alberto stared at the blond man with watery eyes.

"I already knew Aldomein was part of it...but Maxine refused to help her. She...she still..."

He felt anger forming in the pit of his stomach. It made his heart beat too fast. He tried to regain control, but all he could hear was his heartbeat and the music. The melody was soothing enough, but, like him, he could hear an undertone of rage in the chords.

"She was going to leave us, but Reaver convinced her to stay?" His hands clenched into fists and blood dripped through his fingers. "If she had left, I would have gone looking for her. I could have taken

88

Chloe with me. I would have never gone to Trosloth, I could have protected her. Maxine would have never been at Leviathan Pass..." Alberto stopped as something else wormed its way into his mind. A laugh that wasn't entirely his started in his chest and climbed out of his mouth. "Ha! You see, you filthy son of a whore, none of it can be changed. The past is set. Chloe died and Maxine betrayed us!"

Then anger shot up from his stomach and into his throat like a phantom heartburn. He was at his boiling point. The blond man knew it. His notes perfectly matched every emotion, even as they changed. Everything around Alberto grew fuzzy and he heard a faint voice in his head.

*"You have to control your emotions, Alberto. It's the only way we're going to be able to communicate."*

Alberto opened his eyes and found himself in front of one of the boat's main supports. Several terrified pairs of eyes stared at him from the darkness below deck. Something dark and sticky inhabited the three deep dents in the pillar, and it took Alberto a moment to realize it was his blood. His knuckles were split and bleeding. He looked around, opened his mouth to apologize to his fellow passengers, then reconsidered. He slipped into his bunk and closed his eyes without a word.

* * *

The rest of the boat ride was uneventful. Alberto dreamed the same dreams he'd had since Leviathan Pass, and when the ferry stopped, he happily disembarked.

"Bonthon...the one place I'm glad to see wiped off the map," Alberto muttered to himself.

"Did you say something, young man?" a croaky voice asked.

Alberto looked to his left and found himself face to face with an overgrown tortoise. "What the hell?" he shouted in surprise.

"His name is Corsair," an old man announced from the tortoise's other side, "and he takes up quite a bit of room if you haven't noticed. Would you mind stepping aside? I've got a big shipment of cabbages here."

Alberto stepped out of the way as Corsair walked down the ramp with three carts of produce harnessed behind him.

"Sorry about that," the merchant continued with an honest

smile. "The name's Ordell, and cabbages are my game! What brings you to—"

"If you want to be helpful, old man, tell me where the nearest place is that I can get a drink," Alberto grumbled.

"Have we met before?" Ordell asked as he squinted at Alberto and seemed to ignore the big man's tone.

"Don't think so," Alberto said quietly as he fiddled with his pack.

"No, I've definitely seen you some—"

"My hair's black, dammit!" As soon as the words had left his mouth, Alberto regretted it.

"Sorry?"

"People always say that," he said, but then quickly began to recant. "I mean, they tell me my hair should be red, as if they recognize me from somewhere. But my hair's not red, so it isn't me. Now," Alberto turned abruptly, "where's the bar?"

"I'm actually headed there myself," Ordell answered as he eyed Alberto suspiciously. "Nothing like a shot of whiskey after a long trip, am I right?"

Alberto didn't budge.

"The place is called 'The Third Tent on the Right,'" Ordell added.

"Sounds easy enough to find," Alberto said. He turned and started down the path away from the docks.

"It's not actually the third tent from anything," Ordell yelled after him. "It's just a name, but like I said, I'm headed there now. You're more than welcome to follow me."

"Shouldn't you be tending to your turtle?" the big man spat back.

"Tortoise, actually. And no, Corsair knows what he's doing."

"Why?" Alberto demanded forcefully.

"Why what?" Ordell asked, confused.

"Why are you trying to help me? I'm a complete stranger to you."

"It's like you said," the old man explained, "you're looking for a bar. I happen to be heading there. It's a lot easier for me to lead you there than give you directions through this mess of a shanty town, but if you don't want my help then forget it!" The old man stomped past Alberto and mumbled, "Good for nothing…spoiled little…why even bother…no skin off my nose…"

Alberto shrugged and took three long strides to catch up. He let Ordell lead him to one of many identical buildings, this one with the unmistakable shouts of drunken men spilling out of it. Alberto grinned and held the door open for his new friend as he took a minute to look around the bar.

The building was one large, simple room with stained walls and wooden floors. Dirty, mud-spattered workers sat at a bar that rested against the south wall. Across the room was a section of raised floor that acted as a stage, and three tables took up most of the room in between. A group of well-dressed men sat at the cluster of tables.

Ordell led Alberto to a pair of empty stools, where he ordered two shots of whiskey. He passed Alberto a drink and sipped on his own.

"Where ya from, boy?" Ordell asked. "The Federation?"

"Not a chance," Alberto replied. He raised the glass to his lips and tilted his head back. "This is the farthest north I've ever been. Spent my life hunting gorillas in Callula."

"So what brings you to Lilith?" Ordell asked.

"Business," Alberto answered abruptly.

Ordell sipped his shot as a soft voice carried from across the room. Alberto followed the old man's gaze to a boy on the stage. His hands looked as if they had been stained black, and smears of dirt covered his arms and face. Grey fabric, almost like a pillowcase, hung from his malnourished frame. He cast timid glances at the wealthy men in front of him as he sang for the bar.

*"For lands so rich and pure*
*For love to all endure*
*The gods saw fit to craft a man*
*Gave unto him the very land*
*With a heart so proud and true*
*An empire fit for them, he grew."*

"That's funny," Ordell said as he clinked his empty glass on the bar. "You're the second person I know of heading upriver without a cart or a single bag of goods to trade."

Alberto threw a sideways glance at the old man. "Who was the first?"

"Oh, just some drifter. He helped me sell some produce." Ordell caught the bartender's attention and ordered another round. "Cabbages are m'business, after all. Care to buy some greens for the trip ahead? I managed to get my hands on these carrots, see—"

"Ladies, join the boy!" a high-pitched voice yelled out. Its owner wore a tall top hat, and as the three women around his table danced their way to the stage, the man threw a handful of gold at the singer. He laughed as the boy flinched and dove to retrieve the coins.

Alberto watched the sad spectacle as the boy gazed helplessly toward the men at the bar. When he caught his breath and steadied himself, he continued to sing.

As soon as the bartender set his glass down, Alberto took his second shot. "No thanks," he finally said, answering Ordell's half-forgotten question. He set his glass down and stared at the old man with all the malice he could muster. "I want to hear more about the guy who went north."

Ordell stared right back. "You know, I've been in some hairy negotiations before," he said between sips of his whiskey. "Nearly lost my ears once to a Svirdarker...no dirty look from some kid is gonna make me crack. Besides, would you look at that?"

The old man pointed to the women dancing clumsily in front of the stage. Alberto, however, turned his sights back to the short man with the top hat.

> *"Lawrence, Lawrence,*
> *Cygnus, they reigned.*
> *With fire and ice,*
> *Our land they claimed.*
>
> *Ragmor, he came*
> *From o'er the seas.*
> *The humans, they reigned,*
> *Klyntar displeased."*

"Alright, that's enough," the short man commanded lazily.

The boy continued to sing and the women continued to dance.

"I tell you," Ordell interrupted, figuring it was the women Alberto was staring at, "forty is the sexiest age a woman can be. There's just something about it, like they finally know what they want.

You know what I mean?"

Alberto turned back to the bar with a look of pure hatred on his face. Ordell's smile slowly faded.

"Now see here," the old man said, "he was an employee of mine, and I am not at liberty to speak about his personal life."

Alberto cracked his scabbing knuckles. Ordell had become little more than a buzzing in his ear. The lullaby repeated in his head, reminding him of everything he'd lost.

"Okay, well, he might have been the Blue Bandit. Alright?" Ordell twiddled his fingers obnoxiously against the bar.

At the mention of the "Blue Bandit," Alberto's stupor broke. He remembered why he was in the tavern in the first place. He ordered two more shots as the old man blabbered on.

"...tell you, nobody believes me. I don't see why you should either."

When the shots were poured, Alberto tossed a few pieces of gold on the bar. "The drinks are on me tonight," he said. Then he sat a pregnant sack of gold in front of Ordell. "And this is for the name of the captain of the boat that took your employee north."

Ordell opened the bag a bit and closed it just as fast. Then he stared at it as if he were struggling to make up his mind. "I want double," the old man finally said, but Alberto's focus had moved back to the other side of the bar.

The workers all sang along, swinging their mugs and raising their voices as loud as they could.

"I said that's enough, dammit!" the man with the top hat shouted. He looked over his shoulder at the singing workers and yelled, but his voice was easily drowned out.

*"Though our feet are not chained,*
*And our hands are not bound,*
*We're prisoners all the same,*
*Trapped in the ground.*

*Ardänia, Ardänia,*
*Your spirit, it dwells here within,*
*Ardänia, Ardänia,*
*Your kingdom will rise once again."*

The man rose from his seat, grabbed a cane resting against the table, and calmly made his way to the stage. The singer backed away, as did the dancing women, but the man continued to limp forward. He climbed the stage, shoved the boy onto the ground, and beat him with his cane.

"I said—" A loud crack resounded and the young man's body went limp. "Enough!"

The singing ended abruptly and the workers turned back around in their seats. Their eyes seemed to dim as they silently sipped their drinks.

"Excuse me," Alberto snarled as he stood from his stool.

He crossed the bar in a few long strides and climbed onto the stage. The man in the hat raised his cane again and Alberto wrenched it out of his hand.

"That is my cane, you stupid oaf!" the little man yelled as seven of his men stood up. "Do you know who I am?"

"Yea. You're Nancy."

Alberto swung and snapped the cane in half across Nancy's face. The top hat tumbled off of his head and rolled away as his body was lifted several inches off of the floor. Nancy crashed headfirst onto the bar's floor with a resounding crack, though his legs were still propped up onto the stage. Alberto left the bottom half of the cane next to the boy's bloody, unconscious body and then rolled Nancy the rest of the way off the stage with his foot.

"Huzzah!" Ordell shouted in awe.

Nancy's seven cronies stared at the gargantuan man and then looked to each other. They stepped forward, scooped up the little man's body, and dragged him outside without a word.

Alberto walked back to the bar and realized he was still holding the top half of the cane. He took a second to inspect the brass ram's head that sat on top of it, then slammed it on the bar in front of Ordell. The big man rubbed his knuckles, slightly disappointed that Nancy's men didn't stay for a proper fight.

"Half now and half tomorrow when the boat is waiting for me at the docks," Alberto whispered before finishing his drink. "And if it's not waiting for me come morning," he added, "what happened back there'll look like a mild game of slap and tickle."

Alberto saw Ordell's eyes lock onto the broken cane and the old man swallowed hard. The big man made his way to the door, but

94

when he opened it his way was blocked by a wall.

"Ordell," Alberto growled when he finally realized what it was, "get this damn turtle out of my way!"

"Tortoise," Ordell muttered, still a little shaken from the night's events.

"Just move it!" he shouted back.

Ordell stepped between Alberto and the door and tapped Corsair's shell with the cane. The sound of the brass ram against the shell was more pleasant than Alberto had expected and the lumbering behemoth started down the road.

"You are a good negotiator, you know," Ordell said. "I could use someone like you."

"Not interested," the big man replied. He left before the cabbage trader could say anything else.

* * *

When they finally reached Lake Effreudia, Alberto offered the rest of his gold to the talkative captain. The man reached for the sack, his eyes wide, but Alberto held it tight.

"You will no longer bring anyone this far north. In fact, retire from boating altogether. Set up shop at one of those abandoned trading posts along the way, and use this gold to get you whatever you need. I don't care so long as you forget that you ever saw me…but most of all, forget about the Blue Bandit."

The captain nodded and Alberto let go of the sack. He turned and gazed at the toppled parapet just past the shoreline as the boat began to drift downstream.

*Someone ought to fix that damn thing,* Alberto thought. He looked away, toward the dark forest. *Where in the moons was that Grand Highway?*

Once Alberto was under the shadows of Quercus' thick canopy, he tried to find some sign that would lead him to the broken stone path. As the sun set and his temper rose, he finally realized the road he was looking for was under him, covered in a layer of twigs and leaves.

*I laughed here once and…Meyral, Maxine…and Reaver, too.*

The memory passed and Alberto kicked a rock. He watched the stone bounce twice and he set off at a quick pace, continuing north.

Considering his past experiences, he didn't want to stay overnight in the forest, but his fatigue eventually won out. When he found a decent spot, he set up camp and built an overly large fire, hoping that the excess light would keep any predators away. He ate a meal of mutton and watered-down wine, and when he was fed and content, he turned his back to the flames and dozed off.

\* \* \*

The music was heavier that night, which did nothing for Alberto's already sour mood.

"You talked last night," he accused the guitar-playing man. "Your lips didn't move, but I heard you. What exactly are you playing at?"

*"It's always the same with you mortals. Why am I here, what do you want, what does this mean...well, I'm what you might call a 'Messenger.' I have no physical powers here, but I have information. And more often than not, people want that information."*

"So what should I call you?"

*"Some call me Iggy. I think it fits."*

Alberto swallowed and there was an audible click in his throat. Iggy nodded, and Alberto turned as the next vision took shape. He saw himself running along the Wall with three figures behind him. At first he thought they were chasing him, but then the Alberto in the vision stopped so that the smallest shadow could catch up.

"Oh no, man, I'm not getting anyone else involved. Not like last time."

No matter how much he argued, all he saw was his shadow running along a grey expanse of stone with the three men behind him. Iggy stared at him and started to play a shrill song.

"Are you saying I'm weak? Is that it?" Alberto yelled as Iggy continued to play nonchalantly. "You don't have a physical body! You can't even lift a damned rock! You—"

Alberto woke as the three moons set together. *This is just...shitty,* he thought. *I'm...I'm not weak.*

# CHAPTER EIGHT: REUNION

After the dream, Alberto was in no mood to dawdle in the deep forest. He packed up camp in the dull morning light and set out before the sun had fully risen. That evening he reached the base of the Wolke, and he continued to travel the Grand Highway as it wound its way up the side of a mountain.

He passed a few carts that were loaded down with cotton, wheat, and other raw materials, all of them led by men or buffalo. Something was subtly different, and it took him a few moments to place what had changed.

*The road isn't weatherworn or crumbling...this looks fresh.*

When he reached the top, he looked up and saw Misty Pass set against the light of the two largest moons. A new wall had been built with wood and steel, and smooth stone had been laid over the rust-filled cracks at its base. The barrier was tall enough that Alberto wouldn't have been able to see over it even if he'd jumped. Torches along the top of the sturdy wall illuminated several banners bearing the Guild's symbol—a circle with an X in its center. The insignia was now woven into the black cloth with silver, rather than smeared on with blood.

"The fort I remember was falling apart," Alberto mumbled to himself. "This...this is amazing."

Three carts were parked in the clearing before a beautifully carved gate. A group of traders were bickering with a man in a strange uniform. The man's sleek, black hair shined even in the low light of the moons. Behind him, four armored men stood guard in front of the gate, watching the row. They each wore different armor, but they all sported a black tunic with the Guild insignia embroidered on their fronts and backs.

"We have gold. I know that's what you want," one of the traders bargained. "Just let us in already."

"Sorry mates, the gates shut at nightfall," the uniformed man said as he swept his hair back. "That's just how it goes."

"Then we'll knock your damned gate down," another trader yelled.

"There ain't no way I'm sleepin' out here after climbin' that mountain!" the third merchant added.

The four guards unsheathed their swords and stabbed them into the dirt, sending a silent warning. Alberto smirked and strolled past the merchants like they weren't there. He walked right between two of the guards, who glared and retrieved their blades. They didn't advance, however, clearly conflicted about attacking an unarmed man.

Alberto approached the gate and ran his hand over it. Someone had carved a detailed rendering of the Wolke Mountains along with a line of caravans, each one bearing a different nation's flag.

"Who the hell are you?" one of the guards asked.

Alberto said nothing.

"You deaf or something?" the guard continued. "What do you want?"

Alberto glanced over his shoulder. All the guards and even the angry merchants now stared at him.

"Talk or leave, or so help me you will be cut down where you stand," another guard called out as he pulled his sword from the ground.

Alberto scoffed, but his grin fell as it dawned on him that they were serious. "Tell Howler he still owes me a beer," he said.

One of the guards looked up and whistled. Alberto followed suit and saw a head of blond, shaggy hair appear over the ramparts of the wall.

"This guy says he knows Howler," the guard shouted.

"Everyone says they know Howler," the blond yelled as he ran a hand through his hair, revealing a twisted scar on his forehead.

"Should you tell someone?" the guard asked.

"I *am* someone," the young man shot back.

"You know what I mean," the guard replied as the young man's head disappeared.

The man who had been arguing with the merchants casually approached Alberto with a slight grin. He had a kind look in his eyes, but something about his cloak made Alberto uneasy. It consisted of four panels of black silk with gold trim. At the bottom of each panel was a Guild patch. The coat was old and didn't quite fit—it reached just past the man's ankles. It was also missing a few buttons, exposing coarse, black chest hair. Alberto thought he had seen one like it before, but he couldn't place where or when.

The man in the coat smiled and broke the tense silence. "Well...what can the Guild help you with, mate? With nothin' but a rucksack, I'll wager you aren't a merchant."

"No," Alberto answered. "But I am here on business."

"You look familiar," the slick man said. His mane of black, shiny hair waved in the slight breeze.

"I get that a lot," Alberto replied.

"Shouldn't your hair be red?"

"Shouldn't you be starving?"

The man laughed hoarsely, each inhalation marked by what sounded like a strangled coyote. Alberto's face must have given his thoughts away, because Howler added, "I was hoping you'd actually remember me at some point. Are we really that forgettable? Had any fish lately?"

"I've never forgotten how hungry I was for the rest of that trip," Alberto grumbled. His brow furrowed and he asked, "Why didn't you guys say anything earlier?"

"Do you know how many people come through and claim to know me?" Howler replied with a wink. "Half of them don't, and the others I usually owe some gold to, so we all play dumb when we're on the wall."

Before Alberto could respond, he heard the sounds of bolts being drawn and the gate parted a bit.

"Alberto!" the lanky blond from before shouted as he ran forward. He clasped his hands on Alberto's shoulders and tried to shake him. "You're alive! It's me, Jake! I...well, I nearly shot you in the foot. We never forgot what you did for us. We all prayed that you'd somehow survived."

Jake held out his hand and ran the other one through his shaggy hair. Alberto shook it slowly as he noticed the traders whispering to each other.

"We never believed those Nordcross lies about you," Jake continued. "I mean, you practically saved our lives, and then you go off and burn down half the North...I don't think so. Not our Bert."

"You talk too much, kid," Alberto said as Jake continued beaming.

"Emperor's balls!" Howler let out more of his obnoxious

laugher. "That's all you remember. You'll have to forgive Jakey here, he's…excitable. And most of the time, he doesn't think before he speaks."

"Shut up, Howler," Jake said with a smile. He turned back to Alberto. "Let's go see my dad. He'll be happy to see you. So much has happened since you came through last."

"What about them?" Howler asked Jake as he pointed a gloved hand over his shoulder, motioning to the merchants.

"Let them all in," Jake announced as he led Alberto through the gate. He raised his voice and shouted back to the traders, "Everyone is welcome, just this once. Tonight we celebrate a hero!"

"We don't want to be breaking any rules now," one merchant said hesitantly. "We'll, uh…just wait out here 'til morning, if that's alright with you."

The other merchants nodded their heads in agreement.

"That settles that," Jake said with a shrug. "Let's go."

Alberto took one last look at the traders, who did everything they could to avoid his gaze.

*Let them tell whoever they want. I wonder how much I'm worth these days. Judging by the fear in their eyes and tents in their pants, it must be a lot.*

As Jake and Howler led their old friend through the pass, Alberto took in the fully rebuilt fort that seethed with excitement and movement. Jake began pointing and talking about it like a kid choosing his dessert.

"We rebuilt the north and south walls about four years ago, although we just recently got the gates installed and now we have…what's that kid's name?"

"Aiden," Howler answered.

"Right, we got this orphan carving the history of the Guild into them. We've been cleaning up the rest of the place building by building, and I tell ya, every time we complete one, it seems like a merchant moves in the next day and the rooms above it are occupied by the end of the week. We've got about three hundred people living up here full time…and get this, we've even expanded our horizons a little." Jake pointed as they passed a forge. "We finally have a proper blacksmith—"

"Oi!"

"Sorry Howler, but you sucked," Jake said with a grimace.

"It's the truth!" Howler shrugged as Jake pointed to another building with blocks of granite sitting in front of it. "We have a whole family of masons, too."

"Yea, it's a bloody drunkard and his three sons. A right pain in the arse they all are."

"Yes, Howler, I know."

"Well he don't know!"

"Why would *he* care about pains in *your* ass?" Jake asked.

"I dunno, why would he care about that orphan's name?" Howler asked as he swiped his long hair out of his face.

"Shut up," Jake said with a chuckle. "Anyway, the mead hall is pretty fantastic…"

Alberto was distracted by all the people moving about with their buffalo-driven carts. There was even a man advertising wives for sell, although it seemed a little shady that there were no women around him to speak of.

"…in fact, the only thing that hasn't been fixed is the old temple."

"That wanker over there," Howler pointed to the man selling wives, "wanted to turn it into a whorehouse—"

"And you would have let him if my dad hadn't threatened to exile you!" Jake shouted.

"You're a right git, ya know that?" Howler huffed.

Alberto suddenly fell to his knees. Phantom music played in his head, loud enough to cause him pain. He blinked several times and got to his feet as the noise quieted down. The two Guildsmen stared, waiting for him to say something. Then Alberto noticed a sapling under the wife peddler's cart, its trunk bent as if trying to hold the vehicle up.

"Move your cart," Alberto growled as the music picked up again. He ground his teeth as he repeated his command to the merchant. "Move…your…cart. Now!"

The man took one look at the giant before immediately and visibly soiling himself. Alberto picked the merchant up by his shoulders and shoved him toward the cart.

A blade came down between them, its flat side smacking Alberto's forearms, and the big man was forced to let go. An instant later, a fist collided with Alberto's face, splitting his lip and knocking him on his ass. When Alberto rolled onto his hands and knees, blood steadily dripped from his mouth and chaos swirled around him. He could hear Howler nearby, trying to calm the crowd down.

As Alberto looked up at his attacker, he found a well-muscled man with giant horns staring down at the merchant.

"This is last time you fight at Misty Pass," the horned man said. He used Commonspeak, but it came through a thick accent that Alberto couldn't place.

"It wasn't my fault," the soiled man cried. "He came out of nowhere…"

"You have two options," the horned man snarled. "Leave willingly or be forced. You are no longer welcome here."

The trader paused for a second, as if debating with himself. When his eyes caught Alberto's, he cursed and started to pull his cart toward the northern gate. His rear wheels ran over a spatter of Alberto's blood, but they missed the little tree that Alberto couldn't stop staring at.

A small hand suddenly reached under Alberto's armpit and pulled him to his feet. When the big man turned his head, it was Jake at his side.

"…and last on our tour is the Trade Office," the kid said with a nervous laugh, ignoring Howler's rushed explanation to the horned man. Jake pointed to a two-story building in front of them. "I think we've had enough excitement out here, don't you?"

Alberto followed Jake through the Trade Office's double doors that had the Guild insignia carved into them. A tall, old man emerged as Alberto tried to focus through his splitting headache. The music was steadily amplifying.

"What's going on here?" the old man demanded.

Just then Howler stomped through the doors, followed closely by the horned man from before. "Bloody hell, you'd think they'd never seen a fight before. No worries though," he said as he flipped his hair back, "it's all under control."

The horned man wore elaborate scale armor, and his dark arms were as sinewy as any Alberto had seen. He stormed about with his sword still in his hand, yelling angry gibberish. Jake apologized profusely, but Alberto wasn't sure if the man understood, because he only seemed to be getting angrier. When a few more candles had been lit, Alberto realized that the foreigner's horns were part of an ornate helmet he wore.

"Whack fol de dadeo…to the hells," he finally managed in his accented Commonspeak.

When he sheathed his sword, Alberto noticed that its cross-guard was perfectly square and had an elaborate knuckle bow covering its hilt. He removed his helmet, and underneath he was completely bald. His black eyes seemed to be half closed, and he surveyed Alberto before locking eyes with him again.

"Why should you be allowed stay, brute?" the man demanded.

The old man stepped between them and spoke in the foreigner's language. It sounded a little less guttural coming from him, but the other man seemed to understand him well enough.

"Dad, this is Alberto," Jake interrupted with an overly cheery tone as the horned man backed down. "He's alive!"

"Is that really him?" the grey-haired man asked in almost a whisper as he turned to the big man. "Alberto?"

"Yea, it's me. Xander, right? Good to see you again." Alberto took the Guildmaster's hand in his own thick fingers and shook it before he was pulled into a hug.

"I knew you'd come back one day," Xander said. "Is your sister with you?" He looked over Alberto's shoulder expectantly, as if she were shyly hiding behind him.

"Maxine…she—" Alberto coughed, but it was no use. Tears welled up in his eyes and his voice caught in his throat.

Before he left Arntim, Alberto hadn't even acknowledged that he had had a sister. Before Iggy, he refused to let her even cross his mind. She had betrayed them, but….

Alberto ground his teeth. His throat became too clogged to say anything. The pain in his head spread down into his chest and his stomach as the floodgates of his eyes opened. He felt like his soul was being torn into pieces. A deep, burning sensation found its way into his heart, and it took every ounce of strength he had to not pass out. Xander tried to support Alberto's bulk, but it took both Howler and Jake to help hold him up.

The big man didn't even notice. He was so consumed by confusion and sorrow that nothing around him existed. Eventually two loud sobs escaped his throat, and he looked around with bloodshot eyes and a face wetter than water. He finally realized that he was practically being carried down a hall.

"My condolences, friend," Xander murmured before Alberto

completely passed out.

* * *

Alberto woke up on a couch in a room he didn't recognize. He couldn't see any sunlight, so he assumed he'd only been out for a few hours.

"Good, you came back to us," Xander said softly as he patted Jake on the shoulder. "You had me worried for a bit."

"Your mate Kitsune left to wake Gary," Howler added from the other arm of the couch.

Alberto rose to his feet as the foreign man entered the room with Gary in tow. The four former criminals surrounded Alberto and clapped him on the back, shook his hands, and hugged him like old friends. Kitsune stood in the doorway with his fingers just touching the hilt of his sheathed blade. His dark eyes, barely visible under his lids, never left Alberto.

"Kitsune, right?" Alberto asked as he stepped away from the rest of the Guild.

The foreigner nodded, but he didn't move his hand from his sword.

"My name is Alberto." The big man hesitated and looked from the sword to Xander. He swallowed hard and said, "I'm sorry about yesterday. That sapling though, the one growing by the temple? There's something…just something about it," he stammered. "Make sure it lives."

"What sapling?" Xander asked.

"There is a tree, possibly ash," Kitsune explained. "It grows out in the yard." He slipped into another language, yet Xander continued to nod.

"Yes, well, that certainly *is* a strange thing to brawl with someone over," Xander answered with a grin. "But I've seen stranger. Either way, Alberto was one of the people that saved the Guild when it was at its darkest, so if he says protect that tree…we'll protect it."

"Was that Arthur's or something?" Jake whispered.

Alberto overheard and turned just in time to see Howler shrug. Before he could give it any thought, Xander said something to Kitsune in that strange language. When he finished, the foreigner bowed, put his helmet on, and exited the room.

"We'll build it a planter, perhaps," Xander said as he turned to Alberto with a reassuring smile. "In any case, welcome to my office."

Alberto finally took in his surroundings. He was in a comfortable room with a glass door that led to what looked like a private garden. Two armchairs sat in front of the Guildmaster's formidable desk, while a leather wingback chair sat behind it. The Guildmaster's overstuffed chair had such a high back that Alberto had to look up to see its top.

The couch Alberto sat on was across from Xander's desk, behind which sparsely populated bookshelves decorated the wall. A long, low cabinet sat against the west wall next to the door Kitsune had just used.

Jake pulled one of the armchairs to the glass door and sat, but Howler immediately pulled him away. He motioned for Gary to take the vacant seat, then took the second armchair for himself. Jake relocated to the couch next to Alberto until he saw the look on the big man's face. He finally settled on the low cabinet as Xander sat behind his desk.

Everybody seemed unsure of where to take the conversation. In the eerie silence, Alberto reached a hand up and touched his lip with the tip of his finger. He hissed and moved to the rest of his face, but he seemed to be otherwise fine.

"A nasty cut like that'll sting a bit," Howler muttered.

"A nasty cut?" Alberto repeated. "This is a wound! It'll scar..." He gingerly felt his mouth again and sighed.

"Welcome to the club," Xander said.

The Guildmaster moved his long hair away from his forehead and gestured to the noticeable scars that each of them had on their faces. Each was shaped like three bundles of wheat, bound so the tops curved away from each other—the ancroas. Alberto laughed and the tension that blanketed the room dissipated.

It seemed like several lifetimes ago that he and Maxine had given a group of marked criminals all of his prized fish so that the Guild wouldn't starve. It felt almost like a faded dream.

"After you left last time, things got really interesting around here," Xander started. "The official reports say that you three and two men tore down most of the Gate Cities and two towns in only a couple of nights..."

All four ex-cons looked at Alberto expectantly.

"Even if it's true, we'll still let you pass, mate," Howler said with a grin.

"It was Nordcross," Alberto answered quietly. "We tried to stop it, but we were too late."

"I knew it! You *are* good people!" Jake nearly shouted. "I knew you were innocent the whole time."

"Well, because of all that," Howler continued, "the Northern Federation overreacted. It was worse than when the war had started. They shut down the bloody Wall, which meant no one in, no one out. Except the officials, of course, and anyone who gives those thieving wankers enough gold to get the right paperwork—"

"And that's where the Guild stepped in," Jake interrupted proudly.

"The Guild's primary job has always been to keep the trade routes open," Xander explained.

"Yea, and thanks to our past, we knew a thing or two about getting around laws," Howler said with a wide grin.

"Before long, we were the only way to get goods in and out of the Northern Federation without the added expenses of ships and port tariffs," Xander said. "Now we're rich! We've put the money to work rebuilding the fort and the stairs. About a month ago we found Kitsune who had nothing but a rusted sword..."

"And now look at 'im," Howler interrupted. "He found some cells underground that we thought had been used for storage, but Kitsune disagreed. He took one look at the suit of armor and sword in there and he laid claim to it. That bloke's convinced that it was a jail—which is exactly what he wants to use it for. That'd be ironic, eh, us keeping prisoners?" he laughed obnoxiously.

"In fact, we're even talking about rebuilding the Grand Highway all the way to Lake Effreudia, and maybe even adding a dock," Jake said.

"Look, we control who goes where. If you need to get by, just say the word," Xander finished and crossed his arms smugly.

Alberto looked slowly around the room, and something finally clicked inside his head. "Weren't there six of you? Arthur and Cathari, right?"

The mood suddenly plummeted. Gary, who hadn't said a thing, twitched a little and looked through the glass door.

"Arthur and Cathari are gone," Howler answered as he stood

from his chair and paced around the room. "Arthur was like a son to Gary here..." He patted the old man on the shoulder as he passed by him. "Well, we're all practically family."

A long pause followed.

"See, a couple of years after you three came through," Howler explained solemnly, "Cathari disappeared in the middle of the night. All we found in the morning was a note that read 'Don't follow me.' Nobody ever found out where she went or why she left. It tore Arthur apart.

"He waited for a whole year, but she never returned...the bitch didn't even send word. Arthur couldn't handle it, so...so..." Howler's voice escaped him as tears filled his eyes.

"We should have seen it coming," Xander said, taking over as Howler choked back his sorrow. "Arthur stopped coming to dinner, and he started locking himself in his house. He...he even stopped taking care of his garden. All of his plants began to wither. And then one night, Gary watched him jump into Devil's Gorge. Ever since then, Gary hasn't spoken a word."

Silence ensued for several minutes, until Xander stood and beckoned to Alberto to walk with him. They left the three other men in the room. Alberto followed the Guildmaster down a long hallway with several empty rooms leading off of it.

Xander whispered, "After you came through here, Nordcross sent in a small contingent of soldiers."

"I know," Alberto said without thinking. "We came back through and made Arthur and Cathari promise not to tell you guys."

"Well, it seems that's not the only secret that woman kept," Xander muttered. His expression became grave as he continued. "Don't tell the others I told you this, but just days after Cathari let out, the soldiers packed up and left as well. For better or worse, I'm pretty sure she had something to do with it." His face brightened a degree. "But that kind of worked out for us. See, we actually befriended a few of those guys, and some of them got relocated to the Wall."

"Nordcross soldiers guard the Wall?" Alberto asked.

"The North is practically run by them these days," Xander said with a sigh.

Anger smoldered inside Alberto, but he suppressed it as much as he could. The Guildmaster led him through a dark room, then through the double doors of the Trade Office. A pair of men, one with a sword and one with a spear, stood over the small tree that had caused such a fuss. As Alberto looked on, the strange melody started to play in his head again. His stomach began to twist itself into knots.

Finally Xander cleared his throat, and when Alberto looked his way, the music died as quickly as it had started. The Guildmaster smiled and nodded at the building across the way. The structure was built into the mountain, and as Alberto stared up to its top, he found that it disappeared into a thick ring of clouds.

"We call it the Cloud Canopy," the Guildmaster said. "It's a boarding house. We have so much business these days that we're running out of places to put everyone. The pass started to look like a tent city, so we made this. It's just a place where you can rest for the night and take a hot shower in the morning."

Alberto imagined the layout of the building and figured it had no rear exit. The southern gate would be the nearest route if he needed a quick escape. Claustrophobia started to set in and Xander put a hand on Alberto's shoulder.

"The beds are comfortable and it is safe, my friend," the Guildmaster added.

As Xander led him past the ash sapling, Alberto didn't even notice that its trunk was perfectly straight, despite its burden from a few hours before. He was too busy eyeing a dark-skinned man with short, purple hair standing near the lit doorway of the Cloud Canopy.

"What's his deal?" Alberto asked with a nod toward the man.

"We don't actually know much about him," Xander told Alberto as he followed his gaze. "He showed up with Kitsune one day. Poor guy had one of those slave brands on his feet. Must have come from the Island Nations—I've heard they brand feet so that when a slave bows, they're always reminded of their services..." He shook his head and shivered. "I was only in captivity for a small amount of time but...I can't even imagine what it must be like to spend your whole life like that."

Alberto hung his head and silence followed. By the time Xander spoke again, they were standing in a vacant room inside the Cloud Canopy.

"I'm sure you want to get some rest. I'll see you tomorrow."

Xander left the room, and a few moments later Alberto could see him through the window striding through the courtyard.

Alberto took advantage of his solitude and toured the room. He patted the bed and a small smile formed on his lips. It had been a while since he'd slept on anything truly decent. In the bathroom he turned a lever and watched a stream of clear water pour into a tub. Then he walked back to the only window, which was set next to the front door with a perfect view of the main yard.

Jake and Howler were speaking to the two guards keeping watch over the tree. Alberto nudged the window and it opened a few inches, but it was all he needed.

"...only temporary," Jake's voice wandered in. "Just until we can get the masons out here to build a planter or a...a fence or something."

"Bloody hell," Howler let out a bark of his laughter, "the bloke saves our lives and we build him a planter. Strange days we're havin' here mate, bloody strange."

* * *

Light poured in through the Cloud Canopy's window as Alberto tried to fight the urge to wake up. After a few minutes' worth of struggling, he stood slowly and looked out at the fort. Lumber had been piled near the tree and a rope had been strung up around it. The Islander that Alberto had noticed earlier watered the sapling with a small bucket.

The man's dark arms glowed in the morning light and Alberto rubbed his eyes. When he looked again, the purple-haired slave stood with his arms crossed over his bare chest, and nothing about him glowed. Then his head turned and his obsidian eyes stared right at Alberto.

The big man hastily put his clothes on and left for the Trade Office. He pushed through the double doors and found himself in a room that was two stories high with ten large windows looking out onto the grounds.

Alberto headed for the massive, U-shaped counter that separated the lobby from the workers. A handful of men and one shady-looking woman stood in line with papers and bags of goods, waiting to talk to one of the six people behind the counter. The walls were covered in gold, and four crystal chandeliers hung from the ceiling.

A light hand rested on his shoulder and a voice quietly said,

"Welcome to the Guild."

Alberto turned and found Xander and Kitsune next to him. The old man had a smile on his face that didn't reach his eyes.

"Alberto," Xander started, "I think we need to talk about why you're here."

The big man eyed Kitsune for a moment, then nodded. He followed his hosts through a small door in one of the two waist-high counters. In front of him, a woman played with a dial on a metal door until it opened. She walked inside with a sizeable bag under one of her arms. Alberto caught a glimpse of a dark room piled high with similar bags, stacks of gold, a few raw jewels, and what looked like an old crown.

"We actually thought this was just a storehouse until Jake excavated the counters and chandeliers. Next thing you know, we found that," Xander said as he pointed to the open metal door.

As they walked by the vault, Alberto noticed that the thick door had a complicated set of gears on the inside, like a giant machine. Several dials with interesting symbols carved around them were set into the smooth outer layer.

"What is it?" Alberto asked.

"That is what you would call the mother of all safes," the Guildmaster answered happily. "Took me the better part of a month to break into it. Honestly, I was amazed the thing still worked. Anyway, once we found it, I figured this place must have been the old Trade Office." Xander held out his arms and grinned. "So why not restore it, right?"

Once they reached his office, Xander seemed to lose his good humor. He offered one of the chairs to Alberto with a wave of his hand. Kitsune planted himself behind Alberto as they waited for the big man to sit.

"Well," Xander began as Alberto took his seat, "Howler tells me you have come here to collect a small debt he owes you. I personally think he's a bit egotistical—it's quite a long journey for just a drink." He waited with his hands folded on his desk.

"A contract," Alberto said after a moment's hesitation. "I'm here on a contract."

"Kusa ramadi!" Kitsune growled as he grabbed his sword.

A knock at the open door announced Howler's arrival. He put a hand on Kitsune's shoulder and sighed. "Come now," he said, "Bertie isn't here to hurt us. Relax, mate." After a moment of tense silence, Howler's smile dropped and he asked, "Right?"

"I'm after the Blue Bandit," Alberto announced.

"A bounty hunter now!" Howler whistled. "And going after the Blue Bandit to boot…is the normal life really that boring?" He nudged the big man in the ribs, but Alberto's face remained stony. "Blimey, not all full of zest like you were. No wonder you're hunting."

"We're familiar with the contract," Xander said as he began wringing his hands together. "But it says the Bandit is out in the Vigrid Desert, attacking merchants."

"The desert, huh…?" Alberto closed his eyes and remembered his short trek through that place so many years before. "I really hate sand."

"Well, that's what the contract says," Howler chimed in. "But he's not there anymore."

Alberto raised his eyebrows. "You know where he is?" he asked as anger boiled away in his stomach, an emotion he was at least familiar with.

"He went north," Xander answered. His smile faltered when he saw the concerned look on Alberto's face. "Wait, you don't know? …no, I guess you wouldn't. We just found out ourselves, after all."

"Know what?" Alberto demanded.

"How about we take this into the mead hall?" the Guildmaster continued softly. "I think we could all use a drink."

As Alberto allowed the others to lead him out of the office and across the yard, he noticed that the guards around the tree were gone and the planter had been finished. He stopped walking as he stared at the sapling, which had become less of a sprout and more of a tree. Since the previous day, it seemed to have doubled in both girth and height.

Alberto turned back to the others, but before he could get their attention, Jake bounded toward them from the southern gate. Xander put a hand on his son's shoulder and they entered the mead hall. Howler stopped at the entrance and beckoned Alberto with a wave.

The Islander stood by one of the mead hall's side doors with his arms crossed over his chest. His purple hair was done up in short, sharp spikes that stayed stiff despite the breeze blowing through the pass.

Alberto's steps faltered as he realized that the dark man was watching him. As he turned in his direction, he heard someone clear their throat behind him. Alberto turned and found Kitsune staring at him with his horned helmet on again.

"Come," the foreigner muttered with a nod toward the mead hall.

"Sure," Alberto replied as he looked back to the Islander.

Only a few minutes after Kitsune and Alberto entered the mead hall, the Islander joined them. He took up a spot near the entrance and just leaned against the doorjamb. Alberto kept the guy in his peripheral as Xander passed around a pint of mead.

"Why are you looking for your old friend, Alberto?" Xander asked.

"My old friend?" Alberto responded.

He gawked around the table and noted the stern faces staring back at him. At some point Gary had joined them, but his expression was little more than an exaggerated frown.

"You mean Meyral? No, I'm looking for..." Suddenly everything came together in Alberto's mind. "Meyral is the Blue Bandit?"

Xander nodded, but his cold eyes never left Alberto's face.

"Wait," Alberto slammed his mug down, sloshing mead all over the tabletop, "how do you know? Nobody else seems to have any idea *where* the bandit is, let alone *who* he is, but you do?"

"*He* told us," Xander said simply and pointed to the man by the door.

"Him?"

"Islanders make for terrible liars—that particular talent is usually beaten out of them when it first emerges," the Guildmaster continued.

Alberto thought of Aldomein and realized the Guildmaster was right. Aldomein was almost pathologically honest. "So how does he know Meyral then?" Alberto asked.

"He doesn't. He knows Jaspar, and he said he saw Jaspar's son cross the Wolke a moon's turn ago."

Silence blanketed the table as Alberto mulled over this new information.

*This must have been Drazin's plan from the beginning. I hunt down the Blue Bandit, and when it turns out to be Meyral, we go off and fight Nordcross. Gotta give that son of a goat credit for this one.*

"What will you do if you find him?" Xander finally asked. "We said we'd do anything to repay you, but the same goes for him."

"I thought we repaid him with that planter," Howler whined.

"At the rate that tree is growing, we may owe him another in a week," Xander said with a smirk. He turned back to Alberto and waited for his answer.

"I have to find him…" Alberto said after a slight hesitation. "To at least know he's alive."

"He's right," a new voice chimed in. Everybody turned to see who spoke, but it wasn't until it started again that anybody recognized Gary's dry, tremulous voice. "If we heard Arthur might still be alive," the deaf Guildsman said, "we'd search all of Cygnus for him…I know I would, at least." His face had transformed from a long frown into a determined grimace. "Alberto is looking for his friend. We will help him."

Gary's light eyes dropped to his twitching hands. His face fell back into that permanent frown and his shoulders slumped. Gary was once again an old, defeated man covered in uneven, white scruff.

The Guild sat openmouthed, watching Gary with intense curiosity.

"Blimey…" Howler murmured. "Beautiful. Heart o' gold, that one."

The Guildmaster nodded. "You will need a guide then— someone who knows how to get through the gates and where the Blue Bandit was heading…" Xander patted his son on the back. "Jake knows his way around, he can get you where you need to be."

"I don't know, mate," Howler chimed in. Jake turned to Howler with narrowed eyes, but the ex-con continued. "You read the papers these days? The North hasn't exactly been paradise since Meyral passed through." He shrugged. "Not blamin' him or anything, just sayin' shit's rough about now. Don't you think this could be dangerous for the little guy?"

"I'm not little!" Jake yelled at Howler with an indignant stare. "And I outrank—"

"Only 'cause I don't like giving orders."

"You order me around plenty!"

"That's different," Howler said. "Sometimes you need it."

"Howler's right," Alberto nodded. "I'm not really cut out for the whole babysitting thing."

"I'm not a baby, I'm eighteen!" Jake shouted. "I can take care of myself, thank you!"

"I have already given this much thought," Xander told Howler.

"Hey," Jake waved a hand in front of the other Guildsmen, "I'm right here, you know."

"We know," Howler answered.

Alberto groaned and dragged a large hand over his face. He took a long drink from his mug and watched as Howler pulled Xander close.

"You realize I'll have to go as well? I suppose you don't care about that, eh?" The serious look seemed so foreign on Howler's face.

"I expected as much," Xander replied with a nod. "I don't want you two wasting your lives here on this mountain. You're young. You should see the rest of the world. Should you decide to come back, the Guild will always be here waiting for you."

Howler and Jake turned to Alberto, who set his mug down. He opened his mouth to protest but Xander cut him off.

"You will need our help to pass through the Gates anyway, Alberto. These are my terms," the Guildmaster demanded.

Alberto had never liked being told what to do, and even though Xander was right, this was no exception. The music had started playing in his head and his mind raced, working a mile a minute.

*The three shadows, huh? But Jake and Howler only make two...*

Alberto looked from Xander to Gary. The goofy old man he'd met years ago had nothing left. His bent frame and tiny, tilted spectacles gave Alberto the impression that he wouldn't survive one night outside of Misty Pass.

"What about you, Kitsune?" Alberto asked reluctantly.

The bald warrior only stared until Xander translated. Kitsune shouted more of his gibberish and left the table.

"Bertie," Howler said as he watched the foreigner leave, "I don't think he wants to go on holiday with you." He laughed loudly and Jake joined in a second later.

"Kitsune is a man of…discipline, one might say," Xander explained. "He abides by different codes than you or me. He told me when he arrived that he owed us his life, but I never got a reason why. The very thought of leaving offends him, apparently."

Alberto looked at Jake and Howler, still doubled over laughing, and he sighed. "Just don't slow me down."

The Guildmaster stood and patted the big redhead on the back. "Wonderful!" he announced. "Gary and I will take care of the Guild while my son sees the world. When this is all over and you return, we'll prepare the biggest feast of your life!" The old man raised his glass and the others followed suit.

# CHAPTER NINE: DEPARTURE

That afternoon, Alberto feasted on fish and drank the Guild's finest honey wine. Howler and Xander dropped the big man into his bed as the last bit of sunlight disappeared from the sky.

"I said we should show him a good time," Xander laughed while Howler pulled Alberto's shoes off, "not drown the man in mead!"

Howler covered Alberto with a blanket. "Don't yell at me, this guy was on a mission tonight. Besides, look at him, I bet that's the first time he's smiled or laughed like that in ages."

Xander suppressed a chuckle as he led Howler out of Alberto's room. Just before he closed the door, the Guildmaster placed a small basket by the big man's pack.

When the two men were gone, Alberto rolled out of bed and checked the window. He waited until he was sure they weren't coming back before he sat on his bed and rubbed his temples.

*Meyral is alive...Jaspar is alive. I need to find them. Help them. After all, family isn't about blood, it's about who cares for you. I need to help my family.*

He stood up again and navigated around the room with the help of the moonlight pouring in through the window. As he reached for his pack, he saw the basket Xander had left. Inside was a jar of honey, a razor, a pair of scissors, a note, and a bundle of cinnamon sticks. Alberto opened the note and held it in the light. It had been so long since he'd read anything it took him a few failed starts to decipher it all.

*Perhaps if you wash that indigo out of your hair, you'll feel more like yourself. The cinnamon and honey should help.*
*—Xander*

Before he left, Alberto did as Xander suggested. He used the cinnamon and honey to wash his entire head. When he finished his bath, he cut his hair and trimmed his beard short. After he toweled off his face, he stared in the mirror for a long time. His lip was still healing and his hair was the color of old rust, but he already started to feel more like himself than he had in years.

He slipped into his bed, and as soon as his head hit the pillow, he fell asleep. Before long, the music was back. Iggy visited once again.

* * *

Alberto felt the familiar sensation of floating until his surroundings came into focus. A grey, rocky surface seemed to stretch on forever, and above him the black night swallowed the sky. Stars twinkled back at him, and the redhead started to count the pinpricks of light.

It had been decades since he had first tried to count them. Alberto was a restless kid while he was awake, but at night it was even worse. When Maxine discovered his insomniac habits, she convinced him to sneak out with her. She led him to the roof of the old temple, where they lay and watched the night sky. It was the first of many nights like it; whenever he couldn't sleep, she would take him to the roof and tell him stories while he counted the stars. He never remembered what number he had counted to because he always fell asleep at some point during the story. Then somehow every morning he would wake back up in his bed.

As his eyes welled up with tears, the sky began to play the stories as he had imagined them. They were always tall tales about Maxi and Bert, world-renowned criminals looking for their next big score. He watched his memories flash in the sky as he laughed. Alberto didn't know how long he spent watching, but they eventually faded away until he was staring up at the stars again.

"If it wasn't for Nordcross...for Jaspar...then maybe..."

A tinkling sound met his ears, like coins falling into a cup. When he brought his eyes back down, he found Iggy seated in his chair with his guitar held loosely in his hands. The small medallion that hung around his neck gave off a ghostly gleam that made Iggy's skin seem paler than it really was.

"I've got a question for you."

Iggy didn't answer.

"Why don't you just talk to Meyral and finish this? It's him and Jaspar, isn't it? Not me?"

Iggy shook his head and continued playing.

"What, you have rules or something?"

*"Even if I could tell you, I probably wouldn't."*

"Fine. What's in store for tonight?"

Iggy continued to stare at the ground and he strummed faster. The five remaining orbs rose up in front of him, and one on Alberto's left shot forward. It shattered at his feet and fog swirled up around him. Through the mist, he could see the temple where he and his friends had been captured so long ago.

He saw himself chained next to a sleeping Meyral deep inside the dungeon. The image itself moved throughout the maze of passages so quickly that it made Alberto a little dizzy. It came to a stop at the top room, where Sera was holding Maxine.

"Relax, Maxi," Sera said softly, "I won't hurt you…unless you want me to." She leaned forward and nipped Maxine's ear, earning her a sharp gasp.

The blonde temptress sat down in a chair across from Alberto's sister, letting her emerald and white dress part. Her long legs were exposed completely as she ran a hand up her creamy thigh. The effect was immediate; a groan left Alberto's lips as a small whimper left Maxine's.

"All I want to know is…well, you know what I want to know. Just one word could end this all."

"Don't hurt them, any of them," Maxine pleaded. Her voice wavered, but her face was determined.

"Why would I hurt them? They've done nothing wrong…except keep you from me." Sera stood and leaned forward until her pert nose touched her prey's more substantial one.

Maxine looked to the ceiling, trying to avoid her gaze.

"You know this war doesn't have to go on. All we want is Jaspar and his son, and everything will be alright. We'll even pardon your brother's crimes."

Maxine shook her head, her lips pursed and her eyes shut tight. Her knuckles were white from clutching the sides of her chair.

"Why so coy, Maxi? It's just…one…word…"

Sera leaned forward and covered Maxine's mouth with her own. Her tongue pried Maxine's lips apart and met her clenched teeth. As their lips met, her jaw relaxed. Maxine was nearly shaking out of her chair when the blonde broke the kiss.

"How about this?" Sera asked sweetly. "You tell me where Jaspar is, and I'll let you know where more prisoners are being kept."

Sera gave Maxine another kiss—this one was so passionate that it made Alberto's jaw drop.

A single word escaped Maxine's lips as Sera pulled away. "Arntim," she whispered.

Alberto's heart dropped as he watched his sister's betrayal. The feeling intensified when Sera covered Maxine's lips again. The blonde sorceress used her long, white fingers to caress the sides of Maxine's sun-kissed face. Suddenly she stopped and strode away, leaving Maxine openmouthed. The look on his sister's face reminded Alberto of the time he'd convinced her to eat a beetle and she ended up liking it.

"Thank you, Maxi," Sera purred. Maxine snapped out of the trance when Sera pointed to a large map. "Beldin. That's where—"

Just then, footsteps echoed outside. Sera rose up to her full height with a malicious look in her eyes.

The vision broke apart and Alberto found himself biting back his own bile as he glared at the man with the guitar.

"I'd already guessed that she told Sera about Arntim. But I'm still not following. First you showed me that Maxine was refusing to help, and now...now you show me the opposite? What are you doing, trying to manipulate me? Is that what you do?"

Before he had time to process his thoughts, the orb on his far right shot out and surrounded him again in translucent smoke. Images swirled around him, but before they settled, he could already hear Maxine yelling.

"Everyone's pushing and pulling and telling me what to do, and I can't take it anymore! I'm going to make my own damn decisions, got it? You can't tell me what to do, you can't control what I feel, so forget it, you musical freak!"

The Iggy from the vision didn't flinch or even acknowledge that he heard the screaming woman. The music played faster and louder, and it mixed with the music from Alberto's dream in a sickening tune like metal on concrete.

"I listened to you and look what happened! We were captured by Sera!" Maxine screamed. "If it wasn't for Meyral and that...that staff, we wouldn't have been able to get away!"

Maxine went quiet for a moment. She bit her lip with her arms crossed, her eyes fixed on the mesmerizing way Iggy's fingers seemed to glide over the strings.

"Then that bitch lied to me! They were innocent...I didn't know! The whole place was on fire. I couldn't stop it even if I tried. I told her where Jaspar was, and she gave me a training camp. What have I done?" She dropped to her knees and sobbed. "I just wanted it all to end. Sera said she wanted the same thing..."

Alberto's stomach churned as he remembered their surprise attack on Beldin. He had fought to stop Meyral's blue inferno, but it was futile. He only managed to save a few horses, and for some reason, Maxine was absent from the raid.

"Wait..." Maxine's eyes lit up. "That kid warned me...but I didn't believe him. You sent him, didn't you? You sent him to stop me from...I should have listened. If it wasn't for him, I would have...Meyral's staff would have killed me, too."

Maxine stood and looked at Iggy for the first time with contempt—absolute revulsion lined her face.

"But why didn't *you* tell me? Where were *you*?" she whispered with deadly accusation in her voice. "Night after night, you give me these visions of a damn desert. Of Jaspar! I don't care where Meyral's dad is, what about mine?" She dropped to her knees again and put her hands on the ground. "Nobody should have to die...it's all so unnecessary...I don't want to have to fight anymore."

A vision appeared of Maxine and Alberto playing with their father when they were toddlers. Then it swirled and was replaced with an image of Jaspar with a noose around his neck. The final image showed Meyral lying on the ground, a desperate and awful look on his face.

"What about the countless soldiers that will die? What about their kids!? They have families too!" she shrieked at the phantom musician. "Damn you...damn you!"

The sky split, and in the fissure Alberto could see Maxine hanging from a cliff, waves of dark water crashing below. The body attached to the arm she was hanging onto was obscured, but he already knew who it belonged to. It was his.

Tears streamed down the face of the Maxine in the vision as she dropped down into the raging sea below. The hand in the sky disappeared as she fell for what seemed like hours. He watched as her body, once again, disappeared into the frothy waters. A hollow feeling wound its way into his gut, and he fought back vomit with all his might.

*"Is this the path you choose?"*

"This isn't my path," Maxine snapped back. "You're making things up to manipulate me. You're probably the reason Meyral has those visions too!" Understanding lit up her face. "You're the reason we left Mantrych!" Maxine frantically looked around, as if searching for a weapon to strike with. "I...*we* were happy there!"

The vision in front of her restarted and the music grew louder.

"I finally found someone who understood me, people who cared about me because of who I am. Not just because I'm their sister, not because they grew up thinking of me as a replacement mother...just me! And you took it all away!"

Maxine pointed at Iggy, but the vision shifted slightly so that Alberto was the one in front of the accusatory finger. The prophetic image of Maxine falling to her death played again. Alberto pitied his sister. He had no idea that she'd felt so conflicted and alone.

"You're the monster!" she shouted. Her eyes were transfixed on her own death in the sky, playing over and over. "I hate you!" she screamed as she balled her hands into fists.

The vision broke away. Alberto found himself in front of Iggy again as the dream dimmed.

*Had she known all along that she would die? Was she really just trying to help? Was she just a victim...or something more?*

Alberto shook his head violently and finally lost the battle—his dinner launched itself out of his mouth and onto the rocky ground.

"You...were you the reason we left Mantrych?" he whispered as he wiped his mouth.

Iggy didn't respond.

"Why?" Alberto panted. "Not gonna answer me either, huh...? Fine. Take me back."

*"As you wish."*

Alberto woke and cried like a baby for the first time in years. He didn't give a damn if anyone heard him.

* * *

On Alberto's second morning in the Cloud Canopy, Jake bustled into his room and woke the sleeping redhead. Four thick pieces of rawhide covered the kid's torso. The smaller chunks covered Jake's shoulders, and they were buckled to two bigger pieces that protected his front and back. The Guild insignia was emblazoned on these larger bits, but the armor looked as if it had been molded for someone much larger. Underneath he wore a simple white shirt, and his smile was as sincere and jubilant as always.

"Get up, sleepy! It's time to go!" Jake shouted with glee.

"Don't get too excited," Alberto grumbled. "All we know is that he went north, which means he could be in a million places."

"Righty-o! So...let's go, let's go, let's go! We have a lot of ground to cover, and you're wasting time. C'mon!" Jake bounced up and down and held his bow like it was a brand new toy. He almost slipped out of his armor on the last jump, and he had to fiddle with the buckles for almost a whole minute before fixing it.

Alberto sat up. "Whose idea was all this?" he asked as he pointed at the unfitted leather armor.

"You like it?" Jake asked as he rechecked the buckles by his ribs. "Howler got it, said I could grow into it." He looked back up and smiled. "Come on, you can't sleep all day!"

Alberto shook his head and stood up. He watched as Jake bounded down the hall, but he was distracted by the Islander from the night before. The dark man stood completely still just outside the doorway, his bright eyes staring ahead unblinkingly. Alberto grabbed a black shirt and pulled it over his head, and when he looked back, the Islander was gone.

Xander wasn't in the office when Alberto stopped by, but he found Kitsune standing at his door.

"I give you these," the foreigner said as he handed Alberto a small stack of papers. "And I give you this," Kitsune added. He pulled a crystal shard attached to a leather string from his pocket and handed it to the big man. "It is shama...an apology," he explained before he turned and left.

Alberto set the papers down on Xander's desk and took the thumb-sized gem. He held it up against the light pouring in through the glass door. As he stared at the translucent rock, it seemed to dim and then go black. Alberto blinked, and when he refocused, the outline of a glowing building appeared. Then another. Then a whole city lit up inside the crystal.

He moved the shard left, then right, and it was like he was moving a window into another world. The big man brought it close to his face and squinted, and he could have sworn he saw little shadows moving about. The image inside the jewel faded and he could see right through it and the door behind it, where Gary kneeled at a flowerbed and dug in the dirt.

Alberto put the thong around his neck and walked out into the garden. He sat on a bench near Gary, but the eldest Guildsman didn't even acknowledge him. Gary continued planting his bulbs as if Alberto wasn't there, his back to the bench. After a moment, Alberto reached out to pat Gary on the shoulder but decided against it. He rubbed a hand over his face instead and began confessing to Gary as if he could hear him.

"I'm sorry about Arthur. I know...I know how it feels to lose someone. My sister, Maxine...if you remember her...she died too. The truth is, it was my fault. I..."

For the third time, he felt his soul swell with grief. His eyes streamed tears relentlessly and his voice caught in his throat. He sniffed loudly and wiped his face with his hand.

"I envy you, Gary," he said quietly. "Not because of your circumstance, but because you have something tangible to remember him by. Something you can work with and maintain in his memory." Alberto let out a sigh and leaned against the back of the bench. "I don't have anything but a dagger. It's not even a reminder of her life, just her death. This dagger practically...it..."

Alberto lost his voice again and stood up angrily. He looked down at the old man, still digging in the garden, oblivious to the emotional turmoil erupting behind him. A thumping noise from inside the Guildmaster's office caught Alberto's attention and brought him back to reality.

He followed the noise and re-entered the building, where he found Howler leaning over Xander's desk with his hands clenched on its sides. His hair hung down in front of his face in a stringy, sweaty cascade. Alberto considered trying to sneak away, but before he could move, Howler shoved something into his coat and turned.

"Somethin' I can do for ya, mate?" the ex-con asked with shifty eyes.

"What's that?" Alberto asked, pointing to the wooden handle

that was still sticking out of Howler's jacket.

Howler's face was unreadable. He stuck his hand into the pocket and pulled out what looked like a few silver pipes pushed together over a sleek handle. A golden snapping turtle was engraved at its base.

"It's called a gun." Howler's mouth twitched, but his eyes watched Alberto unwaveringly. "It's a weapon. My weapon. And it's also a heavy reminder of my past. I don't expect you to understand."

"I thought I recognized your coat. I've seen some Nordcross engineers wearing the same thing, although it fit them a hell of a lot better. I bet there are snapping turtles under those patches, yea?" Alberto stared at the Guildsman, waiting for an explanation.

"You gonna tell me about the two birdies you were yelling about last night? Maxine and Chloe…?" Howler asked. When Alberto didn't answer, the ex-con continued. "I didn't bloody think so. But I will tell you this—I will stop at nothing to protect Jake, so stop whatever thoughts are working their way through your head. Forget 'em, because I'm going with him!"

"Well, since we're being so honest, I want you to know that if I even think you'll betray us, I won't hesitate to rip you apart," Alberto shouted back. He hadn't felt so fired up in years, and he couldn't quite tell if he liked the way his blood boiled.

After a moment, Howler nodded. He replaced his gun in his pocket, then slicked his hair back and adjusted his jacket. "Glad we have an understanding, mate." He strode past Alberto and turned back when he reached the glass door. "We're not so dissimilar," Howler added. "Difference is, I don't hate Nordcross. But I can't forgive them, either."

Alberto was left alone in the office with a couple of crumpled sheets of paper in his hand. After a moment, Jake entered the room with Xander close behind him.

"Whatever you hear or find out there, don't think ill of me," the Guildmaster told his son. He placed a hand on his shoulder and added, "Promise me that."

"Dad, you were marked for death. How could I think ill of you?"

The two smiled at each other and finally realized they weren't alone. Xander nodded to Alberto and grabbed a box from under his desk. He handed the package to Jake, who ripped into it. The blond pulled a leather quiver from the box and hugged his father tightly. Xander pulled the straps around his son and buckled them together. Jake gave his dad another hug and ran out into the garden.

Xander turned to Alberto and sighed. "Thank you for taking him. I'm an old man, and I fear I don't have much time left."

The Guildmaster led Alberto toward the glass door that looked out onto the Trade Office's garden, where Jake was showing Howler his new quiver. The blond was so excited that he accidentally stepped on the plot of land Gary was working on earlier. The old con jumped from his spot and chased Jake out with a stick. Howler stood back and let out some of his notorious laughter.

"Keep the boy safe, Alberto. I…"

Alberto nodded and allowed Xander to battle with his speech. Eventually he gave up and headed down the hall, his grey hair trailing behind him.

When Alberto exited the double doors of the Trade Office, the sun had disappeared behind a layer of clouds and light snow had started to fall. Alberto walked over to the ash tree, which had grown at least six more inches seemingly overnight, and he looked up into the dark sky. Snowflakes landed on his exposed cheeks and melted, and he closed his eyes as the cold water trickled down into his beard. At one point in his life, he would have loved the impending storm, the promise of a new adventure, the endless possibilities ahead of him.

*I guess I'm not that kid anymore.*

Alberto turned away and noticed the Islander standing across the way. As usual, his arms were crossed and he was leaning against a doorway, wearing nothing but what appeared to be pants made from a burlap sack.

"Ready for adventure?" Jake asked as he joined Alberto.

"Ready for certain death?" the big man replied darkly.

He watched through a window as Xander and Howler discussed something inside the office. Howler made a lot of wild, angry gestures, but Xander didn't let any emotion show. When the Guildmaster noticed Alberto watching, he made his way outside with Kitsune on his right and Howler practically stomping behind them.

"Well, this is where we part," Xander announced with a smile. "Gary doesn't like goodbyes, but he wishes you the best, as do we all."

Jake and Howler gave Xander one last hug. Alberto shook the Guildmaster's hand and thanked him, then stepped back. He locked eyes with the Svirdarker in his full armor.

"May the moons always be ahead of you," Kitsune said through his accent. When he noticed Alberto's questioning look, he added, "I like to wish people a good fortune in the way…the way…" The solemn man switched to his native tongue, which Xander translated.

"Kitsune finds it respectable to wish people good fortune in the way that they are accustomed," the Guildmaster explained. Kitsune mumbled more gibberish and Xander chuckled. "He also says he has a feeling you'll need all the fortune you can get."

* * *

The sun reached its zenith and Jake's feet ached already. Every few steps it felt like a couple small rocks had gotten into one of his boots. He looked over his shoulder at Alberto and Howler, but they both walked in silence. When he caught the big redhead's eye, a scowl immediately formed on Alberto's face.

"By the moons," Alberto said as Jake turned away, "if you ask when lunch is one more time, I might kick you in the—"

"Devil's Gorge!" Howler shouted as he punched the air.

"That's a bit harsh," Jake muttered.

Howler laughed and shook his head. Jake turned around, and just past the next bend, he could see darkness stretching across their path. It had been ages since Jake had been that far away from Misty Pass, and he sprinted ahead of his companions, spurred on by excitement and curiosity.

The path narrowed, though it was still broad enough for two wagons to pass through, then it blossomed into a wide beach just before it reached the ravine. A thick cherry tree sat just beyond the opening, its branches sparsely sporting a few blossoms despite the cold. The beauty of its frosted bark and bright pink blooms set against the dark stones of the mountain easily paralleled that of Devil's Gorge.

"Oi, that shouldn't be blooming," Howler said as he caught up. "It can't be…"

Jake touched the lonely tree's twisted trunk where it branched off in three directions. "Yea, I remember this one," the blond murmured. "It's Arthur's. He could always get them to bloom no matter what season. How'd this get out here? Gary hasn't been this far since…well…"

"Maybe Cathari planted it," Alberto suggested as he stared at the ice-covered bridge that spanned the chasm.

"No she bloody well didn't!" Howler yelled. He let out a loud curse, then turned away. "Gary must have done it. She wouldn't have."

"Well," Jake cut in, "it's much more proper than a tombstone would have been. Arthur would love it." He wiped a tear from his cheek and touched it to the tree.

"Too right," Howler said. A blossom fell in front of him, slowly dancing its way to the ground. He held out his hand and let it land in his open palm. His lips moved, but no sound came out at first. "Let's go," he finally said. "We have a lot of traveling to do, and it ain't gettin' any warmer."

Jake watched Howler stomp away toward the bridge, and then he turned to Alberto. "You know, he probably just needs to eat."

"I warned you," Alberto muttered. Before Jake could react, Alberto swung his leg around and kicked him in the ass.

# CHAPTER TEN: SERVITUDE

By the end of the first day, Alberto was cold and wet, and he'd already had to stop himself from smacking Jake in the face at least four times. He knew the trip to Gate Seven should only take another day, but his nerves were fried and Jake's mouth ran a mile a minute. Alberto didn't see a trace of Howler's anger from earlier—in fact, the Guildsman's overly jovial attitude seemed to only egg Jake on.

The only time the blond kid didn't talk was when he was practicing with his bow, but even that pissed Alberto off. It was a constant reminder of his sister. The fact that Jake couldn't hit a thing made Alberto feel like he was disgracing her memory.

*He's going to get me killed,* he thought. *And maybe I'd deserve it.*

\* \* \*

The sleet stopped as the sun went down, and they made camp in a muddy field. Howler and Jake were soon eating, drinking, and telling crude jokes around the fire. For the first time in his life, Alberto lost his appetite. His mind strayed to Maxine and his last tangible memory of her—the old dagger in his bag.

He pulled the blade out and held it in his hands for a moment, all the while scowling at the dried blood. "I need to piss," he yelled to the others. "I'll be right back." Alberto got up, stumbled over to a large bush, and unbuttoned his pants. He froze as he felt a pair of eyes watching him.

*Could it be…?*

He thought he could smell juniper, but he dismissed it as paranoia. A moment later, a man emerged from the dark and startled him.

"Shit, can't a guy get some privacy out here?" Alberto shouted. He looked down and cursed. "Damn the moons, I got piss on me!"

"My apologies, sir."

Alberto recognized him as the Islander from Misty Pass. He

reached for the dagger and let go of his pants. "What the hell do you want?" Alberto demanded as he pointed the blade at the man.

"I would like to ask you something."

Alberto stood with his pants around his knees, pointing the dagger at the half-naked man who seemed to be struggling with some sort of internal conflict.

"By the moons, what is it?" Alberto asked.

The Islander crossed his arms. "My name is Lee. I'm not here to hurt you, sir."

Alberto started to pull his pants up while keeping an eye on the man. He stuffed the dagger in his belt and sighed. "Alright, I'll ask one more time. What do you want?"

Lee uncrossed his arms and slowly began to speak. "Mr. Alberto and his companions are searching for the son of Jaspar, correct?"

"Why do you want to know?" Alberto asked as he clenched his fists.

"Please, sir, as I stated previously, I do not wish to fight." A long pause followed, and then he continued in his slow and deliberate speech. "Jaspar is the man that freed me."

Alberto looked for the brand that he expected to be on Lee's forehead. "I don't see any markings," he said skeptically.

Lee lowered his eyes and Alberto remembered what Xander had said. He looked down at the brand on the Islander's foot.

"You aren't marked for death, but for life," Alberto muttered. He knew what it was like for someone to try to lead a normal life after Island slavery.

Lee didn't move. A faint tune began to play in Alberto's head. *The third shadow!*

"Instead of stalking us, why don't you join us?" he asked.

"Sir?" Lee looked at him as he crossed his arms again.

"Fight with us," Alberto commanded.

He knew Lee would agree, and when he returned to camp with their new companion, the others didn't show any sign of surprise.

"Dad said this might happen," Jake said happily.

"Xander has a way of knowing a person's intentions," Howler added. "How do you think he's made it this far, eh?" He let out another round of barking laughter and Jake joined in.

By the firelight, Alberto noticed a canteen made from what

looked like lizard's skin hanging around Lee's neck, but he didn't dwell on it. He was just happy to see that his newest companion wasn't laughing with the others.

\* \* \*

The next day, the sun failed to break through the dark clouds once again. The weather was dreary and the snow was intermittent—it reflected Alberto's mood quite well. He sighed as they reached the top of a hill, giving them a clear view of the Wall. It'd been years since he'd last seen it, and Maxine was already back on his mind.

*Maybe that's why my nerves are so shot.*

Just as the thought crossed his mind, Jake lost his footing and grabbed the tail of Howler's coat, sending the two of them sprawling down the muddy hill. When Howler hit the bottom, he let out a bray of laughter. All Alberto could do to not hit the two of them was shut his eyes and tell himself he would ditch them later.

When they reached Gate Seven, the sun had set and the entire place was locked up tight.

"Where's the tent city?" Jake asked Howler.

The ex-con shrugged. "Maybe they cleared 'em all out. Xander said they might. I bet they all moved to Piscar...it's only a few more miles down the road."

"Excuse me?" Alberto whispered venomously.

"There's a town just down the way from here," Jake explained with a bright smile. "It's a little out of the way, but it sure beats sleeping in front of the Wall."

"There's a town?" Alberto clenched his fists. "I was so hungry last time, and there was a town here? And you didn't tell me? What in the moons is wrong with you?"

"Oi," Howler held out his hands, "what Jake means is it's a town *now*. Back in the day, it was a bloody gallphyre colony. The whole place used to be four buildings owned by two brothers and about a dozen of their wives. Or sisters. Or daughters." Howler scratched his chin. "I forget. But the flood of refugees fixed all that," he continued. "Now it's a right pleasant place, so long as you keep it in your pants."

"When the refugees find somewhere more permanent, Dad says Piscar will probably disappear." Jake waited for Alberto to say something, but he only stood there.

After a few tense moments, Alberto shook his head. "Fine. Let's get going then."

* * *

Piscar was little more than a small hamlet that hugged the coast, and the whole thing looked like it was made of driftwood.

"It'd only take a small storm to blow this whole place away," Alberto muttered.

"They have fish," Jake sang.

The big man shrugged, and they walked down the cramped, muddy roads until Howler stopped. They stood in front of a building with a sign that looked like it had been salvaged from a shipping crate.

"Twenty Pounds of Flour," Howler announced as he held the door for his companions. "Best place to get a bowl of chowder this side of the Wall."

Someone yelled from inside, "The only place, he means!"

The rest of the shop burst into laughter. Alberto immediately hated the place.

*I don't have time for this shit. I need to find Meyral before he does anything stupid. Well, more stupid. He might die or get caught or...or he...that smells delicious. Maybe I have time for just one bowl.*

* * *

A gallon of chowder later, Alberto crawled into one of the four beds Howler had managed to procure for them. Before he shut his eyes, he already knew Iggy would be waiting for him.

"How do I know this isn't just another dream?" Alberto asked.

Iggy continued to play his guitar as the remaining three orbs rose.

"You're right, this is way too boring to be one of *my* dreams."

As the big man turned, a flash of green blinded him. When he could see again, he was in a small room with a wooden floor. A shabby table stood in the center, where two women sat across from each other. The tension between Sera and Aldomein was easily discernible, even in the hallucination.

"I need one more thing from you, Aldomein."

"That's what you said last time. Do you remember my response then?"

Sera smiled, but there was nothing pleasant about it. "We both know you can never 'be done.' Being told what to do is just how you work, my sweet Aldomein."

The purple-haired huntress swallowed hard but made no other movement.

"Go to Leviathan Pass," Sera continued, undaunted. "Rescue Jaspar, but do *not* harm the emperor. I know it's a little different from my usual contracts, but it must be done."

"I said—"

"I'll make it worth your while," Sera interrupted.

Aldomein sat back and glared at Sera. "What are the conditions?"

"There will be a boat at the bottom of the cliff. I will have one of my men waiting to take Jaspar to the Islands. All you have to do is get him on that boat alive. I cannot stress how important it is that the emperor stays unharmed as well."

"You know I'm going to want some serious compensation. Protecting people is a difficult business in times of war. People of significant interest increase the risk...and how much will you offer?"

"Triple what it was last time."

Aldomein bit her cheek. She grabbed her axe and rubbed the blade with one of her long, slender fingers.

"Remember, you will always be welcomed into the guard with open arms. I urge you—"

"Not joining, Sera," Aldomein cut in. "Give up on that. But I will take this contract...under one condition."

Sera's face contorted in anger.

"Or you can do it yourself," Aldomein said as she stood up and holstered her axe onto her back.

"Alright," Sera said quickly. "What's your condition?"

"Tell me something. I know you got the staff after the attack on Mantrych, but somehow Meyral got it back." Sera's eyes narrowed, but Aldomein continued. "And now you want me to rescue Nordcross' most wanted criminal, whom you spent so much time and energy hunting? What *are* you playing at?"

The blonde hesitated. She leaned forward and put her fingers together in front of her face. "I was exiled from my homeland a long time ago," she began. "And I have done everything in my power to get back. Nothing has worked. Recently, I made some progress," she smiled as her eyes drifted to the ceiling, "but it didn't work as well as I'd hoped. Then I discovered that as long as the bloodlines of the people who caused my exile still exist, I may never be able to return. I've been hunting for these maggots ever since…but they are still out of my reach."

"So this whole dance that you're doing is to lure these people out of hiding?" Aldomein crossed her arms with a sour look on her face.

"Yes," Sera answered. She stood to leave, but she paused as she reached for the doorknob. "Give this to your redheaded friend." She pulled a folded letter from one of her pockets and tossed it on the table.

The vision faded again and Alberto saw only darkness for nearly a whole minute. One of the orbs appeared, then transformed into a girl no older than fifteen. Her purple hair was tied up in a ponytail, but her familiar, green-and-gold eyes were filled with fear. The ocean lay behind her and stretched past the sandy shore to the horizon.

Aldomein, younger than Alberto had ever seen her but just as dark and beautiful, stood flanked by two men. One had a whip coiled at his waist while the other smacked a thick rod softly against the palm of his hand. The man with the rod had a long mustache that curled up as it trailed past his nostrils. His grey eyes stared intently at the grove of trees in front of them. The other man's face was shielded with a layer of scruff that reached most of the way down his dark neck.

"They're late," the mustached man said as he looked toward the dimming sky. The clouds began to transition to a darker pink as the sun set. "Wonder what's holding them up."

"They'll be here," a female voice said.

Alberto turned and found a woman standing a few feet away from the others. She dressed conservatively, wearing a long, beige dress that almost blended with her tan skin. Alberto noticed her feet were bare, and as he turned to look at the others', only Aldomein and the man with the whip had slave brands.

"I apologize for the inconvenience," another female said from behind Alberto. This woman's voice was slightly huskier with more than a tint of arrogance. "After all this time, the mysteries of the

Islands still distract me."

Sera stepped out of the grove of trees with a man in black walking cautiously behind her. The assassin stopped and folded his arms, though Alberto didn't find a weapon on him. Sera continued toward the Islanders and headed straight for Aldomein.

"I'm very pleased that you agreed to my proposition," Sera continued as she scanned Aldomein's body. She lifted one of the slave's arms and trailed a long talon along her skin.

"We agreed on ten rhino tusks," the woman reminded Sera as she eyed the two newcomers warily. "Svirdarker ivory sells for a high price in these parts…"

"I am quite aware," Sera replied distractedly.

A few moments of silence passed as Sera inspected the Islander. The mustached man shifted uneasily and switched the rod to his other hand.

"She's a damn hard worker," the man began, "I'll tell you that. Never one to complain," he glanced at the man on her other side, "and she always does as she's told." The hint of a smirk reached the edge of his lips and the other man frowned.

"Her uses go beyond just physical labor," the woman explained. "She has a knack for finding our livestock when they run off—I never understood it, but she always manages to bring them back."

Sera locked eyes with Aldomein, who stared back with a mixed amount of pride. "A Tracker, perhaps?" she murmured.

"And my guests have been known to pay upwards of one hundred gold coins for her other services," the mustached man added with a full grin.

At this Aldomein's eyes finally dropped. Sera reached up, put her first two fingers under Aldomein's chin, and lifted her face. Aldomein squared her shoulders as the mustached man rested his rod in his palm.

"Is that right?" Sera mused.

Aldomein nodded firmly.

"Upwards of one hundred gold?" the blonde asked. "And what services would those be, exactly?"

"In these parts, it's common—"

Sera held up her hand and stopped the other woman midsentence without taking her eyes from Aldomein's. "What services?" she asked.

"Pleasure," Aldomein answered simply. "They pay for the use of my flesh."

Sera frowned. Her eyes darkened and she turned slowly to the woman. "And you were aware of this?"

"Well," the woman replied uncertainly, "yes. When she is your property, you may do as—"

"Property!" Sera barked.

"Yes, property," she continued irritably. "And until I see my ivory, she is still my property."

"You mean this?" Sera asked as she pulled a small tusk from her waistband. She took three long strides toward the slaver and the two men followed anxiously. "You want your ivory?"

The woman hesitated. "I thought we agreed on the trade already," she said.

"You're right," Sera admitted. She paused, then stabbed the tusk into the woman's eye.

The two men darted forward but the unarmed assassin quickly pinned the slave to the ground. He pulled the whip from the man's waist and used it to catch the mustached man by the ankle. The man in black yanked and he pulled the slaver to the ground.

Sera continued to stab the woman in multiple places as her assassin finished off the two men. He snapped each of their necks, and as he rose to his feet, Sera let the woman's body fall to the sandy ground.

Alberto watched as Sera wiped the tusk on the assassin's outfit and replaced it in her waistband. She approached Aldomein, whose wide eyes were locked onto her former owners' lifeless bodies. Her lip trembled as she stared at the other slave's corpse.

"Now, now," Sera muttered, "no need for that. You're one of us now. There's no need to subject yourself to such treatment anymore."

Aldomein bowed until her ponytail rested just above the sand. "What would you like me to do, master?"

Her fear shot pain directly into Alberto's soul and he screamed out loud. Every chord that Iggy struck beat along with his heart, and he could feel a fire burning inside of him.

Alberto let out a roar of pain. When he stopped to breathe, he was on his feet in the small room he'd fallen asleep in. Howler stood in front of him, waving in his face, and Jake sat a few feet away with a blank stare. Lee leaned in the doorway as the inn's other guests shot nervous glances toward their room.

"…mate. Are you in there? Hello! Red?"

"I think his brain exploded," Jake said.

"What makes you think that?" Howler asked.

"Well, that's the sound someone makes when their brain explodes."

"You're telling me you've heard someone's bloody brain explode before?"

"Shut up!" Alberto yelled, making the two Guildsmen flinch. He rose to his feet and grabbed his rucksack. "Somehow I wouldn't be surprised if someone's brain had exploded around either of you idiots. Come on, we should have left for Gate Seven already."

* * *

Howler had slowly fallen back, trying not to draw attention so he could have some space to get his head straight.

*Even before prison I didn't do stupid shit like this. Open country? Hunting a murderous bandit? Granted, he might have saved my life at one point…*

He looked around, but Lee still walked steadily behind him. Howler listed to the left, slowed down, and glanced at Lee again. The damn Islander was just as far away as before. It was like he refused to put himself ahead of anyone. Howler reached down and fiddled with his boots, but Lee stopped beside him and waited.

"Blimey…can't I get some privacy here?"

"Hey," Jake shouted from somewhere up ahead, "we have a problem, Howler!"

Howler and Lee both ran to catch up. Jake and Alberto stood side by side, staring at the guards huddled around the Gate.

"What is it?" Howler asked.

"I don't see our contact," Jake said.

The four travelers approached the Wall cautiously, but Howler still didn't see their guy among the three guards.

"He's right, Red," Howler said in a loud whisper. "Our bloody contact is missing. It means this whole process just got a little more interesting, if you're pickin' up what I'm puttin' down." Howler realized after a moment of silence and a confused look from Alberto that he was not in fact picking up anything. "We might not make it through," the ex-con clarified.

Alberto shrugged. "We came this far," he said simply as he strode forward.

When they reached the Gate, Jake spoke first. "Where's Captain Dallas?"

"He was dismissed," the oldest man said as he gave them a scrupulous look. "I am the new commanding officer of this gate: Captain Ballard."

"Why was Dallas dismissed?" Jake nearly whined.

"You haven't heard?" Ballard asked with raised eyebrows. "Things have changed. The senate was assassinated. Well, except for one man. It was a bloodbath."

"As per Northern regulations," a guard who looked as young as Jake explained, "the eldership goes to the next senior official. Hence the only man who survived has taken over." The guard kicked a rock. "That lucky son of a boarhound…"

The last guard scoffed and added, "It'll be a while before the new senate can be assembled."

Howler turned slowly, flipped up his collar, and stared at a grove of trees in the opposite direction. The guards didn't say anything, but Alberto somehow noticed. Howler cursed under his breath as the big redhead took a step closer.

"So," Alberto muttered as Jake rambled about politics with the guards, "which one did you piss off?"

"The bloke on the right is named Oliver," Howler answered with a smirk. "I met his wife in Gaffe once."

"Does he know?" Alberto asked.

Howler laughed quietly for once. "Don't know, and I'm not trying to find out."

"…so until then," the youngest guard continued, "what Elder Harold says is law."

"So, no more Nordcross troops," Jake summarized tentatively.

"Then he reconnoitered the Gates," the young guard added, "and he released a slew of decrees concerning something he calls 'boundary sanctuaries.' It's all very complicated—"

"Wonder where you heard that," Oliver interrupted.

Howler hazarded a glance. The look Oliver gave the young

guard was something like disdain mixed with disappointment.

"The Wall is open now with virtually no restrictions," Ballard finished.

"What?" Howler's wide mouth fell open as all thoughts of anonymity vanished. "Why didn't anyone tell the Guild? We're providing an obsolete service, how do ya think that makes us look, eh?"

"The Guild has not been relevant for more than two hundred years," the old guard answered. "Apparently how the Guild *looks* isn't pertinent. Now, if you're done, may I see your papers?"

"What papers?" Jake demanded. "You just told us this is now an open border."

Howler felt a tinge of pride at the kid's argument.

"Formalities must still be taken," Ballard explained. "Names must be documented, tariffs levied if—"

Alberto cut him off and handed him his crumpled, mud-spattered paperwork. The captain handed it off to Oliver, who flipped through a couple pages.

"These are forgeries," Oliver announced.

Ballard drew his sword and Howler's hand dove into his coat for the gun. Jake tried desperately to set an arrow, but he couldn't keep it straight. Fortunately for him, the youngest of the guards spent as much time trying to draw his blade from its scabbard.

Oliver chuckled as he flipped through the documents a few more times. "They're the best I've ever seen," he said, ignoring the turmoil, "but no less fake. I'm guessing Dallas was your man then?"

Alberto and Lee hadn't moved, and Howler's fingers rested carefully on his weapon.

"However," Oliver continued with a wide grin, "these papers were faked for an edict that no longer applies." The veteran spat out a stream of black goo and nodded. "I guess you haven't broken any laws…today. You're free to pass."

"That is not for you to decide," Captain Ballard interrupted. "I am your commanding officer, I will decide if they may pass."

Oliver rolled his eyes as he handed their paperwork back. "Then you can be the one to tell them to leave." He hooked a dirty finger in his mouth, pulled out a wad of something dark, then threw it on the ground.

Ballard gave a sideways glance at Alberto and relaxed his

sword. "Regardless, we must still take record of your arrival. And would you fix your damn weapon already, private?"

The youngest guard dropped his sheath and his whole belt fell to his ankles. Oliver cackled and helped the kid buckle his equipment back on. Once the private was situated, he joined his superior and snapped to attention.

"Nobody is allowed to import weapons into the North without the proper permits," the youngster recited. "Please disarm yourselves."

Oliver walked away and the other two guards checked Alberto's luggage. They seemed disappointed that he had no weapons in his bag, and judging by the looks they gave each other, Howler didn't think either of them was brave enough to search Alberto up close and personal. Howler knew he and Jake wouldn't be so lucky.

After Alberto gave his name—Russell of Arntim—they waved him through and turned to his companions. Lee was first, and Howler watched as disappointment turned to anger when the guards realized that the only things attached to Lee were his pants and the canteen.

They asked where Lee was from and Howler saw the Islander open his mouth to answer. Honestly.

"He's an Osdorf native," Howler explained quickly. "Lots of ash up there, you know how it is," he whispered.

Ballard glared at the ex-con for a moment before continuing. "And your name?"

"Lee," he answered. "Just Lee."

The young guard nodded and scribbled on a scroll of parchment. "Just Lee...of Osdorf..." he muttered to himself.

Howler's turn came next. Ballard was less than gentle and Howler got the feeling that he wanted an excuse to abuse his power. After he emptied his pockets, the young guard took an extra moment to inspect the gun.

"It's a bloody toy for my nephew," Howler hissed through clenched teeth.

"A Nordcross toy!" the private shouted as he pointed to the insignia on its handle.

"I thought trade was open," Howler said with a shrug.

"Fine." Ballard tossed the gun back at Howler, and his eyes lit up when he looked at Jake. "The arrows stay here!"

Jake turned to Alberto, who shook his head. "Just leave it," the big man told him. "We can get you more at the next city."

Howler watched the blond dump his quiver on the ground. He looked like a spoiled child who had just been told "no" for the first time.

"Your bow too!" the young guard added.

"What danger is a bow without arrows?" Jake demanded. He stood where he was and ground his teeth.

Captain Ballard placed his hand on the hilt of his sword.

Jake reluctantly tossed the weapon to him. "Can we go now?" he pouted.

Howler steered him through the gate as Alberto and Lee followed behind.

While they were still within earshot, Jake turned to the others and added, "Is it me, or is security a little old-fashioned around here?"

"Doesn't bother me, mate." Howler jumped and kicked his heels together in midair.

"You're just happy 'cause you got to keep your thingy! They took my bow…and my arrows!" Jake stomped along the road.

"Shut up! You guys are givin' me a headache!" Alberto pinched the bridge of his nose and sighed. "Look, the senate was murdered by the Blue Bandit. We need to find this last remaining senator they were talking about."

"Then we need to go to Vent," Howler announced. "It'd be northeast from here."

Alberto glared at Howler and stomped away. The ex-con was just happy that he listened—he was stomping northeast.

"I think he hates you," Jake whispered.

"That much tension can only mean one thing," Howler muttered seriously. "We need to get him laid."

"You think that'll bring back the guy we met all those years ago? Because…I don't like this Alberto so much."

"It's worth a shot."

"Oh, don't say shot," Jake whined.

# CHAPTER ELEVEN: PREMONITION

During their exodus from the chambers of the Northern Senate, Meyral and Rubi found stables occupied by boarhounds. Most had been bred for the cavalry, Rubi told Meyral—their telltale white fur was ideal for camouflage—but they managed to find and commandeer a pair of common, brunet boarhounds.

That was a week ago. Now the wall of dark green Meyral had been leading Rubi toward for the last day was growing in front of them as they rode across the plains. The Talvy—a name Rubi had only heard locals use—was a forest filled with evergreens that stretched hundreds of feet into the sky. When they reached the first line of trees, its legend did not disappoint. The forest dwarfed the riders on their boarhounds, and in that moment of awe and wonder, Rubi broke the silence that had blanketed her and Meyral like an icy fog.

"We've been riding for quite some time now," she said. "Where are we going?"

"*I'm* looking for my father."

"Right," she shot back. "Where is the legendary Jaspar supposed to be hiding this time?"

"I've heard he's in the Island Nations," Meyral muttered into his black rags. "I know it…my father's waiting for me."

*Again with the I, me, my,* she thought. *It's like I'm not even here to him.*

"I hate to tell you this," Rubi said as she fought back a grin, "but we're going the wrong way. And we can't get there on boarhounds. I don't think they can swim through the Ardänian Ocean, you know."

"Then what do you suggest?" Meyral asked.

"There are merchant ships that head to the Islands every so often out of Frazier Bay. We can hide out in Nasabin until the next one comes—we're heading in that direction anyway. I should still have a room there, and I can probably get us some gold for the trip."

Meyral nodded. His hound started forward, but Rubi took the lead, patrolling the border in search of something. After a few minutes, she found a path between the thick trees. A wide, muddy rut, left by the sturdy paws of other hounds, cut through the melting snow.

The Talvy was as deep and dark a forest as any Rubi had been in, but there had always been something different about it to her. Perhaps it was the way the thick matt of needles silenced footsteps, or the way the light fell in shafts thought the snow-covered branches, or the heavy moisture in the air. The Northern Cypresses seemed to touch one another with their arching branches that began about fifty feet overhead, and the trunks of these trees were wide enough that people were rumored to have made homes inside of them.

It reminded her of a druidic temple her father had taken her to see years before. Even at such a young age, she found herself in awe of its magnificence. She turned to her companion, yearning to tell him all about it, to describe the stonework and carvings…but all she could see was that ragged cloak.

"You know Meyral," Rubi started tentatively, "the sun's out. It's pretty warm. You could take that old rag off."

"You mean my cloak?"

"If that's what you want to call it, then yes, your cloak."

"You don't have to pretend. I know I'm a monster. I keep this on because nobody should have to see me."

"But out here, it's just me," Rubi said softly.

"I don't want you to see me like this either," he whispered.

Rubi pulled her hound to a stop and Meyral's followed suit. The two beasts grunted and pushed the muddy snow around them with their snouts.

"What's wrong?" Meyral asked.

"I know what you look like," she answered. "But it doesn't bother me, because that scar is a part of you…and you might be the only thing left of my old life."

Meyral sat up stiffly as she reached out and pushed back his hood. His blank eye stared at her unblinkingly.

"That's better," Rubi murmured. She surprised herself by saying it and meaning it.

She kicked her hound back into a trot and Meyral rode alongside her. Every few seconds she glanced over at him, trying to read his expression, but it was useless.

"Do you think that Harold will fight against Nordcross?" Rubi asked, trying to push for something, anything.

"You're the one that wanted to spare him," Meyral answered coldly. "I still think we should have killed all of them."

"Well, he said he had nothing to do with Nordcross' plot in the first place. I think he'll fight. I just wanted to know what you thought." She sneaked a peek at him in her peripheral, but he was still just as impossible to read. "Even if I'm wrong, he's the only chance we have of saving the Northern Federation…anyway, you're the one with the magic eye. What did it tell you?"

"Nothing," he muttered. "It's not like I control this thing." Unhappiness came from him like a wave. A long pause followed, and then he added, "Don't lose hope. Never lose hope…somebody told me that once."

"Who?" Rubi asked as she slowed her hound.

Meyral hesitated. "Taryn, I think," he said slowly.

"Do you remember her telling you anything else?"

He shook his head and pulled his hood back up. Then he kicked his boarhound into a gallop and stayed in the middle of the path so that she couldn't ride next to him.

*I know you're still in there, Meyral,* Rubi thought. *Somewhere…*

\* \* \*

Meyral refused to admit to himself that he was happier with Rubi around, but the relief was slowly worming its way into his heart. He was out of the desert, his life had purpose again, and he had a companion—something he couldn't remember having since Alberto and Maxine. He felt the happiness, but he fought it. Pleasure would only distract him. It was the hate that drove him and the southern light that guided him. He needed it to find his father.

But when Rubi reached for his hood, he had felt warmth roll over him, a strange feeling that seemed so foreign. Even when she pestered him about the senator, he could only feel displeased at best. All he could do to keep himself focused was try to stay away from her.

Nevertheless, he found himself staring at Rubi whenever he could. He still didn't remember much about her, yet he knew what had changed. Her auburn hair was no longer a short, curly mess. She had let it grow, and it had become a slightly wavy, silky curtain of fire that flowed down her back. Her freckles were gone and her skin was flawless. Her eyes, once the bright, starry eyes of a child, were replaced by deep wells of wisdom that captivated him regardless of what she was saying. And there was no denying that Rubi was a woman now—she had the curvy figure to prove it. Meyral continued to ride ahead of her to avoid distraction.

* * *

As the sun sank beyond the horizon, a faint glow ahead of them lit up the forest.

"What's with the light?" Meyral whispered.

"Looks like we made it to Gaffe," Rubi said. "We should be able to find a warm room for the night there."

They rode to the city gate, where a man in silk robes met them.

"No beasts within the gates, please," he announced as he raised a gloved hand. "You may keep them here at the stables for ten gold pieces."

"Ten gold," Rubi repeated with a sigh as she reached for her coinpurse.

"Per hound, per night," the man continued.

"Twenty gold pieces, then," she said as she gave up a handful of gold.

He counted out the gold and nodded, then beckoned them to follow. When they reached the stables, he took the reins from them and led the hounds inside.

The man returned, set their bags on the ground, and walked away. Meyral and Rubi grabbed their luggage and headed back to the road, but when they crossed the gate, Meyral noticed that something was different. They turned a corner and he finally realized what it was.

"Where'd all the snow go?" he asked gruffly.

Rubi laughed quietly, a sound that Meyral didn't find all that unpleasant. "They clear the streets daily in the winter, sometimes twice a day."

Meyral contemplated how tedious it must be to remove all the ice and slush, and then he froze. He stared at the nearest building and a faint glow illuminated the inside of his hood.

"Those are glass castles," Rubi explained as she walked forward. "They serve as shops, hotels, bathhouses...I've seen some taller than these trees and as big as Mantrych's town square."

146

"They're the playthings of the North's rich and affluent," Meyral growled in a voice that didn't seem his own. He rubbed a hand over his face and the glow faded. "This place belonged to the senate and their dirty gold."

Rubi stared into the dark obelisk. The streetlamps around her looked like tiny, orange blotches in the reflection. The forest was a sea of jade, and below that she could see two dark, human-sized smears.

"The senate is dead," she said deliberately, "and Gaffe belongs to the people again. So relax."

"But for how long?" Meyral asked darkly.

"Well..." Rubi started, unsure how to answer. Finally she decided to simply move the conversation along. "There's a small inn for the help down this way."

It wasn't long before they reached the building, which was little more than a two-story, wooden shack. The first floor consisted of a kitchen and a common room, where a large fireplace took up most of its far wall.

A middle-aged woman with round cheeks walked forward and smiled. "Welcome," she said as she curtsied. "How can we help you?"

"We're just stopping by on an errand for James of Nasabin," Rubi replied. "I didn't expect it to take this long, and we just need a place to spend the night."

"We have several open rooms," the innkeeper said as she grabbed a silver key on a ring from the board behind her. "I'll just put it on the butcher's tab then?"

"Yes, thank you," Rubi answered with a bow.

A few minutes later, the two travelers split a less than substantial meal of hard bread and a meat stew in the common room. A chubby man about Meyral's age snored on a nearby sofa.

"We should hit Nasabin around tomorrow evening," Rubi said. "It's quaint, so don't expect too much."

"Sounds like paradise," Meyral whispered into his bowl.

As the night marched on, the inn filled with cooks, pages, maids, and chauffeurs. When the assistants for the North's elite started to pass around the ale, Rubi and Meyral headed to bed. They shared their already cramped room with two traveling bards and a butler. Rubi was just happy everyone had a bed to themselves.

\* \* \*

Meyral woke to total darkness and slowly rose to his feet. He could see nothing, but he heard the deep breathing of drunken sleep all around him. He left the crowded room and walked downstairs to the empty commons below. The fire had dwindled into little more than embers. Meyral righted a chair and sat in it, then finished someone's abandoned beer from the table beside him.

Ever since he'd reunited with Rubi, something had been tugging at his mind. If she was still alive…did that mean Alberto and Maxine were as well? So many questions still lingered in his broken thoughts, but they had changed recently. It brought his entire world into question.

*Who am I, really? Where is everyone I used to know? How did Rubi find me?*

As he stared into the dying fire, he tried to concentrate on his memories. Every candle in the inn suddenly flared, and then the fireplace spit a shower of ashes onto the hearth. He heard a chuckle behind him and found the young man with curly, brown hair that had come to him during the blizzard.

The man sat on the staircase with an eerie grin that split his otherwise calm face. His hands cupped the spine of a leather-bound book, which fell open as soon as Meyral noticed it. The man flipped through a few pages, then cleared his throat and began to read.

*"The monster under my bed,*
*The creature inside my head,*
*The It that wants me dead,*
*It fills me with dread.*

Meyral watched with admiration as the man's eyes never left the pages, even when he made his way downstairs. His bare feet danced between the refuse and the drunks that hadn't made it to bed.

*As long as I run, it can't catch me,*
*When I'm done, I'll become the enemy.*
*Stay fast, this feeling can't last.*
*When the die is cast,*
*Forget the past."*

It made as much sense as it had years before, but it comforted Meyral in some slight way. "What does that mean?" he asked the man.

"Poems mean nothing until the listener hears them," he replied as he shut the book.

"I heard it just fine," Meyral said. He stood up and took a step toward the man. "What do you want with me?"

"What I want is neither here nor there," the mysterious man answered with a garbled chuckle. He vanished, then reappeared just outside the now open front door. "The important question is why, Meyral, are you here?"

Then the phantom faded into the distance, whistling a jaunty tune that echoed throughout the empty streets. Again Meyral felt a familiarity in the melody, but he couldn't place it.

Meyral stepped outside and shouted after the man, "I'm going to find my father!"

There was a laugh, but the young man was nowhere to be seen. "No," the disembodied voice continued, "you have more important things to do."

"Nothing is more important!"

Meyral ran out into the night. A flash of brown drew his attention and he hurtled down several streets and an alleyway, but no matter how fast he ran, the curly-haired ghost was always ahead of him.

"I never listened to what my dreams told me at first, either," he taunted. "When you give up, come and find me."

Meyral cursed and turned back to the inn. He looked at the trees, shops, and glass castles around him, but he didn't recognize any of it. Panic overtook him as he sprinted through the muddy streets, looking for the lopsided shack where Rubi slept soundly.

He headed down a few more alleyways before he found himself in a courtyard. The ground around him consisted of large pebbles that were spaced out just enough to let little tufts of silver grass peek through. In the center of the yard, a marble statue of a winged woman cradled the phantom, who held a hand to his forehead dramatically.

Meyral leapt at the man, wanting nothing more than to cause as much pain to him as he could. He punched with his right hand and the statue's arms shattered to dust, but the phantom had disappeared again.

"You're right," the man's voice rang out. "We do learn best from our own mistakes."

Suddenly Meyral was inside of a giant temple made from the same stone as the Wall. He stood in a ring of men, each wearing hooded robes of a different color. In the center, Rubi slept on a soapstone altar, over which a Northern banner had been laid. A man in scarlet robes stepped forward and held his arms out over Rubi's body.

Meyral tried to move, but he was rooted to the spot as if his feet had been nailed to the ground. The druids around him started to chant softly. The leader gently stroked Rubi's ginger locks and Meyral's entire body tensed.

The man lowered his hood, and Meyral was not at all surprised when the ever-smiling face that appeared was the same as the phantom's. He softly traced Rubi's neck with his fingers, then undid the top two buttons of her gown.

"Don't worry," he murmured with a sly look toward Meyral, "I would never harm something so…beautiful. But you will. I could warn you until I was blue in the face about the tragedies you will bring into this woman's life, yet you would still go through with the dance that you have so unwillingly started." He chuckled as he tugged at the top of her gown, exposing her pale collarbone. "After all, that *is* how love goes. Nothing but pain awaits…for both of you. I would know."

The chanting turned into a low hum as the man produced the leather-bound tome from his robes. He held the book in one hand and raised the other as he finished the rest of the poem.

> *"Don't let It get you,*
> *Don't let It win.*
> *Their numbers are few,*
> *And stained in sin.*
> *I lowered my defense*
> *And let the pain commence,*
> *It got so intense,*
> *It stopped making sense.*
> *If you should go,*
> *Abandon this hate.*
> *What I do know…*
> *This is my fate."*

Meyral felt something inside of him shift this time. He looked around at the men, but their faces were all hidden underneath their hoods. The chanting stopped as the druids revealed themselves one by one. They were all the same tan, curly-haired man from before, silently laughing at Meyral. One of the men held up a mirror, and Meyral screamed as he saw the phantom in his own reflection.

He woke up again, unaware that he'd been dreaming in his bed. Meyral searched for the man, but he was nowhere to be found. Instead, his eyes were drawn to Rubi.

*Did he call her beautiful? Those tragedies...he didn't mean...*

In the dim light of morning, Meyral could make out Rubi's full lips as she pouted in her sleep. He rose and packed what few things he had as anxiety and sorrow filled his heart. When he found the book from his dream, he shoved it into his cloak with a gruff curse that woke Rubi.

She jumped from her bedroll with her knife already in her hand. She pointed the short blade directly at Meyral's throat. "Who...what? Show yourself!" she screamed frantically.

"It's just me," Meyral said.

"Sorry, Meyral...I was having a nightmare, I guess." She fell silent and gathered up her things.

# CHAPTER TWELVE: DECEPTION

Shortly after Meyral and Rubi left Gaffe, a mossy, vine-covered cliff blocked their way. It took Meyral a few moments to realize that the colossal barrier was manmade and that they had reached the Wall. The mighty marvel that encircled the Northern Plains as a triumph of man over nature had been devoured by the encroaching Talvy. Though the Wall towered over them, it was nothing compared to the snow-covered trees that Meyral could see on the other side.

"Gate Two," Rubi announced as she led her boarhound into a clearing near the town wall, which looked like a fence for children compared to the barrier just beyond it.

The Gate City still stood, although it looked completely deserted. When they reached the opening in the town's wall, Meyral found the left door of the gate shut tight, but vines had ensnared it as if it hadn't been used in ages. The right side had been left permanently open, and a tall shrub held what was left of the wooden door in place. Beyond the archway, fresh snow blanketed the Gate City in a smooth, uniform sheet.

Meyral's eye seemed to have stopped working again, but he had a heavy feeling in his gut. "This place looks abandoned," he muttered to Rubi as he dismounted. "I don't like it."

"Abandoned?" Rubi repeated as she gracefully slipped down from her hound. She pointed to muddy tracks in the snow that led down the main street. "Well, technically. But the North usually leaves a few soldiers to maintain the fort."

Rubi looked at Meyral somberly, with a question hiding behind her eyes. He knew she wanted to explain the dynamics of the fort, so he studied the tracks to busy himself.

"Gate Two used to be important, back when the Northern towns were mostly made of wood."

Meyral's anxiety began to rise. He could picture soldiers lying in wait in every shadowy crevice, and he shivered with excitement or fear—he couldn't tell which.

"...Nasabin and other places like it supplied lumber from the Talvy, which had to pass through this Gate. But now the Federation has become all about steel and stone...and a few glass castles."

As Meyral inspected the footprints leading down the road, he thought he heard a voice echo from somewhere nearby. He paused, looked up, then shook his head and turned back to the muddy tracks.

"...Gate City, like many others, was forgotten. Only the soldiers that are ordered here even bother. Aside from a lone trader every now and again, this place doesn't see many humans. All that's left past the Gate are a few families who are too proud or too poor to go anywhere else."

There was a sadness in Rubi's voice that barely registered with Meyral. As he followed the tracks to a pair of ruts left from a wagon, he heard the other voice again and he stopped. His mind began to race.

*The North usually leaves a few soldiers. That's what she said...but that can't be right.*

It was then that he realized what was bothering him. The footprints they had found were round and shallow, not what he would expect from soldiers in heavy boots and armor.

"Something's wrong," Meyral muttered as he straightened up and drew his knife.

"The forest used to extend into the heart of the Northern Federation," Rubi continued. Although she was a fair distance behind him, he could still hear her. "But after years of building, all that's left out there is grass. There are even a few places where you can see all the way to the beginnings of the Frozen Wastes. Lots of strange things—"

Meyral watched an old man stand next to a wagon. When Rubi finally noticed his gaze, her feet stopped along with her story. The man stared back at them and Meyral sized him up. He didn't look very big, but it was hard to tell because he seemed to be wearing several jackets. Two flaps on either side of his buckskin hat crept down over his ears and covered most of his ruddy cheeks. The rest of his face sported light wrinkles underneath grizzled scruff, and his hair fell on the nape of his neck like a short, silver curtain. If not for the heavy, double-bladed axe in his hands, Meyral might not have been worried.

The two buffalo attached to the man's wagon scraped at the snow with their hooves. There was a heavy tarp over the cargo in the back, but Meyral didn't care what the man was selling. Silence continued as the three of them stared. The man spun his axe in his hands, but Meyral and Rubi stood completely still.

"We don't want any trouble," Rubi finally said.

"You don't?" he asked. "Oh, praise the gods. I thought you were bandits." He swung his axe up and rested it on his shoulder, then walked toward them with one extended hand.

Rubi shook the man's hand and he smiled. He had a kind look in his eyes, but Meyral didn't trust him. The newcomer stood as taut as a bowstring ready to fire, and he only relaxed a tiny degree when they broke their handshake. He turned for another handshake, but Meyral didn't budge.

"Okay, not a toucher," the man muttered. "Don't worry about it. I had an uncle once who was like that. Oh, sorry!" He laughed and a carefree smile lit up his face. "Where are my manners? The name's Billiam."

"I'm Jewel of Nasabin," Rubi answered. "And his name is Christophe. He's my bodyguard."

Meyral scowled, but his companion didn't seem to notice.

"Ah, Nasabin," Billiam mused. He set his axe down and checked a few of the straps on his tarp. "Never been myself, I've always preferred the forests."

"Anyway," Rubi continued, "what would make you think we were bandits?"

"Well, with the guards gone I figured it was only—"

"There aren't any troops stationed here?" Rubi interrupted.

Billiam let out a hearty laugh. "There hasn't been anyone manning Gate Two since what happened with the senate. It's fine by me, though. Now that this place is empty, I can work mostly uninterrupted."

"And what would that work be?" Meyral asked, speaking to Billiam for the first time.

"I'm a lumberjack. Just dropped a load in Kö, lovely little village. They make this wonderful beet soup that makes it worth the trek, let me tell you. Anyway, I'm heading back out into the Talvy to restock my pinecrest supply."

"What's in the wagon?" Meyral asked warily.

"That's what some might call the secret to my success...and that's just how I intend to keep it. Secret."

"Watch it, you two," Rubi scolded. "We'll get through the fort together and go our separate ways."

"I think that's the best idea I've heard since my granny invented the goat-powered butter churn," Billiam said with a smile. He slapped one of his buffalos and his carriage started down the road.

* * *

Rubi walked between Meyral and Billiam purposely. It wasn't that she didn't trust her companion, but she could never be too cautious with the new Meyral. The inner and outer doors to the fort had been left ajar, and the three travelers passed through easily.

"Well, look what we have here," a voice rang out as they reached the other side.

The doors behind them slammed shut. The boarhounds and the buffalo spooked, but the buffalo didn't get very far before they stopped. Billiam chased after them and hopped onto his wagon as two dozen men in Northern uniforms stepped out from behind the trees on either side of them. Some stepped out onto the wooden walkway above them that protruded from the top of the Wall. They all had their weapons drawn, most of which were crossbows.

Rubi immediately reached for her own bow and notched an arrow, but there was nowhere to run to or hide. She pressed herself against the Wall, though Meyral hadn't moved.

"By order of the Northern Federation," the leader said as he stepped forward, "you must each pay fifty pieces to pass through Gate Two. There is no use resisting, we have you surrounded."

He wore a spiked helmet, but no shoes. The man next to him had infantry armor, but an officer's cape was slung over his shoulders.

"Imposters," Rubi muttered so only the other two could hear her.

"News does travel fast, doesn't it, *Jewel?*" Meyral sneered. "Harold kicks out Nordcross, but they were the ones protecting his people. He might as well hand the North over to bandits."

Rubi gave Meyral a hurt look, then turned to the imposters. "You're nothing more than charlatans, you swine!"

"Prove it!" someone yelled back excitedly.

"Just pay the tax," another one implored.

"You know damn well the North doesn't tax at the Wall!" Rubi shouted.

"How dare you speak to the Northern Militia like that!" the leader snapped.

"If you really are soldiers, then what color is the eagle on your banner?" Rubi asked calmly.

"Blue!" someone shouted.

"Wrong," she shot back. "Only Blackbird Units guard the Wall. Who are you?"

She heard the twang of the crossbow before she saw anything. A bolt caught Meyral's hood and pulled it back. If his right ear had still been attached, it would have been torn off. Rubi's aim was better, and before the man who fired could reload, he fell in the powder with an arrow sticking out from his chest.

Meyral dropped his cloak and used his knife to cut away his old, grimy shirt. Rubi already had another arrow notched, but none of the bandits noticed. The shirtless monster stomping across the road drew their full attention.

"Shoot him," the leader gasped. He fell back a step and cleared his throat. "Shoot him!"

Rubi fired and the leader's neck spurted blood onto the pristine snow. Crossbow bolts filled the crisp air as the bandits fulfilled their dead leader's order. Most of the missiles missed their target entirely, and the others Meyral batted away like he was swatting flies. One managed to hit Meyral in the chest and Rubi's breath caught in her throat.

The hit knocked his shoulder back, but it didn't slow him down. He held up the bolt, and its tip had become as blunt as if it had hit the Wall. Meyral tossed the missile back and laughed as a couple bandits sprinted away.

Billiam tore the tarp from his cargo as the bandits reloaded. Two copper globes sat underneath, connected by several lengths of coiled tubing. They took up almost the entire space in the back, and small fires sprang to life underneath the coils. The woodcutter roared as he strained to lift a metal box with a six-foot blade protruding from it, its edges lined with gleaming teeth. A bundle of hoses led from the box to the giant spheres, and a shrill hissing noise started as the teeth on the blade whirled faster and faster.

The crossbows swung in his direction, but before they could fire, Billiam leapt behind his wagon. He swung the blade against a support for the upper walkway and hacked at an upward angle. As he held it, the blade ate away at the wooden beam, and a moment later Billiam kicked its bottom portion across the road. The walkway shook and groaned under the weight of the snow and the bandits until it started to collapse. When it landed, the crash created a miniature snowstorm around the fort. The bandits shrieked as some were smashed and others became tangled in the wreckage.

A loud, high-pitched scream echoed around the yard as the hissing machine quieted. Meyral immediately tackled Rubi to the ground as more bandits cried out. The screaming continued, as if a banshee had been let loose, and something heavy landed next to them. Meyral crawled toward the Wall and dragged Rubi as she tried to focus on what was making that noise.

The snow started to settle and she saw what had landed near them. One of the bandits, his face frozen in an eternal scream, lay on his back only a few feet away. His body was covered in blood and giant gashes stood out against his pale skin.

"Run!" a voice screamed from far away.

Suddenly silence surrounded them. Billiam led his buffalo around the scattered debris, but then a dark shape leapt over him. Rubi screamed—she couldn't help herself. A cat slightly larger than Billiam stalked toward them, its hungry jaws open and dripping with saliva. It was a Northern lynx, only much bigger than any Rubi had ever seen. Meyral shrugged his cloak back on and held up his knife while Rubi notched another arrow.

The lynx watched them with narrowed, ravenous eyes. The grey-furred beast's paws were almost as wide as a boarhound's, but its body was much leaner. Its thick tail swept back and forth, churning a flurry of snow behind it.

"Whoa! You two better lower your weapons or you're gonna get hurt now," Billiam yelled. He stopped the buffalo and held his hands out. "Easy girl," he muttered as he inched closer to the giant cat. "Everyone just calm down. Give me the rabbits."

It was then that Rubi noticed the two fat hares dangling from the cat's mouth. It dropped its prey and mewled as Billiam swooped down and snatched the rabbits. The lynx slinked back and purred loudly. It sat on its haunches, still watching Meyral and Rubi.

"That was a close one, yea?" Billiam asked. "Sorry about that, she's a…rather temperamental creature at times. Those bandits really riled her up." He looked over his shoulder at the cat, who was too busy licking one of its terrifying claws to notice.

"Is she yours?" Rubi asked tentatively.

"That kitty cat? I wouldn't say she was mine—at least not within earshot of her," Billiam said with a wink and a smile. "No, it's really more of a partnership."

Rubi glanced at Meyral, but he only stared at the cat.

"Would ya look at that…" Billiam muttered.

A strong wind blew through the trees and Rubi followed the lumberjack's upward gaze. The spots of light green poking through the clouds dwindled as a wall of white swept across the sky.

"Looks like another blizzard!" Rubi shouted over the wind.

"You're right!" Billiam called out. "We should stay here tonight, traveling could get us killed!"

"This crumbling fort could get us killed," Rubi replied as the wind died down a little.

Bits of hail started to fall around them and Billiam shrugged. "Nah," the lumberjack said, "only the walkways are made of wood. The fort is stone…she'll hold."

Out of the corner of her eye, Rubi saw Meyral standing as still as a statue. He clutched his knife tightly in his hand and a faint glow emanated from his hood. Rubi walked back to the Gate and pulled on one of its heavy doors to draw Billiam's attention away from the Blue Bandit.

Billiam led his buffalo toward the Gate and the lynx followed. He looked at Meyral, then turned back to Rubi. "Is he just gonna stand out here?" he whispered when he got close enough.

"Just give him a minute," Rubi replied. "You know how bodyguards are, always so cautious."

Billiam laughed. "You know, my brother was like that. Always went on and on about how he didn't like being inside. Always said he felt like the walls were closing in on him. Last I heard, he was living somewhere in the Clarion Swamp."

Rubi laughed as she opened the other door to the fort. She gave Meyral a worried glance as the wind whipped his cloak around him.

\* \* \*

Snow started to fall. Lightly at first, then the wind picked up and the flurries painted the sky white. When Meyral finally regained control of his body, he was ankle deep in fresh powder. He looked around, startled to find himself once again alone.

The sound of Rubi's voice floated to him on the breeze, so faint yet familiar. He followed it through the fort, then followed the buffalo tracks to a large building. He opened the thick, creaky front door and the smell of stew assaulted his nostrils.

"Hey, I was getting worried!" Billiam said, his wide smile wrinkling the skin around his eyes. "The snow's really comin' down out there," he added as he looked over Meyral's shoulder.

"Yea," Meyral said.

His frozen, aching joints rejoiced in the heat of the blazing fireplace across the room. A large table took up most of the open area, but it seemed as if some chairs were missing. Then he noticed the woodcutter's axe in a corner next to one chair's broken legs.

Billiam closed the door. The overgrown lynx opened its mouth and yawned, letting out a wildly loud meow in the process. It laid its head back down on the hearth next to Rubi, who reached over and scratched behind its ears.

"Now that we're all here," Billiam announced, "why don't we take a seat at the table and eat?"

Rubi stood and walked around the lynx. Billiam left through a side door, through which Meyral could hear the stew boiling in the kitchen. When he returned, he carried a platter with three bowls of jackrabbit stew. Meyral and Rubi took their seats, and a bowl was set in front of each of them. Billiam sat his bowl at the head of the table and left the room again.

"What did your eye show you?" Rubi whispered.

"A lot about Reaver and the cat we used to keep at Number Twenty-Eight," Meyral answered with a glance toward the lynx. Then he remembered his new name. "My name is Christophe?" he asked indignantly.

"Could be worse," she said. "I almost called you Tristan."

Just then Billiam returned and set two bottles of wine and some crusty bread on the table. The woodcutter sat and Meyral pulled a bottle to himself before digging into his stew.

"Back there," their host said, "you mentioned something about the elder. Do you know him?"

"I wouldn't say that," Rubi said as she shook her head. "I've only met him once."

160

"So what was that thing you used earlier?" Meyral asked to change the subject.

"It's called a chain-driven saw," Billiam said proudly. "I bought it back in Gate Five...from a Nordcrosser, I think. Well, they're the ones that make these things, anyhow."

At the mention of Gate Five and Nordcross, Rubi dropped her smile and took a deep drink from her wine goblet. Meyral's spoon, full of steaming broth, stopped halfway to his mouth.

"So you two are heading home I take it?" Billiam asked. "Gonna...settle down, start a family?"

"No," Meyral said before he could stop himself. When he saw Rubi pull her hand off the table and look away, he added, "We aren't staying long, I mean."

"Oh?" Billiam looked at him curiously. "Why's that?"

"Uh, fishing, and..." Meyral stumbled over his words, kicking himself for saying anything.

"Hey, you don't have to tell me if you don't want. I won't take offense, it's probably smart of you. After all, you have no idea who I am and I have no idea who you are. See, my brother's second wife, Kim, she's too trusting like that." Billiam sat back in his chair and laughed. "She'll tell anyone anything. I told him, I said Jet—my brother's name is Jethro, only I call him that—I said, 'Jet, if you marry that woman, she's gonna be a danger to you and the traders.' See, Jet's part of a caravan. I think they're due up this way in about a month or so, come to think of it. You oughtta meet him."

"Oh, we won't be here by then," Rubi said.

Meyral kicked her foot under the table and took another drink of his wine.

"Well, wherever you're going, don't go east. I heard the Blue Bandit's out there, and that he's the one who caused all the ruckus with the senate."

"We're on the west coast of the Federation," Meyral snapped. "Where are we supposed to go if we don't go east?"

"I get it, yea, but I'm just sayin' if you're going to Padscott, you might want to take the scenic route."

"Look, we're not going to Padscott!" Meyral yelled.

"I know, but after that, on your way to Padscott, I'm telling you—"

"And I'm telling you ships don't sail from Padscott, they sail from Frazier Bay! Which is *west!*"

Rubi gave Meyral's cloak a sharp tug and he realized that at some point he had stood up. Then he realized that he had just told a complete stranger where he was going. He slowly sat down and finished his bottle of wine.

"In any case, west, east or what have you, I'm sure it'll all work out," Billiam said as his grin returned. "It always does." Then with a nod to Meyral, he added, "Eat up! There's plenty more where that came from."

\* \* \*

After they'd burned all but one of the chairs and the howling of the wind had died down, the fatigue set in. The lynx was already fast asleep in its spot near the fireplace as Billiam continued to tell his guests very detailed stories of his family and his life as a lumberjack.

"I'm turning in for the night," Meyral muttered as he stood. "I'll be across the way."

"Stay here, you'll freeze to death," Rubi said as concern lined her face.

"There are worse things," he mumbled as he opened the timber door and stepped across the threshold.

"We'll leave the door unlocked in case you change your mind," the woodsman said with a wink and a generous smile.

After testing a few of the other buildings around the fort, Meyral found one that was surprisingly well insulated. He lay on his back, wide awake and anxious. He'd kicked his blankets into a bundle at the foot of his bed, and his thoughts raced faster than the freezing winds outside.

The deserted fort had given him a bad feeling, but as the night wore on, that feeling only intensified. He knew Rubi felt something, too. She'd been quiet ever since she had finished her stew. He could tell something was on her mind, but he didn't want to ask her until they were alone.

*Why can't I shake this feeling?*

Meyral rolled onto his side as his mind turned down a path that he found himself exploring more and more often.

*Is it Rubi? Is she the reason I've been feeling so…uneasy lately?*

*"We could never harm something so...beautiful,"* another voice echoed in his mind, the sound garbled and distant. *"Remember? She's beautiful. And you would hate it if something* awful *happened to her."*

The other voice was mocking him. He thrashed around until he was sprawled out onto his stomach, sweating despite the biting cold.

*Who are you? Why are you here? Leave me—*

"...up," he heard a voice whisper.

Meyral's eye shot open. His breathing stopped and he lay perfectly still, listening with all of his concentration. He heard Billiam's voice drift in through an open window. Meyral slid out of bed as silently as he could, then grabbed his cloak and threw it around himself. He slinked toward the window and watched Billiam lead the lynx down the alleyway right next to him. When the woodcutter and his beast were far enough in that they were protected from the storm, Meyral saw something glow in Billiam's hand. The cat watched it intently, its tail swishing back and forth with a furious kind of disquiet.

"...heading to Nasabin for less than a month. They plan on taking a ship out of Frazier Bay. We couldn't get anything else out of them." Billiam stopped, as if he were listening, and then his face contorted. "Yes, she would make good bait," he continued. "There's a definite connection there, even if they don't see it."

Meyral leaned forward, closer to the window, and he saw the dim light in Billiam's hand disappear. Without the glow, he could see what it was—it looked like a rock that had been split in half, but the flat surface shined like crystal.

"So, Sis, what do you think?" Billiam asked as he slipped the rock into one of his pockets.

The lynx rose onto its hind legs and squared its shoulders. Its ears and sharp teeth retracted, and its thick, grey fur melded together to form a dark suit. Meyral watched, mesmerized, as the large cat transformed into a woman. She tugged at the sleeves of her suit and yawned lazily, her mismatched eyes watching Billiam from under her heavy eyelids.

"You heard her," she answered. "We've done what we need to. From here on out, it's up to the Tracker."

"I'm still curious," Billiam said as he removed his hat for the first time. With it came his hair and a thin, clear sheet that peeled from his face. His wrinkles were suddenly gone, and Meyral finally recognized the two Nordcross agents from the senate. "Why not assassinate him here and now? There were plenty of things in this fort that I could have slipped into his stew."

"You saw that bolt earlier," Farah replied with a yawn. "Maybe he can't be killed…which reminds me, didn't you tell the men not to harm our prey?"

"I think killing them was a fair punishment for disobeying, don't you?"

"More of a slap on the wrist really," she said. "We could have done a lot more." Farah reached a hand into her ratty, coarse hair and pulled her sharpened fingernails through it.

"Forget the blood and guts for a minute, would you?" Will pleaded with a sigh. "I'm trying to have an intelligent conversation here."

"Proceed."

"Why is Sera so interested in this guy?"

"Who knows," she answered. "We've got better things to worry about, though. You heard the redhead—they met Harold. They *let* him live. Let's go."

Farah began to transform again as Will turned away. Meyral slipped back and squatted near his bed.

*"Kill them,"* the voice from before muttered.

Without grabbing his boots, Meyral sprinted outside. He ran haphazardly through the fresh powder, urged on by violent impulses. By the time he reached the alleyway, all he found was a large spot on the wall of the cottage that had been brushed clean of snow.

Rage overtook him and he ran into the night. Meyral quickly found the massive lynx tracks heading back toward the forest. He followed them as the night grew darker and darker, and then he blacked out.

* * *

"Meyral?" Rubi asked as she gently touched his shoulder. "Meyral, wake up."

When she had first realized that she couldn't find Billiam or the lynx, she started to worry. When Meyral turned up missing, she started to panic. She headed out to search for her old friend, but luckily she didn't have to go far. Meyral was right in front of the fort with one of their boarhounds huddled on his side. He was buried in the snow, wearing nothing but his cloak, which barely covered him. His exposed, naked body had lost all of its color, but the cobalt in his scars glowed brightly.

Rubi slapped Meyral across his face. "Don't you dare leave me again," she muttered as she pulled her hand back. "Don't do this to me..."

Meyral stirred weakly before she swung again. His good eye opened, bloodshot and unfocused, and then he suddenly leapt up. He spun around twice, looked at Rubi, then quickly pulled his cloak shut.

"Did they come back?" he asked, his voice still deep and raspy from sleep.

"No," Rubi answered hesitantly. "Meyral, where did they go? Where did *you* go?"

"I'm not sure. But I know that Billiam and his cat were actually the two NIB agents from the senate," he said quietly.

"You mean...the cat was really a woman?"

"It changed *into* a woman. Or the other way around, but—"

Rubi sighed and pressed her hands against his face. "You're freezing. I had a similar experience not too long ago, remember? I saw things...you've seen some too. It happens."

"I know what I saw!" Meyral shouted. "It was them!"

"We should get you properly dressed and restart that fire. Once you're warmed up—"

"I feel fine. I don't need a fire," he snapped. "We need to leave."

# CHAPTER THIRTEEN: NASABIN

After scouring Gate Two, Rubi found Meyral a crisp, black tunic to replace his old shirt. They left the abandoned fort, and before long, the sea came into view from between the trunks of the ancient trees. As Meyral looked out upon the grey ocean, a single wave crashed onto the sandy beach, and with it a memory flashed into his head and disappeared as quickly as it'd come. His gasp was lost in the salty breeze whipping around his face as two buffalo pulled his new wagon along.

"Tell me again why we're keeping this thing," Meyral grumbled.

"We lost one of the boarhounds and that thing in the back could be useful…if we can figure out how to use it," Rubi said. "Or we could sell it, Nordcross machines are in high demand out here."

"Why should we have to depend on Nordcross to—"

"Look, there's Nasabin!" Rubi interrupted, pointing west.

It was a quaint town, like she'd said, with only eight wooden buildings and a few more tucked away in the surrounding forest. Meyral rode ahead, and when he reached the center of the small town, a dozen or so people came out to greet the complete stranger and his cargo. When Rubi finally caught up, shouts arose from the small crowd.

"Hey! The blacksmith is back!"

"Jewel, we missed you!"

"Where ya been?"

"Who's this, your husband?"

"This is Christophe, my bodyguard." Rubi gestured to Meyral, who had abandoned the cart and pulled his hood so tight that his face was barely visible. "You can trust him."

"How long will you be in town this time?" a grubby man asked as he wiped his hands on his greasy apron.

"I'm waiting for the merchant ships that head to the Island Nations," she replied. "When can we expect one, James?"

"Well," the grubby man said as he raked a hand through his

shaggy hair, "you've got at least a week before the next ship swings by, give or take a few days." His powder blue eyes lit up. "Are you reopening the shop while you stay?"

"I might as well," she answered with a smile. "Bring over whatever you have and I'll see what I can do."

"Liz will be very happy to hear this," James added.

Rubi's smile faltered a tiny bit, but Meyral noticed. He slipped away from the crowd as a young girl led the boarhound to the stables and more people peppered Rubi with questions. After a few minutes of wandering toward the forest, he found a small creek with perfectly clear water.

Meyral sat on a warm boulder bathed in sunlight. His hand reached for the leather fold Ordell had once given him, but the pocket was empty. It was a moment before he realized that he no longer carried that burden. His fingers squeezed into a fist and he looked down to watch his scars flex.

*Why didn't I die? I was naked in the snow for an entire night...I should be dead, or at least sick. It took Rubi an entire day to recover, and as far as I know she was only in the snow for a few hours with thick clothes on. I feel fine...how is that possible? And the crossbow bolt...what if the NIB agent is right and I can't die?*

He stared down at his right hand, then pulled his sleeve up. It had never occurred to him how thick the scarring must have been for his flesh to be as tough as it was.

*What is it about these scars? How deep do they go?*

That other voice snickered in his head, an eerie sound that lasted far too long. Meyral shivered as he raised his eyes and stared out over the running stream. The water pitched and bubbled around the frozen stones. The silence there was different from that of the desert, but the peacefulness still calmed him.

A twig snapped nearby and he jumped down from the boulder. He stood straight and looked across the creek. The figure of a man stood in the shadow of a tree, completely still. The two of them stared at each other, but the strange man was too far away for Meyral to discern any features.

A striking image of black eyes ringed in red flashed in his broken mind and pain stabbed at his heart. He blinked frantically to try to rid himself of the agonizing vision, and when he finally looked back, the man was gone.

*It's bad enough I dream about people that don't exist, but now I'm seeing them during the day? Moons be damned!*

"There you are," Rubi exclaimed from behind him. "I've been looking all over for you. My old place is still in my name, we can stay there."

He could feel her waiting for him to respond. Solitude was all he wanted at that moment, and she was in his way.

"Well," she continued after a moment, "it's on the other side of town. If you follow me, we can get settled."

Meyral shrugged and turned. He followed Rubi through the tiny village until they reached a two-story building with a forge attached to its side and the chain-driven saw parked out front.

"Home, sweet home," she announced with a sigh of relief.

The shoddy workplace was tucked under a rickety roof, but the house itself seemed sturdy enough. As they walked into the dusty shop, Meyral closed the door behind them. It made a comfortingly solid thud, and with the four walls shielding him from the outside world, he sighed quietly.

"So…Jewel the blacksmith?" he teased.

"I'm good enough for what these people need," she said curtly as she pulled a sheet covering one of the counters.

"And what would that be?"

"To survive," Rubi whispered.

"Survive against what?" Meyral asked as he pulled his cloak off and draped it over his arm.

"They need panhandles and gardening tools. They need their saws sharpened and they need nails. If you're asking about weapons and armor…no. These people are farmers. They have plenty of fight in them, just not in the way you're used to. I won't let this become another Mantrych."

"Last I checked," Meyral sneered, "that was Nordcross' fault, not mine."

"Is it that simple in your head?" Rubi rounded on him with fire in her eyes. "You're not culpable because you didn't strike first? *You* brought Nordcross to Mantrych. Tyler renounced his duties because of *you*, so the back gate wasn't guarded. And I…I ran." Her cheeks glistened with tears. "We are all at fault in our own way."

"So you blame me?"

"Yes!" Rubi shouted.

Meyral was amazed by how much that hurt him. His skin was nearly impenetrable, yet a single word could stop his breath.

"I have also forgiven you, Meyral," she said, lowering her voice. "But that doesn't mean I will ever forget what happened. This will not be another Mantrych." Rubi pulled a dusty tarp off of a bare display case. "Let's just focus on making a little coin while we wait for the ships to come in." The redhead lifted the last sheet off of a stack of boxes. "Then we'll be out of here…"

Meyral turned away and stomped up the stairs. He pretended not to hear Rubi stifling her sobs as he explored the second floor. It was a long hallway with a room on each side, a bath at one end, and a large room with a kitchen at the other. Meyral picked a room and found a bare, stiff mattress inside. He lay on it and closed his eyes for a quick nap.

*Still…it beats a blizzard.*

\* \* \*

Meyral didn't wake up until the next morning, when the smell of sausage and eggs drifted into his room. He stalked down the hall and headed toward the privy, but the delicious scent of sizzling pig could only be ignored for so long. His base desires won and his feet took him in the other direction instead. He was ready to give whatever apology was necessary to garner a plate.

The redhead he expected to find had her back to him, but the woman in front of her was something Meyral hadn't accounted for. She was tall and had the same messy, blonde hair as the butcher. Her skinny build and nervous demeanor reminded Meyral of a fox. Two small, closely set eyes flanked a large wedge of a nose. Below that a pair of full, cupid lips covered a bright smile. The woman held Rubi's hands while the redhead prattled on about calluses and sword grips.

As Meyral stepped into the kitchen, the woman's attention finally diverted from Rubi, who followed her friend's gaze. When she saw Meyral, she quickly dropped her hands and turned fully around.

"Good morning, sleepy," Rubi said with a small smile.

"Sorry," Meyral replied. He was just happy she wasn't still upset from the day before. "I didn't mean to sleep all day," he added with a yawn that caused his facial scars to split and twist.

"By the gods," the woman yelped as she stumbled backward.

"She…she told me about your, uh, your face, but…there's not much you can do to prepare for *that*, right?"

"Who's your friend?" Meyral asked coldly as he took a seat at the table.

"Right," Rubi answered. "Sorry. Meyral, this is Liz, and Liz, this is Meyral." The redhead gave a kind of awkward bow.

"I thought my name was Christophe?" he snarled.

"Don't worry," Liz said while Rubi shrugged with a pained look. "Your secret is safe with me."

"Good. Otherwise, I'd have to kill you." Meyral stabbed at a plate of sausages without looking up.

Liz laughed, but it quickly devolved into a nervous chuckle. "That was a joke, right?"

Meyral stuffed a forkful of sausage into his mouth and chewed loudly.

"Jules?" the woman continued as she looked to Rubi for comfort. "Is that…was he…"

Rubi shook her head slightly and sat across from Meyral. Liz swallowed hard and joined them cautiously. When she caught Rubi's gaze, her discomfort faded and a smile crept back onto her face.

"Eat up, because you're gonna need all your strength for what my dad's got," Liz explained. "Almost all of his knives are dull, and pounding out the dents in his rendering kettle is gonna be a bit challenging."

Meyral chuckled as he licked his knife clean. "You're in luck," he said, "because Christophe knows a thing or two about a forge as well."

"Does he know how to light the fires, pump the bellows, and fetch water?" Rubi snapped. She turned back to the blonde. "Don't worry, Liz, I'll get to it as soon as *Christophe* gets the fires going good and hot."

Meyral dropped his fork and knife on his plate loudly. A growl started deep in his throat. "Is that all I am now, the apprentice? Just the beautiful blacksmith's hideous lackey?" Meyral pushed back from the table without waiting for a response and marched down the hall. "Let's hope she doesn't break a nail," he shouted as he slammed the door.

"Beautiful?" Liz muttered. "Did he just say he thinks…you're beautiful?"

Rubi scoffed. "It's nothing," she said, but her bright eyes

dimmed as she stared toward the door.

\* \* \*

Before the sun managed to reach its highest point, Meyral had already lost count of how many buckets he'd fetched from the river and how long he'd spent at the bellows. He was, however, grateful that his work kept him away from the other villagers, especially Liz. He hated the thought of everyone watching him, wondering why he hid under his cloak.

The constant physical activity started to bring back memories. Mantrych, Taryn and Rubi, a goose dinner, a woman named Chloe…bit by bit, memories returned to him, but there were still extensive gaps.

"Worthless, worm-eaten mind," he muttered.

As he bent down to fill another bucket, he froze. The eerie feeling of being watched suddenly overtook him. He turned slowly and stared into the forest until he could see the figure of a man in his periphery. The man stood completely still between two trees, watching him just as he had the day before. Meyral blinked and the man was gone.

"I almost forgot," he spat as he filled the bucket and stomped away, "an eye that sees shit that isn't really there."

Meyral thought back to the night he found the senate. He remembered the satisfaction he felt as he ran each one of those bastards through, finally exacting revenge for their crimes against him and his friends. As a flood of anger surged inside of him, his shoulders fell and he sighed. His whole body seemed to relax as he let the darkness inside of him swell. He picked up his bucket and headed to the forge.

"…left us so suddenly," a man's voice said from inside the shop.

Meyral stopped and leaned against the house to listen.

"I'm sorry," Rubi said. "I didn't mean to worry anyone, especially you or your daughter."

"Hah," the butcher said loudly, "worry me? I was terrified, Jewel! And it brought poor Liz to tears. You know how much she cares about you…" As Rubi fumbled over her excuses, James added warmly, "Look, if you don't want to tell me, that's fine. But I know for a fact that the day Jewel needs the help of a bodyguard is the day the sky turns red again."

Rubi threw her head back and laughed. "Yea, well…what you don't know won't hurt you and all that."

"Is it him? Chris or Meyral?" James asked as he jabbed a thumb over his shoulder. "Is he why you left? And why you're leaving again so soon?"

A tense silence ensued.

"His name is Christophe," she muttered. "And no, we just…I…"

Meyral slammed the bucket down and glowered at them as they spun around. Some of the water had splashed out of the bucket and dampened the front of his cloak.

"Christophe!" Rubi gasped.

"Hey," James started, "I was just saying—"

"Shove it." Meyral stomped forward, forcing the butcher back, and he grabbed the empty bucket next to Rubi. "Don't mind me," he added as he left for the creek.

As he neared the freezing water again, a root snagged his cloak and he stumbled. The bucket rolled under his foot and sent him sprawling. As he sat up in the cold mud, visions of Rubi floated to the surface of his broken mind and he felt tightness grip his chest.

*Get a hold of yourself, Meyral. Is this…am I… jealous? How could I be? I didn't even know Rubi until a month ago.*

He rose to his feet and retrieved the bucket from a particularly dense and prickly bush. Once he was at the edge of the creek, he set the bucket down and skipped a rock out over the water. It bounced twice before disappearing under the surface.

*What a waste of time this all is. I need to find my father. He'll know what to do, how to fix this…fix me.*

The more recent memories of Rubi came to Meyral's mind. He clung onto two of them—Rubi sleeping in Gaffe and the nervous look she'd given him that morning in the kitchen—and then he stood up angrily.

*No, no, no! I can't deal with this! If Liz wants Rubi, she can have her. I just need to wait this out, then I can hop on a boat and leave forever.*

Meyral saw himself, inches away from his companion, his mouth sliding over her soft, pouty lips. His hands slid down her arms, caressing her hands and pulling her close. The hopeful dream flittered away and Meyral cursed loudly.

*Moons be damned...I'm going insane.*

\* \* \*

The delicious breakfast, James and Liz, and the mystery man were little more than faded memories by the end of the day. Meyral's arms felt like they were going to fall off and he couldn't seem to let go of the anger that had surfaced when he had seen Liz with Rubi.

He continued to work the bellows as Rubi pounded out the head of a hoe. She signaled for Meyral to stop as she doused the metal, set her tools aside, and wiped her hands on her apron.

"I don't want to lose the light, so we're done for today," Rubi announced quietly. "Meet me out back before you wash up." She turned and walked inside, ignoring Meyral's questioning look.

Meyral was already waiting for her when she walked through the back door in her training gear. She threw a staff at him and unsheathed one sword from her back.

"Let's see if you remember any of this," she said with a grin.

"Really?" he cried. "I just spent all day lugging water and pumping that damn windbag for you. Give me a break!"

"Yea, because all battles start when we're fully rested." Rubi screwed up her face and mocked him. "No, no fighting, I didn't get my nap today. How does that sound?"

Meyral roared and closed the distance between them in three steps. He swiped at her head and she was just able to dodge the attack. She countered and barely slashed his cloak, which he tossed aside to give him more freedom.

After another flurry of strikes, Meyral managed to get behind her and sweep at her feet. To his surprise, she saw it coming and jumped high, then landed a kick to his face. Rather than letting it knock him over, he used his momentum to ease into a series of back flips and ended in a defensive stance.

"I see you haven't forgotten it all, but you've become slower than armadillo snot."

Meyral gestured to his right arm without a word.

"Excuses, excuses," Rubi tittered.

"I've heard yours, and they're pretty weak."

Her eyes widened. "What do you—"

"Do you think Liz or James really believed you?" he asked as he circled her. "I can't believe you left without letting that poor girl know where or why. Don't you know she loves you?"

Rubi lunged forward and slashed wildly. Meyral preyed on Rubi's emotions like a master playing a violin, using his hate and anger to show her the way into Liz's arms.

He parried each hit until the last. Rubi's sword made contact with Meyral's scarred ribcage. The blade cut through his shirt easily, but when it reached his burnt flesh, it bounced back. Once again his skin refused to break, but a cracking sound like a tree branch snapping filled his head. He took a knee as the pain of three broken ribs floored him.

"Are you trying to kill me!?" he gasped.

"You're still alive," Rubi snarled between breaths, "aren't you?" She stared at him for a moment, then turned and headed inside.

The anger Meyral had felt all day started to dissipate as he focused on the pain in his chest that accompanied every breath he took. "And for some reason," he muttered to himself, "I'm still here."

\* \* \*

The next morning, Meyral woke to low voices outside his window.

"Well here's your problem, hun," Liz said. "There's an arrow in your condenser coil."

"How can you know so much about Nordcross technology, yet not know the difference between an arrow and a crossbow bolt?" Rubi asked.

"Just a skill, I guess."

Rubi giggled, and the sound of it drifting into his room was the sweetest thing that Meyral could think of to wake to. He hated her for it. He threw on his cloak, grimacing at the pain in his chest, and quietly headed down the hall. With a brief visit to the privy, he grabbed an empty bucket and set off to the creek to get started, letting Liz have Rubi to herself.

*If that skinny buffalo turd takes her off my hands, I can get on with my life. I can't afford to have anyone slow me down.*

His first trip to the creek was the most enjoyable part of that day. Everything afterward went downhill. If he twisted or knelt in the slightest way, his ribs exploded with pain.

As Meyral returned with his last bucket of water for the day, he found the forge abandoned. Around the other side of it, he heard the screech of metal and a long hiss. He dropped the bucket and reached for the nearest hammer, then ran toward the sound.

Out in the front yard, Liz stepped back from the wagon. Grease covered her clothes and hands. Rubi bent over next to her, and the two grabbed the base of the chain-driven saw as the teeth spun around the blade.

"Careful," Liz grunted, "this thing is heavier than I thought."

The two women grunted loudly as they lifted, and the blade tilted up to the sky. They lowered it back to the ground and Rubi pulled a thick lever, which caused the contraption to slow to a stop.

Liz pecked Rubi on the cheek with a sigh of relief. "We did it, hun!" she shouted as she kissed Rubi again.

"It was mostly you," Rubi responded with a wide smile. "What would I do without you?"

The joy in Liz's face vanished in an instant. "I don't know," she accused, "you tell me. After all, you're the one that disappeared for two months."

Meyral wanted to walk away. He wanted to leave the girls to their quarrel, but he couldn't. His feet wouldn't move, so he stood and watched.

Rubi set the saw back in the wagon and held Liz by the shoulders. "Honestly…I nearly froze to death without the warmth of your embrace. Without the sweetness of your lips, I almost starved."

Liz gave Rubi a bashful look. "That was a good speech, but it wasn't an answer. I'll get the truth out of you yet, Jules." Then she covered the redhead's lips with her own.

Meyral walked back to the forge and let the hammer clank to the ground. Rubi showed up alone a few minutes later.

"What happened to the water?" she asked as she gestured to the puddle around the bucket.

"I don't know," Meyral replied sullenly. "Guess it spilled or something."

"No worries," Rubi said brightly. "Meet me out back again for more training."

"No," Meyral shouted as the redhead tried to walk away. "I'm not going to let you break any more of my ribs."

"It was an accident."

"Accident my ass. You did it on purpose because I'm right about you and Liz."

"You want me to admit it?" Rubi shouted back. "Fine. After Mantrych, I was alone. My dad, dead. Tyler, dead. You and Maxine, dead. Taryn, dead, for all I knew. Liz was the first person to show any interest in *Jewel.* It made me…it made Jewel feel good. But…"

"But what?" Meyral asked as he stepped closer to her.

"It's complicated," she murmured.

"Not from where I'm standing. The scrawny girl loves you, Rubi. She wants to take care of you and raise your little redheaded babies. Isn't that what you want?"

"What I want is for you to stay alive," Rubi said forcefully. "You're out of shape, not to mention you've forgotten more than some people will ever know."

"I was 'in shape' enough to take out the Northern Senate," Meyral growled.

"Big whoop," she scoffed. "You killed a bunch of old men while they pissed in their robes. What about those two Nordcross agents? Did you take them out too? No, you didn't, and you didn't again the second time we ran into them. So shut up and train, dammit!"

Meyral conceded defeat. He picked up his weapon and waited for Rubi to get her training gear. That night, she only threw overripe cabbages at him while he jabbed at them with his staff.

His body seemed to be healing faster than it should have. By the next morning, he had almost his full range of motion back. He and Rubi spent the rest of the week in a constant cycle—Christophe would fetch water and work the bellows for Jewel, and in the evening, Meyral would train with Rubi. The only variable was Liz, constantly working her way back into her lover's arms.

* * *

One night, as Rubi took her leather armor off after a particularly intense sparring match, she noticed Meyral staring. She stopped and stared right back, which shook him out of his trance.

"It's…my eye."

His face was unreadable, but she was sure that it wasn't his eye. For one thing, it usually turned blue when he zoned out.

"Well, whatever it is, get it fixed," she said, "because we're leaving for Frazier Bay early in the morning. I also suggest you get packed. We won't be coming back here for a long time."

"Did you let your *friend* know that we're leaving?" he asked with a smirk.

Rubi turned around to keep from saying something stupid. Meyral did as he was told, and long after he'd fallen asleep, Rubi met Liz down in the shop. The ice and wind blew through the dark night, but the fire in the hearth danced merrily. It gave just enough light and warmth for the two of them.

"I won't let you leave this time," Liz said in a harsh whisper. "If I have to, I'll fight him for you."

"He'd only kill you." Rubi shook her head. "It took me over an hour after I told you his name to convince him to let you live."

"You think I'm afraid?"

"If you're not, you're a bigger fool than I already know you are."

The butcher's daughter held her with her deep blue eyes. Rubi gazed back, the firelight dancing across her pale, determined face.

*Her eyes are the same color that Meyral's used to be,* she thought. *They may not have that same sparkle, but at least I see more than death when I look into them.*

Liz leaned in and kissed the redhead. Rubi felt Liz's hands on her waist, and she let them disappear beneath her shirt.

*Soft hands from years of dealing with a knife, not a sword or staff. Hands made smooth from being smeared with lard rather than the bile of a vanquished foe.*

Liz broke their kiss just as her hands found Rubi's sensitive nipples. They hardened and pressed against her palms.

"I can go with you," Liz whispered. Her breath was hot against Rubi's neck, and it sent chills down her spine. "This town doesn't need two butchers. We can go anywhere you want, and I can make enough gold to support us. Imagine a life where you don't have to slave over a hot forge anymore."

Liz's hands wandered down Rubi's ribs. The redhead's back arched and she let out a small moan. Her lover grabbed her hips and held her close while her body ached for more. Rubi pulled Liz's shirt over her head and then pushed her onto her back. She pressed a finger against the blonde's lips, then covered Liz's neck and shoulders with soft bites and long kisses.

"Do you really want me imagining other lives, or should we stay in this moment?" Rubi asked.

Liz grabbed the back of Rubi's head and brought her face right in front of her own. She pulled the redhead close and kissed her with as much passion as she could.

*Not as much as Meyral could.*

"Do you love him?" she asked when the kiss broke.

"No," Rubi answered immediately.

"And do you love me?" the half-naked woman continued.

Rubi admired her bravery, but she knew Liz was playing with fire. "I don't know," she whispered. "I could."

# CHAPTER FOURTEEN: INSTINCT

Rubi woke Meyral before the sun was even up. She led him and Liz, whose hair was a wild, tangled mess, to the cart with the chain-driven saw. The boarhound they had left at the stables was already waiting for them next to the wagon. Meyral saddled and mounted his hound as the other two harnessed the buffalo and checked the straps over their cargo.

There were no people to wish them luck, no last minute pleas for Jewel the blacksmith to stay. In the early morning gloom, the tenuous threesome left Nasabin while the town was still fast asleep.

As the sun rose, they rode along a strip of grey sand that separated the Northern Federation from the Frozen Sea. Strange balls of white fluff padded about in the surf, looking for food, while various gulls cried overhead. By midmorning, the Wall came into view.

"So where exactly are we going?" Liz asked.

"I'll let you know when we're on the boat," Meyral interrupted as Rubi tried to answer. "You've already proven that you can't keep your mouth shut."

Liz did nothing to defend herself. She just kept riding as they followed the salt-stained Wall.

Meyral fell back to two hound-lengths behind Rubi, and an awkward silence settled on the troupe. His hand strayed to his pocket, where it pulled out a brown book. Reading through his fold had become such a habit that he didn't even realize he had the book open until he heard himself murmuring aloud.

*"A gale overtook me,*
*And in its wild fury*
*I was lost*
*For so long*
*The tempest became me*
*And I became it*
*The stormrider*
*Until I found solace*

*In the eye of the storm."*

Meyral looked out over the bleak ocean. Then he faced forward, and a stab of anger ripped through him as Liz whispered happily in Rubi's ear. He looked back down and finished the poem.

*"A voice asked my broken heart,*
*'Why do you fight your nature?'*
*I had no answer*
*As it deplored of me*
*'Why weep for that which is not lost?'*
*So I climbed the wind*
*To meet the voice*
*And answer its question*
*'All is lost, upon our birth,*
*For our lives have been decided.'*
*The voice howled in the wind*
*'Fear not,*
*For your nature will always shine through.'"*

A smile cracked Meyral's face. *My nature will always shine through...good. I'll be alone soon enough.*

\* \* \*

After thirty miles of roaring waves and cold, salty spray, the sun set and the troupe made camp. At the base of a grove of trees that seemed tiny in comparison to those farther inland, Liz and Rubi continued to chat. Meyral left and walked along the beach to gather driftwood that had been speckled with bits of tar. Before long, he had built a sizeable fire near the wagon, but without food, the sleeping hound was his only comfort.

When the moons rose and lit the landscape enough for them to see clearly, Rubi threw Meyral his staff. He wasn't entirely disappointed that she was continuing the nightly lessons. For reasons Meyral didn't try to understand, the spar became less and less about strategy and more about physicality.

The fight came to a head when Rubi tackled Meyral around the waist and wrestled him to the ground. The fighters rolled around in the sand like animals until Meyral managed to mount and pin Rubi, his arms on her shoulders and his shins across her knees.

Meyral's face hovered just over Rubi's. The flames reflected perfectly in her round eyes as her struggling ceased. As they stared at one another, their heavy panting synced. Meyral's arms felt heavy, and just as his nose touched hers, Liz cleared her throat.

The two combatants untangled themselves quickly. Meyral snatched up his cloak, shrugged it on, and headed for his bedroll, his thoughts immediately pulling him to his book. Rubi walked in the opposite direction—right toward Liz's arms.

* * *

The next day, Meyral kept his distance in an effort to not hear anything the women were saying to each other. By the time the sun had fully risen, they reached Gate Four. A small town had already formed out of the ashes of the city before it, and the smell of smoked fish hung in the humid air. Meyral pulled his hound to a stop as a memory started to worm its way into his mind.

*A city...its name was Tem, and a man...no, a king...his daughter was with him, and...*

Rubi pulled the buffalo to a stop. "You need a break?" she called over her shoulder.

"No!" Meyral shouted. He shook his head, clearing the remaining tendrils of the vision. He knew Rubi would want to talk about what he saw or what was wrong, but he was in no mood for either. "I thought all the Gates were abandoned?" he asked as he sped up and rode alongside them.

"Not all the Gates were rotting cesspools," Liz said loudly from atop the wagon.

"Some of them were actually quite unique," Rubi added. "Gate Twelve, high up in the Black Iron Mountains, is more of a mine than it is a gateway."

"That's right," Liz beamed. "My mother used to tell me tales about how that mine was built by dwarves."

"Mine too," Rubi added.

"I never knew my mother," Meyral said with a scoff. He looked to the Gate while Rubi and Liz stumbled over their apologies. Where a road should have run under the arch of the fort, a wide, lazy river spilled through instead. They approached the Gate City, and as they made their way to the Gate, Meyral murmured, "This one's on the wrong side of the Wall."

"You're right," Rubi answered. "The rich fisheries of the Frozen Sea are what drew them to this side. The only other places along this coast are the Frozen Wastes and Ardänia," she gave a sideways glance at Meyral, "so there isn't much of a threat from building near the sea."

"That fish smells great," Liz said with an eager smile. "You want to stop for a bite?"

"No," Meyral growled as he pointed his hound to the Gate.

Two young boys and a crippled sailor manned the fort, but they didn't even bother to search the riders as the trio passed through. Liz and Rubi rode behind Meyral as he followed a road that led away from the sea.

He pulled out his book, flipped to a random page, and read to himself.

> *"Like reaching out in the dark,*
> *In the middle of the night*
> *To touch your lover*
> *But there is only emptiness.*
> *Like talking to someone you've known for ages,*
> *But when you look away*
> *For only just a second,*
> *You find that they were never really there.*
> *Like waking from a nightmare*
> *To find that you weren't even dreaming."*

\* \* \*

The travelers stopped just outside of a small farming commune. As soon as they dismounted, Rubi pulled out both of her blades. Meyral used his staff to stretch, then took a few practice swings. He set his weapon aside and bent over, flattening his palms against the muddy grass. His hood fell over his head, and when he straightened up, he caught Liz eyeing Rubi while chewing the inside of her cheek.

"Could you teach me to fight?" Liz asked tentatively.

"You?" Meyral laughed before he could stop himself. "With

what weapon?"

"Maybe one of these," the butcher's daughter muttered as she reached under the wagon's tarp. She pulled out a leather roll and opened it. The thing was the size of a bedroll and had knives of all shapes and sizes buckled inside, along with a few hammers.

Meyral whistled.

"What are you doing?" Rubi hissed in Liz's ear.

"There's no reason I shouldn't be able to fight with you," she replied fiercely.

"Yea, Rubi, let the woman fight," Meyral cut in. He grabbed a chef's knife the size of his forearm and held it up. "Good heft, full tang...I think this one will do nicely."

The skinny woman nodded and Meyral tossed the blade to her. Liz reached for it, but pulled her hand back at the last moment. The tip of the blade missed her fingers by mere inches, and the handle hit her in the chest before landing with a soft plop in the mud.

"You did that on purpose," Rubi snarled as she rounded on Meyral. She shoved him back and glared, waiting for a response.

Meyral grinned and leaned back against the wagon. Rubi turned to Liz, who was still checking her fingers. The redhead picked up the knife and handed it to the other woman.

"No," Rubi muttered as she grabbed the blonde's hand, "hold it like this." She turned the knife around so that its spine ran along Liz's forearm and her thumb covered its pommel.

Liz smiled and said something quietly, to which Rubi responded with a short snicker. Meyral's grin faded and he wished he had buried the blade in the girl's heart rather than the mud.

*This is what you want, remember?*

Meyral repeated the thought, but Rubi's laugh cut through his concentration like a startling cry. He stomped away and laid out his bedroll before turning in for the night.

\* \* \*

After riding through what seemed like countless miles of Northern farmland, they arrived at a plateau with a spectacular view of the shore beyond the Wall. Directly below them was the immensity of Frazier Bay.

From the eastern bluffs that overlooked the inland sea, Meyral still had to turn his head to see both sides of the city. He stood and stared at the ugliest thing he had ever set his eyes on. There was a large gap in the Wall where the ocean had forced its way into the continent. A band of rust hugged the bay while spewing muck into the water. On each side of the gap, atop their respective peninsulas, were old, crumbling forts that climbed into the sky.

"Those forts were built back in a time when Ardänian pirates were a problem for the North," Rubi droned on as if she'd heard it a million times.

"Deimos and Phobos," Liz added.

"And now they rot in the salty air," Meyral murmured as he sat back down atop his hound.

"They're still important pieces of Northern history, Christophe," Rubi snapped.

He hated the look of triumph on Liz's face as the redhead scolded him.

*This is what you want,* he thought. *Get rid of the baggage so you can find your father.*

Meyral shook his head and turned his hound toward the city. He silently left Rubi with the butcher's daughter, hoping deep down they would just turn around and decide to go home.

He descended into the mess of narrow streets, and after a few turns, he realized that any beauty that might have existed there had long since been stripped away. Instead it had been replaced by a rusted jungle of scrap metal.

It looked to Meyral like the Northerners had even managed to violate the bay itself. As he rode toward the piers, he saw long dead ships sleeping with their hulls exposed and masts poking out of the bay's surface like ancient monuments. Frazier Bay was nothing more than a derelict tribute to a dying civilization.

Liz and Rubi's conversation started up again and Meyral realized that they had stayed behind him. They continued to delve into a tale of industrialization and civil war, neither of which Meyral cared about. After having seen Drum, Frazier Bay was nothing short of atrocious, and he couldn't find any appropriate excuse for such a place to exist.

The shacks made from scrap metal eventually gave way to sturdier structures as the travelers made their way toward the main harbor.

"We should sell the boarhound here," Liz suggested as she pointed to a stable that marked the end of the paved roads and the beginning of the metal docks.

"That's not a bad idea," Rubi agreed. When she noticed Meyral's scowl, she added, "What do you care? We'd have to pay extra to bring it aboard. Look at it as a win-win."

Liz found the stableman and began haggling as Meyral automatically pulled his hood back a little. He knew they were right, but he would never admit that anything the butcher's daughter did was a good idea. Instead he opted for silence and waited for Liz to finish.

A cold fog rolled in and blanketed Frazier Bay in a perfectly grey haze. Rubi and Liz asked around about a shop that might buy their chain-driven saw as men in dingy uniforms lit the streetlamps, although it was barely past midday.

"Even the sun avoids this place," Meyral muttered as the women led him around town, seemingly without direction.

Despite the fog and terrible directions, Rubi eventually found a shop underneath a giant sheet of corrugated steel. The sign over the door read "Marla's Steam Emporium." Meyral followed Rubi inside while Liz waited with the wagon.

The small office was packed with odd pieces of brass and copper, and long, glass tubes hung above them. Rubi poked through a few boxes full of valves while Liz paced in front of the entrance.

Meyral slowly walked through the narrow rows of shelves. He didn't like the place one bit. It smelled like something strange and unfamiliar, but what really bothered him was that all of those machines, all of those pieces, were property of Nordcross. His enemy. The fingers on his right hand tapped the base of his palm as he scowled.

"Can I help you?" a whispery voice called out behind him.

An elderly woman, pushing just past four feet tall, silently shuffled down the cramped aisle. There was a noticeable hump on her back, and she was shaped almost like a grey brick.

"Are you deaf or something, boy?" she demanded. "I asked if there was something I could help you with."

"You must be Marla, then?" Meyral said with a smirk as he glanced back toward the sign.

"Well, at least you managed to piece that together. There might be hope for an intelligent conversation here yet. Now, for the third time, why are you here?"

"We...acquired a Nordcross machine we thought you might be interested in," he answered.

"You *acquired* one, did you? More like you stole it," she accused, "but that doesn't bother me. Let me see it."

The woman turned and continued her strange shuffle toward the front of the shop, where Rubi and Liz waited. They noticed Marla leading Meyral outside and they pulled the tarp off. Marla's eyes grew when she saw the heavy contraption in their cart.

"That's a Carver Seven, one of the latest chain-driven saws," she said with very short-lived awe. "I'll need to inspect the piece, of course."

"By all means," Rubi chimed.

Marla looked past her as if she didn't exist. Then the old lady pulled a leather cap from her shawl and placed it on her head. Several magnifying lenses, attached to the hat by tiny brass arms, fell in front of her face. She tapped a few lenses and rearranged them until her eyes seemed larger than her entire head.

Marla climbed into the cart, tapped on a few pieces, then climbed back down to the ground. A look of disappointment dominated her heavily winkled face. "It's taken quite a beating," she announced darkly.

"I can assure you, it works," Rubi added.

Marla jerked like she had just noticed the redhead. "I can see that it operates, young lady, but the repair did more harm than good. Leaving it full of holes would have been better."

"But you even said you know it'll still run," Rubi continued, both confused and insulted.

"This isn't just some Northern tool for regular lumberjacks," Marla explained as she removed her strange hat. "This is a Carver Seven. It's bought for its beauty as much as its practicality. In this state, I couldn't pay more than fifteen for it."

"Fifteen pieces of gold?" Meyral snapped. "I'd rather watch it sink in the bay."

Marla tittered. "I can't tell if you're funny or touched in the head. Fifteen hundred, son. You have no idea what you've found, do you?"

"Five thousand," Liz stated simply.

Rubi and Meyral froze, but Marla turned to the blonde. "Ah,

someone with more above their shoulders than scars or beauty," she said quietly. "Five thousand is the price for a new Carver, but this is not new. Maybe if it was still wholly intact I could offer three thousand, but with the cost of the repairs it's going to take..." The old lady used her fingers to count to herself. "Replace the condenser and a few of those bearings, combined with the general service fee for the burners, then I'll need to flush the lines...I couldn't settle with anything above two thousand pieces."

"That price is insulting," the butcher's daughter continued. "Thanks for your time anyway, but we'll go elsewhere." Liz grabbed the buffalo's reins and motioned for the other two to follow. "Let's see...was that a lumber mill I saw coming in?"

Marla's eyes narrowed. "I would rather cut off my own foot than send you to that lying cheat with this...this piece of art! Twenty-five."

"Thousand," Liz said without even turning around.

"Twenty-five hundred, you cheeky twat! But only if you let me get a *good* look at the Blue Bandit here," she added as she stared hungrily at Meyral.

"How—"

"I make it a point to know everything that happens in this city," the old woman interrupted before Meyral could finish. "I knew you were looking for me before you did. Now are you going to let me take a gander at those scars people say you've got?"

"How are we going to carry that much gold?" Rubi asked. "Shouldn't we trade for something more convenient?"

"Don't I get a say in this?" Meyral demanded, but his question fell on deaf ears.

Marla pulled a key from her shawl. She disappeared inside the shop for a few moments and then returned with a lockbox.

"Ten Osdorf Bloodstones," the old lady offered. "The going price is three hundred gold pieces per stone."

Rubi raised her eyebrows, silently begging Liz to make the deal before she pulled out. The blonde grabbed the box reluctantly, although Marla's eyes didn't stray from the cloaked man in front of her. Meyral cursed under his breath as he shrugged off his cloak and held out his arm for her.

"The shirt, too," Marla added. "I'm no pervert, but I must see it all."

For a long, tense moment, the three women stared at Meyral. He finally walked past them and into the shop, and when everyone was inside, Liz closed the curtain. Meyral pulled his shirt off, then dropped his pants for good measure. Liz immediately grabbed Rubi and pulled her away, but Marla stayed where she was and inspected the length of his scars.

No more than five minutes later, Meyral was fully clothed and once again following the two women toward the docks. Boats lined the rusted piers that stretched into the bay like giant fishing poles.

"One of my father's friends is the manager of a company that owns a portion of these docks," Liz panted as they reached a tall building. The pack she brought was significantly heavier than her companions'. "If someone tells me where we're going, I can get us a good deal on a ship."

"That'd be great," Rubi said as she pecked Liz on the cheek. She looked to Meyral with a kind of sarcastic plea.

"The Island Nations," he finally managed through clenched teeth.

"Which island?" Liz asked.

"The biggest one," Meyral snapped back. "I don't really care."

"Really?" the blonde asked. "Well, why there?"

With just a look, Meyral shut the scrawny woman up. Liz dropped her pack next to Rubi and almost tripped over her own feet as she walked through the doorway to the building they had stopped at. Meyral and Rubi were left on the busy street, and he could already feel her glaring at him.

"Why are you so hard on her?" Rubi demanded as she planted her hands on her hips.

"I'm no harder on her than I am on anyone else," he answered without returning her gaze. "I'm not the one who sees something special in her."

"What's that supposed to mean?"

"It means giving someone like that a weapon is like giving a soulslug blessed salt."

"You only encouraged her."

"I wanted her to understand," Meyral growled. "I wanted both of you to. She is not one of us." The docks teemed with people, but nobody seemed to notice their public spat. "She's gonna end up getting herself killed, and she may very well take one of us down with her."

"Well in that case, you'll have a fifty-fifty shot at getting exactly what you want," the redhead accused as her voice started to pick up. "No more Liz, no more Rubi. Then nobody will be in your way."

Suddenly Meyral's head felt like it was about to split in two. He hadn't dealt with his eye in some time, and at that moment, a name wound itself into his sight. The pain was so immense that he dropped to his knees. Rubi knelt down beside him, the last few minutes forgotten, and she placed a hand on his back.

"Alright, I get it!" Meyral murmured as he clutched his head.

"Get what?" Rubi asked as she glanced nervously at the noticeable crowd that had started to gather.

A trickle of blood dripped from Meyral's nose and onto the dock. With Rubi's help, he rose to his feet, and the pain began to subside. "Nephi-Uriel," he said quietly, still panting.

"What?" Rubi asked.

"We need to be on the Nephi-Uriel, no other ship is…right," Meyral continued as he finally regained his breath. He blinked several times to clear the residual pain from his head.

"You're kidding, right?" Rubi's face turned from concern to anger in an instant.

"Does it look like I'm joking?" he snarled. "…the Nephi-Uriel, go tell Liz!"

Rubi rubbed her eyes with her free hand. "Fine, I'll go see what I can do. But if Liz already has the tickets, I doubt they'll give us a refund." She left her pack with Liz's and ran into the building.

While Meyral kept watch over their supplies, Rubi reached Liz and passed the message along. When the two women emerged from the building, the blonde had a bounce in her step.

"Thanks again for not asking too many questions, Liz," Rubi said as she glowered at Meyral. She sounded as displeased as she looked. "Since the Nephi-Uriel doesn't leave for another day, we need a place to stay…and we're out of coin."

"What?" Meyral demanded. "We had three *thousand* pieces of gold in bloodstones, how are we out?"

"The Nephi-Uriel is a luxury ship," Liz answered with a smug look. "It costs five times as much as the Red Jolly."

"And there were only two rooms left," Liz added. "So we got what we paid for…but isn't that what you wanted?"

Meyral stood silently as the women turned to each other. Rubi's face lit up as they locked eyes and he looked away.

"Oh, and Jules," Liz said, "I still have some spare gold saved up, so we won't need to slum around tonight. We're a team, so we're sticking together, yea?" The last question was directed more toward Meyral, who was forced to nod. "Good. Now let me find some decent lodging befitting of your beauty while you just sit tight. I don't want to lose you in this fog." Then Liz gave Rubi a peck on the cheek and skipped away.

* * *

When they arrived at the Seapuff Inn, it became clear to Meyral why Liz seemed so happy. The Seapuff was an opulent glass castle, the first level of which was forged from metal that looked much less rusted than its neighbors'.

Rubi played right into the blonde's hand. "This is too much," she said with an ear-to-ear grin. "There was a simple inn down the way that would have sufficed."

"But I insist," the butcher's daughter replied expectedly.

"This must have cost a fortune."

*By the moons,* Meyral thought, *if I have to keep listening to this…*

Rubi's eyes drifted in his direction as she kept feeding Liz's ego.

*Is she saying all of this for Liz's benefit or to hurt me? Is she trying to make me jealous?*

Before Meyral delved too deeply into the women's motives, Liz took Rubi by the hand and dragged her into the lobby. Liz handed their packs to an attendant, along with a gold coin, and then she tossed a key to Meyral. "You're in room thirteen," she told him.

"We all have separate rooms?" Meyral asked, but he knew what she was going to say before he had even finished speaking.

"No, that would be silly," Liz answered. "Rubi and I are staying on the top floor. Together."

Insult turned to injury as Meyral found his lodging. It was more of a closet than a room, and the only furniture inside was a small dresser and chair. There were fist-sized holes in the walls where the room had actually rusted through to the outside. The whole first floor had to share one bathroom, which wasn't much concern for a man who could clear a room just by greeting someone.

"Lucky number thirteen, right, Ordell?" Meyral said aloud as he tossed his pack on top of the dresser. It swayed ominously and Meyral shook his head. "Guess I'm sleeping on the floor tonight."

Meyral closed the door and walked back to the lobby. With the meager pittance that he had in his pocket, he was able to buy a meal. He sipped his bowl of mysterious fish soup in a dank corner of the dining hall before heading to bed. Alone.

* * *

The next morning, Meyral was more than ecstatic to leave the downtrodden city. He waited in the lobby for Rubi and Liz, skimming his book of poetry. As morning quickly approached midday, Meyral grew impatient. He shoved the book into the pack over his shoulder, noticing a few of the Seapuff's employees watching him nervously. Finally the two women emerged from the stairway with an attendant carrying all of their luggage in his arms.

"Mey—I mean, Christophe," Rubi yelled excitedly, then turned the color of her hair. "Wasn't that amazing?"

Meyral didn't respond. He had no idea what Rubi meant, but he didn't care.

"The view was spectacular, and I've never slept in a bed so soft. Which floor did you end up on? And that food—" Rubi finally noticed Meyral's distant look. "You had room service, right? And the featherbed?"

Liz had a slightly worried glimmer in her eyes.

*Here's your chance. Pull her right into your arms!*

Meyral swallowed hard. "Yes," he lied flatly. "It was fantastic. Now let's go before the ship leaves without us. I don't think I can handle any more of this luxury."

The attendant handed Meyral their luggage and walked away as Liz and Rubi strolled outside, hand in hand. The blonde looked at Meyral over her shoulder with a soft, almost thankful smile that went unreturned.

The simple contact between Rubi and Liz gnawed at Meyral worse than any of his returning memories had...but he didn't seem to be the only one annoyed by it. Most people they passed seemed put out by their affectionate display. People pointed and whispered, and one merchant even shooed them away from her cart.

"You two need a coupla' men in your beds to set ya straight," a bearded sailor shouted as he grabbed his crotch.

Liz seemed adept at ignoring these taunts, but Rubi's hold on the butcher's daughter continued to falter. Soon her pinky was all that connected them, and she stared at her feet as Liz led her through the town.

Meyral's mixed emotions bubbled back to the surface, and he simultaneously grinned and grimaced. Then he grabbed Rubi by the arm and dragged her into an alleyway. Liz tried to follow, but Meyral shoved her back toward the street and pulled Rubi deeper into the shadows. The redhead already had her swords out by the time Meyral opened his mouth.

"Good," his raspy voice whispered, "your reflexes are fine."

"What do you mean?" she asked quietly. "What are we doing here?"

"Are your feelings for that girl so fickle that a couple of foul sailors can change your heart?" Meyral asked, knowing that he didn't truly want the answer.

"My relationship with Liz is none of your business," she spat.

"You made it *my* business when you brought her along on *my* journey. You made it *my* business when you held her hand and drew the entire town's attention to *me*—a wanted man." Meyral's speech left a sour taste in his mouth, but he trudged on. "I ask you again, do you own up to the responsibility of your actions?"

Rubi's eyes flashed bright orange as she searched Meyral's face for something. He had no idea if she found what she was looking for, but the redhead pushed past him and grabbed Liz's hand. She turned the blonde around and planted a long, fierce kiss on her lips in front of everyone passing by.

"Oi, why don't you two ladies bring that onto my ship, eh? We'll have a right good time, I guarantee it!" The bearded sailor from before was back, but this time Rubi didn't withdraw.

"Your puny ferry wouldn't stay afloat for more than five minutes," the redhead shouted back. "You wouldn't be able to handle our passion." She pressed against Liz and her hands rose up to her breasts. "Maybe I'm a little more experienced than you on the subject, but these," she gave the blonde's chest a squeeze for emphasis, "feel a hell of a lot better than anything we'd find on you."

The man's mouth shut comically and the two sailors next to him guffawed with laughter.

"Rubi," the butcher's daughter said as she blushed, "I think you made your point." She pointed to the redhead's hands, which were still clutching Liz's breasts.

* * *

By the time they reached the Nephi-Uriel's mooring, the day had taken a much more pleasant turn. It seemed that Rubi's newfound confidence in her relationship shut the townsfolk up, and the Nephi-Uriel lived up to its title as a luxury ship. When the two women kissed aboard the ship, not a single passenger batted an eye—Meyral guessed that was because the others had their own affairs and scandals to worry about.

Meyral wandered the deck and its halls, taking in all the glamour of the oversized boat. It was made out of lumber from bow to stern, but unlike the weather-beaten barges and riverboats that he was used to, this ship was expertly cared for and the wood still had its original luster.

He began to notice small details as he continued to explore. The railings had golden leaves, the likes of which Meyral had never seen, embellished on them. There were several walls with murals carved into them, depicting fanciful sea creatures and other nautical-themed portraits.

Meyral followed one large illustration of two women attacking a giant squid, and he found a young man scrubbing the deck just around the corner. The kid whistled a jaunty tune and had a huge smile on his face.

"Welcome to the Nephi-Uriel, good sir!" the worker announced cheerily as he looked up.

Meyral tried to smile back, but the young man's face blanched and he immediately went back to his work. The Blue Bandit scowled and marched away.

*Of course, the girls go unnoticed, but I'm still a monster.*

He wasn't purposely avoiding Rubi and Liz at first, but when he found them having a private conversation at the bow, he let them be. By sunset, he'd grown accustomed to being alone—something he was already so familiar with. Then when he saw them coming up, he went down. If they strolled onto the same side of the ship as him, he would briskly walk to the nearest door and cross to the other side.

Meyral had covered the entirety of the Nephi-Uriel twice before he decided to search for the door to his cabin. Before long, he was deep in the hull of the ship where the only light came from tiny, circular windows about a foot in diameter placed near the ceiling.

He found the right door quickly and entered. The room was bright, and it took his eyes a moment to adjust to the light. Then Meyral realized he was in a large, open room with pillars scattered throughout for support. Hammocks hung between these, serving as makeshift beds for the poorest of the passengers.

"I'll wring her scrawny neck," Meyral muttered under his breath. "Only two rooms left my ass…"

"Excuse me?" a man asked.

Meyral looked toward the owner of the voice and found a man in a similar uniform to the scrubbing kid from earlier. He stood near the doorway under a lantern and eyed Meyral curiously.

"Nothing," Meyral responded as he pulled his cloak tighter. "I wasn't talking to you."

"Ticket, please," the uniformed man requested with an outstretched hand.

Meyral handed him the ticket Liz had given him upon boarding. The man studied it for a while before pointing to a hammock near one of the round windows.

"Your spot is over there, near that porthole. Put your pack wherever you like, but keep an eye on it. The Nephi-Uriel and its affiliates take no responsibility for your possessions."

Meyral scoffed and pulled his hood back. The chatter in the room came slowly to a stop, and he calmly and deliberately approached his hammock. He set his pack down and basked in the effect he had on the room.

*No one will touch the monster's things…and at least I have a bed this time.*

His window was too high up to see through, so he grabbed a crate and stood on it. The porthole gave him a meager view of the filthy bay. As he looked out at the scenery, trying not to think of Rubi, the city started to dwindle behind the ship. A strange and exciting feeling gripped him and he sprinted out of the room. He sped up a ladder and two flights of stairs before he reached the main deck, where he watched the dark sea unfurl before him.

# CHAPTER FIFTEEN: LUST

"First time?"

Meyral turned to greet the voice, and he found a woman that looked about his age standing behind him. She was a head shorter with olive skin that glistened in the setting sun. Her straight hair was as white as the Northern snows, then slowly transitioned to deep lavender toward the ends, which matched her bright, heavy-lidded eyes.

"On a ship, I mean," she added with a giggle.

Several memories swirled in Meyral's broken mind and he fought to stay focused on her. All the visions seemed to center on beautiful women in some state of undress, and each one shared her sultry eyes and tinted skin. He realized too late that he was staring and hadn't said a word.

"What's wrong with you?" the girl huffed. "Haven't you ever seen a Svirdarker before?"

Despite her pouting, she didn't walk away. She waited, and in her playful anger, Meyral thought she had become even more striking.

Her tight, leather pants stopped just below her knees, and on her tiny feet she wore black wedges. Her shirt looked one size too small, and an expanse of her flat belly showed from under the white blouse. But what mesmerized Meyral most were the two rings she had in her bottom lip and the tattoos decorating her arms and calves.

"Is it a race thing?" the Svirdarker whined. "Next you'll try to buy me or something…"

"I'm not sure," Meyral muttered. He tugged at his hood, making sure his right side was still covered.

"Not sure about what? Whether or not you want to buy me?"

"…about being at sea," he continued slowly. His head, for the first time in years, seemed to have completely emptied. "I didn't really follow the rest."

The young woman stared at Meyral, who assumed the conversation had ended. He turned back to the ship's rail and watched as one of the forts came into view. A scoff escaped him as he noticed how much the relic looked like a stack of mismatched rocks and sticks.

As the ship slid silently past Deimos or Phobos—Meyral had no idea which was which—he saw the shadow of the man that had plagued him in Nasabin. He strained his eyes toward the base of the fort, but before he could properly focus, the girl started again with a sigh.

"I remember my first time," she said. She leaned against the rail next to him and rested her chin on her hand.

Meyral smelled her without meaning to, and it was like he had dipped his head in a bucket of the sweetest lilies. He turned back to the fort, but the shadow was already gone.

"It's a little scary at first, but…you get used to it. And eventually, you just can't get enough." She glanced sideways and winked at him with an eye surrounded by dark green makeup. "I just think there's something so…adventurous and exciting about being out at sea, don't you?"

The ship broke out of the bay and into the open ocean before Meyral could answer. He marveled at how much it resembled the desert he'd spent so much time in. The lack of life on the surface and the rolling of the waves looked so much like the ever-shifting sand dunes that it brought a sick feeling to his stomach. He shook his head to clear it and looked back into the woman's questioning eyes.

"Sorry, I was just reminiscing," he muttered. "What'd you say?"

She pouted a little and then turned her body so that he could see her right calf. On it was a tattoo of a mermaid with a multicolored tail, but Meyral found himself staring more at the curves of her backside.

"I said that I got this on my first voyage across the Narrow Sea," the petite Svirdarker repeated with a smile. "We landed in Hastrum and I walked into the first shop I found."

"Hastrum…" Meyral muttered. "You were in Nordcross?"

Something in his tone must have given his disposition away. "Only for a stint, and it's not as bad as some people say it is," she explained. "Then I went to Ardänia, then moved to the Northern Federation, and now…well, who knows. Home is where you make it, after all." She waited a moment, but when Meyral didn't comment, she held out her hand. "My name's Sakura. You are?"

Meyral stared at the tattoo of a calla lily wrapped in a chain with an ornate, silver lock on her right forearm. "Mey—my name is—

Chris."

"Chris, huh?" She scanned him up and down. "Tell me, why the huge cloak? Overcompensating for something?"

"There was an accident a few years ago. The scars are…" he trailed off, unsure how to finish his thought.

"How bad could it be?" she asked. "Give me a peek…please?" She clasped her hands, put them between her legs, and batted her eyes.

Meyral hesitated, then moved his hood back a little and waited for her reaction.

"That is *so* badass!" Sakura exclaimed. "Why would you want to hide that?"

He pulled his hood back over his face and grunted. "Like I want that kind of attention?"

"Well, I don't know about you, but everyone needs to get noticed every once in a while. And seeing that kind of…makes me want to see the rest." She bit her bottom lip and her rings clicked against her teeth.

Meyral stared at her again, wondering if she meant what he thought she did.

Sakura stepped back and smiled. "Maybe I'll run into you later, cutie."

He watched as she walked away as if he were caught in a dream. His good eye mostly followed her lower half, where he caught a flash of vibrant, green ink in the sliver of exposed skin between her shirt and her pants. He found himself wondering what the rest of her tattoos looked like. His lecherous thoughts broke apart when he realized someone was standing behind him.

Meyral spun and caught movement in the porthole of the nearest door. He burst through just in time to see a red blur streaking around a corner. He ran down two flights of stairs and followed it all the way back to the ladder below deck, where he caught Rubi and pushed her into a small alcove. The redhead was panting, but she recovered quickly and crossed her arms over her chest. Her face alternated between angry and hurt.

"I came to invite you to dinner," she stated flatly.

"What was with the chase?" Meyral demanded.

"I…what did that darker want?" Rubi asked.

"Darker?"

"I mean—it's not nice—but I'm not here to be nice," she

stammered.

"You mean Sakura?" he asked.

"Is that her name?" Rubi snapped. "She could be a bounty hunter, you know."

"Her?" Meyral snorted. "Not a chance, nobody that hot is a warrior."

Rubi's face lost all of its anger. All that was left was the hurt, and Meyral immediately realized that he'd said the worst thing he could have possibly thought of.

"You're an ass," Rubi hissed as she grabbed him by the cloak and pulled him close. She looked left, then right to make sure that they were alone. "Nordcross hasn't forgotten about all the disasters in the desert, remember? You're still the Blue Bandit, and the price on your head is huge!" She let go of him with a little shove.

"...you really think I killed all those people?" Meyral asked unapologetically.

"Of course not! I just..." Rubi stumbled over her own words.

"Why are you still traveling with me if I'm such a monster then?" Meyral shouted as he banged a fist against the railing.

"I don't...I don't want to be alone anymore," she whispered.

"You're not alone," Meyral snapped. "Or did you forget Liz again?"

"It's different with her than it is with you."

"By the moons, what does that even mean?"

"You're the last remaining connection to a life that was taken from me...I don't want to lose that."

"Good to know I'm nothing more than a convenience to you." Meyral whirled around and stomped away, leaving Rubi behind with tears in her eyes.

* * *

The ship made its way south, and Meyral was back to his strange dance of evasion until that night. He skipped dinner, eliminating any chance to see Rubi or his newest distraction, Sakura, in the dining commons.

With a hollow feeling in his gut, he lay in his hammock and stared at the darkness of the back of his eyelid, hoping to wake early enough to get breakfast without running into anyone. Just then, above the gruff voices of the crowded space, he heard the steadily growing beat of someone stomping toward him.

"You can't avoid me forever!" Rubi yelled as she yanked Meyral, still half asleep, to his feet. "Being on a ship isn't reason enough to quit training."

"So I take it you're not just here to see how the poor live," Meyral said as he bent and reached for his staff. He had to shove a sweaty, shirtless man aside to retrieve it. "Although you seem to have left your coinpurse at home…what did you call it again? Oh, right, that was it—Liz."

"You don't know what you're talking about," Rubi spat.

"You and lover girl are sleeping in a converted cargo hull then, too?"

"No…we're in a cabin." A shadow of doubt crossed Rubi's face, but it vanished as quickly as it'd appeared. "Liz got this space so we would have room to continue your training."

"So this is for my benefit? Please, thank the butcher's daughter for me. The hammock was a great touch."

"Are you going to whine all night, or are you going to fight?"

Meyral attacked without a second thought. Rubi was just able to spin out of his way and into a group of grimy women before she drew her blades. The rest of the people moved back, but instead of hiding, they formed a circle around the two fighters and started placing bets.

In a series of quick moves and even quicker strikes, Meyral had disarmed the redhead and had her kneeling in front of him. Groans and a few curses rose up as the crowd broke apart.

Rubi looked up at her training partner with a mix of confusion and awe. "When did that come back to you?" she asked.

"I've been pulling punches since we left Nasabin," Meyral said as he dropped his staff and offered Rubi his hand.

"Why?" the redhead demanded.

*"The most feared of all sounds is that of the broken heart,"* his mind whispered. He wasn't sure where that phrase had come from, but he couldn't stop himself. Even with the pain he heard in her voice, he had to continue to push her away. "I don't know," he finally answered. It was a lie—he knew the reason, and it both excited and disgusted him.

Rubi ignored Meyral's extended hand and got to her feet. "I

guess we don't need to do this anymore, then."

"No, we certainly don't," Meyral agreed.

"Goodnight, Christophe," she muttered as she backed up.

"Goodnight, Jewel."

* * *

A young merchant watched Rubi and Meyral spar, then later hired the victor to guard his storage room. Meyral took the job without a second thought, mostly to keep busy. At night he stood watch at a door, and then during the day he would sleep in solitude. It was the perfect way to avoid Rubi and Liz.

It was rare that he ran the possibility of crossing paths with the two lovers, but when those windows of opportunity cropped up, Meyral would wander the bowels of the Nephi-Uriel. But he wasn't the only one practicing avoidance techniques. If he ever saw Rubi, even at a distance, she would turn and walk in the opposite direction.

Regardless of where the women were, he would spend an hour before his shift standing at the bow of the ship and staring at the heavens. Meyral noticed early on that he could see the moons so clearly out on the open sea that they looked entirely different from the celestial rocks he'd looked up to his entire life. He thought he could make out mountains, valleys, rivers, oceans, and even forests. Eventually he started to envision whole cities and roads on their surfaces. If the skies were cloudy, he would look out at the never-ending horizon, where the deep green ocean met the emerald sky in a perfect, infinite line.

A rumor had started to circulate that the ship was haunted by one of its former captains. Meyral was too absorbed in his debate on whether or not he should apologize to Rubi to realize that the alleged ghost was him. During one of his meditative musings, the steady clomp of stilettos on the wooden deck behind him broke his trance. He turned slightly and watched Sakura approach.

"Hey, handsome. Still upset about your woman?"

Meyral didn't answer.

"Isn't that Jewel chick your girlfriend or something? I can't imagine any other reason to put up with her." Sakura gasped and put a tiny hand over her mouth. Meyral had just enough time to appreciate the dark red paint on her nails before they trailed down her neck, revealing her shy smile. "Unless she's your sister...I definitely didn't mean anything—"

"We're only traveling together," Meyral murmured. "She just likes to worry about me sometimes."

"I don't think anyone's ever worried about me. It must be nice." A shadow passed over Sakura's face. She joined Meyral in staring out at the ocean.

"You alright?" Meyral asked when he noticed a tear trailing down her cheek.

"Forget about it." She brushed the tear away from her face with her palm, leaving a trail of dark makeup. "People are starting to say you're a ghost, you know."

He shrugged. "Maybe I am."

"How about you come by my place and I show you how wrong you are about that?" Sakura smiled and ran a hand lightly over his shoulder. She traced her fingers down his right arm until she touched the back of his scarred hand. "Surely you don't have to guard that silly door every night..."

"You've been checking up on me?" Meyral asked as Rubi's warning played in the back of his head. Sakura gave him chills, especially when she touched his scars, and he hoped Rubi was wrong.

"You're gonna pretend you're angry that I'm interested in you?"

Meyral shrugged. Inside he was burning with lust, and he wondered if she could sense it.

"Good. I'm in cabin seven." Sakura pecked Meyral on the cheek and walked back the way she came.

Minutes later, as Meyral made his way to his post, he turned a corner and Rubi ran right into him.

"Where's your lapdog?" Meyral asked before he could stop himself.

"Shut up and read this," Rubi said as she offered him a piece of parchment. It looked like it had been torn out of a newspaper.

Meyral carefully took it from her and read it in the dim light.

# Blue Bandit Body Count Rises

**Anatra 28<sup>th</sup>, 518**

Reported sightings of the Blue Bandit in the Northern Federation seem to be falsified as the body count in the desert continues to rise.

In the last month alone, three caravans have reported violent attacks and even grizzlier murders than the previous tragedies. Six victims from these attacks, all daughters of traveling merchants, were reported to have been sexually assaulted and then stabbed dozens of times. Most of the victims' faces were unrecognizable after the attacks.

Rumors recounted the notorious desert killer in the colder climates of the North, even going so far as to accuse him of the assassination of the senate, but Nordcross officials have yet to…

Meyral stopped reading and looked up. He expected anger—he almost wanted it—but all he got were tears.

"I'm sorry, Meyral," she said quietly as her throat clogged with emotion. She took a deep breath and steadied herself. "I don't know what's going on in the desert, but look at the date. I've been with you this whole time, which means someone is still killing people in the desert."

"And it's not me…" Meyral muttered.

"Maybe this would have made a difference," Rubi said quietly. "Before, I mean. It would have changed some of what I thought—"

"No," Meyral said. His right eye remained blank, but he understood what it all meant. "You thought right, it's just…there is something evil underneath the sands, and it inspires atrocities."

"Evil?" Rubi asked. "What do you mean?"

"I mean just that," he answered quickly. "There's something rotten underneath the desert and it drives people to do terrible things. And I…I…" Meyral lowered his head as he tried to find the right words. "It's impossible to fight those dark urges forever."

"Impossible?"

"Toward the end, I had these blackouts," Meyral explained as he absentmindedly reached up and touched the scars on his face. "When I came to, I was always surrounded by bodies and covered in blood. It *was* me, Rubi. I killed a lot of innocent people. But at the same time, it wasn't me…"

"Oh, Meyral," Rubi whispered with pity shimmering in her eyes. She slipped her arms around his shoulders. "I think I've known that all along, but I don't care. I know you."

There was a lull in the conversation and they let the sounds of the ship cutting through rough seas fill the void.

"I spent the last three days trying to figure out how to apologize to you," Rubi started slowly. "Figure out how to make things right, and then I found that paper this morning and it felt like too much of a coincidence. Only when I finally found you, you were with that…that darker."

"You mean Sakura?" Meyral asked as he held Rubi out at arm's length. "What's your problem with her?" His left hand clenched into a fist involuntarily.

"I…I don't know!"

"You can't be jealous," he added with a weak chuckle.

"Leave me alone." It was little more than a whisper. Rubi didn't even bother with eye contact, but her command had enough force in it to send Meyral away.

With nothing else to do, Meyral started guarding a door that didn't need it. He could hear the merchant inside counting loudly as anxiety ate away at him. His mind kept jumping back and forth between Sakura and Rubi. He couldn't tell if he was hurt or pissed off, but every time he started to feel apologetic, he could hear the redhead's angry voice scolding him. Halfway through the night, thoughts of Sakura won.

*Who cares about this damned door and who cares about Rubi? I just want to feel good for one night, by the moons, just one night!*

When he made his way to the upper parts of the ship, he found Sakura's cabin on the top floor. The richly gilded carpet underfoot was soft, with golden leaves embroidered along its edges. He stood outside of Sakura's room for what seemed like hours, telling himself that it was what he wanted, but knowing it was a lie.

As he was about to walk away, the door behind him swung open. Liz, wearing a thin silk robe over her undergarments, stepped into the hall. The heavy smell of wine wafted out with her.

"…and don't forget the strawberries this time," a familiar voice called from inside the room.

Meyral stepped aside, then pushed Liz against the wall. He poked his head around the corner and saw Rubi lying naked in the bed.

She immediately pulled a sheet up over her breasts and dropped her eyes. Meyral closed the door quietly and turned to Liz, whose eyes were wide with fear.

"What are you waiting for?" he asked darkly. "The woman said strawberries. You don't keep someone like that waiting."

Liz stumbled down the hall, occasionally casting worried glances over her shoulder. Once the blonde rounded the corner, Meyral knocked on Sakura's door.

"Come in," her sweet voice called from the other side.

Meyral turned the knob and opened the door. With one last look toward the other cabin behind him, he shut himself in and turned the lock for good measure.

Sakura's cabin was one room with two doors against the back wall. One was ajar, revealing a small bathroom, and the other was open enough for Meyral to see the balcony beyond it. A four-poster bed lay between the two doors, and a small table set for two occupied the space on his left. The only thing missing was the woman he'd come for.

"Where are you?" Meyral called out.

"I'm out here," she answered from the door on his right. "You should see it, the view is wonderful."

"You shouldn't leave your door unlocked like that," Meyral said as he walked toward the balcony.

"Why?" Sakura asked as she poked her head inside, her white hair trailing down like a curtain. "There's nothing on this ship to worry about."

*She has no idea,* he thought.

"Are you coming or do I have to drag you out here?"

Meyral stepped out onto the balcony, where Sakura stood in a royal blue dress with black hemming that showed off a fair amount of her golden thighs.

"Look," she said as she pointed toward the small ribbon of sand on the horizon, a section of which was interrupted by jagged rocks. "You can see what's left of Leviathan Pass."

Sakura turned and caught Meyral staring at the colorful tattoo that extended from the nape of her neck down, but most of it was covered by her dress. He shied away and stared down at the water, which was riddled with jetsam from the cliff.

"That means we should be in the Island Nations in a few days.

Have you ever been?" Sakura asked with a mysterious grin.

Meyral shook his head.

"I stopped there once," Sakura said as she turned toward Meyral. "This is my first time this far south since…"

The Svirdarker shivered, but it wasn't cold out. Meyral instinctively put his arm around her and let his cloak cover her back.

"I was with someone once, but we were poor. All we had in this world was each other." She looked up into Meyral's eyes. "He volunteered for some meaningless war with the promise of riches when he returned. It took the empire an entire year to tell me that he'd been killed, and I'd had his daughter in that time. On her first birthday, I…"

Meyral squeezed her shoulder lightly. She put her head in her hands and sobbed, then turned and buried her face in Meyral's chest.

"I couldn't take care of her! I was all alone. I couldn't even support myself. How was I supposed to raise a child?" Another sob racked her body. "I left her on the steps of a temple. For all I know, she died right there, right where I left her."

Sakura looked up again and Meyral noticed her red eye makeup was running. It looked almost like she was crying tears of blood. A long silence followed as the Svirdarker regained her composure. Meyral stood with one arm loosely around her shoulders, not knowing what to do or say.

"Sorry," Sakura said with a weak smile. "I just…I get a little emotional around this time of year. She'd be eight years old this season."

Meyral was a statue. Sakura pressed against him and pushed herself up onto her toes. She kissed him on the mouth and he could feel his feet curl in his boots.

"I'm a mess," Sakura said as she broke the kiss. "Would you excuse me for a bit while I freshen up?"

Meyral could only nod, and then Sakura kissed him one more time before she disappeared into the cabin. Alone once more, Meyral stared at the cliffs until his right eye blurred and his vision was quickly overtaken. The images were stronger than they had been in a long time, but they were little more than a swirl of neon colors. Meyral tried to concentrate until the colors began to form shapes. Two figures were running through the desert and arguing, but Meyral had no idea what they were saying.

His breath caught in his throat and he panted like he'd just run ten miles. His ears started to ring and the pain began to eat away at the rest of his senses. He started to pass out as he ran from her room, but he barely made it to the ladder at the end of the hall when he lost consciousness.

He felt a small, cold hand touch the scarred part of his face and his vision returned.

"I'm so sorry, Meyral."

When his eyes focused, he saw that the hand belonged to Rubi.

"You don't have to apologize," he groaned.

"Maybe I do," Rubi whispered. "Look, Liz—"

"I get it," Meyral interrupted. "You have needs and she fulfills them better than…than someone else would."

"But what if I'm wrong?" she continued. "Maybe if you had a good reason for me not to see Liz, I could…I would…"

Meyral looked into Rubi's eyes for the first time in so long. Her amber irises almost begged him to say something, but he couldn't find the words to tell her what she needed to hear. Instead he did the only thing he could think of, the same thing he'd been doing the entire time.

"I found someone."

"That Sakura girl?"

"Yes."

"Something about her doesn't feel right," Rubi mumbled weakly.

"It never will." Meyral rose to his feet and climbed onto the ladder. "Rubi," he added with a glance over his shoulder, "stop following me!" Then he left before the tears in her eyes could fall on him.

\* \* \*

As the sun started to rise the next day, Meyral opened his eyes to find Sakura standing next to his hammock. First her skin wrinkled and paled, and then a swarm of maggots burst from her eyeballs. Meyral jerked and fell from his hammock as the demonic apparition cackled.

"Was it that bad?" Sakura's soft voice asked.

Meyral looked up and stared at her unblemished, lavender eyes for a long time. "Sorry," he mumbled as he studied her face. "I had a strange dream, I guess."

It was then that Meyral noticed the skintight, crimson dress that stopped above mid-thigh. He stared at her legs as he dragged himself off the floor, and then he fumbled with his hood and rubbed his face.

"Look," Sakura said with a smile, "I'm willing to overlook getting ditched if you can get past whatever it was that made you run last night."

*I don't think she knows what she's really asking for.*

"Tonight is your night off, I checked. If you're not at my door by sundown," Sakura bit her bottom lip, clicking the rings against her teeth, "I'll be very disappointed."

Before Meyral could answer, she spun around and sauntered away. Her white hair settled and almost reached the small of her back, which swung back and forth in a rhythm that had Meyral almost hypnotized.

\* \* \*

Meyral made his way to Sakura's cabin that night with no voices arguing in his head. The door was already slightly ajar when he got there, and the soft light of candles poured out of the thin opening. He could smell the sweet fragrance of food and something that he couldn't place.

When he fully opened the door, the scene that met his eyes stopped him in his tracks. Hundreds of candles had been set up around the room, and sitting at the small table was Sakura. Her hair had been braided into two long pigtails, the tips of which were now bright pink. She wore a dress as black as the makeup around her eyes, and sleek, silver buttons lined its front.

Meyral cleared his throat as he stepped forward into the cabin. Sakura's dress was already partially unbuttoned at the bottom and the top, revealing much of what little cleavage she had. As he admired her bosom, Sakura pulled off her silver necklace. The long pendant on it looked like a key, and she put the jewelry on top of her nightstand. Then she shot him her bright smile and gracefully danced over on bare feet.

"I've been waiting," Sakura whispered seductively into Meyral's ear. She pulled him in for a kiss, then grabbed his hands and led him into the room.

Meyral's eye blurred again, but nothing came into focus. That odd scent returned, a smell that took him straight back to his childhood, but he still couldn't place it. Before he could dwell on it, Sakura kissed him deeply and pulled him to the table. She eased him into his seat and pushed a plate of food in front of him.

"These are called oysters. They're a...kind of delicacy," Sakura said. She bent forward and popped one into her mouth before offering one to him.

Meyral gazed at her perky breasts, now almost completely exposed, and the sultry way she bit her bottom lip and clicked the rings against her teeth. It was a long moment before he finally slurped down whatever was on the shell Sakura was holding.

She turned to grab something else, but Meyral couldn't bear it anymore. He reached out and grabbed the back of her knees, and in one swift motion, he buckled her legs and sat her in his lap. Her shock lasted only a split second before she smiled mischievously and grabbed another shell.

Meyral started to notice that all of his senses, not just his right eye, were starting to go a little fuzzy. "By the moons," he took a deep breath, "what is that intoxicating smell?"

"You like it? It's from Svirdark."

The young woman placed her hand on Meyral's cheek and kissed him again. This time Meyral's tongue darted into her mouth. As they tasted each other, Meyral's eye kicked into action. The girl in his arms repeated her transformation from that morning, then continued until she became a hideous grey slug. He pulled away and blinked furiously, trying desperately to stop the vision.

When Meyral's eyes managed to refocus, Sakura was standing with a curious look on her face. Then with a wink, she turned the curiosity into seduction. She turned and unbuttoned her dress, letting it drop in a small pile at her feet. Sakura wasn't as curvy as Rubi, but she was naked and standing in front of him.

Meyral finally saw the tattoo that spanned her entire backside. The tail of a serpent started at the nape of her neck and twisted itself in knots along her spine. The snake continued down to her right hip, then across the tops of her shaped butt cheeks, where its diamond-shaped head rested. Its scales had the same multicolored pattern as the mermaid on her calf, but something was different.

The serpent almost looked like it was alive. He couldn't tell if it was moving or not, and the colors started to blur together and shine too brightly. Meyral fleetingly thought of Rubi, but the shifting tattoo and the woman he intended to bed helped make the redhead a distant memory. When he finally looked away from the tattoo, Sakura was watching him over her shoulder with her thin, violet eyes.

She turned fully around and strolled toward him. Her flawless skin glistened and her breasts practically quivered with excitement. She leaned over and kissed him, but his lips felt numb and awkward. Drool left the side of his mouth, but that didn't stop Sakura. The tiny woman ripped Meyral's cloak open and dragged her nails down his chest.

Meyral groaned and let his head fall back as she reached up and slid her hands across his shoulders. He wriggled a bit and she freed him from the rest of his cloak, and then his shirt, both of which she haphazardly tossed to the side. Sakura leaned in and kissed his scarred neck, then worked her way down his shoulder and onto his chest, following the scar to the top of his pants. He hated that half of him was a disfigured monster, but he loved that she didn't mind.

"Looks like you got lucky," Sakura said with a grin as she rubbed a hand between Meyral's legs. She grabbed his thick bulge and squeezed, earning her another groan.

The room started to spin and Meyral quickly stood, almost knocking Sakura over in the process. He pulled the Svirdarker against his chest and tried to regain control of his breathing. Then he dipped his head and kissed her neck, her shoulders, and back up to her mouth. His hands cupped her pert breasts and he enjoyed the way her flesh squeezed between his fingers.

Sakura pushed Meyral onto the bed and knelt in front of him. Her small hands went down to the lacing on Meyral's pants, and soon his member was free. The Svirdarker bit her bottom lip as she stared up at him, then buried her face in his lap.

Meyral was lost. The room spun once again and his vision faded as the thought of those rings in Sakura's lip ran through his mind.

\* \* \*

When Meyral came to, Sakura was still on top of him, but he

was on his stomach with his hands behind his back. The Svirdarker snaked something cold around his wrists while mumbling to herself.

"Thank the gods he passed out. I was afraid I'd actually have to go through with it and let that monstrosity into my little muffin."

"Hey, I'm as adventurous as the next guy, but shackles?" Meyral asked groggily.

"How in the hells are you awake already?" Sakura growled as she stood. "There's enough poison in this incense to put a whole pack of doxyls to sleep!"

"Poison? What...why didn't it affect you?" His speech was slurred, but he knew she understood him.

"I told you, it's from Svirdark. My homeland. I've spent most of my life building up an immunity, dipshit." She reached down and pulled her dress back on. "Well, at least you're caught. Hope you enjoyed yourself, because that's all you'll be getting for a while."

"A bounty hunter...really..." Meyral's eyes glossed over for a moment, and then he fell off the bed. "I should have known when you gave me that garbage sob story!"

A look of pain crossed Sakura's face before she resumed her calm speech. "Believe what you want, ugly, but you're the Blue Bandit. When this ship pulls into Nordcross territory, I'm going to be rich! I'll finally have enough to get my daughter back! You're lucky that contract wants you alive, or I would have killed you the second I saw you."

"You know what?" Meyral wiggled on his back a bit, but he remained on the ground. "If getting drugged is what it takes to dip my tip in you..." Meyral grinned with his hands still bound behind his back. "It was worth it."

Sakura frowned for a moment, and then she realized Meyral was staring right up her dress. She tried to stomp his face with her bare foot, but he managed to roll out of the way.

"Dirtbag!" she shrieked. "You're forgetting the part where you're either executed or you spend the rest of your life in prison. Still worth it?"

"Death or prison...for you? No," Meyral said with a chuckle. "But neither of those are going to happen."

"How—"

"You forget." Meyral's face split into a wide grin. "I'm the Blue Bandit."

"Oh please," Sakura said with a laugh. "Wanna explain how you see this going, then?"

"I think I'll just kick your ass with my hands literally tied behind my back," he started. "And then hopefully you can swim, because I'm going to throw that same hot ass of yours overboard." Meyral hopped to his feet and laughed at the look of disbelief on her face.

Sakura whipped two short, curved blades out from under the table. "Asshole! I'll kill you and dance in your blood!"

She swung with both knives, but Meyral evaded her effortlessly. Every time she missed, her face became redder with anger and frustration, until she sloppily lunged with all her might at Meyral's gut. He spun at the last second and kicked her in the small of her back, sending her to the floor. She rolled and hit her nightstand, knocking several bottles onto the bed, some of which rolled off and shattered on the ground. A few candles fell as well, lighting the whole mess on fire.

Meyral jumped and swung his cuffed arms under his legs so that his hands were in front of him. He ran for the door, but at some point she had locked it.

"What about the contract?" he shouted over the roar of the fire as he looked around the room for the key. "Don't you need me alive?"

Sakura finally made it to her feet. She lunged at him, this time weaponless, and Meyral easily knocked her to the side with another kick. As she fell to the floor once again, more candles dropped and the bed was set ablaze along with part of Sakura's dress.

Meyral jumped on his would-be assassin to put out the fire and find the key. His hands explored what remained of her dress, but Sakura misread Meyral's intentions.

"You pervert!" she screamed with rage as she bucked him off.

Her attacks became fast and unpredictable. She became little more than a whirling mess of fists, knees, and elbows. The back of her dress fell away and the rainbow serpent seemed to reflect the firelight. He managed to dodge each of her attacks, despite his poisoned state.

Suddenly the snake from her back struck out at him and he leapt backward to avoid it. He blinked several times, but the serpent was still inked on Sakura's skin. Meyral rolled aside and realized that the flames were inches away from his pile of clothes.

Something stirred inside of him and he didn't think he had the willpower to fight it. It fed on his anger, and as he bit it back, the

Svirdarker landed a quick kick and several punches. He shoved her away and got to his feet.

"Sakura," Meyral shouted, "we're going to burn to death in here! Let's finish this later!"

She only smiled with a distant look in her eyes. The bed and curtains were engulfed in flames that were spreading to the rest of the cabin; the heat was undeniable, but Sakura didn't seem to notice. She struck him three more times and he could feel the other presence inside of him rising to the surface.

"I think you're being a tad unreasonable," came a dark voice that didn't belong to Meyral, although it used his lips.

"If I have to die to kill you, so be it you son of a bitch!" Sakura shrieked.

Meyral dodged another kick and sent Sakura sprawling with one of his own. It took all of Meyral's strength to resist pounding the Svirdarker into nothing. The cabin was filled with enough smoke that his eyes stung and his breathing came in ragged gasps.

"Think about your daughter!" he pleaded as he battled the beast inside of himself.

"Don't you dare!" she warned as she found one of her curved blades. "You have no right to mention her!"

She pounced and he slipped under her knife and between her arms. He knocked her out with a swift headbutt and her body went limp. A glimmer of light caught his eyes and he finally found the key. It was attached to the necklace on the nightstand where the blaze had begun.

Meyral stuck his hands into the flames, protecting his left with his scarred arm. He wasn't at all surprised when the cobalt cracks lit up. There was no pain as the flames licked his skin or as he grabbed the silver key. Meyral crossed the room and unlocked the door in a matter of seconds. As soon as the fresh air from the hallway rushed in, the inferno flared up and smoke billowed out.

He stopped at the door and cursed as he watched his shirt and cloak turn into kindling. Then his eyes landed on Sakura, only a few feet away from the nearest blaze. "I guess I can't just leave you here."

Meyral reached down to drag her out, but something exploded and sent him sprawling to the ground out in the hall. For a short moment he looked at the room, which had become a roaring inferno, and then he backed away as people began to run everywhere.

"It's you!" one man shouted as he pointed at Meyral. "Guards, come quickly! The Blue Bandit is onboard!"

For a split second, Meyral considered silencing the shouting man, but the violence left his mind as the door behind him opened up. A pair of small hands pulled him backward, and all he could see were Rubi's wild, orange eyes full of fear. Once he was in the room, she shut the door and quickly locked it.

"What did you do? Where's your shirt? Are those shackles?"

"My shirt, my cloak," he rasped as he shook his head. "Dammit! We need to go below deck and grab my—"

"There's no time for that," she whispered.

Deep voices came from the other side of the wall, then someone began pounding on the door. Rubi reached for the lock and slid it back.

"Rubi, no!" Meyral shouted, but the redhead didn't listen.

When the door opened, a skinny, blonde woman ran inside and locked the door behind her. She handed something to Rubi and hugged her. "The guards have arrived," Liz said before turning to Meyral. "We need to get out of here."

"I'm not leaving without my—" Meyral started, but Rubi held up the bag Liz had handed her. "My bag..." he finished as he finally recognized his own pack.

"Liz saw you going into that cabin again—"

"I wasn't spying or anything," Liz explained apologetically. "Jules told me about Sakura, so..." she shot the redhead a nervous glance.

Meyral groaned.

"Care to explain?" Rubi asked as she examined her half-naked, soot-streaked friend. More banging and shouting came from the door, which rattled on its hinges.

"Nope," he answered flatly. "I don't suppose you have an extra shirt for me, though?"

"No time!" Rubi shouted over the noise. She grabbed Liz's hand, then Meyral's bound wrist, and she pulled them toward the balcony. "It's our only way off," she said with a glance back to the door.

"You're right," Meyral answered.

"You're right?" Liz whimpered. "You mean we're *jumping?* Please, tell me I'm wrong."

"Fire, huh?" Rubi said, ignoring Liz. Adventure sparkled in her amber eyes as she gazed over the railing at the long drop into the ocean.

"Why's it always my fault?" Meyral responded as they continued to disregard the babbling blonde behind them.

Rubi smirked at him. "Blue Bandit," she answered in a singsong voice.

"Right. Well, it was technically the bounty hunter's fault…"

"I told you that darker was a bounty hunter," Rubi said simply as the pounding on the door grew louder.

"You were right, are you happy now? How did you know I needed help?" Meyral asked as Rubi disrobed and Liz followed suit. "I thought I told you to stop following me."

"It's kind of hard to ignore screams and explosions when they're outside our door," Rubi yelled. She helped Liz put one leg over the railing before swinging her own body over to the other side.

The blonde's face paled. "Where are we going?" she asked.

"We're just south of Leviathan Pass," Rubi said. "It should be an easy swim."

Liz began to shake.

"Don't worry, I won't let you die," Meyral said with a smile. Then he shoved her and shouted, "Try not to land flat!"

Rubi rolled her eyes and dove into the sea after Liz. As Meyral stood shirtless and alone on the balcony, the door behind him splintered. He heard the sound of heavy metal boots clomping on wood and he turned. As he was about to jump, a tan man with curly, brown hair caught his attention. He stood among the soldiers, staring at Meyral with an ear-to-ear grin.

"Did you do this?" Meyral asked as the guards closed in around the door to the balcony.

"I told you, you weren't going to see your father," the phantom answered.

Suddenly a name flashed in his mind with no other memory to accompany it.

*Shraka.*

For some reason, all Meyral wanted to do was kill the mysterious man. Another explosion erupted from across the hall, this one strong enough to push Meyral over the railing. He toppled in midair before the cold ocean bit into him. When he came up for air,

Shraka was standing on the water and laughing at him.

"When you give up," the smiling man said, "come and find me."

A wave crashed over Meyral, and when he resurfaced, the phantom had disappeared. Meyral looked everywhere, but all he saw was the ship billowing smoke and Rubi practically skimming over the water with Liz in tow. He started after them, making his way to the rocky cliffs of Leviathan Pass.

It had been years since either of them had had endurance training with Taryn, but Rubi was still able to drag Liz through the surf for half of a mile before helping her climb the ridge. Meyral, on the other hand, had fallen behind the moment they started. With his hands bound, he managed to float on his back and propel himself with his legs, all the while holding his pack above the surface to try to keep it dry.

* * *

Rubi reached a small ledge just below where the pass used to be as Liz struggled behind her. She helped her lover up over the edge, and as she let Liz catch her breath, she saw a quick movement out of the corner of her eye. Rubi turned in time to see a figure draped in shadow slip behind a rock on the far side of the cliff. She wanted to investigate further, but Liz's breathing had slowed and she looked hurt.

"Are you okay? Rubi asked.

"No, no, I am *not* okay," Liz snapped. "I had no idea your life was this exciting, Jewel. Or should I call you Rubi?"

Rubi looked back to the ship, then watched the Blue Bandit climbing steadily twenty feet below. She wondered if she should tell Liz the truth. She didn't want to risk Liz's safety by telling her everything, especially since she'd already proven that she couldn't keep a secret, but Liz deserved to know.

"That's what Christophe or Meyral or whatever his name is called you back at the cabin," Liz continued. "I heard it, so don't deny it. Who *are* you?"

Liz took a step forward. The rocks beneath her groaned, then shifted and finally gave way. The butcher's daughter shrieked as she reached out for her lover. They both fell into the pit, but Rubi landed alone until the rocks shifted again. Liz fell on her and rolled away. A loud snap resounded and Rubi's leg exploded with pain.

"Liz!" Rubi shouted. "Liz, are you alright?" She dragged herself over to her unconscious companion, careful not to move her leg too much, and she checked Liz for injuries. Rubi squeezed one of the blonde's thighs and she woke up with a groan.

"There are easier ways to get into my pants," Liz said with a chuckle that turned into another groan when Rubi touched her arm.

"I'm so glad you're okay," the redhead sighed. "One of your ribs might be broken and you dislocated your arm, but you'll be fine."

"And you?" Liz commiserated.

Rubi sighed. "My leg is broken."

"You're down a leg, I'm down an arm," Liz said. "How are we supposed to get out of here?"

Rubi reached for Liz's arm and quickly relocated it. Liz yelped and pulled away.

"Gods be damned!" the blonde shouted. "What was that for?"

"Can you move it now?" Rubi asked calmly. When Liz nodded, she continued. "I reset your arm. You should be fine soon, aside from your rib…"

"Thanks," Liz said. "So how do we get out of here?"

Rubi looked up at the giant hole they fell through. The entrance was little more than a miniscule speck of green sky above them. "I don't know if we do."

The tiny pillar of light shrank even more and Meyral's voice echoed down to them. "Hey," he shouted, "Rubi, are you there? Are you alive?"

"We're alright," Rubi yelled back, "except my leg is broken and Liz is pretty banged up."

"What happened?" he asked as he dropped a rope down to the women.

"Some kind of cave in," Liz muttered as Meyral rappelled down the wall.

"I've heard that Leviathan Pass has been plagued by tremors ever since you blew it up," Rubi told him. When he touched down next to them, Rubi could just make out the anger on his face. "It's time to cut the crap, Meyral."

"You're the one who blew up the pass?" Liz said with fear and wonder in her voice.

220

"I remember that article," Meyral said as he gave Rubi a scrupulous look. "I even dreamt about it once, I think I was on fire...and that would make sense," he raised his right arm and stared at it, "since these scars had to have come from somewhere."

Liz looked at Rubi with wide eyes, but then a crumbling noise came from above them. Meyral covered Rubi and Liz with his body as shattered rocks fell around them. Liz moved out from under him and stood to her feet.

"We need to get the hell out of here!" the blonde shouted.

Rubi could barely see her lover's scared eyes.

"That's what the rope's for," Meyral said.

He reached down to feel Rubi's leg and she braced herself for the pain, but it never came. Something moved behind her and Meyral froze. Liz pulled out the chef's knife she'd been working with as Meyral grabbed a nearby rock.

Scaly arms reached into the pillar of light and grabbed for the knife and the rock. Hands with three thick fingers and a black talon on the end of each easily broke Meyral's and Liz's grips. The stone and blade were lost as the limbs retreated into the darkness.

"Intruders?" a rough, strong voice asked. "Tell me, are you the tzęprön?"

"I don't know what you're talking about," Meyral said.

"We don't want to fight," Liz added. "My...my friend, she's injured badly."

Rubi couldn't help the twinge of pain at being referred to as a friend. The boulders above shifted and a trickle of dust fell, reminding her of the pain she'd feel if they didn't get out soon.

Despite the urgency of the situation, a scaly arm tugged on Meyral's rope. Three oversized fingers fiddled with the lifeline and Liz twitched nervously.

"This place is collapsing!" the blonde shouted. "Are you going to help us or not?"

"We only wish to allow the tzęprön entry," the voice insisted. "Are you him?"

Rubi was quickly becoming irritated. She was more powerless without the use of her leg than she ever imagined.

"My name is Meyral," her old friend explained quickly. "My friends need help and we need to get out of here, whether or not we are who you want us to be."

Rubi heard more shuffling behind their emissary, then what sounded like several people speaking in hushed tones. The owner of the first voice stepped forward into the small circle of light. Rubi's heart dropped into her stomach. The man, if you could call it that, was nearly seven feet tall. He looked as rough as the rocks around them and his skin was covered in brownish scales.

The creature took one more step forward, now fully immersed in the dim beam. Rubi looked up into his face and found milky white eyes that seemed to look right past her. His nose and mouth protruded together in a short kind of snout.

"Help?" he hissed. "The kasmömig need help?"

As the beast spoke, the broken redhead could make out several rows of teeth that looked sharp enough to break stones. She dropped her eyes from that hideous grin and noticed that the lizard-man's hands and feet looked identical. Quick movement brought her eyes to a thick tail that hung to what should have been the man's ankles. The nightmare was complete.

*This thing is going to kill us all,* Rubi thought.

"Kirth," another voice spoke out, and although this one was slightly more effeminate, it was still just as rough, "these two, the female and the juvenile, are injured. I don't think these topsiders mean any harm."

"Juvenile?" Liz huffed, as if forgetting their current proximity to death. "I'll have you know that I'm—"

The words caught in Liz's throat as the owner of the second voice stepped into the light and nudged Kirth forward. The new lizard looked just like the other one, only she had bright green scales and was slightly shorter. The curve of her body reinforced Rubi's first instinct that this one was female, even though both creatures seemed to lack the defining features of their respective genders.

"Kallö," the female lizard commanded as she continued to push Kirth.

"I already planned on helping them, Pläblé." The lizard-man slapped her hand away. "I just want to know if they are the ones we dreamt about."

"What chance is there that these topsiders aren't? How many stumble in like this?" Pläblé's condescending tone made even Rubi cringe.

As the two beasts argued, more cracking and grinding came

from above.

"Kasmömig," Kirth said as he turned to Meyral, "I will help you. But in return, you must stay with us. Your arrival has been foretold. There are things that must be done, for both your sake and our own. However, daz anręxmömig are free to leave," he finished as he glanced to the others.

Between his tone and Rubi's knowledge of the old language, she was pretty sure that she had just been insulted. When Pläblé elbowed Kirth, she knew she had been. Before she could voice her indignation, a crash came from above and the light disappeared.

The whole cave started to shake as boulders fell from all around them. Rubi quickly climbed to her feet, using the wall as a support. Then she felt a pair of skinny hands push her with so much force that she was lifted off of the cold ground. She heard Liz scream as a three-fingered hand closed around Rubi's arm. Liz's cry was cut off as a stream of boulders crashed to the ground.

The rough claw dragged Rubi farther into the blackness. Dust filled the air as the shaking came to a stop. A moment later the deafening roar of the last few rocks falling and bouncing ended as well. In the darkness, Rubi found a familiar hand wrought with scars. The cold metal around its wrist confirmed that it was Meyral, and she breathed a sigh of relief.

"Rubi, is that you?" Meyral's detached voice seemed to come from everywhere and nowhere at the same time. "Are you alright?"

"Yea," the redhead, "but…where's Liz?"

"I tried, Rubi," Meyral whispered. "I had her and then something ripped me away. I couldn't—"

"What? You couldn't what?" Rubi demanded. She turned and shouted, "Liz, where are you? Say something, make a noise, anything! Where are you?"

Tears fell freely from Rubi's eyes as she crawled along the wall back toward the rubble. She continued to call out while she pulled at the fallen stones that blocked their exit.

"Enough," Kirth demanded firmly.

"Don't you dare touch her!" Meyral shouted.

Rubi couldn't see anything, but she heard a scuffle break out near her. She felt someone place a hand with three fingers on her shoulder. The touch was so gentle that Rubi thought it was impossible to belong to the monsters standing before her.

"Your lamömig did not make it," the female lizard announced solemnly from behind her.

# CHAPTER SIXTEEN: HAZE

Alberto found that if he kept up a milder pace from sunrise to sunset, Jake wouldn't start whining until late in the evening and Howler wouldn't have enough energy to get the kid riled up. It had been a few days since they had crossed through Gate Seven and Alberto's mood was already lightening. In fact, he was almost enjoying himself. Maybe it was because things finally seemed to be turning in his favor, or maybe it was because Iggy was leaving him alone. What he did know was that the air was fresh and crisp out on the Northern Plains. Nobody was hunting him and the exercise was doing his body and soul some much needed good.

Valdis was a quickly fading memory, but not Aldomein. Every once in a while, the big redhead was sure he could smell his lover's scent on the breeze. His short-lived joys were always accompanied by a pain in his heart and strong bouts of paranoia or confusion—sometimes both.

"What's wrong with him?" Jake asked.

Alberto turned to see what he was talking about. The blond pointed to Lee, who stood as still as a statue a few feet behind Howler.

"Lee," Alberto shouted, "are you coming or what?"

The former slave didn't budge. His eyes were shut tight and his head slowly bowed.

"Oi, are we gonna have to wait for that wanker to finish whatever he's doing?" Howler asked as he took a seat in the grass.

Alberto cursed and set his pack down before turning his back to his companions. "I've gotta piss anyway," he said as he stomped off, leaving Jake and Howler snickering by the statuesque Islander.

When he returned, Lee took a sharp breath like he'd been underwater for several minutes. The Islander was covered in sweat and breathing hard as Alberto approached him cautiously.

"Sirs," Lee panted, "we should go that way." He pointed southeast, away from where the dirt road was leading them.

"Dammit Lee," Alberto said as he snatched his pack off the ground, "we wasted all that time so you could point us in the wrong direction?"

"My apologies, sir, but there is a haze ahead that I would advise you to avoid."

Alberto looked to the others in disbelief. Neither of the Guildsmen moved. Jake's eyes were as large as saucers, and Howler looked ready to believe whatever cryptic advice came out of Lee's mouth next.

"Absolutely not," Alberto said.

Howler and Jake shook themselves from their temporary trance.

"Maybe—"

"We are not taking the scenic route because of some fog," Alberto said loudly before Jake could finish. "Let's go, we have a lot of ground to cover."

Uncertainty crept into Lee's eyes, but the former slave swallowed hard and followed Alberto. Jake looked to Howler, who shrugged, and the two strolled forward to catch up to their companions.

\* \* \*

The four travelers reached the edge of a valley late in the night. To their left, the Clouded River cascaded into the depression and filled the shallow bowl with fog. Howler let out a low whistle and Lee nodded silently.

To the north, the river flowed out of the mist and skirted around some low hills. The fog in the valley reflected an abnormal amount of moonlight, making it glow, and Alberto could just see glimpses of the bottom of the basin. He turned to make his way down one of the hills, but Lee placed a hand on his shoulder and shook his head.

"I'd listen to 'im, Bertie," Howler said as he neared the edge. "I thought this place was a little farther west, but there's no doubt about it. This is Whitewater."

"I think that's actually mist," Jake said dryly.

"I know it's mist. I'm tryin' to tell you that the bloody town hidden down there is called Whitewater." Howler noticed the grin on the blond's face and added, "You're a bloody arse, you know that?"

"My apologies, sirs," Lee cut in, "but you are both

misinformed. This is not mist—there is magic here."

Alberto listened, though his eyes never strayed from the faintly glowing valley. He couldn't see very well, but he was sure there were blue lights inside. "Is it him?" he whispered.

"Oi, like I said, that's Whitewater," Howler answered with a sigh. "It's where the druids come together to do...whatever it is those crazies do."

"I heard they sacrifice babies to a god that looks like a bird," Jake said as he backed away from the valley.

"Is that right?" Howler asked. "I heard they sacrifice virgins...so you'd better watch out."

Alberto thought back to a discussion he had a lifetime ago with Chloe. His stomach immediately twisted in knots as he recalled her angelic face. She had told him about the druids, about how they worshiped four dragons who governed Cygnus' basic elements. It was her way of laughing at his belief in the power of the moons. He winced as the knots twisted so badly that they caused him physical pain.

*She was always doing that...*

He wiped a bit of spittle from his mouth and said, "Druids help the sick and dying. They take in the unwanted. They respect borders and the laws of other nations...what's your problem with them?"

"Well," Jake said as he pulled his hand through his blond hair, "some say that druids practice ancient sorcery and alchemy. Some say they're all powerful. Some say that they can predict the future. Some say—"

"Yea, right. Who says this?" Alberto interrupted.

"The Nordcross soldiers that came through Misty," the kid explained. "Most of them actually seemed...scared of the druids."

Alberto laughed loudly. "Nordcross is a cesspool of liars and hypocrites. They don't know their asses from their faces."

"Look at you," Howler said with a grimace. "You've met how many Nordcrossers in your life? I'll bet you could count them on one hand, yet you're worthy to pass judgment over an entire bloody country because someone on their side wants to fight someone on yours?"

"I've met you," Alberto answered coldly.

"Do I hear the sounds of discontent?" a soft voice called out from just below the edge of a particularly steep cliff. "There is no need for such contempt when one is standing so close to salvation."

"Who's there?" Alberto demanded as he stepped between his companions and the cliff.

"Please, friends, I mean you no harm. Tell me, what has brought you to the dragons' doorstep? Certainly not despair. Allow me to cleanse you with the elements and set your souls on a path of righteousness." A man climbed over the ledge and held his hands up. "I am Marik, Brother of the Forest."

The man wore a brown cloak, its hood lowered into a bundle around his neck. His head was bald and slightly pointed at the top, and his skin was the color of the bark of an old tree. He had thin lips and even thinner eyebrows. The lines on his face curled into something most people would misread as a smile, but Alberto knew better. The happiness didn't reach Marik's eyes. Those hazel orbs surrounded by dark skin bulged out from the druid's face without emotion.

"I invite you to dine in the halls of Whitewater." As Marik spoke, the haze underfoot dissipated, revealing the cobblestone path on which he walked. It followed the cliffs downward until it curved and lost itself behind more of the thick mist. "There is no reason for you to sleep out in the cold when the warmth of the elements is at hand. Would you not spend the night behind the safety of our humble walls?"

Lee shifted his weight. The movement was subtle, but Alberto knew his usually poised companion must have been nervous, and he didn't like that one bit.

"Not tonight," Alberto said, siding with Lee's silent refusal. "My friends and I have a lot of ground left to cover, and we still need to find a way to cross the Skirn River."

"The next bridge is a day's walk from here," Marik continued with that unceasing smile. "We have our own that you may use. You would be hard pressed to find a crossing as sturdy as ours."

It had been a long time since Alberto had looked at a map of the North, and as he thought back to Carter's Archives, his gut twisted some more. He could have sworn he caught a gleam in Marik's eye as the druid watched him lament his lost life.

"Okay, we'll use your bridge," Alberto said. "But we still aren't staying," he quickly amended.

Marik brought his hands together in front of him and bowed. "Allow me to accompany you to the road that will lead you there. I enjoy taking long strolls under the light of the moons, for it always seems to clear my head...but I would be lying if I told you that was my only motive."

The smile finally dropped from the druid's face. Lee shifted nervously again, setting Alberto on edge.

"The fates can be traitorous in the mists of Whitewater, especially to nonbelievers." The druid then retrieved a dark bottle from his cloak, uncorked it, and passed it to Alberto. "Let us bless our journey together, be it only for the briefest of moments."

"If you want to question them," Lee said slowly as he grabbed the bottle out of Alberto's hands, "just do so. There is no need to ply us with your drink. I have looked into the hearts of each of these men, and their quality is pure."

Howler and Alberto stared at each other. Jake reached for Lee's hand, took the bottle, and brought it to his lips. Howler slapped the small flask out of Jake's hands before he could taste it. The bottle's dark contents spilled onto the grass, where it caused the blades to immediately wither.

"I don't suppose that was whiskey. Am I right?" Alberto asked with raised brows.

"Truth serum," Marik said simply. "You can never be too sure these days." The man descended into the mist unfazed.

Alberto went next, followed by Howler and Jake. Lee took up his usual position at the rear. The fog peeled back and made a sort of grey tunnel. Other than the cobbled path and the druid leading them, they saw nothing but clouds. Once the lip of the valley and the night sky disappeared, the brother of the forest spoke again.

"You should be honored," he said. "Since the war started years ago, we haven't allowed visitors. The mist turns everyone away, lest they know the way of the dragons. You four are the first to reach the rim of the valley in a long time." Marik stopped and turned. "Yet I wonder why the clouds tell me you're a haunted man, Alberto."

"You know my name?" Alberto huffed. "If you're looking for a bounty—"

"No, no, no." Marik held his hands up to calm the big man. "I'm only curious. I like to know both sides of the story. Sometimes, perception is more important than the facts themselves."

"Nordcross hunted down and killed—"

Again Marik held up his hands. "That is a matter of record. Besides, Nordcross can do many things, but it cannot haunt you. I

229

speak of two women, green hair and black."

"My family," Alberto murmured. "I survived. They didn't."

"The dragons teach us that only the dead should seek out the dead."

"So I should kill myself?" the redhead asked. "Is that how your dragons would find peace?"

Marik chuckled. "Quite the opposite, actually. Suicide is a sin against the elements. What the dragons teach us is that the living must live on and not dwell on the things they cannot change."

Alberto shrugged and silence surrounded them for a moment.

"So what does 'Brother of the Forest' mean?" Jake asked.

The druid slowed until he was side by side with the young blond. Alberto watched Marik out of the corner of his eye.

"It is but a title, Jake." Marik waved a hand in front of his face with his dead smile. "You'll always find that what lies just beneath the surface is far more interesting." He looked pointedly at Lee, then sped up to reach Howler. "Some would look at you, for instance, and they might see a simple criminal. But of course, it is not so simple, is it, Robert?"

"Tell me something," Howler snapped. "Xander—I'm sure you know who that is as well, so introductions would be pointless…" He paused and Marik bowed his head slightly. "Right, well, he told me once that the senate always listens to your counsel. He called it faith. I've heard some call it superstition. Me, I call it corruption, but whatever it is, it is. So I find it very curious that the druids never got involved in the war. Even when it spilled into Northern territory, you hid in your little cloud here. What were you all doing while the people you claim to love were dying in the streets, eh?"

"I appreciate your honesty," Marik started. "Not many would speak so frankly while so vulnerable, but have no fear. The elements will always bring peace and love."

"I once attended a funeral where they spoke a lot about peace and love, but that bloke was dead," Howler remarked.

The druid chuckled dryly. "You see, Jake, they are not all what they seem. You might be surprised to find that your friend is a bit of a philosopher. I'll bet there's a lot about the people you hold most dear that you don't know. The dragons tell us to talk less and listen more, so that all may be revealed in time."

Alberto noticed Jake nodding along with what the druid was

saying. He slowed until he was on Howler's other side, though the action seemed lost on the druid as he continued his long-winded answer to Howler's question.

"The senate was wicked, as you know, but it was not because of the druids. It was despite us. Like a storm testing the resolve of a ship's crew, Nordcross was the senate's test. Needless to say, they failed. Their punishment was the Blue Bandit."

Alberto caught the druid's eyes when Meyral's alias left his thin mouth.

"The metal dragon has sent his agent, a reaper of lost souls. Yet he left the worst of the heretics alive as a test for the people of the North, and I assure you, the druids' love will not let those people, those lost lambs, fall into dismay as the senate so willingly did."

Howler frowned and fell silent, but Alberto read the message loud and clear. The druids were not on the new elder's side.

"Follow this path until you reach the Skirn River," Marik announced when they reached the other side of the valley. "A ferry will take you across the way to Vent."

Alberto thought the journey seemed entirely too short. "How do you know where we're going?" Confusion quickly transformed into anger. "Why are you really here?"

"Relax, friend," the druid said quietly. "Secrets are revealed to the druids by the elements. A whisper on the winds, a vision in the night's fire; if you are pure you can see all the people of Cygnus in a single chalice of water. I am a tool of the dragons, and I only know what they deem necessary at the time."

"Oh, perfect," Alberto muttered as he walked away, "a loon."

"It's dangerous to travel the road at night," Marik called out to the travelers. "You ought to reconsider my offer and rest in the cathedral."

"I say we keep going," Alberto said just loud enough for Howler and Jake to hear.

"You should at least set up camp now and start again when the sun rises," Marik almost pleaded.

"I'm not stopping until this place is over the horizon," Howler whispered as he jogged to catch up with Alberto.

"I'm with you guys," Jake added as he caught up, surprised that Howler and Alberto agreed on something.

* * *

The sun had risen before the four travelers felt secure enough to stop. Under the shade of a twisted elm, they rolled out their beds and rested. When Alberto closed his eyes, he already knew Iggy would be waiting.

The moon looked as it always did, but there was something off about the blond. He tapped his foot on the ground incessantly and his music was fast and harsh. Alberto tried to speak, but the music drowned him out immediately.

Iggy played faster and faster, and Alberto felt sick to his stomach. Rather than giving him the option to view as he had always done, Iggy forced the images into Alberto's head.

"No wonder people hate coming to see you!" he shouted as his mind became overwhelmed.

He saw a hall with semicircular tables. A cloaked figure walked between them. The room was decorated with streaks and splatters of blood, and the katana that the man held was slick with gore. The cloaked shadow lifted the only other man in the chamber to his feet and brushed him off.

As the apparition broke apart, only the man in blue-and-gold robes was left. Harold, the man whose name Alberto didn't know how he knew, spun around, and outside of the broken window were lines of soldiers with turtles engraved on their breastplates.

Alberto pounded his fists on the ground, but nothing happened. Then the music broke and he woke up coughing and sputtering. Lee was sitting next to him with his legs crossed and his hands on his knees. The Islander faced west, and Alberto knew that somehow he was watching the valley of mist.

"Bad dream, sir?" he asked without turning.

"You could say that." Alberto coughed. "What did I tell you about that 'sir' shit?" He laid his head back and closed his eyes, then heard Lee shift next to him. "Don't worry about me," he told the Islander. "It's been happening a lot lately."

"I am not worried about you, sir." Lee spoke slowly and softly. "I do not trust the brother of the forest."

Alberto opened his eyes. Lee held his canteen in his right hand and a leaf in his left.

"What are you doing?" Alberto asked.

Lee didn't respond. His arms and stomach flexed and dull, purple glyphs formed around both of his wrists. The leaf hovered just above his palm, and a small stream of water floated up from the canteen. The jet swirled around his hand in a mesmerizing dance. As the water shredded the leaf, the resulting ball of liquid turned a light brown.

"Hold out your hands, sir."

Alberto did as he was told, mystified. "What is this?"

"It is an Island tea. You will sleep like a baby on his mother's milk."

Lee mimed pouring the tea and the warm, brown liquid filled Alberto's cupped hands, which he lifted to his mouth. He drank and, for the first time in weeks, the music in his head stopped.

"Thanks," Alberto muttered.

Lee nodded and resumed his watch of Whitewater.

"We'll talk about that 'sir' stuff in the...in the morn..." Alberto drifted off to a dreamless sleep.

# CHAPTER SEVENTEEN: SPIRIT

Howler could tell that something had happened to his Ardänian companion while he had slept. His mood had become even graver than usual, and there was a newfound urgency in him that nobody understood. Alberto had them pack up camp after lunch, and Howler had been jogging ever since to match the big man's pace. The last light of day went out, and still Alberto dragged his companions along as the moons danced their celestial waltz.

Jake finally dropped onto his back and sighed. "I'm beat! I couldn't go another step." He rolled onto his stomach. "Let's set up camp for the night. Please?"

Howler looked down at the young blond. *This kid's spent most of his life in a prison and in a mountain,* he thought. *He won't last much longer at this rate.*

"Blimey, Bertie," Howler said, taking a seat next to Jake. "We've been running for six hours straight. I think it's bloody time for a rest."

Jake propped himself up on his elbows and looked at Alberto with wide, watery eyes. "We won't make it until daybreak anyway, so why can't we just relax? What's the rush?"

Howler cringed. Alberto listened to reason, but Jake's whining would only serve to irritate him. Sure enough, a breeze carried the redhead's muffled curse. But rather than trudging on like Howler expected him to do, he started to pace back and forth, as if debating with himself.

"I really didn't want to have this discussion," Alberto suddenly mumbled. "I know how crazy it's gonna sound...but I also know that stuff like this has led me in the right direction before."

There was a long pause. Howler leaned forward, surprised at his own intrigue.

"Nordcross is going to invade the North," Alberto finally blurted out. "I don't know when, but I know it's going to be soon. We have to warn the elder."

"Bollocks," Howler argued. "We're in a time of peace, there's no need. It's your own damn prejudices that are blinding you, mate."

"Yea," Jake said, "that's a pretty heavy accusation. The Guild hasn't heard a thing about any invasions."

"You got a spy we don't know about? Tell me, Red, how do you claim to know this?" Howler asked.

"You wouldn't believe me if I told you." Alberto turned away and jammed his dagger into the nearest tree.

"I don't believe you right now, so you've got nothin' to lose," Howler said.

"Yea, try us," Jake added.

Howler looked around and noticed that even Lee was watching Alberto, and that guy never seemed to care about anything any of them had to say.

"I had a dream," Alberto muttered. "A vision, really," he said a little louder.

Howler looked at Jake with wide eyes before he noticed Lee nodding solemnly. He scoffed and said, "You mean like the one you had the other night about your two girlies?"

"Look, I know how it sounds to act solely on a dream, but…" Alberto suddenly yanked his dagger out of the tree and spun around. "You know what?" he yelled. "Stay if you want! I'd actually prefer that! You're just slowing me down anyway."

Howler thought to himself for a moment. Then he hopped to his feet and nudged Jake with his foot. "I'm fine without sleep. Oi, let's go, men!"

The ex-con mimed a goofy salute and gave Jake a swift kick in his ass. The kid reluctantly rose to his feet and grabbed his pack, which Howler promptly took from him.

"How 'bout I take care of these," he said quietly, "and you just follow the big guy as best you can." He shouldered both his and Jake's packs, then turned back to Alberto. "Lead the way, Red. I can't wait to see your face when you realize Nordcross isn't as evil as you want it to be."

Alberto didn't respond. He just stomped away with Jake following closely. Howler led Lee, who remained several paces behind.

"We should get there just in time for bangers and mash!" Howler announced. He looked around, but he seemed to be the only one excited about the prospect of a proper breakfast.

* * *

They continued for the rest of the night until Klyntar dipped below the horizon, leaving its two larger siblings alone in the night sky. They'd reached the banks of the Skirn River when Alberto finally stopped.

"I guess the druid wasn't lying about everything," Howler mused.

Jake flopped down and drank from the slow-moving waters. "That guy gave me the creeps," the blond said between gulps.

"Whatever he was up to, we still have to cross the river," Alberto said as he stared longingly into the water.

Bright rays of light from the sunrise lit up the lime sky as Howler nudged Jake with his foot. He pointed toward a pier made of thick, white stone. "Look, you lazy git," he told the blond, "it's the capital. You don't have to milk it anymore."

Howler was surprised when his words rang true and Jake stood upright with a stupid grin on his face. The kid grabbed his pack from Howler and skipped toward a waiting ferry.

The Northern Federation's capital sat on the banks of the Skirn River where it bent back on itself, forming a broad kind of peninsula. For most of the year the waters were so cold that swimming across would freeze a man solid by the halfway point, and any modestly sized vessel would be caught and grounded on one of the many sandbars that shifted daily. The closest entrance from their side was with the aid of small ferries docked at a pier on the shore, which was guarded by three uniformed soldiers. Unlike those stationed at Gate Seven, these looked a great deal more official in their blue plate armor.

"What is your business in Vent this early?" one of the guards asked.

"I'm the governor of Arntim, in Nordcross' Western Frontier," Alberto answered. "I was hoping for an audience with the senate."

Howler hoped that the big redhead's blank stare went unnoticed. He'd practiced that speech at least a hundred times in the last hour, but he still couldn't get it right.

"The senate chambers won't open for another two hours," the guard continued. "You'll want to head for that building over there, can't miss it." He pointed to a spire off in the distance.

"Thanks," Alberto said as the others stepped onto the ferry. He took a step and hesitated, then turned to the guards and bowed before boarding.

Two ferrymen pushed the small boat out into the lake with long oars. As the west bank fell away, Howler heard the guards chuckle behind them.

"I don't think those blokes were being completely honest with you, Red," Howler muttered.

Alberto threw up his hands. "Do you have a better plan?" When Howler didn't answer, the redhead continued. "Then we check the tower thing to see if he's here."

When they disembarked, they were already close to their destination. It was hard to miss the tallest building in Vent. After traveling through a few streets, they came to a main road that led up to a three-story structure that acted as a wall protecting the spire within. They passed through a large archway and found themselves in a courtyard. The yard itself wrapped around an eight-story tower that stood out from the rest of the shorter building.

Howler could just make out a man and a woman holding each other at the base of the tower near a cluster of freshly planted trees. He jabbed Jake in the ribs and pointed the people out.

"Maybe they can help us," Jake said. He ran forward and approached the couple.

Alberto nodded and followed the blond along a pebble pathway. Howler quickly noticed the dozens of man-sized blocks of white marble all around them. Some had even been carved into the beginnings of intricate statues, but most had been scattered at random throughout the fresh grasses and shrubs.

"Oi, check it out, mates." He nodded to the top of the spire, where a broken sheet of stained glass twinkled in the morning light. "This must be the place where Mey—I mean the Blue Bandit did his thing."

Jake stopped to admire the demolished tip with Howler, but Lee continued to follow Alberto. When the redhead got close enough, he coughed loudly and waved. The couple broke apart quickly and the short man brushed himself off as if he had just pressed up against something dirty. Alberto averted his eyes, as did Jake, only Jake at least busied himself with pretending to read a plaque.

"Excuse me," Alberto finally croaked, "is Elder Harold's office here?"

"Er...yes, it would be," the woman answered. "And you are?" she asked as she extended her hand.

It took most of Howler's willpower not to laugh aloud at the woman's pretension. She was pear-shaped and had more wrinkles and grey hair than Xander, but her silk clothes and ornate jewelry told Howler that she was rather wealthy...or, at the very least, thought she was. The ex-con knew her type, and he wasn't impressed.

Alberto grabbed the woman's small hand with his gargantuan one and pumped it twice. Howler looked away in shame and studied her man. He looked just as ancient, but his clothes were old and worn.

*A fraud, eh? Guess it takes one to know one.*

Howler laughed to himself. The man sat on a small hunk of marble, trying not to draw their attention, and he nervously pulled a handkerchief from his pocket. He spat some phlegm into it, then opened it back up and stared. Howler almost gagged as the old man refolded the cloth and stuffed it back in his pocket.

"Guillaume?" Alberto asked curiously. "I thought you'd have dropped dead by now!"

"You know this guy?" Jake asked.

"You know...who?" Guillaume sputtered as he searched Alberto's face. Then his eyes came to rest on the big guy's red hair. "I remember you! You're one of the—"

"I'd be very careful about finishing that sentence if I were you, old timer," Alberto said through clenched teeth.

"I just remembered..." Guillaume turned to the woman and backed up a step. "I, uh, have some unfinished business I need to tend to." Without another word or a look back, he turned and ran from the group.

Howler and Jake couldn't hold back any longer—they both burst with laughter, Howler clutching his sides and Jake hanging onto a half-finished statue. As Howler caught his breath, he noticed the name carved into the base of the marble bust: "Irgoth of Skirn, Order of the Crow."

Alberto started to repeat his speech from earlier and the old woman's face quickly transitioned into a look of revulsion.

"I'm the governor of Arntim, in Nordcross'..."

*Blah, blah, blah,* Howler thought. He tried to get a good look at the huge ruby on the old lady's middle finger without arousing suspicion. The ruby moved as her hand swept upward, and Howler was brought back into the conversation.

"Your handshake was brutish," she huffed. "And I doubt you're the governor of anything more than a pile of dung. I have met the real governor of Arntim personally, and you are *not* Valdis! Start making sense or stop wasting my time!"

"I'm looking for the elder," Alberto pleaded.

"What do you want with my husband?"

"That man wasn't Harold," Alberto countered as he jabbed a thumb over his shoulder.

Howler slapped his forehead as the old lady's eyes narrowed into slits. He knew that look, and he knew that if Alberto wanted to come out of this without limping, he had some serious backtracking to do.

"That most certainly was not my husband!" the woman whispered threateningly. "Harold is old, weak, and ugly. The only thing he ever did right in his life was not dying..." She looked to the top floor and added, "Which is actually debatable."

Howler stepped forward and inconspicuously tapped Alberto's hand. When he got the redhead's attention, he shook his head slightly. Alberto got the hint and waited for the old woman to continue.

"That coward is out promoting his vision for the North," she said after pondering her husband's death for a moment. "Meanwhile, I'm stuck here fixing the mess that used to be the senate chambers. Can you imagine?"

It was then that Howler noticed the old lady's eyes. They seemed to only watch Jake as she went on and on about how dreadful her pampered life was. She eyed the kid like a buzzard might stare at a dead buffalo.

"...I mean, a woman of *my* talents, reduced to leading a cleanup crew, unthinkable! And don't even get me started on those lazy gardeners, the bastards. Those sculptors though, they sure are a nice change. They're so good with their hands..." She shivered as she finished her thought and looked Jake up and down.

"Help," Jake silently mouthed to Howler.

"So where can we find the senate now?" Alberto asked.

Howler rolled his eyes. Apparently the big guy didn't comprehend half of what the elder's wife was implying.

The hag frowned, creating an infinite pool of wrinkles around her dark eyes. "Are you touched in the head, dear?" she asked with a scoff. "There is…NO senate…they were…ALL killed."

"You must excuse my colleague here," Howler intervened out of pity. "His office is more of a figurehead position, if you catch my meaning?"

The woman extended her hand again. Howler gently bent at the waist to kiss the fat ruby he'd been admiring earlier. He barely brushed his fingertips along hers and straightened back up.

"We're actually an emissary convoy from Qellnorm," the suave ex-con explained. It was the only town in Ardänia that he knew anything about, and he hoped it still existed. "We were hoping to petition a lucrative trade agreement with the Northern Federation. I hoped that the back channels would work faster than trying to cut through all the paperwork that comes with the bureaucracy."

"Of course," the woman responded, then batted her eyes and smiled brightly. "My name is Denali. How may I be of service to you, young man?"

"You were about to tell my friend here where we might find your pig of a husband? The man who is obviously incapable of appreciating such a delicate flower as yourself, that is."

Alberto grimaced, but Denali was too busy basking in Howler's compliments to notice.

"You can find him in Padscott in the east, Mr.…?"

"My name is Robert Nader Quaashie Sibisi Henry Valerie Blue Hlimner Xanthippos von Banger…the Fourth," he finished with a wink.

"Oh, well, Harold should be there for the rest of the month, at least. You have plenty of time…in fact, I might be able to find you a warm bed to sleep in before you set off."

"I appreciate the offer, madam, but our time is short and we *are* in a rush," Howler explained. "We must be off, I'm afraid."

"Perhaps Harold won't come back…and you will," Denali said with another hungry glance at Jake. She paused and then added, "Tell me, Mr. Xanthippos von Banger, how—"

"The Fourth," he interrupted with a playful smile. "But please, call me Howler."

"Tell me, Howler, how do you feel about older women?"

"I find that experience is a must when it comes to the arts:

painting, sculpting, music…these all require years of practice with the goal of perfection. At the forefront of all these, however, is lovemaking."

The old bat giggled while Alberto continued to stare openmouthed.

"Thank you for your help, madam, you've been so very generous." Howler bowed again and turned to walk away.

"Anytime, young man, anytime." Denali waggled her fingers at Howler and sighed.

He grabbed Alberto, who sputtered in confusion, and the four travelers left the spire. Once they were out of earshot, Alberto shuddered and turned Howler around.

"Moons be damned, what *was* all that?" the big man asked with wide eyes. "Where did you learn to do that?"

"Oh, that? It was kind of my specialty back in the day, Bertie. It's called 'schmoozing.' You should try it sometime." Howler tossed his fearless leader the ring from Denali's finger.

"You stole from the elder's wife?" Alberto gawked.

"She was a bitch," Howler answered nonchalantly. "Besides, she'll wind up blaming that Guillaume guy. Or those workers."

"Hey, I hear they're great with their hands," Jake said with a wide grin.

"Ya know, I've heard that too," Howler responded. He laughed hard until he caught the look on Alberto's face. "Look, Red, we're in the clear. Relax."

"Who cares?" Jake interrupted. "Hey, gov'nah, I need a new bow, 'member?"

"When we get to Padscott kid, right now we gotta get going," Alberto said with a grunt. He shoved past Howler and Jake. "This trip is gonna take us the better part of a week on foot. Oh…and no more stealing," Alberto warned.

"That's not fair," Jake whined. He cursed and kicked a rock.

"Life is never fair, and to think otherwise is childish at best," Lee announced.

Everyone stopped and looked at the Islander, who kept walking. Whether or not he even knew he was speaking aloud was anybody's guess.

"The young master would be wise to remember that."

Howler shrugged when Jake looked at him for explanation, but

Alberto nodded. The big guy headed toward Vent's eastern gate as Lee passed him, and the others followed.

"Did you find the senate chambers?" a voice slurred from the doorway of a nearby bar. The guard that directed them earlier stepped forward. "I believe Elder Harold's colleagues are buried in the courtyard if you want a more private conversation!"

Howler smirked, and as he opened his mouth to sing Alberto an "I told you so," the big guy shoved him aside. He stomped toward the guards, who were doubled over with laughter. When Alberto got close enough, he growled, "Are those your boarhounds?"

The laughter disappeared as the guard's eyes filled with anger and flickered toward the hounds tethered to the building. "Yea, so what if they are?"

"I like them. I like them a lot."

\* \* \*

As they rode away from the city, Jake yelled, "And how do you think it looks that an Ardänian emissary posing as a governor is out beating up Northern guards and stealing their boarhounds?"

"Especially after that bloody git just lectured me on my own larceny," Howler added.

Jake sat in front of him on one hound while Lee and Alberto each rode on their own. Unlike the smaller boarhounds Howler was used to seeing in Misty, these were bred specifically for the military. These were bigger, with pure white fur, and they had two tusks on each side of their faces instead of the traditional one.

"Oh, did you want to walk to Padscott?" Alberto asked with the slightest trace of humor in his voice. The big man could barely conceal a grin.

"We really are a bad influence, Jake," Howler muttered. "I mean, Bert here's only been with us a couple of weeks and now he's a bloody thief! You better watch yourself, Lee, no telling what you might do!"

Even Alberto let out a chuckle as they rode eastward.

\* \* \*

Alberto claimed that Padscott would only be a three-day trip by hound, and Howler hoped that the redhead was right. His ass was sore and he was tired of sitting behind Jake—the little guy bounced around too much. On more than one occasion, he managed to crush Howler's twigs and berries. At their next stop, Howler made up his mind to switch seats.

"But I can't see over you," the blond whined.

"Stop being a spoiled brat and saddle up," Howler said as he pushed Jake up the hill toward their hound. "There's nothing to see out here anyway."

Jake spun at the last moment and Howler lost his balance. The ex-con went down, but he refused to go alone. He reached out and grabbed a corner of Jake's ill-fitting armor and they both tumbled. Alberto stood at the top of the hill, glaring at them. Then he suddenly started laughing loudly and clutching his sides.

After a moment, it finally set in. Jake had rolled into a pile of boarhound shit and had taken Howler down with him. Howler didn't care, though. He'd been covered in worse, and he was just happy to see a spark of the old Alberto still in there.

"If I'd known that all it took was that," the ex-con panted, "I would have smeared shit all over myself ages ago."

This time they all laughed, aside from Lee, who remained as stoic as ever.

* * *

As night fell on the second day, Howler pointed out the lights of a town off in the distance.

"It's not Padscott yet, is it?" Jake asked from the back of the boarhound. "Hey, Alberto, hey, do ya think maybe we could get me a new bow here? I don't wanna wait until Padscott..."

"We will also need more food soon," Lee added.

"We could always go back through Whitewater," Howler suggested.

"Not funny," Jake mumbled as he glanced over his shoulder.

Alberto stopped, and Howler could tell he was thinking hard about their next move. As Howler straddled his hound, waiting for their leader to decide, he couldn't help but imagine sleeping in a warm bed.

"We'll stop at the town for the night," Alberto finally announced, "but we leave at daybreak tomorrow."

"You're a saint, Red!" Howler tossed his head back and laughed.

"Don't make me change my mind," Alberto grumbled.

Just then a bird let out a lonesome cry from above.

"Falcons do not fly at this hour," Lee muttered to himself.

"Bollocks," Howler said to the Islander. "How d'you know it's a falcon, mate?"

Lee stared into the sky and ignored Howler. The others followed suit and scanned the sky for the bird, but nobody saw anything.

Another screech came from the village ahead and Howler shivered. He may have been the one to joke about Whitewater, but he quickly realized that he wasn't in a rush to meet any more strangers at night.

"You know," Howler said, trying to keep his fear out of his voice, "I suddenly don't feel so tired. I think we should just keep riding until dawn. There's another town not ten miles east of here. Also, I'm pretty sure I've heard of night falcons devouring entire herds of boarhounds." Most of what he was saying was a lie, but that was what Howler was good at.

"Entire herds?" Jake gawked. "We only have three. He'd still be hungry, and then he'd eat us too!"

"Well, only if he's fully grown," Alberto said with a mischievous grin. "Otherwise he'd just peck us to death over a couple days' time."

Jake stared at the others as fear crept onto his face.

"Emperor's balls, Jake," Howler said with a sigh. "He's lying to you. So was I. There's no such thing as a night falcon."

"Well…that bird still gives me the creeps. Maybe we could still go to that other town?"

"But Jake," Alberto interrupted, "what about your bow?"

"We can get a bow anywhere, right?" Howler asked and Jake nodded. "See, Red, let's just go."

"No, no, this was your idea," the redhead sang. "We're stopping here, evil night falcon or not." Alberto rode ahead and left the others behind.

A second later, Howler cursed and kicked his hound into a

gallop. He caught up to Alberto at a short bridge spanning a steady creek, where they could barely make out six men standing guard on the far side. None of them wore the traditional blue-and-gold armor, yet Howler could just make out the telltale signs of sheaths strapped to their hips. He imagined the sharp, curved swords that were hidden underneath and his hand immediately dove into his coat. The wooden handle inside was both a comfort and a burden.

"Halt! This is the town of Heatherbrook," a short man shouted. He had a thick, black beard that was speckled with grey. "What business do you have here?"

Another man, this one lanky with dirty-blond hair, stepped forward into the light of a torch. When Jake peeked around Howler's shoulder to see what was going on, he nearly fell off of the hound. A large falcon with an orange, hooked beak sat on the blond's forearm. The bird had a snowy white chest, but the rest of its feathers were as black as midnight.

Howler felt the tension rise and looked over at his big leader. Alberto was either gauging the situation or trying to remember a recipe for peach cobbler, Howler couldn't be sure. He pulled his hound in front of Alberto's and took the lead.

"We are weary from traveling," Howler announced, "and all we ask for is a few warm beds and perhaps a bite to eat."

There was a quick discussion amongst the men, and Howler heard mostly angry tones.

"Get ready mates, this might go badly," the Guildsman said under his breath.

"We've been waiting for you to arrive all day," the short man called out.

Howler liked his voice. It was gruff, but not unfriendly. The ex-con quickly thought of an angle he might be able to use.

"What was the hold up? You guys get lost?" the tall blond asked.

His voice was cool, almost cold even, and Howler knew immediately that there was nothing he would be able to say to this man that would win him over. Howler checked Alberto again, but the big man was busy ogling the bird on the lanky man's arm.

*What's the point of having a leader if the wanker never leads?*

"We got here as fast as we could..." Jake said as he turned to Alberto. "Right?"

Alberto shrugged. "I took you with me because you were supposed to know the way," he hissed under his breath, "but you two couldn't find your way out of a tunnel. I haven't seen a map of the Northern Federation in years, so I'd say we're just lucky we aren't more lost."

Jake hung his head in shame and the villager's words finally sank in.

"You were following us?" Howler shouted.

"No," the blond said, "but Avira was." He raised his arm and the falcon took flight.

Howler and Jake ducked dramatically, much to the Northerners' delight.

"We can house you for the night and feed you," the blond announced, "but it'll cost you."

Alberto held up a sack of gold, but Howler shook his head. "That's not how you—"

Avira's screech cut him off. The falcon swooped down and snatched the heavy bag from Alberto's hand. It brought the bounty back to the blond, who laughed loudly.

"We thank you," the bearded man said as the falconer counted Alberto's gold. "Now, if you would hand over one of your boarhounds…"

"We just gave you all our gold!" Alberto snapped. "You want a hound, too?"

"Technically the bird stole it and we retrieved it," the blond explained. "Might sound better on your part if you just say you lost it. You should be more careful."

Howler laughed on the inside, but then he noticed Alberto's skin flush. His blood was boiling; there was a particularly large vein throbbing in his forehead.

"The gold is for the use of this bridge," the bearded man interrupted. "The hound is the price for room and board. We know they're stolen from the Northern Cavalry anyway."

"We only want one," the falconer added. "Do we have a deal?"

Howler picked at his teeth and watched a log bob in the river when he felt warmth on the back of his neck.

"Hey…" Jake whispered.

"What?" Howler asked innocently as he caught Alberto's glare.

"You're the Guildsman," Alberto whispered more loudly than

was necessary, "you do the bartering."

Howler cleared his throat and yelled, "We choose which hound and you have a deal!"

Alberto slumped in his seat. "I could have done that," he muttered.

The men across the way murmured to each other for a moment. Howler already knew they would accept; the desperation was as clear as day in the short man's voice. He'd already played out a few scenarios and had several deals ready to offer when they turned back to the travelers.

"Done," the blond announced.

Howler almost choked on his own disappointment.

*Alberto was right. He* could *have done this.*

The two men who had done all the talking approached them. Alberto and Lee dismounted, followed by Howler and Jake.

"My name's Daniel," the blond announced. "This is Winston. And, as you already know," he motioned to the falcon, "this is Avira."

The bird blinked its orange eyes several times at Howler, and the suave man made faces at it in an attempt to get it to take flight. Daniel threw the sack of gold back to Alberto, who bounced it in his hands a few times.

"Well," the redhead said, "it certainly is lighter."

Winston's beard twitched. "Just be happy we didn't take it all," he said.

"These are my men," Daniel told them. "You can trust every one of them…"

Howler blissfully ignored the introductions. His wandering eyes eventually met the falcon's blinking orange ones again. The ex-con got a weird feeling like he was being judged and he quickly looked away.

"…you can leave our new beast with them."

Alberto caught Howler's attention and they decided to leave the boarhound Lee had been riding with the remaining townsfolk.

"Excellent!" Winston clapped his hands together. "Daniel and I will lead you to your rooms for the night."

He grabbed the reins from Alberto, and Daniel did the same with Howler and Jake's hound. Avira took flight again and disappeared as the travelers followed their new hosts through the sleeping village. Their fatigue caught up with them and the slow walk quickly became a chore. Jake jabbed Howler in the ribs after a moment.

"Right," Howler muttered with a sigh. "Excuse me, sir," he addressed Winston, "if there is one to spare, might we also purchase a bow, seeing as ours was confiscated at the Wall?"

"Oh, that tickles," Winston said with a chuckle.

"Pardon?" Howler asked.

"The smoke you're currently blowing up my ass with all your 'sir' talk," the bearded man answered.

Howler was floored. He thought he'd had Winston pegged, but apparently the beard hid more than Howler read.

"A bow would not be out of the question," Daniel answered, surprising the ex-con yet again.

"Thanks Dan-Dan!" Jake said, though an angry glance from the blond shut him up.

"My name's Daniel. I won't say it again."

Five steps later, the kid was back at it. Howler was used to his undying curiosity, but he knew some people found it annoying. Daniel, he guessed, would be one of them.

"So," Jake said, stretching the word out. "What's with the huge falcon?"

"The young master has a point," Lee cut in. "Your falcon is abnormally large."

"Avira is a Black Iron falcon," Daniel answered simply. "The females are always larger, but they rarely leave their nest."

"How many kinds of falcons are there?" Jake continued.

"Don't know," Daniel responded. Howler hoped Jake heard the warning in his tone.

"Okay," Jake muttered. "If you guys are guarding the bridge, why aren't you wearing any armor?"

"Don't have any," Winston answered this time.

"Have you guys ever heard of night falcons?" Jake continued. "Or the Guild? Misty Pass? Druids that sacrifice virgins?"

"They don't exist, heard of it in stories, no, and we don't talk about druids around here," Winston replied again.

Howler was impressed. The bearded dwarf had no problem keeping up with Jake tit for tat.

"So what's the story here then?" Jake asked.

"The *story* is that the damn senate has been screwing us for the better part of a decade," Daniel snarled.

Winston nodded along as his friend spoke.

"First they disbanded the local militia, which left us jobless," the lanky man waved his arms with wild gestures, "then they closed the Wall and took everything that wasn't nailed down and sold it to Nordcross!"

"Is that why you need the boarhound?" Jake asked.

"You ask a lot of questions, don't you?" Winston interrupted with a chuckle.

"The town's only mule died last month. We were afraid that come spring we wouldn't be able to plant enough food to get us through the year." Daniel's scowl relaxed a bit. "But now we might have a chance. I mean, it's no mule, but it might do the job."

They stopped at a house with walls that were stone on the bottom and then wood until the roof, which was made of slate. Smoke billowed out from one of the two chimneys.

"This is my home," Daniel announced. "You'll be staying here tonight."

They entered the large living room, where a roaring fire filled the hearth. The mantle and brickwork around it took up one whole wall. In the corner, with her head resting beneath one of her wings, Avira roosted on a simple perch with an open window behind her. A kind-looking woman was busy in the kitchen stirring a giant pot.

"Winston, it is so good to see you again," the woman cooed. "Oh, Daniel, who are your friends?" she asked as she noticed the four extra men in the living room.

"Gentlemen, this is my mother, Gillian," Daniel said. "Mother, this is Jake, Alberto, Lee, and—"

Howler darted forward and took the old woman's hand lightly in his own. He bowed and kissed her fingertips. "Howler, at your service."

When he straightened up, Gillian laughed softly. Daniel looked ready to explode, but Howler was distracted by Alberto's eyes studying the woman's fingers.

"I wouldn't steal from those down on their luck," the ex-con whispered as he resumed his place next to Alberto.

"They're just passing through, Mother," Daniel said. "We're trading room and board for one of their boarhounds."

"And a bow," Jake added before Howler could restrain him.

"Yes, and a bow," Winston said. "You're persistent, too, it seems." He laughed this time. It was a deep and powerful rumble that revealed two rows of crooked teeth.

"No offense," Alberto said slowly, and Howler braced himself for something stupid, "but you and your friends don't look like farmers."

Howler sighed and his shoulders fell. He was relieved that their leader wasn't so dense after all.

"It's been a long journey and I'm tired," Alberto continued. "I just want to know the truth before I let my guard down."

"Well, the short story is that we're farmers now!" Winston said. He rested a hand on Alberto's shoulder, but removed it quickly when he saw the look on the big man's face. "...although not the greatest. We make much better soldiers, I assure you, but that was a long time ago."

"I dunno about that," Jake said suspiciously, "that sword looks all funky. I don't see how—"

"It's a katana!" Daniel practically yelled. "Only the best soldiers are awarded the right to carry one."

"Trust me, little one," Winston's eyes were practically lost in wrinkles as his face was swallowed by a giant smile that was visible even through the beard, "we were skilled enough when the North still stood for something."

"Still, that kanta or whatever you called it doesn't look all that great to me," Jake muttered.

Daniel clenched his fists and opened his mouth again, but Gillian put a consoling arm around her son's shoulder.

"So how 'bout this house, eh? Must have cost a pretty penny," Howler said with a grin as he gently pulled Jake out of Daniel's reach. "I'm impressed, mate!"

"It did," the falconer answered when he calmed down. "And now I have to pay an inordinate amount of taxes on it while trying to keep enough food on the table for my mother and me."

"I'm sure you could get your old jobs back now," Alberto suggested.

"And then you could just buy whatever food you need, right?" Jake added.

Winston let out a hearty laugh. "Funny you should say that, because a group of men came through here about a week back and offered us that very thing."

"One of them claimed he was the new elder. He said, 'Things are going to be different.' They looked real enough, with all the guards and whatnot, but…" Daniel trailed off.

"So…" Jake's eyes were locked onto Daniel, waiting for the rest of his story.

"We told him to get lost," the falconer continued. "We don't trust the senate and we don't need a new elder. They're all the same anyway, greedy bunch of motherless goats…"

"We're only looking out for this town and our families these days, and damn the rest!" Winston interjected. "After all the years we spent in their service…where were *they* when *we* needed help?" His face finally lost some of its bright vigor. A moment later, however, his visage reset to its naturally jolly state.

"The journey of a thousand steps starts with but one," Lee muttered just loud enough for everyone to hear. He stood by the front door with his arms crossed and didn't even bother looking up.

"What do you know of it, slave?" Daniel's face turned red as emotion got the best of him.

"He's no slave, mate," Howler stepped forward, "and you'd be wise to listen to him. Just because someone doesn't help you is not a reason to turn your back on everyone else. Someone's got to go first!"

"Do you want a place to stay or not?" Daniel threatened.

"We mean you no offense," Alberto said wearily. "We just have a problem sticking our noses where they don't belong." He looked at Howler as he said the last part, and the ex-con decided the big guy might have a point.

"Try to get a handle on it before you lose that nose of yours," Daniel said. "We'll be back later. We're supposed to be on watch." He opened the front door and waited for Winston to exit, then slammed it behind them.

"Sorry about that," Gillian said, more to Lee than anyone else. "It's been hard around here, for all of us." She forced a smile and motioned to the hallway. "The spare room is down the hall on the left, and the bathroom is one door past it."

Howler thanked their host and followed the others down the hallway. When he entered the room, Jake had already abandoned his pack and was struggling with a buckle on his armor. Alberto sat on the bed across from him, and Howler knew he would be either spooning

Jake or sleeping on the floor that night.

"Go wash up before dinner," Alberto commanded. He had a stony look in his eyes and seemed to be grinding his teeth. A moment later he stood and walked to the door. "You two smell like shit," he added as he left.

"I think he's talking about you," Jake said as he pinched his nose and shooed Howler out of the room.

# CHAPTER EIGHTEEN: FRAGMENTS

Alberto stomped down the hallway toward the living room. His skin flushed as the pounding in his chest matched the pounding in his head. The disdain growing in the pits of his stomach became a roaring blaze of emotion, clouding his vision. It wasn't anger—he knew that feeling intimately—but it was something close.

He balled his large hands into fists and his breath came in quick, ragged gasps. Time slowed to a crawl as Alberto made his way through the house. He felt trapped in his own skin and panic began to overtake him.

The big man wanted nothing more than to leave that place, to be alone with his thoughts to figure out what in the moons was wrong with him, but he couldn't seem to escape the full house. Sweat dampened the collar of his shirt as he stared toward the end of the hall. The opening began to shrink, as if to tell him that he would never fit, that he would never make it out.

A handful of seconds had passed, but Alberto could have sworn it had been lifetimes. The hall finally gave way to the living room, where Gillian gave the redhead a concerned look. She called out to him, but it sounded as if she was underwater. When Alberto didn't answer, she repeated herself, but he still couldn't understand what she was saying.

"W-what?" Alberto asked numbly.

"I asked if you were alright," the old woman answered.

"No," Alberto muttered as if the thought had just dawned on him.

He made his way to the front door and an odd kind of fatigue set in. The big man couldn't find the strength to fight it, and his hand trembled as he reached forward and grabbed the door's handle. An eternity seemed to pass as he waited for the night to come into view. A cool breeze blew in, strong enough to shift the damp hair matted to his forehead. Relief washed over him. He stepped out onto the porch as time resumed its usual pace and his skin rejoiced in the fresh air. Finally his fists began to uncurl and his breathing returned to normal.

Another gust brought a familiar scent—lavender and roses—and his eyes were drawn south, toward the place he once called home, if only for a short while.

It was a rare night where none of the moons were out, and as a result, thousands of bright, shimmering stars littered the dark sky. He started to count them and thought to himself, *One for each death I've caused.*

"Mantrych," Alberto whispered as he let his fists fully uncurl. He took several deep breaths and the last tentacles of panic started to dissipate.

*Why did you have to do it, Maxine?* Alberto thought bitterly. *I still don't understand what your goal was...I know you loved Mother in your own way, but Chloe? Mantrych? ...how could you...if you had a problem, why didn't you just come to me?*

"Why?" he demanded from the night, his croaky voice surprising him. A fat tear rolled down his cheek and into his scarlet scruff. His lips quivered in a feeble attempt to fight his sorrow.

Someone cleared their throat from a shadowy corner behind him, but Alberto didn't even bother turning around.

"I thought you had to return to your post," the big redhead said flatly.

"I needed to take a breather first," Daniel responded. "Calm down a bit."

The blond sighed as he strolled past his guest and stepped down the stairs of his porch. Alberto wiped a hand over his face and stared as Daniel continued toward the road. The night quickly swallowed up the watchman, leaving Alberto to drown in his sorrow.

The redhead cracked his knuckles, freeing the slight numbness that had overtaken his fingers. He looked down at his hands and noticed four crescent-shaped cuts in each of his palms. As the wind shifted and he wiped his bloody hands on his pants, he could have sworn he caught a hint of juniper. He looked up hopefully, but all he saw was the blackness of the night.

"Shit," Alberto muttered as he started down the stairs. "Ah, shit." He picked up his pace and began to run after Daniel.

Alberto caught up to the blond outside of what looked like an old general store. Daniel walked with his hands in his pockets and the sort of shuffling gait that accompanied deep thought. It reminded Alberto of his second day in Mantrych, when he first saw Chloe. The memories renewed the tightness in his chest and he had to strain to call out.

"Wait!" the redhead managed.

Daniel spun quickly, his hand already on the hilt of his sword. The threat of danger cleared Alberto's head and he smirked appreciatively.

"I'm not looking for a fight," he assured the blond. "I just...have some stuff to take care of elsewhere. I need you to look after my friends."

"Your friends?" Daniel asked with raised eyebrows.

Alberto stared, but the watchman didn't drop his gaze. "You're right," the redhead finally said. "They're not my friends. But I need you to look after them regardless."

"I'm no babysitter," Daniel snarled.

"I was thinking more along the lines of jailer," Alberto responded with a grin that went unreturned.

"What exactly is your relationship with the convicts?" the blond asked as he narrowed his eyes. "Did you honestly think I'd miss those brands?"

"I was hoping," Alberto answered honestly.

"Too bad for you then. So what's your story?" The watchman crossed his arms as he waited for an answer that wasn't coming. "They don't act like prisoners, so I doubt you're a bounty hunter. A freedom fighter? A rebel? I can tell from the way you hold yourself that you're no stranger to the battlefield."

All Daniel got was more stony silence from Alberto.

"I don't give two boarhound shits what you're up to. But those two were sentenced to death, and I know Nordcross will come to get what's theirs at some point. What exactly are you trying to get Heatherbrook involved in?"

Alberto reached into his pocket and fished out the ring that Howler had pilfered from Denali. He tossed the heavy loop to the blond. "Just keep Howler and Jake here until I return. Nothing more, nothing less."

Daniel looked down at the ruby in his hand. "What of the slave? Should I keep him on lockdown as well?"

"For the last time," Albert snarled, "Lee is *not* a slave. He can do as he pleases, but..."

"Right, right," Daniel nodded, his eyes still locked on the ring.

"Babysitting…"

"I'll need my boarhound," the redhead added.

"The stables are back the way you came," Daniel replied, "one block south of the bridge. We confiscated the rigs you rode in on. The silver on those cavalry saddles should buy us enough grain to plant at least a few fields. And with this…donation, we just might make it through next year." His eyes finally left the ring as he stared up at the big man. "You can find a decent enough replacement saddle in the stables, help yourself."

Alberto nodded and extended his hand. Daniel shook it after pocketing the ring, and without warning, the redhead pulled the watchman close enough that he could smell the sweat building on his scalp.

"I don't know much," Alberto said, "but I do know this: people like us, we can't hide forever. I know you won't stay out of whatever this is for long. I look forward to seeing you on the battlefield…my only hope is that you're on the right side of things."

He let go of Daniel with a small shove. Alberto could swear he saw a retort brewing in the blond's eyes, but Daniel swallowed and let it rest.

"I'm sure I'll see you soon," Alberto added before strolling off into the night.

* * *

It took Alberto a long hour to find the stables. It wasn't that Daniel misled him—his directions were fine—it was just Alberto's mind. He couldn't keep a single thought in his head for more than a minute without it getting overshadowed by something else. By the time he called on a stableman, he was sure that he'd found every dead end in Heatherbrook.

His mind refused to clear and it took him five attempts to rig his saddle correctly. On his last try, just as he secured the final buckle, he heard something shift in the adjacent stall.

"At least I'm not pissing this time," the redhead called as he slowly turned, "but it's nice to know someone's looking out for me."

Lee stepped out into the flickering light of the torch the stableman had left. The Islander crossed his arms over his chest and leaned against the nearest stanchion. He stared at the big man with contempt, but Alberto shook his head.

"I'm not running away, if that's what you're thinking," he explained. "I'm coming back. I just have to go take care of...some stuff. And I can't do it with *them* around," Alberto said as he jabbed a thumb over his shoulder.

Lee's expression lightened a bit, but he didn't drop his stare. It was the most assertive Alberto had seen the Islander act and it made him slightly uncomfortable.

"You can stay or come with me, but either way, this is something I need to do." Alberto mounted his hound and paused, already knowing that Lee would join him.

He held out his large hand and waited for the Islander to take it. When he did, Alberto was surprised at how cool his skin was. Once Lee was secured behind him, Alberto kicked the boarhound into a trot and left the stables.

*Out there somewhere are the ashes of Mantrych...and Chloe.*

\* \* \*

The next morning, the sun broke free of the horizon and lit up a sheet of wispy, pinkish clouds that had rolled in during the night. He was so focused on his destination that they hadn't stopped once, even for breakfast. The big man was grateful that it was Lee who accompanied him. The former slave was as sturdy as the boarhound they rode and his desire for small talk was as minimal as Alberto's.

The boarhound, despite having run all night with the weight of two men, trudged on without so much as a grunt. The steed was magnificently built, bred, and trained, but Alberto knew it would need to rest at some point. A few hours before dusk, the hound finally stumbled a bit and Alberto decided to stop and set up camp. Lee set out to gather kindling while Alberto tended to a tenuous fire.

A powerful yawn rose up from his chest, and as much as he fought it, his eyes drooped as his mouth closed. Alberto needed to sleep, but he knew Iggy would be waiting with his guitar and visions of tragedy. He waited for the music to start. He knew it would continue until he was back on track doing whatever it was that the man on the moon wanted from him.

Lee returned with an armful of small, somewhat dry sticks and twigs. He set the kindling in front of the fire and sat next to the big man.

Alberto leaned back on his forearms and raised his eyes to the sky, watching the sun set, but he cursed loudly as he fought back another yawn. He sat up and tossed a few twigs onto the paltry fire as he and the Islander watched the flames dance, continuing their futile fight against the brisk, Northern air.

\* \* \*

Alberto woke to the smell of something tangy. At some point during the night, the big man had fallen asleep. But sleep was all he did. Iggy had left him alone.

*Guess I'm doing something right,* he thought. Then his eyes drifted over to his brooding companion. *Or maybe someone really is looking out for me...*

Lee sat cross-legged in front of a bowl that sat on the fire. Inside was some kind of stew with bits of leaves and roots poking through its filmy surface. The Islander looked pointedly at Alberto, then the bowl, then back to the redhead. Alberto's stomach growled, but he shook his head. His mind was so cluttered and his stomach was so unsettled that he couldn't bring himself to eat.

With a nod, Lee turned and carefully pulled the bowl from the fire with two long sticks. He dropped the bowl in a drift of snow and steam hissed up around it. The boarhound bounded over and Alberto watched it slurp the stew eagerly.

They broke camp moments later and rode until midday. Not a word was spoken between the men for the duration of their journey until they approached the remains of a devastated orchard. Severed trunks and burnt tree limbs were scattered across the snowy ground.

"Mantrych?" Lee asked at just above a whisper.

Alberto didn't know how the Islander knew that name, but he nodded nonetheless. He turned his boarhound southwest and skirted around the burnt shells poking up through the fresh powder. Voices from his past called out in the distance, but he refused to turn his head.

Through instinct or providence, Alberto unwittingly led their hound to a hill. All that set this hill apart from the few others surrounding Mantrych's remains was the pair of boulders sitting on top of it, overlooking the plains to the west.

"I guess we're here," the redhead said as he dismounted the

hound. He patted the panting creature on its side as the tightness in his own chest returned. The pounding in his head started next. It quickly became a deafening roar as his peripheral vision faded to black. When Lee grabbed Alberto's shoulder, the big man flinched and spun around.

Lee nodded, urging him ahead. Alberto turned and walked toward the boulders, his feet dragging through the snow. He felt like weights had been attached to each of his muscles. Crossing the short distance to the grave he sought seemed to take hours.

Once he slipped between the rocks, everything else ceased to exist. It was only him and the tomb. Alberto dropped to his knees as he ran his fingers over the inscription he'd carved so long ago.

*Chloe. Taken before she had the chance to see all the beauty in the world that she deserved.*

His fingers began to tremble as memories of a woman with black and red hair surfaced. Alberto's lip quivered and his head spun as he tried to stand. Music began to play in his head, a guitar strumming along to the lullaby his mother used to sing to him. He fell back and Lee caught him.

"Breathe, sir," the Islander said, "you must breathe!"

The invading music dwindled and Alberto realized he'd been holding his breath. He regained control of his body and his eyes focused on the disturbed snow underfoot.

"By the moons," Alberto snarled as he leapt out of Lee's arms, "someone's been camping here! What sick bastard would sleep on a...on a grave..." He trailed off as his own words sank in and the music restarted. "My...my fiancée...I'll kill them." His voice picked up. "I'll rip them apart! I'll—"

Before Alberto could finish describing what he would do when he found the perpetrator, Lee said, "A month has passed since your friend slept here." The Islander then squatted near a pile of blackened wood in the snow.

"My friend?" Alberto shouted.

"Yes," Lee answered as he rose to his feet.

Alberto stared at him with disbelief. A string of purple glyphs stood out against the dark skin of the Islander's neck. As Lee strained, the symbols caught Alberto's eye. They seemed to shimmer before disappearing completely.

"He came alone," the Islander continued, "but...he did not

leave that way." He pressed a hand against each boulder and leaned until his forehead was almost touching one. "He is in great peril. Neither she nor you can help him now."

"She? Great peril?" Alberto asked.

The redhead's doubt was extinguished completely when Lee turned around. His eyes glowed light purple, then dimmed. It reminded Alberto of when Meyral would pass out and his eyes would flash blue.

"My apologies, sir," Lee said. "It is impossible to interact with someone or something and not leave a trace of yourself behind. You spent much time with your friend, and there is still a piece of you with him. If you know how to look, it is easy to see."

"What else can you see?" Alberto wondered aloud. "Who is the 'she' you mentioned? Or the 'great peril'?"

"I do not know," Lee answered as he shook his head. "But there is much death surrounding your friend."

Alberto's eyes drifted back to the inscription. "But he's...he's still alive, right?" he asked quietly.

"I believe that is something you have to find out for yourself," the Islander said.

"We set up camp here," Alberto said. He nodded toward a spot that lay a respectable distance away. He turned back to Chloe's disturbed grave and whispered, "This is what I came here for."

"With all due respect, sir," Lee said as he walked past the big man, "I do not think you have the slightest idea what you truly came here for."

* * *

After clearing Chloe's grave of debris and snow, Alberto lay down next to the small fire that Lee had built. Throughout the day's labors, Alberto tried to think of everything he wanted to say to the man on the moon when he finally came. But when night fell, his sleep went undisturbed again. The big man was almost disappointed.

Dawn broke and his stomach growled loudly. Alberto rose from his spot near the fire, but his appetite was still gone. He hadn't eaten since before Heatherbrook, and he was fairly certain Lee hadn't either. Alberto raised his sights to the former slave, but the place where Lee had slept was now empty.

Alberto took advantage of his solitude and walked back to

Chloe's resting place. He sat in front of it and concentrated, but his mind refused to focus on what he felt.

*Pain,* Alberto thought. *I feel pain. I lost the one person I truly loved...it must be pain.*

Alberto sat completely still, lamenting his loss. As he tried to focus solely on Chloe, his mind strayed to Aldomein and then to Maxine. After a few minutes, he sighed and shook his head.

*That's a damned lie. It's not pain, that's what you feel when you bump your head or get chopped with an axe. No, it's sorrow. I'm still in mourning, I am...sorrowful.*

The big man repeated the last line several times with his eyes shut tightly, but he still felt nothing.

*Moons be damned, what's wrong with me? I can't feel a thing.*

"Dammit!" Alberto shouted. "Even my ass is numb!"

Anger began to eat away at him. His mind refocused on Maxine, but he brought his thoughts back to Chloe. Only a few seconds later, memories of Aldomein resurfaced. His stomach turned and he tried again to clear his mind. He knew what he was supposed to feel, but there was only emptiness.

"I came all this way, and for what?" Alberto demanded. He tilted his head back and roared, and it was several more moments before he realized he was no longer alone.

"You think too much, sir," Lee said. He stood just outside of the tomb with several grey-green balls cradled in his arms, each dotted by small, white flowers.

"That's the first time I've been accused of that," Alberto replied with a small laugh. "What are you holding?"

Lee didn't answer. He sat by the fire and placed a dented pot over the crackling flames. The Islander carefully placed the balls inside, then scooped some of the surrounding snow and filled the rest of the pot. As the snow began to melt, Lee crossed his legs and set his hands on his knees. The outline of a bright, purple rune appeared across his back, then filled in with the same vivid color. As Alberto tried to study it, the tattoo disappeared back into Lee's dark skin.

"What is that?" Alberto asked as he pointed to the pot. "You're not gonna eat that, are you? Smells like my socks..."

Lee's brow furrowed and a light sheen of sweat glistened on his face. Alberto leaned forward to look in the pot, but one of Lee's eyes shot open and he held out a hand.

"Do not get any closer," the Islander warned.

"Why? What does it do?"

"It does many things, sir." Lee let out a long sigh as he broke his meditative state. His eyes flashed bright purple as he opened them and looked at the big man. "For you, I hope it will unlock doors. Emotions are not thoughts, sir. They come from different places and do different things. You cannot simply think pain or happiness into existence."

"Right," Alberto mumbled as he slowly sat back.

A strange feeling began to twist its way into Alberto's gut, like a mix of anxiety and guilt. That old lullaby returned, softly though, as if it were coming from far away.

Lee restarted his meditation. A purple glyph that stretched from his neck to his navel shined brightly and the music in Alberto's head stopped. "Please, sir, do not disturb me again," the Islander said. "This is a delicate concoction, and if prepared incorrectly, its effects could be lethal."

"Oh, that's reassuring," Alberto grumbled. He made his way back to Chloe's grave and sat down again.

For the next hour, the big man sat in silence and was only able to conjure up two emotions: anger and curiosity. Finally Lee approached him, breaking Alberto's already feeble concentration. The former slave handed him a strip of fabric, and half of the dirty bandana was covered in lumpy, grey slop. When the smell hit him, Alberto leaned forward and gagged.

"Good thing I haven't been eating lately," the redhead panted. "You know what? I think I'm done here anyway," he added as he eyed the bandana. "Why don't we just head back to Heatherbrook? I bet Howler and Jake are worried sick."

"You cannot continue to run, sir," Lee said almost soothingly. "Tie this around your head."

Alberto hesitated. His stomach was still turning just from the smell, but when his eyes fell to Lee's left pant leg, he made up his mind. Lee's burlap pants were torn away from the knee down. This man, who had spent most of his life in slavery, had only known Alberto for a few weeks, and he was willing to sacrifice one of his only possessions for him.

Alberto nodded and took the strip of garment, then tied it around his head while holding his breath. Lee stepped back as

Alberto's mouth started to feel like it had been stuffed with the same burlap he had wrapped around his forehead. His fingers began to go numb and the colors around him intensified. At first it made everything look more real, more defined, but then it became too bright to look at. He squinted and fell onto his side. He felt like he hadn't slept in years, but all of his muscles were too tense for him to sleep.

* * *

*Did I fall asleep?*
Alberto's voice seemed to echo back at him in his head.
*What is this?*
All around him was blackness. A bright blue flame burned in the distance.
*Where is this? How long have I been here? Who am I?*
Alberto realized he was standing with his eyes closed. He opened them slowly, letting himself adjust to the brightness of the sun, which shined over a red sky with no clouds. Surrounding him was a field of tall, orange flowers the size of his face, all swaying with an invisible breeze.

He stared at the nearest plant and noticed details that he had never stopped to notice before. It was like he could see every vein in every petal on every flower. As the big man gawked, trying to count the myriad of flora before him, the blossoms began to shrink. The petals twisted and folded, and soon Alberto saw only fist-sized buds topping the stalks scattered throughout the grassy field.

Then the plant itself shrank. The bud was pulled into the stalk, and the leaves disappeared one by one. The plant grew backward and Alberto followed its progress curiously. The big man actually got on his hands and knees as the ground finally swallowed the little green plant. Then the grass beneath him withered, sinking into the ground as the flowers had done.

The rich, dark soil dried up, leaving harsh dust in its wake. A ring of bone-white clay surrounded Alberto, and suddenly the ground began to crack. The stretch of dead ground spread rapidly, cracking the surface into clay plates that curved upwards at the edges. Alberto tried to escape the spreading dryness, but no matter how fast he scrambled, the morphing landscape followed right behind him.

Alberto got to his feet, but it seemed to take several minutes for him to actually stand. When the big man looked behind him, he found that he was standing in a desert. His head pounded as he looked out onto the sand, burning hot in the blazing desert sun.

*I need water. I need to drink something…*

In the distance, he could hear music. Something glimmered far away, and as he squinted at it, he could swear he saw a man in a chair. He stared for what seemed like hours, but he still couldn't tell what it was past a shifting, blurry concoction of colors. It could have been anything.

Suddenly an eye opened up across the sky. Its pupil was blacker than any darkness that Alberto had ever experienced, and the rest of it was so violet that he had to shield his eyes. He screamed as he fell upwards into the center of the massive eye.

His body became weightless, and as the color drained from his world, he realized that he was leaving the desert. The heat that was beating down on him dissipated and he felt relief spread throughout his body.

\* \* \*

Lee opened his eyes as the glyphs covering his body began to fade. He watched as a steady stream of drool fell from Alberto's chin to his shirt. The big man's breath was shallow and rapid, but he was only sleeping.

The Islander knew it would take a great amount of energy to help guide the big man, but he could still tell that someone or something was interfering. It was too late to stop, though, so he continued to sit by the fire, his legs crossed and his hands resting on his knees.

Then Alberto's eyes opened and a dim, purple glow could be seen around his pupils. He reached up slowly to wipe drool from his mouth, but as soon as his hand touched his face, he vomited. A jet of bright, greenish goop spurted from his slightly parted lips and covered his hand. He burped loudly and sat up.

"…are you real?" the big man asked as he rose to his feet.

Lee followed suit. He stood and followed Alberto as he walked down the hill, his eyes unfocused and his words falling from his mouth in a jumbled mess.

\* \* \*

*Where am I? Am I still falling? Am I still me?*

The light returned and a country lane opened up in front of him. He was standing still, but it still felt like he was falling. Slowly the feeling lessened and he started down the road, his legs walking without him telling them to. He didn't need to because he knew the trail by heart—he'd been down it a million times. He was back in Westmore, heading home to his family. Euphoria, like a flood of the purest adrenaline pumping through him, overtook his mind and body. He'd never looked forward to anything more in his life.

He reached their home, a quaint, sturdy cabin that Jaspar and Meyral had helped him build. Its roof was covered with the same jasmine and roses that his mother had planted in the garden around their house. His children, Somnia and Spero, emerged from the side yard, laughing and playing.

"Dad!" Somnia shouted as she ran up to Alberto and hugged his thigh. Her arms were caked with dirt and mud up to her elbows. She loved digging in the garden, just like her grandmother. "Did you bring me back anything?"

"I didn't have time," Alberto answered slowly. "I wanted to get back home to you as soon as I could."

"What about me, Dad? Did you get me anything?" Spero asked. He was three years Somnia's junior, and he was the spitting image of his father, only with his mother's black hair.

"How would that have been fair?" Alberto responded. "What if I had gotten Somnia something and not you? Imagine how you would feel."

Spero grinned and held his hands out, and then Somnia copied him. Alberto kneeled down and scooped both children into his arms.

"Now, where's your mother?" he asked his children. "It's been so long since I've seen her…"

They both pointed toward the porch, where Chloe rocked in a chair overlooking the garden. She was pregnant with child number three, and she was starting to show. Alberto sighed with relief when he saw her.

"How's the greatest cartographer this side of the Wolke been?" Chloe cooed when she saw her husband.

"I'm home now," Alberto replied, his throat clogging with

emotion. "I couldn't be better."

"Is Uncle Carter doing well?" she asked. "He wrote me a month ago when he came to help with the shop, but I haven't heard from him since."

"Carter is here?" Alberto asked.

Somnia giggled at her father's forgetfulness, her red braids swinging in her face.

"Of course he is," Chloe said with a small laugh. "You insisted he come help when you opened the shop."

Alberto kissed his children on their foreheads and set them down. He stepped forward and pulled Chloe into a tight embrace, relishing in the sweet smell of her hair as he brushed it away from the back of her neck. He could see every fine hair, every follicle, every little freckle, and he vowed to himself in that infinitesimal infinity that he would never forget any detail.

"Are you okay?" Chloe asked with a light laugh. "You seem…different."

Her hand, soft and delicate, just like Alberto remembered, trailed down his face. When she reached his beard, her eyes flickered down and the light around him seemed to dim for a moment. He looked past her and caught his reflection in the clean window behind her.

*When did I get so old?*

"I know," Chloe said, "these kids just keep growing, don't they? I feel my age more and more every day." She sighed, sending her sweet smell his way again.

Alberto pulled her close and kissed her deeply. His tongue parted her full lips, and just as it met hers, she pulled away.

"Dear, the kids…" she whispered.

Alberto picked his wife up and spun once. Chloe kissed him as she pulled her legs up and sat in his arms.

"Are you sure you're okay, honey?" she asked as she stared longingly into his eyes.

"I'm more than okay. I want to take you into the back room and rip—"

"Dear, the kids," she repeated, this time with a hint of anger that didn't quite match the smile on her face.

"They need to learn about this stuff at some point," the redhead retorted.

"Not today! Now put me down."

Alberto set Chloe on her feet with a grin, but he didn't let her go. "Put them down for a nap," he said.

Chloe's eyes lit up and she smiled again. She turned away and called their children over, but as they approached, Alberto sniffed the air.

"What is that?" he asked.

"Oh!" Chloe blushed brightly. "I completely forgot, your sister stopped in for dinner. She wanted to make that rabbit stew you love so much."

"Welcome home, Bert," a familiar voice said. It echoed between his ears, playing over and over for hours as he slowly turned toward the front door.

Standing over the threshold, dressed in a purple apron and happier than Alberto had ever seen her, was Maxine. She held a large wooden spoon in one hand and had her other cupped underneath it.

"Taste the broth," she told him. "It's missing something."

Alberto sipped the soup and smacked his lips loudly. "Two bay leaves and a dash of salt," he announced.

"Bay leaves, of course!" Maxine slapped her free hand on her slightly wrinkled forehead. She seemed to have gained some weight as she had aged.

She stepped aside as Somnia and Spero ran through the doorway, both chanting "Dash of salt, dash of salt!"

"You two wash your hands!" Maxine called after her niece and nephew. "Thanks, Stubby," she told Alberto.

His sister disappeared into the house, and as Chloe walked by to follow the others, Alberto smacked her backside. She jumped a bit and smiled, her plump lips curling up into that sweet grin.

He stepped through the doorway, but there was no light on the other side. He could feel his eyes straining to adjust, but he couldn't see anything. Suddenly, as if somebody had lit a thousand lamps, a hallway appeared around him. It looked just like his home in Westmore, only hundreds of doors lined each side of the hall. The room seemed more spacious than a castle and he felt smaller than he'd ever felt before.

Alberto heard someone sobbing faintly down the hall and he called out, "Spero! Somnia! Where are you?"

He barreled headfirst down the hallway, following the sound, but the hallway stretched in all directions. The doors were so tall that he could barely reach the doorknobs, and there was no end in sight.

After what felt like days, Alberto slowed to a walk and then stopped. The sobbing was loud, like it was right next to him. When he turned, he saw a small, green-haired girl crying in the corner. Her face was buried in the crook of her arm, which held her knees close to her chest. Her weeping continued even as Alberto knelt beside her.

Maxine looked up, biting her lip as she had always done when something was weighing on her mind. Her violet eyes sparkled back at him, brimming with tears. She couldn't have been more than ten years old.

"Is this a dream, Maxi?" Alberto asked shakily.

She shook her head and whispered, "It's so much more than that, little brother." Maxine started bawling once again and dropped her head back down.

"Am I dead?" Alberto asked. It felt strange to him that no fear accompanied his question.

"No," she managed between sobs.

"But you're…I mean…are you real?"

Her cries slowed to a stop and she raised her head. "As real as you want me to be," she whispered with a trembling lip.

The lights went out and Alberto fell backward. He fell for so long that he was afraid he'd never stop.

* * *

Lee followed Alberto until the big guy stopped and sat in front of a pile of burnt wood dusted with layers of fresh, powdery snow. The structure may have been a shop at some point, but now it was nothing more than charred wood.

The Islander sat next to his companion as Alberto mumbled to himself. Lee couldn't tell if the big man was crying or sweating profusely…or both.

* * *

The smell of juniper hit him and Alberto realized he must have landed at some point. A thousand candles scattered about lit a dim outline of the bar in Gate Five. It was all the light Alberto needed to see the well-endowed women in various stages of undress all around him. Several danced in nothing more than a couple strips of cloth, while others strutted forward to undress him, massage him, fan him, and feed him. When he tried to focus to see past the thin cloth, his vision blurred and a kaleidoscope of colors blinded him.

Alberto had never felt quite so hungry in his life, but every grape he ate and every cup of wine he drank only made him hungrier.

"So this is where you go when you're not with me," a sultry voice said beside him. Aldomein, fully nude and covered in oil, rubbed her bare chest across his back as she massaged his shoulders. "It's a good thing I'm not the jealous type...although I do appreciate the location," she added. She nipped at his neck and smiled playfully.

"I've missed you so much," Alberto groaned as he let his head fall back.

"And what about your wife?" another voice asked.

Alberto followed the voice to between his thighs, where Chloe's smiling face stared back at him. She crawled up her husband's torso and sat in his lap with an impish grin.

He found himself caught between his two loves, and his mind raced as he felt his heart tear in half.

"Who will you choose, Alberto?" Aldomein whispered in his ear.

"Who?" Chloe demanded as her grin receded. "Your wife or this harlot?"

"Chloe..." Alberto reached up and brushed a lock of his wife's hair back over her shoulder. "You're dead. I watched you...I watched you die in my arms."

As the words left his lips, the other women disappeared one by one. His two loves lingered for a moment, Chloe biting her lower lip and Aldomein holding her breath, and then they faded away too.

One last woman slinked out of a shadowy corner and into the low light of the candles. A soft melody played, and the woman moved with the music in a way that almost brought tears to Alberto's eyes. She was skinny, not usually the type Alberto liked, but the way she danced had the redhead mesmerized.

She bent and glided smoothly across the floor, spinning and dancing lightly on her toes as she went. When the dancer came within an arm's length of Alberto, she stopped and turned around.

Maxine stepped in front of her brother with a look of guilt and shame dominating her face. It wasn't the happy, older version of his sister that would never be, nor was it the child Alberto remembered. This was the Maxine that was at Leviathan pass, the night that Alberto killed her.

"Get out of here!" Alberto shouted as he rose to his feet. "You don't belong here! What—"

"I'm only here because you want me here, little brother," she said calmly.

"Well someone didn't get the message, then!" he continued to shout. "I wanted to see gorgeous, naked women, not my sister! Get out!"

Maxine sighed and looked up to the ceiling. "I always did have to spell things out for you when I was alive. I don't know why I would have expected that to change."

Alberto crossed his arms and pouted. He waited for her to continue.

"What were you thinking about right before you conjured me up?"

"I was in the middle of a titty sandwich," Alberto grumbled somewhere between pride and shame.

"You are so crass, brother of mine."

"Thank you," Alberto said as he folded his hands and smiled.

"Who were you sandwiched between?"

"Aldomein and—" Understanding suddenly dawned on Alberto's face. "I was thinking of Chloe. My dead wife…and then my dead sister shows up."

"Right," Maxine nodded, "only you didn't kill your wife. But you killed me, didn't you?"

Alberto suddenly stood and pointed an accusative finger at Maxine. "You let me think you were helping Sera! Why didn't you tell me something was going on? I could have helped you!"

"No!" Maxine shouted back. "There wasn't a thing you could have done. But I did try to tell you. I told you in a thousand ways, but you couldn't see it. You've never been able to look past my title. I was always the sister and the caretaker. I never allowed myself to be…to be me. I was always looking out for you and Meyral. I was…no. I *am* a person, Bert. You have to acknowledge that."

"Maxine…" he murmured.

For the first time in so long, he felt shame. True, unrelenting torment ripped and tore his insides apart. He grimaced until his face bunched up on itself and he cried. He cried the most honest tears he'd ever shed, and Maxine placed her hands on his shoulders.

"I love you, Bert. I always have and I always will. Everything I did was for you. Don't let my death be in vain. Acknowledge me."

"Maxine," he repeated as snot dripped from his nose. "Maxi..."

"Where is your heart, Bert?" she asked.

Suddenly his sister fell through the floor. Alberto watched her drop into the sea, an image he wished every day that he could forget. Pain seared in the scar on his forearm and he cried out.

"My heart? I don't understand!" he shouted. "I still don't understand! Why?"

*"I can give you the answers you seek,"* a deep voice called out from all around him. *"I can show you truth, but there will be no solace in it."*

Alberto's vision flashed purple, but as it faded, music began to play again. He welcomed it for once, releasing the guilt he felt for ignoring the call for so long.

*       *       *

Lee watched as Alberto suddenly sat straight up. The purplish glow in his eyes was gone when he opened them, and then he started to hum. Lee didn't like the tune. He knew someone was interfering again, but Alberto was beyond his reach this time.

The Islander concentrated as hard as he could, trying to interrupt the new direction the vision was taking.

*       *       *

When his sight returned, Alberto instantly recognized his surroundings: glassy lake, dense forest, and three bodies lying near the shore. He was at Lake Effreudia, almost nine years prior, back when he was traveling north with his sister and his old friend. A wave of nostalgia hit him and the phantom music switched to a string of low, somber tones.

As he watched himself and his companions sleep, he suddenly

273

remembered what happened that night. Just as the thought formed in his head, a dark figure stepped out from the trees. The man bent down by Alberto's sleeping body, then sneaked right past Maxine and circled around to Meyral.

*This is my chance to change it all*, Alberto thought.

He lunged for the dark figure, but when the big redhead was within striking range, a purple flash blinded him for a second and the music skipped a beat. A firm hand grabbed his bicep, but when he turned with his fist raised, he found Aldomein holding him in place.

"This has already happened," she whispered with a wry smile. Her wavy, purple hair fell around her like a curtain of silk, for once not pulled back in a tight ponytail. Her gold-flecked eyes looked to her lover with pity. "Did you come here for answers or to play hero? Just watch."

Alberto relaxed and turned back to the bedrolls. The dark man was lightly running his hands along Meyral's bed, searching for something. Then he stopped and his head snapped up like he heard something. Alberto gasped as the failed thief transformed into a cat and ran away.

Before he could stop to think about where he'd seen the grey feline before, two more men emerged from the forest. They ran forward, dressed from head to toe in black armor, and grabbed Maxine from each side.

Alberto was rooted to the spot until Aldomein walked across the shore and waved to him. After a moment's hesitation, he followed his purple-haired lover into the surrounding forest. They caught up with Maxine as she kicked and struggled against her captors. She managed to let out a short scream before one of the assassins covered her mouth with a gloved hand, but she was too far from camp to alert either of her companions. Then, in a flash of bright green flames, the forest was gone.

Alberto found himself outside of a familiar temple with the two assassins dragging his sister up its steps.

"How in the moons...?" Alberto wondered aloud. "Maxine wasn't gone that long. This is all the way on the other side of Ardänia!"

"Did it look like they walked?" Aldomein scoffed. "I thought she was the one who never believed. You always knew there was more to this world."

Alberto understood. His curiosity was piqued and he continued to watch.

Another flash of purple overtook the vision, and the deafening sound of someone beating on the strings of a guitar filled his head. When the light faded, the music resumed its adventurous pace and Alberto found himself face to face with Sera. She was waiting impatiently, tapping an emerald-tinted finger blade against the wall behind her.

"Finally," she said as she beckoned Alberto forward. It was only after the two assassins dragged Maxine through him that Alberto realized the beckoning wasn't actually for him. "Follow me," Sera commanded.

She walked through the temple, followed by the assassins and Maxine. Alberto hesitated. Aldomein grabbed his wrist and pulled him forward.

"Try to keep up," Aldomein called as she let go of his wrist.

They reached a door at the top of a set of stairs and Alberto continued to follow. They entered the room where Maxine would later give up Arntim. The two men dropped their prisoner on the floor and exited with a bow. Sera circled Maxine slowly, like a buzzard preying on a carcass.

"Don't you touch my sister, you blonde whore! I'll rip your damn tits off and use 'em for slippers! I'll—"

"Ha!" Aldomein put a hand over her mouth to stifle her laughter. "You've always been creative with your insults. It's a shame they can't hear you."

Sera grabbed Maxine by the arm and threw her into a metal chair that was bolted to the floor. The stone doors closed and chains snaked themselves around Maxine's arms and legs. Alberto's sister came to and immediately began to thrash about. Despite her struggles, she couldn't break free.

Sera watched Maxine with a frown, but Alberto could see the pleasure in the blonde's eyes.

"So…" Sera mused. "You three escaped as well?"

Maxine kept her eyes and mouth shut tight.

"Tell me, does the name Jaspar mean anything to you?"

Still no answer.

"Girl, I'm speaking to you."

Sera grabbed the back of Maxine's hair and yanked, pulling her head level with her cleavage. Alberto guessed that the heaving mounds threatening to avalanche over their corseted prison took up most if not all of Maxine's vision. His sister quickly looked away.

"We all have our secrets, Bert," Aldomein said softly. "Did you know any of your sister's?"

"I don't...I don't know," Alberto admitted. "I loved my sister, but...I knew nothing about her."

"Is that right?" Sera said with raised eyebrows.

Alberto almost answered her when he remembered it was his sister the blonde harpy was talking to. A tearing sound brought Alberto back to his vision. Sera used her finger blade to cut away part of the green corset that made up the top of her dress. Her breasts were almost completely exposed, the tops of her pink areolas just visible over the shredded fabric. Alberto stared openly, but Maxine tried desperately to look elsewhere.

"I think we went about this the wrong way," Sera purred as she sauntered toward her prisoner. "After all, kidnapping someone in the middle of the night is a hell of a way to say hello, am I right?"

When the blonde was within an arm's length of Maxine, she reached down and ripped her dress again. Two slits now ran up both of its sides and stopped at her curvy hips. As she walked around the room, her long, shapely legs and creamy thighs peeked out. At one point, she turned so abruptly that Alberto could have sworn that he could see most of her perfectly rounded ass.

"Open your eyes, please," Sera commanded softly, like a mother speaking to an unruly child.

Alberto turned and saw his sister's eyes shut tight. When she didn't obey, Sera simply flicked her hand and Maxine's eyes were pried open magically. Maxine whimpered as she saw the vixen standing before her.

"Now, where were we?" Sera touched the tip of her finger blade to her cheek like she was trying to remember something.

Alberto suspected it was to draw attention to her face, because even though he hated to admit it, Sera was beautiful in every way; the perfect disguise for what was inside.

"Ah, yes!" the blonde devil exclaimed. "I'm Sera. And you are?" When she didn't get an answer, she sighed dramatically and looked to the ceiling. "I don't know what you've heard about Nordcross, but we're not after anything out of the ordinary. We just want the accused murderer Jaspar to stand trial and let justice take it from there. We would never kill someone in cold blood."

"Ha!" Alberto and Aldomein shouted in unison.

Sera walked over to a lit fireplace with several pokers sticking out of the coals. She pulled one out and ran her finger blades down its shaft. A shower of sparks fell to the floor around her bare feet. "That being said, I can tell you that there is a lot a person can go through before they actually die." She paused to let her statement sink in. "The problem I seem to have is that my soldiers can't find the bastard. But, we happen to know two things."

Sera paced around the room. She stopped and stood so close to Maxine that Alberto imagined his sister's entire view was again swallowed up by the blonde's supple curves. Her breasts swayed happily on the edge of what was left of the corset. Sera gently tilted Maxine's head back and stared into her eyes like a lover might.

"First of all, we know Jaspar's son escaped while he attacked our troops."

Maxine stared at Sera with blank eyes.

"That means he's going to try to find his son at some point. I mean, that's what fathers do, right?" Sera sneered.

Her face was so close to Maxine's that their noses were almost touching.

"My question is simple then. Innocent, really." Sera tilted her face so her lips were all but brushing against Maxine's. "Do you know where Jaspar's son is?"

A tense silence followed and Maxine kept her mouth shut. Sera walked away and picked up a glass ball from a desk near the fireplace. As she continued to pace around the room, Alberto found himself mesmerized by the blades along her fingers and how they cupped the glass ball, how her breasts slid past each other as her arms moved back and forth, how her smooth legs reflected the firelight, and how the rest of her dress formed perfectly around her beautiful buttocks.

"Lust can be such a powerful tool," Aldomein said. "It can make people do foolish things."

"Betrayal?" Alberto asked quietly. "Murder? Those are 'foolish things'?"

"Perhaps I'm being too pushy," Sera continued as Aldomein looked away. "Let's start with just the names of the boys you were sleeping with tonight?"

A look of panic found its way into Maxine's eyes.

"Just a couple of names, girl, what's the worst that could happen?"

Sera knelt in front of Maxine and looked up at her with innocent eyes. Alberto followed Maxine's line of sight to the junction of Sera's creamy thighs as they parted.

"Albrecht? No? How about Alberto?" The blonde tittered. "Good, one is named Alberto."

"Did you see the surprise and terror on your sister's face when Sera said your name?" Aldomein asked. "Those are true emotions, derived from her love for you. And that's exactly what Sera hoped for."

"Now, how about Cal? Eli, perhaps? Maybe Meyral?"

Alberto frowned at his sister, pity weighing heavily on his conscience. Then he saw the look Aldomein had mentioned.

Sera stood again and prowled around the room with her glass ball. This time the succubus' effect on Alberto was muted. "We also happen to know that there is an artifact, a staff that Jaspar was protecting. I need to know where it went as well."

She stood behind Maxine and set the glass ball down, then put her hands on Maxine's shoulders. Sera rubbed her way down to Maxine's elbows, until the back of her head rested in Sera's generous cleavage.

"Chances are he's going to look for that staff as much as he'll look for his son," Sera continued. As she spoke, she brought her hands back to Maxine's shoulders, but this time her fingers spread over her captive's front. Sera's metal talons were inches away from Maxine's hard nipples.

"Tell me, do you know where that staff is?"

"I…I don't know," Maxine finally said.

Sera ran her delicate fingers along her prisoner's collarbone, then wrapped her hands around Maxine's small neck. She squeezed for just a second, but Maxine hissed and arched her back.

"Don't lie to me."

Maxine shook her head.

Sera picked up the glass ball and asked, "Did the staff go south?"

"No," Maxine answered.

Sera hurled the globe across the room. It shattered and she

stepped back in front of Maxine.

"Most people flinch when they hear glass break," she hissed. "You're too busy thinking up lies to properly pay attention to the situation you're in. Now tell me, where is the staff?"

Maxine looked up at the ceiling and then down at the floor. She looked everywhere but at Sera. The blonde's eyes suddenly lit up, but Maxine missed it.

"Or does Jaspar's son *have* the staff?"

Maxine didn't say anything, but Sera gasped.

"He does! My, this makes things much easier…one target," the harpy muttered as she paced.

She tore the rest of her dress off as she faced away from Maxine. Sera was close enough that Alberto could study every crease in her skin, every arch of her hair. The blonde slowly turned and walked toward her prisoner, whose eyes were glued to her captor's body.

"I want us to become friends, Maxine," Sera purred. "Would you like that?"

"No," Maxine said with a trembling voice.

Sera thrust herself onto Maxine's lap and shoved her breasts in her face. The blonde tossed her head back and sighed up into the high ceiling as she slowly writhed in Maxine's lap. A low, dark chuckle escaped Sera's throat.

"S-stop! Please!" Maxine cried.

"You don't like this?"

"I…no!" Maxine shook her head, but her body betrayed her again.

"Enough!" Alberto shouted. He ran forward, but he didn't get any closer to the two women. "Leave her alone! Stop torturing her!"

"Alberto," Aldomein whispered, "there is a side to your sister you still have yet to acknowledge. Please, be patient."

"Tell me what I want to hear and I will make this all go away," Sera said. "But not until you help me find Jaspar. He's what we're really after here."

All Sera heard from Maxine was her heavy breathing.

"Look, we don't want to fight. You can understand that, right?"

Maxine's violet eyes met Sera's emerald ones.

"You're a strong, independent, smart woman. Be rational for a moment. The logical choice here is to help me. We can end all of this, together."

Sera waited, but still no response.

"That a girl Maxine," Alberto shouted. "Don't give that bitch a thing!"

"You do remember that this already happened, don't you?" Aldomein asked with a chuckle. "But your vigor is one of the reasons I love you."

Alberto stared at the purple-haired woman, trying to decide if she was telling him the truth or what she thought he wanted to hear. A pained, lust-filled moan brought his attention back to the center of the room.

"Look at you Maxine, you're dripping wet," Sera chortled as she ground her pelvis against her prisoner's thighs. "Now if you tell me where we can find Jaspar, we can do this as much as you want. And if you're a really good girl, I'll even leave your companions alone." Sera slipped off of Maxine and slowly walked to the other side of the room. "Why would you protect someone like Jaspar, I wonder? He murdered the emperor's wife, after all."

Sera looked over her shoulder for her prisoner's reaction. Maxine's eyes widened and her arm twitched. Sera let out a girlish giggle as Maxine stared at the floor.

"That poor girl was being pulled in eight directions at once," Aldomein said. "I'm surprised she lasted this long. The things she'd been through…"

"Of course she's lasted this long," Alberto said as he squared his shoulders. "She's my sister, after all."

"Didn't know that, did you?" Sera asked sympathetically. She leaned over and her pendulously hanging breasts almost touched Maxine's lap. "Oh, yes, it's why all this fighting started in the first place."

"You…you're lying," Maxine accused. She looked up with a glimmer of hope.

"If only," Sera whispered as she covered Maxine's mouth with her own.

Her blade-covered hand disappeared between Maxine's thighs, and for a moment Alberto contemplated the kind of skill it would take to maneuver so delicately. All it took was one slip and she would spill blood.

Sera broke the kiss and pulled her hand back, earning a moan from Maxine. Alberto saw his sister bite her lip as she squeezed her legs together.

"I still want us to be friends, Maxi," Sera said, continuing to grind against Maxine's thigh. "And friends don't lie to each other, so I'll keep it simple—one man or the rest of your crumbling kingdom. You can end this war by sacrificing one life. It's the logical move."

Maxine opened her mouth to answer, but she shut it right away. Sera backhanded her across the face, got off of her lap, and stepped toward the fireplace.

"Impressive," Aldomein said.

"I'm sorry I doubted you, Sis," Alberto mumbled. He turned back to his lover. "But I still don't understand."

He could feel himself being pulled away, out of the vision, but then the music came back, a crescendo of fast, syncopated chords. Alberto tried to focus as he watched a trickle of blood trail down his sister's cheek, but it was no good. The music couldn't be ignored. The staccato progression refused to be denied.

He stared back at the scene, but Aldomein no longer accompanied him. With a flourish of her hand, Sera made a new and identical dress appear on her body. The music cut off abruptly and Sera's voice filled the void.

"You leave me no choice," Sera said. "I would apologize, but I'm really not that sorry for this next part." She raised her hands and clapped.

Seconds later, the stone doors opened and the music returned gradually. An assassin with a whip attached to his waist dragged a badly beaten man into the center of the room and immediately left. It was hard to distinguish the other prisoner's features, but dark green hair hung in his face as he spat blood onto the stone floor.

"Dammit…just kill me already!" the man pleaded angrily.

"I don't think so, Derek," Sera said. Alberto and Maxine both gasped as soon as his name left the sadistic blonde's lips. "You have a purpose now."

The music in Alberto's head picked up, matching his heartbeat perfectly.

"Papa?" Alberto and Maxine yelled.

"That's right, *papa*. He's my personal prisoner. And to think, I considered killing him just this morning." Sera laughed as she walked behind her desk.

"Maxine…sweetie…help me. Make her let me go."

Sera looked pointedly at Maxine and said, "Tell me what I want to know, Maxine, and I'll let your father go. I give you my word. On top of that, you and your brother's crimes for harboring a fugitive will be pardoned. Then you can rest easy knowing that you made the right choice—for Ardänia."

"Jaspar's son…" Maxine started.

"No, don't do it!" Alberto yelled.

"Maxi…please. I can't take it anymore," Derek whimpered as he sobbed on the ground.

"…is Meyral." Maxine spoke so softly that Alberto could barely hear her, but Sera had no trouble.

"Jaspar's son is traveling with you?" Sera asked with a glimmer in her eyes. "Perfect! Tell me, where are you headed?"

"To Mantrych." Maxine hung her head and tears fell into her lap.

"And…"

"He also has the staff."

"Much, much better, I'm so glad you're cooperating." Sera clapped her hands again, and Derek was dragged away by the assassin. "Back to the dungeon with you, *Papa*."

"You said you'd free him!" Maxine shouted at Sera.

"And I will. Eventually," Sera said with a sneer. "See, the deal was also not to harm…Meyral, wasn't it? So I can't have my men capture him, because they're too rough around the edges. Since he'll be out wandering on his own, I'll need someone on the inside to keep track of things."

Maxine sighed and looked up.

"That's right! I need you to give me information. Keep me updated and I'll treat your father as right as rain. Once I have Jaspar, I'll let what's left of your family go free."

Maxine sat and thought for a long time, biting her lip and trembling. Finally she looked back up and nodded to Sera.

"That's more like it! But one last thing…not a word of this to the boys. Got it?"

When Sera saw Maxine nod, she raised her arm and shot a blast of green flames at her. The blaze vanished and Alberto's world went purple once again.

There was no music when Alberto found himself back at the

lake with his sister, who lay unconscious in the bushes where the others would find her a few hours later.

"Sera was holding my father prisoner?" Alberto asked.

Then it all began to disappear. The forest, the lake, the music, everything faded away. Alberto was surrounded by complete darkness, a black so deep that he knew he must have been inside of his own tormented soul.

"Why would she keep so many secrets from us…from me?"

Alberto rubbed his forearm where the dagger had scarred his flesh. He reached for the weapon in his belt, the same dagger that Rubi had given his sister and the same one that Maxine had stabbed him with, but it wasn't there.

"What have I done?" Alberto yelled into the darkness. "My father…my sister…I've killed them both."

\* \* \*

Alberto's shoulders slumped. He returned to his altered state as whatever was interfering let him go. Lee's body relaxed in response and the purple runes scattered across his body dissipated. He panted heavily and continued to sit by the demolished building with his companion.

Lee looked to the sky and watched the sunset. White rays splashed across the pale heavens, and dark clouds hovered over the plains to the west.

\* \* \*

Alberto could hear the strings of a lute being played somewhere in the distance. He immediately recognized the melody as the Kings of Men, and then he could hear the words being sang.

*"Celeste, Celeste,*
*Three moons, they reign.*
*Klyntar, smallest,*
*Sent down four kings.*

*Lawrence, Lawrence,*
*Cygnus, they reigned.*

*With fire and ice,*
*Our land they claimed.*

*Ragmor, he came*
*From o'er the seas.*
*The humans, they reigned,*
*Klyntar displeased.*

*Waters rose and winds fell,*
*Old ways were lost.*
*This story I tell,*
*For humans forgot."*

When the lullaby finished, the familiar voice echoed from behind him, "My poor Alberto."

He turned slowly, not entirely sure he wanted to know who the owner of the voice was.

"Maxine's love betrayed her, which in turn betrayed you."

"Mom?" Alberto gasped.

"Yes, dear," Eden responded with a sweet smile. Her chestnut hair was thick and healthy, done up in a complicated braid that Alberto hadn't seen since his father had left. Her hazel eyes looked up at her son with so much love that it hurt the big man to stare at them. Eden extended a soft hand and gently brushed away her child's tears. "You're so much like your father," she cooed. "So temperamental and angry, so quick to fight. What good is all this yelling going to do?"

"It'll make me feel better."

"Well…do you?"

"No," Alberto answered honestly.

"The pain you feel may lessen over time, it may change with knowledge, but it will never go away," his mother continued. "It's time you stopped running from your problems. You have to face them."

"Maxine was trying to free him," Alberto managed after a long pause. "She was trying to free Dad."

"I would like to believe that you would have done the same thing," Eden said. "You may be selfish like your father, but you still have a piece of me inside of you. When it comes down to it, that has to count for something."

284

"But I...I killed her," he whispered. His voice caught in his throat and his lip quivered.

"Alberto Bluesummers!" Eden hissed. "You should know better. Maxine was her own person who made her own decisions. If she had just asked for help instead of trying to carry the weight of the world on her shoulders, she may still be alive. And now I see you about to make the same mistake!"

The big redhead gawked at his mother for a moment, then sat down heavily. "I just don't understand. I'm too stupid for this."

"No, you're not," Eden said. She placed her hand on her son's scruffy chin and raised his face. "You're just stuck in the past, in your own selfishness. Stuck behind your imaginary titles."

Alberto shut his eyes tightly. He didn't want his mother to see the fear inside of him.

"You are not Alberto the warrior god, a man so strong he can take whatever this world has to throw his way. Just as Maxine couldn't think her way out of every situation, you can't singlehandedly punch your way through either.

"You can't stay the happy, selfish boy that I remember and love. You need to be complete, and that comes with pain and sacrifice...and eventually understanding. It comes from recognizing our past mistakes so we may learn from them and move on to a brighter future.

"Don't forget your heart, Alberto. Stop mourning your losses and start learning from them. Become the man I always knew you could be."

\* \* \*

"I love you," Alberto mumbled through snot and tears, rousing Lee from his meditation.

It was the first coherent thing Alberto had said since they had left the hill. The sun was down and the Islander was exhausted. The constant meditation and fasting wore him out as much as the toll he imagined Alberto's journey was taking on him.

Lee heard something in the distance, something like chains and carriages, and he forced his body to move. He took a long pull from his canteen and stood.

\* \* \*

The hand that held Alberto's chin disappeared. When he opened his eyes, he saw his beautiful, pregnant wife in place of his mother. He relished in the joy he felt, but he cursed as his mind began to clear.

"This isn't real," he said.

"It's as real as you want it to be," Chloe said softly.

"You died."

"Yes, I did."

Alberto looked up as blood seeped from an unseen wound in Chloe's belly. "I never got to tell you goodbye," the big man said through clenched teeth.

"You could tell me right now."

"I don't want you to leave me again."

"I may have died, but I never left you." Chloe shook her head with a sad smile. "You told me once that you believed in the power of the moons," she continued as Alberto stared into her angelic face, trying to remember every feature. "So now I'm telling you to believe in the power of *us*. I will always be by your side."

Guilt, a dark and ugly storm, brewed in Alberto's chest and rose up into his throat. Aldomein stepped out of the darkness and the two women looked at each other, then back at him.

"I understand," Chloe said. "She's not what I expected, honestly, but she is a fine woman with a good heart. I couldn't live with myself if I didn't let you move on. I would be flattered, but I wouldn't be happy, because you wouldn't be happy. You're alive and I'm not. Live your life, Bert. Live it for me."

"And for me," his mother's voice said as she appeared behind Chloe.

"For all of us," Maxine added as she slowly faded in beside Aldomein.

"Remember us, but don't dwell on us," they said in unison.

Chloe wrapped her arms around Alberto and kissed him. It felt more real than anything he had felt before.

When they broke their embrace, Chloe smiled her perfect smile and said, "And remember, don't come back to me unless you're a hero…with treasure."

"Goodbye, Chloe," he sobbed. "I love you."

"I love you," her voice echoed back to him as the vision fell apart.

* * *

Alberto suddenly woke up and vomited all over himself. The yellow bile that dribbled from his mouth was all that was left in his stomach, and it stuck his shirt to his skin like some kind of stinky sap.

It took a while for his head to stop spinning, but then the pounding in the back of his mind began. The big redhead blinked furiously and tried to stand, but he couldn't. As soon as he lifted himself, his head collided with something metal and he fell backward.

He rolled onto his side, vaguely aware of the chains and cuffs binding him. His head bobbed limply as a wagon carried him along.

# CHAPTER NINETEEN: DARKNESS

"Centuries ago, when the trees of the Northern forests were no more than saplings, Ardänia's reign stretched from shore to shore. These were gentler times. The weather was predictable, the waters were calm, and Cygnus bore much fruit. It was also a time of magic. For some, it was as simple as lighting the fires at night. Others would come together to battle the wrath of the sea. Yet there were some who warned against the growing dependence on magic, though their warnings were seen as little more than superstition.

"Our home, Ardan, was the capital city of our beloved kingdom, and King Theodore was our ruler. It was because of the king that Ardänia had become so powerful. Under his rule, the citizens were never restless or unruly. Poverty was a foreign concept, and hunger never touched the golden shores of our lands. We praised the king as any citizen would, and he was pleased. Everybody was united in the common cause.

"It was paradise, but it would be unfair to say King Theodore did all of it alone. Like every king before him, Theodore had a court magician. The love that the king had for his kingdom was equaled by the love that his advisor, Svaark, had for magic.

"Like every advisor before him, Svaark had an apprentice, and together the three men stretched the boundaries of the powers of our world. They applied all that they discovered to the land in order for everyone to become even more prosperous.

"Like all good things, this paradise was not to last. Svaark's apprentice, Saul, disappeared. He was Svaark's youngest brother. Many people had been skeptical of their relationship, claiming that a court magician and his apprentice should not be so close. In hindsight, they were right. The disappearance of his brother changed Svaark.

"Rumors spread like wildfire and speculation ran rampant. Svaark ignored his duties to put all his efforts into finding his apprentice. Months passed, and Svaark still hadn't found any clues of his brother's whereabouts. He slipped into a deep depression—so deep that King Theodore had to reluctantly dismiss him and take upon himself a new advisor. That man's name was Spencer.

"From the moment he entered the royal court, Spencer was never very well liked. There were many who believed that it was by his hands that Svaark had fallen from grace. But as the kingdom returned to its path of prosperity, speculation dwindled until it blinked away completely one night, like a small fire in a snowstorm. Once again, Ardänia was at peace.

"Then the day came that the moons aligned, and Saul reappeared in the middle of the palace courtyard. He called to Spencer, blaming him for his absence. He demanded revenge. The king had Saul arrested to avoid civil unrest, claiming that this apprentice was an imposter. When Svaark heard of this, he freed his brother and challenged Spencer to battle. King Theodore forbade it, but none of the sorcerers would listen to reason.

"When the king understood that a confrontation was inevitable, he evacuated Ardan in an attempt to minimize casualties. The first to leave were the royal family and their court, followed closely by their guard. The king planned to later lead the rest of the citizens out of the city himself.

"As the procession approached the gates, Svaark appeared. He allowed the king to cross before he turned the gates into a solid wall. Only a few of the citizens near Theodore made it out. On that day, the king failed his people and rode away, leaving them at the mercy of the magicians.

"Everyone left behind was caught in the crossfire. Spencer killed Saul quickly, which enraged Svaark beyond anyone's wildest imagination. He unleashed an immense arsenal of magic at Spencer. The two sorcerers continued to battle until their magic combined in a way that nobody had ever seen before—until they could no longer control the powers flowing through them.

"It was never known who had actually caused the final explosion. The two mages were consumed in a fiery maelstrom that swallowed the city whole. No citizen was touched and the buildings were left unharmed, but as a result, the city sank below the planet's surface.

"Soon after the battle, we all realized that the magic we'd grown so fond of had left us forever. We had to learn to toil with only our hands to maintain our existence. It was hard work, but we managed, and our population was able to sustain itself.

"Years after the sinking, while we attempted to continue living as we had on the surface, we came across a large cavern filled with crystals. In the center of the chamber was an orb that gave off a cerulean light so chilling that we tried to seal it back up the same day we found it.

"But alas, the crystals refused to stay contained and managed to grow outside of the cavern, and soon they overtook our city. Ardan still functions today; all around you is what was left behind. The buildings of old merged with the caverns and tunnels that we have dug out of the solid rock. However, now our buildings are covered in the crystals like sea anemones that cover the rocks of a tide pool.

"Slowly we learned how to harness the power of these crystals. Instead of having to search for food or, Klyntar forbid, having to eat one another, we simply allowed the power of the crystals to flow through and sustain us. Like all other things in life, this came at a price. It is our belief that these crystals are what have altered our appearance into what you have undoubtedly seen before you. Our bodies were transformed.

"Despite all odds, we have survived. We honed our skills of digging and tunneling, and we've learned to rely on senses other than the five we once had. We have long forgotten what taste is, and light is a foreign entity in this place. Like the blind man whose hearing becomes inconceivably keen, we have found other ways to cope.

"We know how it sounds, but we lived through this whole ordeal. Death has not visited this underground utopia but thrice since the beginning, and since the discovery of the orb, new life avoids us as well. But soon, this will all change."

The old lizard-man finished his speech as Pläblé continued to set Rubi's leg.

"Yiddi and his brotro," Kirth growled. "Are you finished? We have business to tend to with our new d'römmömig."

"Yes, we've just finished," the old lizard answered. "How is the other kasmömig doing?"

"She will be fine," Pläblé said as she finished. "I've reset the bone, but it'll be a long time before she'll be able to use it like she used to." The lizard stood and brushed dirt off her scaly knees.

"You two," Kirth pointed to Meyral and Rubi, "follow us."

Kirth waited as Meyral helped Rubi stand and then led them into the tunnels. Rubi relied heavily on Meyral as they hobbled after the lizard, who continued through the pitch black corridors at a frighteningly normal pace. He seemed to forget that Meyral was blind in the dark and that Rubi was nearly crippled.

A few times Rubi thought they had lost their reptilian guide completely, but Meyral continued to lead her forward until they reached a small ledge overlooking a deep cavern. When they finally found Kirth, he turned and spoke.

"This is our ręxträg, Ardan."

After a few seconds, Rubi could just make out the faint glow of a thousand dots of colored light that hinted at the outline of a mighty city. "It's beautiful!" she said just above a whisper.

Although Meyral was holding her, she couldn't see him at all. It took Rubi a moment to realize that Kirth was walking away from them, and a moment later, Meyral urged her forward, following the sound of the lizard's footsteps.

After half an hour of walking downhill, the ground began to level out. Rubi begged for a break, but Kirth kept walking. She lost her footing twice and would have fallen if it wasn't for Meyral.

"I can't keep going like this…" she pleaded.

Meyral reached his other arm under her legs and lifted. She almost passed out when her good leg bumped into her damaged one. Defeated, Rubi buried her face in Meyral's neck as he carried her along, but her tears wouldn't come.

*Liz…it's all my fault,* she thought. *I knew I shouldn't have let you come along.*

They stopped outside of a large, green door made from granite. It was the only tangible piece of civilization they'd seen since the outline of Ardan.

"This is where the two of you will be staying," Kirth said.

Meyral gingerly lowered Rubi. She propped herself against the wall with her good leg.

Kirth opened the door and handed Meyral an unlit torch. "We'll be back soon with food," he told them as he turned around.

"We?" Meyral asked.

"Yes, *we*," Kirth muttered with exasperation. "The two of us."

Rubi's head was swimming. "I'm not going anywhere," she slurred. "And Meyral…no, please don't go." She swallowed hard and reached for his hand. "Stay here…with me. Please."

"I should have guessed the kasmömig wouldn't sense you,"

their guide said mysteriously.

A dark figure brushed past them as it moved down the hall.

"He's been with us the whole time." Kirth shook his head as he disappeared into the darkness as well.

Meyral helped Rubi into her room, where she had to strain to see. Crystals lay scattered across the walls and gave off just enough light to make out the faint shadows of their environment. Rubi ran a shaky hand along a small, glimmering shard embedded in the wall next to her.

"They're pretty...so comfortingly warm, yet they give me an odd feeling. Like I'll never see the sky again." She shivered.

As Rubi's eyes adjusted to the low light, shadows gave way to actual outlines. Eventually she was able to distinguish furniture in the main chamber. It was devoid of any object from the surface. Clay frames, carved from the walls and floor, stood in for chairs, tables, and shelves. Next to the door was a hole in the wall the size of the torch handle Meyral was holding. She pointed it out and he stepped forward, set the torch in the crevice, and turned to Rubi.

"Got anything to light this?" he asked.

Rubi shook her head and Meyral shrugged. They both looked around, but they couldn't find even a stray hunk of flint. Meyral gave up on the torch and walked back to the granite door with a worried look on his face.

"Wanna place a bet that they locked us in here?" As he spoke, he grabbed the handle. Despite its size, the door seemed to glide easily inward. When he closed it again, the torch lit itself, illuminating the entire room much more than the crystals had.

"What—" Rubi started. "I guess there's some leftover magic in this place after all."

"They're a little more trusting than I would be in their situation," Meyral grumbled.

"Is that a bad thing?" Rubi grimaced as she lay down on a large lump of stone that might have been a couch. "Do you think there's room for all three—" Her voice caught in her throat and she fell silent. The piece of her heart that had been torn apart still hadn't really registered with her.

An adjoining room branched off of the main chamber behind a door made from polished rose quartz. Rubi watched as Meyral pushed the door open. The dark bedroom beyond was furnished with a cluster of old, wooden furniture and what looked like a comfortable bed, despite the thick layer of dust.

"Shit," Meyral suddenly shouted, "there's no kitchen or bathroom!" He pounded a fist against a wall. "There isn't even a chamber pot."

"Maybe you should file a formal complaint with the innkeeper. You know, I'm sure they have a bucket somewhere," Rubi mumbled. She shut her eyes and tried to slow the throbbing in her leg and her chest.

* * *

Meyral sat on the stone table with Rubi's pale hand resting on his scarred one. She had slipped into hysterics for only a few moments, and then she passed out.

It seemed like hours had passed before a knock at the door drew his attention away from her steady, shallow breaths. He rose to his feet and opened the door, and two lizard-women stepped out of the darkness. They were the same height and their scales were the same shade of dull orange with identical black stripes. Their milky eyes stared past Meyral, yet he still felt like he was being watched.

The first woman carried a silver platter, on top of which sat two cups, an assortment of mushrooms, a few cuts of raw fish, and a salad made from long, slimy leaves.

"Welcome, Tzẹprön," she said. "I am Sascha. And this," she motioned to the other lizard-woman, who held a clay jug, "is my twin sister, Syndell."

"These are the kasmömig?" the twin asked. Her voice was slightly higher than her sister's.

"Hush now, Syndell," Yiddi said as he entered and stepped in front of the girls. He stared at them for a moment, then took the tray and jug from them and placed it all on the table. "We hope that you find the accommodations to be to your satisfaction."

As he spoke, the sisters turned and exited the apartment.

"Please, come eat," Yiddi said. He sat in one of the chairs and waited.

Meyral lightly stroked Rubi's cheek. She woke slowly and squinted up at her old friend.

"They've brought us food," he told her. "You need to eat."

Rubi sat up and eyed the food warily. After a few seconds of hesitation, she scooted forward. Meyral sat in the newly vacant seat and grabbed a mushroom. As he held the smelly fungus to his mouth, he took a minute to stare at Yiddi in the light.

His scales were bright yellow on his back and arms, but they were much lighter on his chest and stomach. Faint scars peppered most of his body, while a long, thick scar ran from his neck to his thigh and cut right through his torso. A jade cane leaned against his chair, and Meyral noticed that it looked like it was missing a chunk from its tip. Despite his twisted posture, there was a sense of pride and power coming from the old lizard.

Meyral finally looked away and bit down on the fungus. As soon as he moved, Yiddi reached for the jug and poured two glasses of wine for his guests. Meyral finished the mushroom and then downed his glass in one drink.

"That's not half bad," Meyral admitted.

Yiddi turned to Rubi. "Klynmö," he said, "do not be afraid. We have plenty."

"The fish is raw," she whispered, "and that's a pile of seaweed. And my leg—"

"That is precisely why you must eat," Yiddi cut in, making Rubi jump a little. "That leg will not heal properly otherwise."

Meyral watched Rubi pick up a slice of fish and pause. A light sheen of sweat covered her pale face, and she had deep, purple circles under her eyes. Her hand trembled as she took a bite, then another, and then she shoved the whole thing in her mouth. Her appetite was back and in full swing. Meyral, however, had just lost his. Watching Rubi eat raw fish reminded him of a happier time with Alberto and Maxine.

While Rubi shoveled food into her mouth, Meyral took the opportunity to talk to their host. "I don't know if you're familiar with these things called bathrooms, but—"

"Kirth didn't explain? Our apologies," Yiddi said. "There is a small stream just down the tunnel from here. There we have all that a kasmömig would need. It has been a long while since that bathhouse was last used, but it should still work. Now please, eat!"

Meyral took a small bite from the seaweed salad and his mouth erupted with pleasure. He attacked the rest of the food with much more voracity, and he realized how long it had been since he'd eaten something decent. After they finished the urn of wine, they began to talk more freely.

"Tell me how people who haven't eaten in hundreds of years still know how to make such delicious food," Rubi demanded as she leaned back against the couch. She let out a small burp and covered her mouth to stifle a giggle.

"Simple," Yiddi answered. "Sù kìttęza d'sävv—we remember forever. Yet another curse from the crystals, we think."

"How could that be a curse?" Rubi asked.

"You never forget the people you lost or the mistakes you made," Meyral answered for the old lizard.

"That is correct," Yiddi added. "We all have things that are better forgotten, yet still they remain."

Rubi stared at the floor for the next few minutes, lost in thought. Meyral wondered if it was shame or comprehension that had changed her mood.

"How about the tzęprön, we must have a question or two, yes?" Yiddi inquired.

"Sure," Meyral said with a nod. "First of all, what the hell is a tess-pee-ron? Second, I want to know where all your scars came from."

"These scars? First, I must admit that I lied to you. The history I told you earlier was more of a fairytale that we are fond of recalling. It is a superficial legend that neglects the darker parts of the story.

"When the city was first buried, there was much anger and hopelessness. The people split into factions pitted against one another for space and resources. This led us to a time of much strife." Yiddi ran a scaly hand along the arm of his chair. "Only through combat could one assume the role of leadership...and there were many skirmishes."

"And you won them all?" Meyral asked with genuine interest.

"Yes. As for the tzęprön, or the person who sits before me..."

Meyral turned around to see who the old lizard was talking about before he understood it was him.

"The dreams foretold of a topsider that would be led to us by a green fury."

"Well," Meyral growled, "Rubi's hair is red, not green. I must be the wrong guy."

"Is this the first time you have been down here?" Yiddi responded carefully.

Meyral racked his brains, but he couldn't recall ever being in a dark, lizard-infested hell before. Then something in his mind clicked. "Maxine was kind of my guide years ago. Does that mean—"

"It does not mean a thing," the lizard answered. "If we had said a purple fury, you would have undoubtedly recalled someone with purple hair, or a purple coat, or possibly purple skin that at some point aided our journey. The important thing is that the tzęprön is here. The one who will return glory to our land. But first, we must help him see the light."

"See the light?" Meyral scoffed. "This is probably the darkest place on the planet! If you want me to see light, get me out of here, dammit!"

Yiddi laughed. "Not that light. *Our* light, the ká'ahan. It is a light that lives in each of us, a light that only we have trained ourselves to see."

"I'm not following," Meyral said with a scowl.

"Do not worry, Tzęprön," the old lizard stood and walked to the door, "in a year's time, you will understand."

The door shut as Meyral opened his mouth to argue. The thought of spending a year down in the tunnels was more than enough to turn his mood sour.

"So it looks like more training for you while my leg heals," Rubi murmured. She rose carefully and limped toward the quartz door. "Enjoy sleeping out here."

"What?" Meyral stood up, but Rubi wouldn't look him in the eye.

"There's only one bed, if you haven't noticed," she said curtly. "If you think I'm going to share it with you…maybe there's a bounty hunter down here who'll share her bed."

Rubi slammed the door behind her and Meyral almost expected it to crack. Before he could decide what to do, the torch went out and darkness bathed his broken skin.

* * *

Meyral woke with a start as a clawed hand clamped on his shoulder. He struggled a bit until Kirth spoke.

"It's almost noon," the lizard-man growled. "Do you plan on wasting the entire day?"

"Noon?" Meyral groaned. "How can you tell?"

"Get up. It's time for tù raysnít'n...your training."

Meyral looked back at the door to the bedroom, and even though he couldn't see a thing, he knew the door was shut.

"Don't worry, boy," Kirth assured him. "Your lamö will be fine. She's in good hands."

"My what?" Meyral asked.

"Your woman," Kirth explained with what Meyral though was a smile.

"Rubi is not my loo-moo or whatever you said."

"Is that why the tzęprön sleeps on the couch? Come now, we have much work to do."

Meyral followed Kirth through the granite door and into the tunnel, where another clawed hand grabbed him from the darkness. He couldn't tell what bothered him more—being at such a disadvantage, or worrying about Rubi being left alone with those lizards. There could have been a hundred of them in the room, and apparently they'd all be able to see him even though he couldn't see them.

"This is Luka," Kirth announced. "You met kìtsävv. Now follow me."

Other than a small cough, Meyral hadn't heard Luka make a sound. As far as he could tell, the second lizard was nothing but a hand. But that hand gave him a small push and he walked after Kirth. If Luka hadn't been constantly pushing Meyral when he fell behind, he wouldn't have known anyone else was with them.

After a few minutes of following the sounds of footsteps, Meyral was completely lost. Still he continued on, occasionally nudged by the other lizard, until he felt soft sand under his feet. There was some shuffling and then the cavern lit up with torches.

Kirth stood in front of him with Yiddi at his side. Luka stepped forward and stood next to his brethren. He was short and stocky, and his body was covered in scales as black as ink.

Meyral looked around and saw that they were all standing in a circular pit filled with sand. He couldn't see a door, and he vaguely wondered if he would be able to escape from this place if he wanted.

"What is this?" Meyral demanded.

"We will get to that soon, Tzęprön," Yiddi answered.

"You brought me down here to talk?" Meyral snarled. Spending his time underground wasn't bringing him any closer to finding his father.

"We aren't *talking* about anything!" Kirth shouted. "We're *telling* you what's going to happen."

Meyral folded his arms.

"Like we said," Kirth continued, "your arrival was foretold in daz kas'n. Dreams like these are not to be taken lightly."

"The tzęprön will stay here for exactly one year," Yiddi added. "In that time, your lamö will be able to fully heal and your raysnít'n will be complete."

"Let's clear some things up," Meyral said as he uncrossed his arms. "Rubi is *not* my loo-moo. And there's no way in Klyntar I'm staying in this shithole for an entire year. What makes you think that you would be able to teach me anything I don't already know?"

"Anręxlig!" Luka finally spoke.

Meyral's first encounter with the lizards' style of fighting was swift. Luka took a step back, then jumped into a ball and shot forward at him. Suddenly a foot or an arm, Meyral couldn't tell which, came within an inch of his face. He lunged in the other direction and moved right into the path of another of the lizard's limbs.

When Luka returned to his feet, he attacked with a flurry of fists, elbows, and knees. Meyral dodged with some effort, and when he saw an opportunity, he took it. He swept at the lizard's legs, but one of Luka's feet grabbed his ankle and pulled him forward. Meyral moved with it, spun, and kicked Luka in the back of his head.

"Röm, röm," Kirth practically sang. "You are not completely useless, it seems."

"Come at me and I'll show you just how *useful* I can be," Meyral shot back.

Before he'd even finished his threat, the arena was engulfed in darkness. Luka hit him from behind and he could hear the other lizard closing in.

"Yes, very useful," Kirth mused.

"Had the tzęprön been able to use daz ahan other than his sight," Yiddi said calmly from somewhere behind them, "he would have easily seen such an elementary attack coming."

Meyral heard a sound like two stones hitting each other.

"That's for hitting our guest with such a cheap move," the old lizard growled.

"But he should be grateful for such an honor!" Luka's gruff

299

voice had taken on a slight tone of annoyance.

"This is true," Yiddi interrupted. "Not many come from the topside to train with us. The tzęprön will come to understand this in time."

Luka or Kirth cracked their knuckles—all twelve of them.

"Well, the tzęprön better get used to it," Luka said. "When we decide on something, we stick with it."

Another scaly fist hit him in the head and he fell backward into the sand. Meyral was sure it was a foot because of all the sand that filled his mouth. Though the hit took him by surprise, he was back on his feet seconds later.

"That time it wasn't a cheap shot," Kirth said from somewhere behind him. "Raysnít'n has begun."

He could hear Luka and Kirth coming at him from both sides, but he had no idea where exactly they were. Meyral swung out into the darkness and a cold hand wrapped itself around his arm, then pulled him to the ground. Luka laughed somewhere on his right, so he guessed it was Kirth that pulled him to his feet.

"This will not be easy," Yiddi explained. "The ká'ahan is a sense the tzęprön is not aware he has. Use it. *Feel* around. Touch everything with your mind and soul."

Meyral bit back a retort about how ridiculous Yiddi sounded. Instead he shot out his fist and barely clipped the side of what felt like a rock.

"Not good enough!"

Meyral couldn't tell who'd said it, but he punched in the direction of the voice. His fist met nothing and he focused on the laughter on his left. Meyral lunged, but again he hit only air. Then a knee collided with his gut and he lost consciousness.

* * *

Meyral awoke in hot, slimy water with Rubi standing over him.

"You feeling okay?" she asked as she swayed a bit.

Rubi still wasn't entirely comfortable using the crutch that Syndell had given her earlier that day. It was made of steel and stone, yet it seemed as light as wood. The stone parts were encrusted with so many different gemstones that they reflected rainbows when the torchlight hit them. She set the crutch down and sat gingerly next to the edge of the pool.

"They really ran you through the ringer. This hot spring should help. They told me it had magical healing properties." Rubi waved her hands in front of her like she was casting a spell.

"Where is this place?" Meyral grumbled as his head fell back against the edge of the pool.

"It's next to the bathhouse. And it seems like they had this planned the whole time…kick the crap out of you, heal you, and then do it all over again." A distant look overtook Rubi's eyes. "But at least you're alive…"

Meyral sighed and felt the warmth of the waters penetrating his sore muscles. He already felt better than when he'd woken up. Just as he was about to relax, he realized that he was naked.

"By the moons, Rubi, where are my clothes?" He reached his hands down and tried to cover himself, despite his protesting muscles straining from the sudden movement.

"Relax, I can't see anything," Rubi muttered. "It's dark, the water here is completely murky, and it's not like I would look! Anyway, Luka was the one that helped you get in. I'm just making sure you don't drown."

"I didn't ask to be dunked in this shit stew, you know." As Meyral spoke, he finally noticed the grim look on Rubi's face as she stared out into the nothingness around them. "Well I'm not going to drown, so you can stop worrying about me." He didn't mean to be harsh, but his mood was as foul as the water smelled.

"Fine," Rubi said flatly. "There's a drink on the table back home that Yiddi wants you to finish before you go to sleep." She picked up her crutch and hobbled away with the torch.

"*Jackass,*" Meyral distinctly heard her mutter as she left him alone in the dark.

*Home? She thinks of this…this dungeon as home?*

Something about that thought calmed Meyral down a little. He couldn't remember ever having a place where he belonged.

His relaxation was cut short as he imagined Luka undressing him. Shivers ran down his back and he crossed his arms.

When Meyral got back to the apartment, which took a lot longer in the dark than it should have, the quartz door was already shut and Rubi was nowhere in sight. His dinner sat on the table in the corner. Raw fish and a drink that looked like split pea soup and smelled like fermented cabbage simultaneously drew and repelled him. He drank the broth in one gulp and felt a thick, warm sensation as it went down. Sleep found him shortly after.

\* \* \*

Pläblé woke him the next morning. The only reason he assumed it was morning was because he'd been sleeping, but it could have been the middle of the night for all he knew. He hated not being able to see the sky, although the torch in the apartment that somehow burned nonstop was some consolation.

"I apologize if my rexlamig, Kirth, offends you," the lizard-woman said. "But please, try to listen and consider his words. You might learn something. He is the captain of the guard, after all."

"It's less what he says and more what he does that offends me," Meyral muttered. He found it hard to sit, but he was happy that he wasn't covered in bruises. "I guess that gnarly green drink works," he added as he rubbed his hands over his body. Aside from his scars, his flesh bore no signs of recent battle wounds.

"You must be speaking of the lödran—the healing tonic we left last night."

"Right...you probably don't even know its green." Meyral looked back at the quartz door.

"Your lamö has requested a tour of Ardan proper," Pläblé said as if she'd followed his gaze. "If you would like, we could send for her—"

"She's not my loo-moo," Meyral repeated for what felt like the hundredth time, "and she can do whatever she damn well pleases." He grabbed his pants and began to get dressed—not that Pläblé would have even noticed. "So what do they have in store for me today? Throw me in lava and see if I can resist burning? Maybe hold me underwater and tell me to grow gills?"

"No, you are to meet Yiddi by Grey Lake." Pläblé walked across the room and began chopping the raw fish that she had brought in. "Though it's not so grey anymore…"

"How can you tell?" Meyral's foul mood had a knack for finding its way to his mouth.

"We weren't always blind." The tone of her voice shut Meyral's mouth until he was standing on the shores of a lake that stretched into the darkness.

Yiddi sat under the light of a torch on its bank. Pläblé gently pushed Meyral toward him, then disappeared like all the other uncanny lizards tended to do. Meyral expected to hear bugs or birds by the lake, but there was nothing except for the occasional splash from a jumping fish and a constant dripping somewhere in the distance.

*This place gives me the creeps,* he thought. *I wonder if they have some kind of giant sea monster in here waiting to eat me.*

"Hello, Meyral. Our apologies, but there is no hungry sea beast. Today we thought we might try a different approach. Have a seat."

Meyral sat next to the ancient lizard, trying to recall if he'd said anything about a sea monster out loud.

"The fish in this lake live such a wonderful life. We come down here to just feel them sometimes." Yiddi laughed an old man's wheezy laugh.

"You feel fish?"

"A different kind of feel. The ká'ahan is a sense between sight and touch. It is a thing that only your mind can do, and this is what we would like for the tzęprön. To be able to feel the world around him." Meyral stared blankly at Yiddi, who continued calmly. "So we close our eyes, empty our minds, and try to fill them back up with something else."

The rest of the day was spent in silence as Meyral tried to empty his mind and meditate. The seconds dragged on. Nothing happened as Meyral felt time blur together, minutes melding into hours, until he heard Yiddi shift next to him and sigh.

"We guess that will be enough for today," the old lizard announced. "Maybe we'll do better next time."

* * *

Once again, Meyral returned to an empty apartment, but it didn't bother him. For doing nothing all day, he was surprisingly drained, and all he wanted to do was sleep. He shuffled toward his stone couch and accidentally kicked his pack over. What few possessions he still owned scattered across the floor. He cursed as he reached down to pick up his belongings, but he stopped suddenly as he touched the first item—the book of poetry.

Meyral had completely forgotten about the gift the phantom man had given him—in fact, he'd forgotten about Shraka altogether. His thoughts turned to the curly-haired man and his book, and sleep quickly became a distant memory. He got up and walked over to the torch, where he flipped through the pages randomly. He quickly found the strange poem that both terrified and soothed him.

Meyral read it three times before something finally clicked in his head. He remembered an almond tree and…nothing else. Frustrated, he slammed the book closed. He shoved it back into his pack and he returned to his spot on the couch. As he drifted off to sleep, a piece of the poem echoed in his mind and provided him with some comfort.

*When the die is cast,*
*Forget the past.*

\* \* \*

The next morning, it was Luka who woke and retrieved Meyral. Then he and Kirth beat the piss out of him for the rest of the day. They dropped him in the hot spring when they were done. Meyral was hoping that Rubi would be there, but she was nowhere to be found. The day after that, it was back to the lake.

And that was to be Meyral's life for several months—back and forth and back and forth, without any sign of improvement. The only change Meyral noticed was that he was becoming increasingly more resilient to physical pain, which the scarred man had become fairly intimate with. What bothered him most was how rarely he and Rubi saw each other.

# CHAPTER TWENTY: ARGENTUM

A low, clay wall surrounded an enormous courtyard littered with fragmented flagstone. Rubi stood in the center of a fairy ring of crystals that poked up through the cracks in the slabs. Her pale, sweaty face lit up with varying shades of blue from the luminous stones.

Rubi stared at her feet and chewed her lip. Circles of sapphire radiated outward from where she stood and illuminated the courtyard. The steady, pulsing rhythm drew Rubi's thoughts from her scaly guide.

*Liz would have loved tinkering with these lights...*

Her shoulders slumped and she slowly closed her eyes.

"This courtyard is where the ręxsnít'n that sank Ardan took place," Sascha announced from somewhere behind Rubi. "It was..."

*She would have known why it sank,* Rubi thought as she felt the sting of hot tears, *she always had an answer.*

"Kasmömig?" Sascha asked after a moment.

"I'm listening," she muttered quietly as she leaned on her crutch. Rubi heard the lizard, but her attention was elsewhere.

*I can't think about her down here, I have to be strong for Meyral. I can't burden him with my sadness. He needs to finish his training.*

The redhead blinked hard, but she couldn't stop what she knew would happen. Then Sascha placed a claw under trembling chin.

"Kasmömig," the yellow lizard repeated gently, "z'aha."

"I told you, just call me Rubi," the redhead whispered as she raised her head.

Through a veil of tears, she could barely see the outline of a magnificent building. The structure stood in the middle of a cavern so high that she couldn't see the ceiling. Rubi used the heel of her hand to wipe away her tears and she began to make out more details. The walls were patterned with clay, stone, and crystal. The structure alone was the size of several city blocks, dwarfing Ardan Palace, which stood just across the courtyard. Its parapets reached into the darkness above, and Rubi imagined that it held the whole thing up.

"That's Argentum Academy," Sascha continued as Rubi slowly peeked out of her world of regret. "It used to be the most prestigious university in all of Ardänia. People from all over Cygnus would travel here to learn the basics of taraha and Ardänian lore."

Rubi had never seen a building like it before. It had flying buttresses and arches all throughout. "It seems so frail," she murmured as they approached a wide set of chipped stairs that led toward an empty foyer. "How is it even standing?"

"Some things are stronger than they appear," Sascha replied as Rubi ran her hands over the surface of the nearest wall and looked up. "But it wasn't strong enough," the lizard continued. "Parts of the building are in ruins."

Rubi gazed at the multitude of huge, glassless windows that stared back at her despondently.

*It wasn't just her that died. Jewel...I lost a part of myself. All because of the Blue Bandit.*

Rubi's sorrow was tainted with a hint of resentment. The glow of the crystals that barely brightened the sunken city suddenly lit the cave completely. Rubi could see the ceiling and knew that the academy's towers stopped several feet short of touching.

*Of course they don't hold the place up,* she thought angrily. *I've been wrong about everything, everyone...*

The colossal building glowed so brightly that Rubi had to look away. As she blinked to focus, a cold claw gently touched Rubi's shoulder.

"Sù anarr, anna sù tur antzę. Xùn sù anray yamömig sù tur, xùn sù tur so'o yunträg."

Rubi hesitated for a moment. "What does that mean?" she asked.

"It does not translate well, but it means: we may stumble, but that is not the same as failing. When we forget who we are is when we are truly lost."

Sascha didn't give Rubi a chance to respond. The lizard walked away, listing the various scholars that had studied at the university before its demise. Only the gleam from Sascha's jagged teeth remained visible as the cavern darkened.

Rubi's eyes trailed upward one last time, and then she remembered something Meyral had said on the ship. "There is something evil underneath the desert..." she mumbled.

"Pardon?" Sascha asked.

"Meyral—the tzęprön," Rubi continued, "he told me once that he could sense something in the ground that made people do terrible things." She could feel Sascha's eyes staring past her, but she was too focused on the ceiling, wondering how deep underneath the desert they were.

"There are many things beneath the sands, both alive and inanimate, that are not what you might call normal," Sascha finally said. "I want you to remember this, however: just because something is different, it does not necessarily mean it is evil."

The hint of a smile reached Rubi's lips after a moment. "You're right," she said. She shifted her weight, then winced as her bad leg touched the ground. "I'd like to see it...the *abnormal* stuff."

"Would you?" Sascha asked warily. "Don't be so eager to go looking for danger."

*But I am,* Rubi thought. *I want to feel alive again, and the only way to do that is to be close to death...to be close to her again.*

Rubi finally looked at her guide and saw Sascha staring directly at her from only a few feet away. The look on the lizard's face was something akin to concern or fear, though Rubi wasn't sure whether she was just imagining it.

After a moment of silence, Sascha continued. "Perhaps we have seen enough for today. You don't want to injure your leg more than you already have."

"You're right," Rubi said with a smile. Then she shook her head and laughed quietly. "I don't know what came over me. Let's head back."

\* \* \*

After almost two months of living in the dark, the lizard brothers—Meyral's almost endearing term for Kirth and Luka—accidentally broke Meyral's left arm. Yiddi led him to Pläblé to set the bone, then to the spring for him to soak. Meanwhile, Luka and Kirth stayed behind to fight over whose fault it was.

Rubi hadn't talked to Meyral much since their first night, so it was a pleasant surprise when Meyral heard the chip-clump, chip-clump of a person using a crutch and saw the glow of torchlight approaching the springs. Though he thought it might be comforting to talk to somebody other than his sadistic trainers or Yiddi, the last thing he wanted was Rubi's pity. He watched through a half-closed eye, pretending to be asleep, to at least give Rubi the opportunity to pass through unnoticed.

When the redhead stopped and sat down next to the water's edge, Meyral finally stirred. Rubi smiled down at him.

"I hear we have something else in common," she joked as she held out her casted leg and pointed to his arm. "I thought they were training you, not just kicking the shit out of you."

"I guess the two are one and the same," Meyral mumbled groggily. "How's your leg? I haven't seen you in a while."

"Still slowing me down," Rubi answered, "but I'm getting better at using this crutch."

Meyral felt like the conversation was forced, like both he and Rubi were skirting around their intended topic.

"This place is so…magical," Rubi offered.

"Yea," he said simply. He gave a half smile, then imagined how his crooked grin and odd, one-eyed stare must look to her. His face dropped and he tried to fill the silence. "Do you want to join me? It might help your leg. I won't peek, I promise."

Rubi chewed her cheek and studied his face for a moment. "Turn around," she said finally.

Meyral did as he was told and turned his back. The soft sigh of fabric rustling over skin and the clank of a crutch hitting hard ground reached his ears. Then a splash of water told Meyral that Rubi had finished.

"It's safe to look now," she announced.

Meyral turned to find his old friend submerged up to her shoulders with her leg propped up on a rock outside of the spring.

"This is so nice," Rubi muttered with a soft sigh. "Why didn't I do this a long time ago?"

"Maybe if you stopped by more—"

"I know," Rubi interrupted, "I'm not here for a fight. Let's just say I had some things I had to figure out and leave it at that."

Meyral nodded and he let his body relax again.

"How long are you going to be broken?" Rubi asked.

"Pläblé figured it might take a week or so."

"A week?" Rubi exclaimed as she practically leapt out of the water. "I'm in a cast for another month and you're going to be all healed up in a week?"

Meyral clenched his jaw and his good eye went round. Standing in the torchlight was the muddy outline Rubi's naked body.

Rubi finally realized her mistake while shadows danced across her bare chest. "Turn around!" she shouted as she dove for her clothes.

"Right," Meyral murmured as he obeyed.

There were a few grunts as Rubi pulled on her clothes and then the steady chip-clump, chip-clump returned, only this time it faded away. Meyral shook his head and slipped under the thick water.

* * *

It took Rubi a considerable amount of time to traverse the city, given the state of her leg and the fact that she had only the slightest idea where she was going. She pushed on, because she knew that if she stopped, even if only for a moment, her mind would wander and fixate on darker thoughts. The only way she knew to fight it was to explore more of the sunken capital.

The buildings stopped abruptly and what remained of the city's border entwined with the walls of the great cavern that imprisoned Ardan. Rubi turned left and walked on until she reached an old outpost, where she found a large tunnel leading away from the sunken city.

A short trip down the tunnel and Rubi found herself in a low but wide cavern. A gem the size of a boarhound sat in its center, but unlike the other crystal growths, this one had been purposely placed.

Rubi turned slowly and noted a dozen black holes just like the one she had entered leading away from the lit cavern. She picked up a small rock and marked the way she came with an X, then chose a tunnel at random and marked it with a circle.

Minutes, hours, or days later—time meant nothing down in the dark—Rubi added an X in the middle of the circle. The tunnel had twisted and turned, but it never branched out. She eventually reached a pile of sand at its dead end and had to turn back. Undeterred, Rubi picked another tunnel and made a circle at its entrance.

The tunnel forked before long and she could clearly hear the ping of pickaxes and the crunch of falling rocks echoing faintly from one passage. As she followed the sounds, more gems cropped up and lit the pathway.

Rubi pressed against the wall as a lizard-man ran past her with a wagon full of dirt and ore. Moments later, a cavern full of rubble, boulders, crystal clusters, and a mob of workers hammering signaled the end of the tunnel.

A short, reddish lizard addressed the newcomer without turning around. "Roke didn't know the kasmömig was allowed to roam freely."

This earned him a good round of laughter among his fellow excavators.

"I'm not entirely sure I am," Rubi replied honestly. "Why are you digging?"

"We're rebuilding," Roke stated simply. He kicked a nearby stone and sent it skidding. Another worker easily scooped it into a wheelbarrow. "Yiddi has Roke and the others trying to regain the ground that was lost."

Rubi leaned against the wall to get out of the way and to relieve the pressure under her arm. "What lost ground?"

"About a century ago," the worker said loudly, "an earthquake tore down most of our tunnel system and collapsed a lot of our oldest caverns. We've been trying to reconstruct what we once had, and we were almost finished, until another earthquake about ten years back destroyed even more of our tunnels. But Yiddi never lets Roke rest either way, that yid art." He swung his pickaxe and smashed a crystal on the wall next to him. "And to top it all off, more of these crystals are growing in places that they've never been before."

"Don't you need the crystals to survive?" Rubi asked as she picked up a shard. She glanced at its smooth, glowing surface and slipped it into her pocket.

"We have plenty," Roke shot back and earned some more laughter from his coworkers. "The only thing these crystals do is get in the way of Roke's digging."

A few of the lizards around him grunted in agreement.

"So why are you digging?" Rubi asked again.

"The orb reappears in one of many caverns, so Yiddi wants access to them all. Not sure how that yid art knows where these caverns are, but Roke wishes he knew where the next one was so Roke wouldn't have to dig for no reason, as the kasmömig has pointed out."

"The orb?"

"Are you deaf as well as broken? Yes, the orb. They say it is *the* orb, the one that caused all of this," Roke explained as he motioned around him. "Of course, Roke wasn't there, because Roke is too young," the red lizard puffed his chest out with pride, "born after the city sank."

"Roke, shut up and get back to work!" the largest lizard Rubi had encountered so far shouted. "We don't pay you to tell d'anlönmömig brotro."

"And stop referring to yourself in the third person, anręxlig!" another miner yelled.

"Roke will talk as Roke likes, and we don't get paid for anything, fools!" Roke turned his attention back to Rubi. "That orb is nothing but trouble. It reminds the elders of days when they had hope, but not daz klynlön—"

"Klynlön?" Rubi interrupted.

"It's someone who was born after this place sank," Roke answered. "Only a few of us around, and we know that orb is a disease. It always brings the Harbinger of Dreams with it, and something terrible always accompanies that—the Harbinger of Death. Every time we find it, someone ends up dying. The first victim was a man guarding the cave where it originally appeared."

"But maybe this harbinger is the true tzęprön," another lizard shouted mockingly. This one was green, though his belly was covered in blue scales. "Maybe things will be different!"

A few lizards around them laughed.

"What does that mean?" Rubi asked.

"This Meyral, he's not the first," the green-and-blue lizard said.

"Not even the second," Roke added. "It's hopeless!"

"A fool's errand," the large lizard from before agreed. Then he added, "But it's better than sitting in the dark and doing nothing. We've seen what happens from that."

A shudder seemed to pass among the workers.

Roke nodded and turned back to Rubi with what could have been a sneer. "Ever since the kasprön—"

Work stopped and a tense silence fell on the cave.

"What is a kasprön?" Rubi asked as she pushed away from the wall.

"I wouldn't expect a dran to know the old language."

Unlike kasmömig, which seemed more proper, Rubi could tell that dran was meant as an insult.

"You don't even know me," Rubi hissed harshly. "How can you be so quick to assume anything about me? The topside isn't so bad, you know, maybe you should try it!"

"Was that a joke?" the green lizard asked.

"Roke does enjoy the stories the yidmömig tell," he said loudly. "Roke would love to feel the grass beneath his feet, or to lay in the shade of a…what were those things, the ones with the shade?"

"Trees," the large foreman added.

"Right! …and to lay in the shade of a tree," Roke continued. "But it's all a story. Roke doesn't really expect anything. This is where Roke belongs."

In the dim light, Rubi could make out a few of the miners nodding while others resumed the excavation.

"If you're so good at tunneling, why don't you just dig your way out?"

"The dran would like to know why we don't just dig our way out!" Roke shouted before laughing obnoxiously.

"So it wasn't a joke," the green lizard muttered with a laugh.

More lizards stopped listening and turned back to their digging.

"Tunneling was a necessity for survival in the beginning," the large lizard began gently, as if he were explaining something to a child.

"But that was before Roke," Roke interrupted in his boisterous manner. "By the time Roke grew up, it had become a sport. We dug everywhere we could and it was a matter of pride to have the longest or widest or tallest cavern. Roke's tunnels held a few of these titles more than once."

"But it turns out that if we dig far enough," the large lizard continued, "the tunnel eventually fills with sand."

"You can't dig through sand?"

"Sure you can, topsider. Dig all you want," Roke said and offered his pick to Rubi. "But you won't be able to tunnel through the stuff. It's just too…shifty."

"Anyway," the foreman said, "after several attempts and a few close calls, Yiddi forbade anyone from trying to dig out. He said that we're meant to be down here, and Ardan was peaceful for a long time. Then the kasprön came and promised us the tzeprön."

"Yea, she just forgot to mention how to tell them apart," the blue-and-green lizard added.

The cavern exploded in laughter. The large lizard shouted something in the old language, and before Rubi could ask another question, the sounds of mining drowned her out.

\* \* \*

When Rubi returned to the low cavern, she marked an X in the circle she'd carved earlier. She turned around and saw the twins waiting for her, illuminated by the single gem in the center. One lizard leaned against the giant crystal while her mirror image paced back and forth.

The leaning twin straightened up and said, "Is the city not interesting enough for you?" From her tone, Rubi could tell it was Syndell.

"Have you been following me?" Rubi asked more out of curiosity than anger.

"Everyone knows where everyone else is when you live in a cave, even one as big as this," Sascha answered as she finally stopped pacing.

"So the tzęprön·already knows there is something else down here," Syndell stated firmly. "And he thinks it is evil?"

Rubi shot Sascha an accusatory look as the other twin continued undeterred.

"I do wonder, why do you assume that the orb is the evil?"

"I don't," Rubi said flatly.

"And why are you down here with the excavation team?" Syndell asked.

"This was just the first place I came to," Rubi answered. "One tunnel looks like all the rest to me."

"That explains the graffiti," Sascha said as she pointed to a circled X across the room.

"Sorry about—wait, how did you see that?"

"Felt," Syndell corrected.

"Well, she's pretty set on it," Sascha told her sister. "So we can either help her to make sure she doesn't further injure herself," she motioned to Rubi's leg, "or we can leave her to her own devices and hope it all works out."

The two sisters stared toward one another for a long, silent moment while Rubi waited.

"Fine," Syndell finally said. Then with a nod to the redhead's broken leg, she added, "But we're not exploring until you can get around on your own. Deal?"

"Sure," Rubi lied. She had no intention of waiting.

*This evil...it's what got Liz killed. And it's somehow connected to Meyral and...and the fewer people that get hurt, the better. This is something I'll have to do on my own.*

# CHAPTER TWENTY-ONE: DESPAIR

When Rubi woke the next day, she headed to Argentum Academy without a word to anybody. She hobbled through the rocky courtyard as quietly as she could, and when she entered the massive building, she paused to let her eyes attempt to adjust. There were no crystal growths inside of the academy, and she'd left the torch at the apartment. Minutes passed, but the void was darker than she could imagine.

As she thought back to the day before, the image of the lone gem in the middle of the low cavern lingered. She reached into her pocket and pulled out the crystal shard that she had taken from Roke's dig. Rubi held the broken sapphire up and an almost nonexistent glow lit the wall next to her.

Rubi carefully leaned her crutch against the entrance. She held up the shard with one hand and rested the other on the wall for support. The minimal radiance the shard emitted comforted her some small amount, and as she focused on the gem, pinpricks of light shone from inside of it. When she moved her hand, the lights disappeared. She brought the shard back up to her face and the lights returned.

With a renewed sense of hope, she set off into the empty academy, feeling her way through the corridors. Rubi passed three open doorways; at each one, she held up the gem, but the rooms were as empty as the rest of the building. At the end of the hall, she reached a pair of wooden double doors with thick, iron handles. Only one of the doors opened, and as it swung inward, it scraped against the slightly uneven stones underfoot.

Before she could raise the shard, a chandelier holding six torches lit the chamber. Rubi quickly put her hands over her eyes to shield them from the sudden light. She squinted as she moved her hands, but her eyes quickly widened in awe.

The Thalamus Library was more magnificent than she had ever imagined. The chamber was circular and had two mezzanines above the ground floor. Each wall was lined with bookshelves filled with tomes of various sizes. Six spiral staircases, evenly spaced throughout the room, led up to the higher floors.

When Rubi finished gawking at the library's immensity, she noticed large, clawed footprints in the dust on the ground, each with a clean line between them. *What use do blind lizards have for a library?* Rubi thought. One of the ground floor's tables had lost a leg at some point, but it had been replaced by a clay rod. *Then again, I went searching for a library without a torch...I guess it helps to have something to occupy your time.*

She walked the bookshelves on all three levels of the library and pulled books at random. The ones she couldn't read she put back to peruse later, but the ones in Commonspeak she carried to one of the tables. Rubi had a sizeable stack on the third floor by the time she was too exhausted to find more. She sat at a table and propped her leg up on another chair as she reached for the books.

By the time she fell asleep with her head resting on ancient parchment, she had read her way through five tomes. The first four were about various mythologies relating back to ancient Ardänia, but the last had been written about language. Most of the book had been written in Commonspeak, a dialect popular among peasants at the time of the sinking, but parts had been written in the old language.

When Rubi awoke, she limped her way back down the stairs, shut the heavy door behind her, and ventured back toward the entrance. She reached the courtyard and paused by her crutch. Rubi drew the knife she'd brought with her and cut off her cast, then took a few steps. The sharp pain that she had experienced before was gone, replaced by a dull throbbing. A small smile formed on her lips as she tossed the cast aside and grabbed her crutch. She set out to meet her half-scarred friend exactly where she knew he would be—soaking in the smelly muck of the hot spring.

* * *

"You got your cast off?" Meyral asked as he watched her approach, heralded by the familiar chip-clump, chip-clump. "I thought you said you had another month."

"That was yesterday." The redhead's response was deliberately cryptic.

She saw that he wanted to know more, but she cut him off with a circling motion of her finger. Meyral understood and turned around.

A moment later, Rubi laid her head against the rim of the pool as the relaxing waves of heat soaked into her body. She could feel Meyral's eyes on her but she didn't bother opening her own, instead opting to wait for him to break the silence. After a few moments, she gave up and opened her eyes.

"How are you doing in the dark these days?" she asked.

Rubi knew he still ran into walls a few times a day. It was mostly when he wandered through tunnels that lacked the dim luminescence of the crystals or the low light of torches. She still heard him cursing at the walls on his way back from the bathhouse from time to time.

"You need to stop fighting it," she said. "Once I accepted it, I found it a lot easier to get around. I still trip, but now I don't really need the torches to walk down the corridors to get to the city or the hot spring."

"I'm guessing it has more to do with your crutch than acceptance," Meyral replied in an almost friendly tone. "If I had feelers like you, I wouldn't hit the walls either."

Rubi noticed that talking to her sullen friend had become less of a chore. Not yet a pleasure, but better than any time after she'd woken up half frozen. Although she appreciated the change, she delved into a subject that she knew could ruin it.

"You told me that there was an evil under the desert, remember?"

Meyral nodded once.

"And as far as I can tell, we are underneath the desert—"

"Underneath," Meyral repeated softly.

His blank eye started to glow light blue, but Rubi wasn't sure if it was just a trick of the dim light.

"The lizard-men believe there's something down here too, some kind of orb. They said that a long time ago, a man guarding the cave the crystal was in was found dead…and ever since, whenever the orb disappears, somebody dies. Some believe it calls to the kasmömig, and when one comes, death accompanies him."

The glow was gone from Meyral's eye as he stared at his roommate. Rubi continued to face forward, hoping that no emotions were showing.

"A lizard by the name of Roke called you the 'Harbinger of Death' more than once…have you even wondered what tzęprön means?"

"No." Meyral shrugged. "Why should I care what these *people* call me?"

"Literally translated," Rubi continued, "Tzę means 'To finish,' and prö means 'To deliver.'"

"To finish deliver?" Meyral scoffed. "That sounds like gibberish."

"Well, the old language doesn't translate well to Commonspeak. There's a lot of context that's implied."

"Did Roke tell you that, too?"

Rubi imagined Roke contemplating language, referring to himself in the third person, but her laugh never made it to the surface. She could feel the tension in Meyral's voice and didn't want to push too hard. She was surprised when Meyral spoke next.

"Yiddi says it means that I'm their salvation." Meyral's eyes were closed and his head was resting against the rim of the spring. "He said it means the Harbinger of Ends. Doesn't sound any different from what Roke said."

Rubi watched as Meyral rubbed a wet hand over his face, lingering a few seconds longer on his scarred eye.

"Yes and no," Rubi said delicately. "It all depends on how you look at it. Destruction, death, and end are nearly synonymous with finish. Yiddi thinks you'll end their suffering, meaning you'll free them."

"Sounds to me like they expect me to kill them. I've seen this before out in the Vigrid. Diseased men who know nothing but pain will beg for death…beg *me* for death. And to be honest, I didn't care either way. It was just something that needed to be done and…I could do it." Meyral said the last part quietly before he lifted his head and looked across the spring. "I'm already the Harbinger of Death."

"Maybe it means the end of Nordcross. It's not specific about who or what—"

"So I'm supposed to drag these people into the war too?" Meyral climbed out of the spring and gave Rubi a full view of his partially scarred ass. "Great, that's just perfect," he said before stomping away into the darkness.

\* \* \*

After Meyral cut his soak short, Rubi headed over to the twins' home. They lived in a corner of Ardan Palace, in the two topmost floors of its southeastern parapet. Sascha was curled up in one of the open windows, and her sister was sprawled out on her stone bed. Rubi leaned awkwardly near the doorway, reading the thickest tome she'd found in the Thalamus Library.

"Is that all you do now?" Syndell asked as she let her head fall upside down over the edge of the bed.

"I sleep, too," Rubi shot back playfully.

"What's that like?"

Rubi thought the question was a joke until Sascha took a seat next to her sister. Both of the twins looked at her expectantly.

"You don't sleep?" Rubi asked quietly.

"We sleep, anrex—"

"But we don't dream," Sascha interrupted.

Rubi could feel the sorrow in her friends' voices.

"You're a kasmömig, a dreaming one," Sascha continued. "We call you that because we no longer dream."

"Well," Rubi began slowly, "last night I dreamt about you, Sascha."

Sascha and Syndell looked at each other, then turned back to Rubi.

"We were down in a tunnel with no crystals. You were moving fast, I could barely keep up with you."

"Where was I going?"

Rubi shrugged. "Seemed like a random tunnel. I think you were looking for something."

"Looking for what?" Sascha asked breathlessly.

"The orb."

"Not this again," Syndell cried in exasperation.

"You asked."

"What is it with you kasmömig?" Syndell asked. "Every time that orb shows up, you follow like moths to a flame."

"It's not all that simple," Rubi answered. "In our case, it wasn't even a choice. It just happened, and it happened as a consequence of a thousand other things. Don't you think there might be something more to this orb?"

"I think it's dangerous," Syndell said quietly.

"Sister, listen—"

"No, you listen," Syndell snapped. "Every time this thing appears, one of us dies!"

"Coincidence!" Sascha said as she crossed her arms.

"You can't deny it, sister. The orb is dangerous, yet we can't help ourselves. We keep digging and searching, as if it's our responsibility to shield it from the world…or the other way around."

"So this orb *is* evil?" Rubi ventured.

"Evil?" Sascha replied. "It depends on what evil means to you. I don't think an inanimate object can be evil."

"Is it inanimate, though?" the other twin continued. "When so many lives are lost for it, does it not take on a life of its own? Maybe it is evil. Maybe—"

"Let's go find it." Rubi said with a wild look in her eyes. "This evil has something to do with the tzęprön, my partner, and I want to figure this all out."

"Your partner or your lamig?" Syndell asked with a mischievous grin.

"Anyone I loved died," Rubi answered quickly. "All I have left of them are their ghosts. Now," she looked pointedly at Syndell, "are you going to help me like you said you would?"

Syndell turned to her twin and asked, "Do you want to hunt down an ancient, possibly evil artifact, in a series of underground tunnels with someone who has no business being there?"

Sascha looked at Rubi and her snout curved upward in a smile. "Absolutely." Before Rubi could respond, Sascha added, "But we also told you we'd go looking *after* your leg healed."

"And I told you I'm good to go!"

"Then jump," Syndell commanded as she sat on the windowsill.

Rubi hopped on her good leg and landed with a triumphant look.

"Is that really as high as you dran can jump?" Syndell yawned.

It was the first time one of the twins had called her a dran. Something about it infuriated Rubi so much that she jumped with all her might. When she landed, she immediately knew the twins had been right. Pain shot through both legs and her injured leg buckled.

"Your leg would heal much faster if you stopped using it so much," Sascha scolded. "You need to let it rest."

"Okay. Okay," Rubi said from the ground. "You made your

point. But I did dream about the tunnels and the searching. That's gotta mean something, right?"

"It means you kas and we don't," Syndell answered simply. She turned to face the city from her window and curled into a ball.

Rubi noticed the lizard's tail was twitching irritably, like a cat's might, and she decided to give up. She remained sitting on the ground and she reached for her book. When she resumed her place, she almost immediately let out a small squeak of excitement.

"What is it?" Sascha asked.

"Nothing…thought I saw a rat," she murmured as she stared at the page in disbelief. She couldn't have hid her smile if she'd tried, but she hoped that the twins didn't catch her lie.

*I think I found it. Soon Liz, soon I will give your loss meaning…I love you.*

\* \* \*

Rubi woke to the sound of the stone door opening. Shuffling footsteps and the plunk of a cane told her that Yiddi had come to escort Meyral to their training session. She waited until she heard the door close, then she quickly dressed and headed out into the tunnels.

The book she had found mentioned a secret passage that the Thieves Guild operated. All she knew is that it was somewhere in the northwest section of Ardan and that it had collapsed long before the city sank.

She followed the city wall for what seemed like hours, looking for anything out of place. Finally she found an old postern decorated with intricate carvings of vines and flowers, though it wasn't the carvings that caught her attention. A steel gate that once shielded the entrance sat eternally open, and a flood of sand flowed from the gap. As Rubi stared at the sand, Roke's voice played in her head.

*"Dig all you want. But you won't be able to tunnel through the stuff. It's just too…shifty."*

Rubi grabbed a handful and tossed it aside. "I'll show that little red anrexlig," she said aloud. "Something is down here and I will find it."

Barely an hour later, Rubi was nearly convinced that Roke was indeed telling the truth. With every scoop of sand, more fell to take its place. Finally she caved and lay against the pile, panting for air. As she rolled onto her back, she noticed that the carvings led all the way into the tunnel.

*How did I not notice that before?* she thought to herself. *How did...*

Before she could finish her thought, she realized that more of the tunnel was visible near the top of the pile. The burning desire that drove her before was reignited by hope and she went back to work. Eventually she found something completely out of place, something she hadn't seen anywhere else in the sunken city: wood. Someone had boarded up the tunnel, and she had a feeling it was done after Ardan sank.

When she could easily fit her body into the space between the sand and the tunnel's ceiling, she reached in and grabbed one of the boards. The wood was remarkably well preserved, though it broke away fairly easily when she pulled. There was enough space for her to see the other side of the pile. As she stared into the tunnel, she saw the familiar glow of pulsing crystals.

Rubi dragged herself forward and dropped into the tunnel. Directly in front of her sat a mound of dusty equipment, and Rubi plucked a pickaxe from the batch. Chunks of stone were scattered throughout the postern, and when she reached toward the entrance to grab her torch, she felt sand falling onto her arm. With the help of a chunk of flint she'd brought, she lit the torch and looked up. The ceiling had caved in, just as the book described, and a steady stream of sand poured onto the pile.

*I'm not turning back,* she thought as claustrophobia gnawed at the back of her mind.

Rubi turned, ignoring her shrinking exit, and she headed into the tunnel. The deeper she got, the brighter the tunnel got. More and more crystals littered the walls around her until she no longer needed the torch. She set it on the ground and followed the tunnel around a tight curve.

The tunnel widened a little and the clusters of crystal grew so densely on the walls that they almost covered the entire rocky surface. It reminded Rubi of the orchards after snowstorms, when the trees would be encased in ice, yet their detail could still easily be seen. The caves were beautiful and morbid all at once.

Two tears dropped onto Rubi's cheeks and trailed down to her neck. She could almost hear her own heartbeat in her head, and the pulsing glow seemed to match it. Curious, she reached into her pocket and retrieved the shard that she'd kept from Roke's dig, and it pulsed in sync with the others.

"Inanimate?" Rubi asked a lizard that wasn't there. "Looks plenty animated to me."

She continued on and eventually reached an opening that was big enough for a small entourage to set up camp comfortably. The crystals here grew out from the walls in thick hexagonal patterns. Several paths met in the room, just like the tunnels that she had found Roke in. Rubi grabbed a rock and made to mark the wall, but there were too many crystals for her to even reach the surface.

"Okay, which way from here?" As the redhead spoke, she became aware that there was no echo.

She stood still and chewed her lip for a moment. Her mind strayed to Liz, the way her arms moved when she worked, the curiosity in her bright eyes, the way her lips felt against her cheek...

In an act of desperation, she held up the shard and looked into it just as she had done at Argentum Academy. The pulsing from her chunk stopped, and for a moment, it seemed as if she could see all of Ardan inside. Then it vanished and the surface of the rock was again an obsidian veil.

"Son of a—" Rubi stopped mid-curse as the blackness in the shard cleared. She held the rock up to the tunnel on her left, facing away from Ardan, and an image sharpened. In it she could see a dingy room, made from cracking stones with thick moss growing inside. The room bobbed up and down, as if floating, and then it shifted. Half of her view was obscured by dark, red hair, through which she could barely make out a sleeping man's face.

*"Why would she keep so many secrets from us...from me?"* a voice asked from inside of her head as she stared at his face. It continued to repeat itself until Rubi turned to the other tunnel. In an identical cell, a slender figure with shoulder-length, blond hair sat huddled in the corner.

"Liz!" Rubi shouted into the shard.

*"Maxine?"* the deep, familiar voice from before asked.

"Liz! Liz! By the moons, Liz!" Rubi shouted again and again, until the image of her lost love floated out of view and was replaced with blackness.

"This way," Rubi said, more determined than ever as she

lunged down the second passage.

The clusters started to break apart as Rubi wandered on, which dimmed the tunnel. Before long, darkness engulfed the redhead and she continued on with outstretched hands. Her steps were slow and deliberate as she felt for sudden drops.

*Why didn't I keep the damn torch with me?*

Rubi eventually came to a bend in the tunnel, and then another. Only a few feet later did she run into a wall.

"It's a dead end," she cried aloud. "But the shard...Liz...it has to be here."

Her hand clenched on the handle of the pickaxe and she swung in frustration. Rocks skittered across the floor and the dim glow of crystal underneath her mark shone through. She swung again, shattering a rock, and on the third swing, she knocked a small boulder free that landed on her good foot.

The redhead collapsed and cursed everything she could think of. As one hand caressed her foot, the other automatically reached into her pocket. She quickly fished the stone out and held it up to her face. The crystal shard made its own light and once again, the outline of Ardan lit up in its smooth surface. Rubi got back to her feet and turned. The vision of the sunken city disappeared, but she continued to spin slowly until she saw the redhead again.

She put her mouth next to the rock, almost touching it with her lips. "Wake up," she whispered to the sleeping man.

He didn't budge.

"Help me," she said a little louder.

The man shifted a bit and the vision floated back to her love. Liz now paced her cell, but her face was still hard to make out. Rubi didn't care. She knew it was Liz, but she didn't know why she was in a cell or who the big redheaded man was. Rubi tried to turn the shard to see, but all she got was blackness. She gave up on the vision and resumed digging in the direction that she'd seen her love. Deep in her heart, Rubi knew that she would find retribution in the tunnels, whether through vengeance or death.

She pounded into the wall without restraint. Crushed stones rebounded and pulverized crystals shattered into dust and tiny gems at her feet. There was a sizeable hole in the wall when Rubi stepped back and wiped her brow. As she caught her breath, she heard a voice call out faintly. Rubi spun around and listened, but the voice stopped as quickly as it had begun. She turned and continued digging, but then she heard a man's voice and realized it was coming from her head.

*"It was dark,"* the voice started, *"and this woman...digging. I had a bad feeling, like something terrible...chasing me...of rock."* The muffled voice faded in and out, then vanished altogether.

As if the man's bad feeling was contagious, Rubi's pulse rose. She stepped away from the hole when she heard a loud cracking noise around her. The tunnel began to moan and the wall in front of her bowed.

"This was a bad—" was all she managed before the wall came apart in front of her.

A beacon of light emerged from the rocks where she had just been digging, but the wall didn't collapse. Instead, a creature nearly ten feet tall and made of stone stepped toward her and unfurled its long limbs.

Crystal growths, just like those lining the tunnels, covered most of its body. It was shaped like a lean man, and its shoulders bore pointed prisms. The top half of its head glowed with a neon crown of crude sapphire, which brushed against the ceiling. It hunched over and roared so loudly that Rubi fell backward.

Rubi scrambled away as the golem shuffled forward. As she half ran, half limped away, the stone beast picked up speed. A few steps later, it was sprinting through the tunnel toward her. She glanced over her shoulder and saw the golem bearing down on her, its bulk shaving crystal from the walls as it went.

Although she continued to run, a small part of her wanted her body to stop and collapse, to just let the stone beast crush her into oblivion. She sprinted as fast as her legs would let her as the crystals lit her path more and more.

Suddenly, only a few feet from the entrance to the giant cavern, pain shot up her leg and through her hip. She limped to a stop, and that small part of her smiled as she turned to face her death.

*I'll be with you soon, my love.*

A clawed hand pulled the redhead around the corner and slammed her against the wall. Rubi realized that she was staring into Sascha's face. Syndell stood at the entrance to the tunnel with her feet and tail planted squarely on the ground as she waited. The orange lizard moved in a blur, and in the confusion, Rubi had no idea what she had actually done. But a moment later, she heard a crash, followed by Syndell whooping triumphantly. The tall golem skidded through the chamber, a pickaxe embedded in its face, and it smashed into the opposite wall.

"You anray'n," Sascha told Rubi as her sister climbed onto the silenced rock to retrieve her tool.

"I'm sorry," Rubi said quietly. "I can't do this anymore. I can't keep living like this. I want to die. I'm worthless," she continued as she motioned around her.

"No, you're reckless," Sascha corrected her. "I sensed your pain, but I never thought it would lead you to this."

"Enough sniveling," Syndell snapped as she approached them with the pickaxe in her hand. "Where did the golem come from?"

"Did you summon it?" her twin added doubtfully.

"It came from down there," Rubi pointed to the ruined arch and the tunnel beyond. "I reached a dead end and dug a bit. Nothing else, I swear." She noticed the crown on the rocky corpse continued to glow in sync with the rest of the room, whose rhythm still matched the one in her chest. "Was that...the evil?" she asked.

"It's not evil," Sascha said as she shook her head. "It was simply guarding something. That's what they do. But they haven't been around since kìtlön." As she explained the golem's purpose, she shot a meaningful look at her sister.

"Where do they come from?" Rubi asked.

"Blood magic. It links the elements with a person. It doesn't bring the beast truly to life, but the ritual leaves it with enough energy and purpose to stand guard almost indefinitely."

A rumbling came from behind the twins as the lights began to pulse more brightly. The blood golem rose to its feet and let out another horrific roar.

Sascha jumped into her sister's hands and launched toward the golem in one fluid movement. Syndell picked up her pickaxe with her tail and rushed forward on all fours. The sisters struck the monster at the same time and knocked it back. Syndell's weapon lodged itself in the golem's leg, knocking a few rocks and crystal shards to the ground, but Sascha still had hers.

Rubi slid down the wall as her leg seized up again. "Do golems have a weakness?" she cried out.

"Technically, yes," Syndell answered. She snaked forward and jumpkicked the golem before it charged again, then snagged her pickaxe from its knee on her way down. "They only have so much power. If you can outlast them, they'll eventually just stop."

"If?" Rubi asked quietly as her eyes dropped.

The twins nodded in unison and ran to opposite sides of the chamber. They leapt from their opposing walls and caught the golem in the arms with their axes. They swung around the stone giant like a circus act, hammering and shouting as they went.

"Once activated…"

"…a guardian can last for a few seconds…"

"…or a week…"

"…depending on who made the thing."

Rubi lost track of which sister was which and who was shouting at her.

"All the golems were exhausted a long time ago…"

"…which is why this is so strange."

"I have no idea who possesses enough power to sustain something this powerful and durable."

The twins were on the golem's front and back, hammering away with their pickaxes. The living rock reached its left arm forward and right arm backward, grabbed each of their tails, and hurled them toward Rubi.

"Why won't it go down?" Sascha panted as she joined her sister at Rubi's side.

*Why did you come?* Rubi thought. *It was just supposed to be me. No one else was supposed to get hurt.*

A barrage of rocks cascaded from above as the golem used its boulder-like fists to punch the cavern's ceiling. As the three women watched, the monster scooped up the rubble in its huge hands and straightened up. The lizard-women crawled up the walls again, and Rubi scrambled sideways as fast as her busted leg would let her. Stones, some as large as Rubi, rained down toward them as the golem hurled fistfuls of rock.

*Think Rubi, think. How does it get its power?*

Rubi dove out of the way as a storm of shattered crystals peppered the wall above her. It was then that she remembered the little shard in her pocket.

*It had the power to lead me here. The damned crystals in the wall have their own power to glow, and the golem is covered in them. Which are for show and which do something? Do they all do something?*

"Give me your axes!" Rubi shouted.

Sascha and Syndell snaked their way toward Rubi and hesitated for only a second.

"Do it!"

They simultaneously rolled to avoid the newest barrage of flying stones and hurled their weapons to the redhead. Their picks embedded themselves at her feet as the golem threw the last of its ammunition. Rubi ripped the pickaxes out of the ground and hobbled forward. Her leg continued to cramp in protest, but she knew she had to do it.

*This is my vengeance, my recklessness, my responsibility.*

"Come and get me, you overgrown pebble!"

The guardian touched its fingertips together, making a sort of wall in front of it, and it brought its hands down to the ground. It pushed forward, intent on smashing the redhead into the wall.

"Here we go," Rubi murmured to herself. Then with a motion toward the twins, she yelled, "Throw me at its head!"

The twins clambered down from the walls and sprinted to Rubi as the golem picked up speed. They pulled Rubi to safety and heaved her toward the beast's head. Rubi caught the moving mountain under the chin with one axe, and before it could react, she used her momentum to swing around onto its back. With no tail for it to grab, Rubi was able to hold on safely. The golem gave up on her and pressed toward the twins. Syndell and Sascha again took to the walls to avoid the deranged guardian's attacks.

"If you're going to do something…"

"…do it already!"

Rubi held onto the golem by the axe still sticking out of its neck and used the other to smash the sapphires on its head. The golem roared as if it was in pain and Rubi continued to smash its crown. As the last few crystals burst, the conjured guardian crumbled to pieces.

Rubi fell as the golem collapsed and she lay awkwardly in the rubble. The twins rushed to her side and pulled her from the mess of stones.

"By the moons," Sascha muttered in awe, "how did you know that would work?"

"I got the idea from you," Rubi admitted. "When you first brought it down, it was because you shattered one of the sapphires in its crown."

"A kasmömig with an injured leg felled a rock guardian?" Syndell whispered. "Perhaps I misjudged you, Rubi. I'm sorry."

"You shouldn't be. You know why I came down here…it was selfish, and I almost got the both of you killed."

"So now what?" the twins asked in unison.

"Now…well, when I was lying in the rubble, I remembered something my old teacher once told me. She said, 'Life isn't about any one thing. It's simply the joy of experiencing each thing and the pain of losing those experiences. Life is a journey without destination.'"

The twins looked at one another before turning back to the redhead.

"I've heard Yiddi say that before," Sascha murmured.

"I guess it's more common than I thought." Rubi smiled as the twins helped her to her feet.

"He first heard it from the kasprön," Syndell added.

\* \* \*

When the twins gingerly laid Rubi down on the stone couch, all she wanted to do was sleep. A moment after they shut the granite door, however, it swung right back open and slammed into the wall.

"They tell me a blind, half-crippled topsider was stupid enough to go after a magical guardian and, only by the luck of the moons, lives to tell about it. Do you have any idea who they might be talking about? If you wanted out—"

"Shut up, Meyral!" Rubi shot to her feet despite her leg's very prominent protests. "You have no idea what I wanted," she snarled. "You have no idea because you don't let people in, so you can't understand. I lost a part of my life, dammit! I lost a part of *me*!"

"And so have I! But you don't see me hellbent on my own demise!" Meyral shot back.

"No, you haven't. You forgot everything you lost. I lived it. I'm still living with it."

"Mantrych?"

"That's the start. Then there was Tyler and you, and then Liz."

"I'm right here, Rubi."

"No, you're not. I have the shadow of you, but the young man I knew…that Meyral. He's lost to me. That guy would understand that the rocks in these forsaken tunnels killed someone I cared for deeply."

Rubi watched Meyral's face intently. He didn't speak, but he didn't back down, either.

"I only wish that you understood, Meyral. I wish that you understood that the only reason I had the drive and the ability to take down that golem was because of you." She paused as complete confusion riddled Meyral's face. "What could I possibly have left to fight for? I won't just stand around while people I care about are threatened, and for better or worse, you are someone I care about. I don't even try to understand it anymore, but I know it's true. So I want to live...and I want you to live, so I will fight. Moons be damned, I will."

Rubi pushed past Meyral. She bumped into his scarred shoulder as she stormed out of the apartment, leaving her companion openmouthed.

# CHAPTER TWENTY-TWO: JUSTIFY

Howler stepped out onto the porch that wrapped around Daniel and Gillian's home. He pulled his long coat closer around him, then leaned forward and rested his forearms against the porch's banister. His breath left little clouds of vapor that hung in the air until Jake waved a hand in front of his face.

"Didn't Alberto say that we're supposed to stay?" Jake asked.

"It was Daniel that told us that," Howler answered solemnly. "Our useless leader either deserted us or died during the night. And now we answer to the captain of the watch."

"Died?" Jake repeated. "You don't think—Daniel wouldn't—" The blond hastily threw a glance over his shoulder, making sure they were alone.

"No." Howler shook his head and continued looking out across the plains, which were a mix of dark mud and brilliant snow punctuated by an occasional stubborn tree. "That Northern bloke is too much of a straight arrow for murder. And then it begs the question of why he's keeping us around."

He turned to Jake, who was picking at a stain on his shirt. When the kid realized Howler was watching him, he looked up and yawned.

"So it wasn't Daniel?" Jake asked.

Howler leaned in and whispered, "We could make a run for it. Maybe have a spot of fun while Red's away."

"I'm waiting for Alberto," Jake pouted.

"You're a right tosser, so unreasonable," Howler said with a sigh. "I guess I've got no choice…"

"You could always leave and do whatever it is you want to on your own."

"I would never leave your side, Jake," Howler said seriously. "We're staying."

Jake gave the Guildsman a confused look. "I'm not a kid anymore, you know. I can take care of myself. Isn't that why my dad sent me out here?"

"I still don't know why Xander did that, but I have a hard time believing that it's because he thinks you've matured."

"If you're just gonna mope," Jake argued, "then go. I'll be fine."

"We're sticking together and I don't wanna hear another word about it," Howler snapped. "And when Red gets back," he continued, "I'm gonna box his bloody ears!"

"Right!" Jake laughed and ran out into the snow, leaving Howler behind to dwell on dark thoughts about punishing Alberto.

A door slammed and Howler spun around. Daniel stepped onto the porch with a package under his arm. His eyes were red and slightly squinted, like he'd just woken up.

"What's that?" Jake asked as he doubled back, red-faced and panting.

"It's for you," Daniel replied as he held the long box out. He opened its lid and tilted it so Jake could see inside. "We made a deal. It's a bow."

Jake gawked at the weapon that was almost as long as he was tall.

Daniel took a step forward and held it out for the kid. "It's a Northern bow with a few embellishments," he explained. "It was going to be a gift for my son…"

Howler noticed tears in the falconer's eyes, but Jake only stared at his bow as he turned it over in his hands. The morning light hit its limbs just right and reflected the gold scrollwork that ran their lengths onto the young ex-con's face.

"This is a big house for just you and your mum," Howler told Daniel.

The captain of the watch stared slightly above Howler's head for a bit before he looked Howler dead in the eyes. "I built it as a gift," he finally said. "It was for my wife, so she would have a place to raise our son. They're both…they're both dead now." Daniel turned toward Jake, who still seemed completely oblivious to the other two. "He would have liked you, you know," he muttered to the kid.

"Sorry, mate," Howler said softly. "I didn't know."

"Wow," Jake finally whispered. "Thanks! This is awesome!"

"Treat it well, kid," Daniel said with the hint of a smile. "It may save your life someday."

"You got it!" Jake yelled as he sprinted out into the yard. He immediately started shooting at trees with imaginary arrows.

"Oi, don't dry fire the bloody thing!" Howler shouted. He turned back to Daniel. "Is there some place where he can practice his aim? Preferably, ah, somewhere secluded, and with actual arrows?"

"We have some leftover targets and spare arrows in the barracks' yard," Daniel answered with a nod, though he was avoiding Howler's gaze. "North end of town."

"Thanks, mate," the ex-con said. He put two fingers in his mouth and whistled to get Jake's attention. When he came running up the porch steps, Howler grabbed the scruff of his neck and turned him north.

"What gives?" Jake asked as he squirmed.

"Look kiddo," Howler explained, "you suck as an archer. There, I said it, now stop with the sad face. If you insist on following Red and fighting Nordcross, I'd rather we died with some dignity. So, I need my best friend to become an archer that can hit more than just the broad side of a cow house."

Jake smiled at Howler, but there was still some doubt behind his eyes. The two Guildsmen waved to Daniel and headed for the barracks.

Their trek across town was shorter than they expected, and the barracks was as desolate as the snowy tundra beyond. Three targets, which were nothing more than frosted bundles of straw strung up like men, stood in a thick layer of slushy ice.

The barracks itself was an open-air facility. The stone walls remained but the wooden roof had rotted away some time ago. Jake ran through a doorway with no door to search for arrows, but Howler hung back and examined a stout structure made from old bricks.

Metal slats covered openings in the brickwork, and whatever their original function was, they no longer served a purpose. Howler circled around to the other side and found a large hatch. He grabbed its handle and pulled, but nothing happened. He pulled harder and the sound of rust grating against the metal hinges grew until the door broke away completely from the sizeable fireplace.

"You don't say..." Howler murmured to himself.

Weather and a layer of ash had eaten away the iron grates and hooks that used to serve the stove or forge—Howler wasn't sure which it had been used for. Inside the ex-con found a piece of flint and a rusted striker. A pile of tinder sat in a neat stack near him, and he had to dig through the first couple of layers to reach the dry wood.

By the time Jake came back with a full quiver, Howler had a smoldering blaze going. He had leaned the broken door against the hole as best as he could, and was pleased to find that a small amount of heat flowed from the vents.

"Stand over there," Howler commanded as Jake hopped up and down. "Away from the fire," he added when he noticed Jake's eyes stray toward the bricks. He knew that look—that slightly smirking frown, the glimmer in his eyes. It was the look he had when he wanted to do something stupid. "Flaming arrows aren't for novices. Maybe later. For now, pretend that the closest target is a Nordcross bloke."

Jake notched an arrow and lined a shot down his sights, but Howler could see his arms shaking. His eyes flickered with the same rhythm of the dancing flames and Howler already knew he would miss. As soon as the arrow left its place along the bowstring, Jake stomped his foot and cursed.

"Well, you hit it!" Howler said cheerfully. An arrow stuck out of the wooden stand that held up the target. "And that would certainly slow down a soldier...but we're looking more for a head or chest wound, mate. How 'bout you start off a little closer and we'll work our way up from there."

Jake walked toward the target and Howler turned back to the fire. He held his hands over one of the vents to warm his numb fingers.

*Bollocks!* Howler thought to himself as he listened for the twang of Jake's bowstring. *What did I do to deserve this life, eh?*

He heard Jake shoot, followed by another loud curse.

*He's bloody awful. Xander gave him a bow to keep him away from the fighting. If we keep following Alberto, we're gonna need all the manpower we can get.*

As the ex-con shook his head, something flew past his ear and ricocheted off of the vent nearest to him. Jake had just narrowly missed severing Howler's fingers.

"Blimey!" Howler shouted. "The bloody target is over *there*! How in Cygnus did you end up nearly shooting me?"

Jake blushed and hung his head. "It slipped," he murmured just loud enough for Howler to hear. Any zest and energy inspired from his new present had vanished.

"Try to relax, mate," Howler said as he pulled his cloak tighter around him. "Just aim and fire, aim fire, aim fire. That's all."

Jake's next shot was closer, seeing as it at least went in the direction of the targets, but he still missed by at least two men's widths. The shot after that hit a dummy dead center, but it wasn't the one he was aiming for. His fifth shot showered sparks over the snow when it glanced off of a lone pole near the barracks wall.

"Go get your arrows back," Howler called out lazily after a few more minutes.

Jake had shot almost a dozen arrows, but he hadn't hit his target since the first shot.

Several hours later, when the sun was high and Howler no longer needed the warmth of the small blaze, Jake still had yet to show any improvement. Howler suspected that he might actually have been getting worse. The young Guildsman only managed to hit the target once more, but it was because a bird had flown in front of his face and spooked him.

"It's gotta be this bow. I swear I was never *this* bad!" Jake grumbled as he and Howler picked up arrows from around the yard.

"Don't blame the bow. You just need some practice, that's all." Howler turned so Jake couldn't see him grimace.

"Maybe it's these weird arrows..." Jake said as he inspected the arrow he'd just picked up, which was as straight and flawless as any Howler had seen.

"It's not the arrows," a gruff voice called out from near the barracks wall.

Howler turned as a short man with a bushy, black beard walked into the yard. It was a moment before Howler recognized Winston without his armor on, even though he still had his katana sheathed at his hip. Without a helmet, the short man's head appeared to be buried in hair.

When he reached the two ex-cons, he snatched an arrow from Jake's hand and said, "It's you."

Jake opened and closed his mouth a few times, but no sounds came out.

"Thanks, mate, that's bloody helpful," Howler said in Jake's defense. "Why don't you just hit him next time?"

"Right," Winston said with a chuckle, "keep coddling the boy. You plan on pullin' his string back for him, too?" The hairy man turned back to Jake. "First off, you need proper gear."

Winston pulled something out of his thick coat and handed

Jake a pair of leather cuffs. They had the same gold scrollwork as the bow in the kid's hands.

"These armguards were given to me by a druid," he explained. "They're lousy with magical spells that guarantee a sure hit in an emergency. They'll also protect your arm." Winston grabbed the hand Jake had been using to hold his bow and turned it over. The underside of the blond's forearm was mostly red, but there was an angry, purple welt in the center.

Jake slipped his arms into the bracers, but he quickly realized that they were backward. He pulled his hands out, flipped the armguards around, and put them back on. Winston joined Howler at the fireplace as Jake took aim.

"Magical spells, eh?" Howler asked with a raised eyebrow. "Thought you folks didn't talk about druids here."

Winston winked, but it almost went unnoticed underneath his bushy eyebrows. "Relax now," he yelled as Jake pulled the string back. "Remember, it's not you who matters. The bow, the arrow, the wind…forget yourself and become one with your weapon."

"One with your weapon," Howler mouthed silently as he tried to hold back his laughter, which came out in sneezes that sounded a lot like snickering.

Jake closed his eyes and Howler saw his hand steady. He also noticed a slow, calm rhythm in the kid's breathing that hadn't been there a minute earlier. Jake opened his eyes, exhaled slowly, then let the string go. The soft thump of an arrow hitting its mark reached Howler's ears a second later and his mouth opened slightly.

"Lucky shot," Howler murmured with a frown. "Do it again."

Jake turned his head and Howler saw a cocky smirk on his face. He knew the kid would miss the next shot, so he rounded on Winston. Before he could yell at the hairy Northerner about giving him false hope, he heard another soft thump behind him. Howler turned and looked at the arrow that now protruded from the center of the target, right next to its twin.

Jake notched another arrow and aimed before Howler could voice his skepticism again. The kid was completely calm and confident. The bow sat as steady as he'd ever seen it. Jake let his arrow fly, but this one didn't join the other arrows. Instead it pierced the target in what would have been its head.

"Jake…what in the world?" Howler asked as he gaped at the

three arrows.

"Winston is right," Jake said with a sheepish grin. "It's a mental thing."

Howler looked down at Winston, who crossed his arms smugly and shrugged.

* * *

Two days later, while Jake and Howler pulled arrows from the targets, the young Guildsman finally addressed what had been bothering him.

"He isn't coming back for us, is he?"

"Pardon?" Howler asked.

"Alberto," Jake continued. "He isn't coming back."

Howler bit his cheek. He wasn't sure what Jake was getting at.

"Lee's gone too, if you haven't noticed. I'm sure they ditched us because they think they're protecting me, just like you and just like Dad. But look at the progress I've made in just the last two days! I don't need protecting all the time, dammit!"

"We just don't want to see you hurt," Howler said after a moment.

"I know why my dad sent us," Jake said forcefully. "We broke out of prison to live our lives, right? Well I haven't lived mine. This is the longest and farthest I've been from Misty Pass, this is the most I've ever lived, and that's pretty damn sad because we haven't done a whole lot."

Howler couldn't think of any argument. When it came to Jake, he was powerless.

"If we just wait around to die, it'll be no different than prison for me. I need to be able to act on my own, Howler," Jake explained. "I need to make mistakes. I need to learn. I need to lose a fight, get laid, have my heart broken, laugh at danger, and find myself. I can't do those things trapped in one place and you know it."

There was a long silence where Howler tried desperately to think of a retort. Three came to mind, but they were lies. The kid was right.

"So what do you propose?" Howler asked honestly.

"They went ahead to Padscott without us," Jake answered. "We need to go and meet them there."

"Head to Padscott alone?" Howler mused. "It's a gambit, but it beats sitting around doing nothing."

Winston coughed and the two ex-cons jumped like they'd been planning a heist.

"I might be able to help you with that, you know," the bearded man said with a smile.

\* \* \*

Something warm dripped onto Alberto's face. As the dripping became a stream, he realized he was awake. His eyes were closed, and when he tried to open them, it felt like someone had tied them shut.

A hot, rank smell reached his nose a moment after the stream stopped. Alberto coughed and gagged, then tried to wipe his face with his hands. It took him three tries before he understood that his hands were restrained behind his back. The big man groaned and managed to open his eyes. The light was so bright that he had to squint.

Two other men sat with him in the back of a wagon covered with a thin, white tarp. Alberto couldn't see well enough to know if he recognized either of them, and his aching muscles told him that he'd been riding for days. As he shifted his weight and tried to stretch his legs, something behind him growled. It became a snarl as he turned his head and came face to face with a doxyl-sized badger guarding the tarp's flap.

The beast glared at him, but it didn't get any closer. The sour smell from before hit him again and Alberto finally realized what it was.

"Did you piss on me?" he croaked at the badger.

"Yes," a female voice answered.

"By the moons," Alberto groaned, "I'm still out of my mind. Talking weasels?"

"Just as I thought," the voice continued. "You *are* as stupid as you look."

The other two men cowered away from the wagon's entrance. The badger scooted sideways as the tarp flap opened and a woman walked in. Alberto turned his head from the strong daylight, and when his eyes adjusted, he looked back at the woman. She wore a dark green, hooded cloak, and she stared at him with narrowed eyes.

"Who are you?" Alberto asked their mysterious captor.

The woman made a low rumbling noise and the badger growled in response. Then she whistled and it let out a yelp. Its large paws made a clicking sound against the boards of the wagon as it crawled outside.

Alberto turned and found that he could now see who the others were. He recognized the one closer to him as the man who was selling wives back in Misty Pass. The other man was dressed well, like an aristocrat, but Alberto had never seen him before. His unkempt beard and matted hair didn't seem to suit him.

"She's a hunter," the aristocrat whispered.

"A what?" Alberto asked.

"She's a hunter," he repeated slower and louder.

"A druid enforcer," the wife trader explained. "It's said they speak to animals, and each always travels with some kind of demon, one trained specifically for them. Maniacs, the whole lot of them." He shuddered. "They kidnap innocent men in the middle of the night so they can feed their gods or fertilize their forests with our bodies."

The woman scoffed and shook her head. Alberto turned away from the wife trader as the other prisoner dropped his head and wept.

"Is that true?" the redhead asked his captor. "Are you some kind of witch?"

She pulled her hood back, revealing a thin curtain of jet-black hair with streaks of white throughout. It draped down to her shoulders, then looped back upward and met a bun on the back of her head. A string of black, twisted runes trailed from her neck to the left side of her face, ending just under the far side of her eye and matching the charcoal color of her irises.

"I am Karin," she said with a cold look. "This is Fujin. My companion is not a demon, and I am not a witch. We seek justice for those who cannot seek it themselves."

Fujin crawled back into the wagon with something in its mouth, which it dropped at its master's feet. It was a bident whose shaft had been engraved with the same runes marking the hunter's face.

As Karin picked it up, her cloak parted down the middle. Underneath she wore tight shorts and a thick brassiere made from what looked like rabbits' pelts. Alberto stared openly at her, and even as Karin's eyes caught Alberto's, she didn't seem to notice.

"Justice..." the big man muttered. "What kind of justice?"

"That man," the hunter used her bident to point at the aristocrat, "sold medicine to refugee camps."

"That's illegal?" Alberto asked.

"It is when the medicine is nothing more than a mixture of pepper oils and excrement," Karin explained. "He always made sure to leave town before the concoctions were supposed to take effect. The local authorities can't track a criminal once he leaves their jurisdiction, something Mr. Bosely took advantage of. I, on the other hand, can."

The aristocrat whimpered and pulled himself into a ball.

"This man," Karin said as she turned her weapon to the wife trader, "is a human trafficker."

"I get it," Alberto said with a nod, "they're scum, but that doesn't explain why I'm here."

"You were found under the influence of Devil's Root. Since you survived, that means that you or someone you are acquainted with knows how to properly brew it. But," Karin's tight lips curved upward slightly, "I do know that you're also wanted by the Empire of Nordcross for war crimes, Alberto Bluesummers."

The big man felt the color drain from his face. His hands clenched into fists as he started to involuntarily strain against his cuffs.

"And the Northern Federation wouldn't be opposed to trying you for those, either."

"I didn't...I didn't do—"

Fujin circled around Karin and snapped at the big man's face.

"I know you didn't," the hunter said. "That's why I've only charged you with brewing and consuming Devil's Root."

"You know?" Alberto asked.

"Everything has a voice if you just listen," she answered.

The badger backed up and sat in front of Karin. It licked its large, grey paws and purred quietly.

"And everything leaves a trace if you just look," a familiar voice called from outside of the wagon. "You see, sir, there is more to this world than what you know."

The badger jumped out of the wagon and Karin calmly stepped back through the flap. As she exited, her bident caught the tarp and pulled their cover down off of the wagon. She tossed the canvas to the side and approached Lee, her weapon raised over her shoulder. Karin glared intensely at the Islander, like she might be pondering the best way to castrate him.

Lee crossed his arms, but he didn't back down. "Ma'am, I would appreciate it if you let my friend go free."

"You must be the cook," Karin said as Fujin circled the Islander, sniffing all the while. "And now that you're here, you're under arrest."

"Dammit, Lee," Alberto yelled, "just run!"

"Keep your trap shut, Alberto," Karin warned.

"Or what?" the big man shot back. "You'll arrest me again?"

Without taking her eyes from Lee, she growled in her throat. Fujin immediately leapt back into the wagon and bared its teeth at Alberto.

"Okay, okay," the big man said. "No need for the weasel to get excited…"

As Fujin slinked off of the wagon, Alberto started to feel dizzy. Then he realized that the wagon was actually rocking slightly. He looked over his shoulder and saw a rusty nail in the wife trader's hands, which he was using to try to saw through his restraints.

Both he and Mr. Bosely gave Alberto a pleading look. The big man shrugged and turned back to Karin and Lee.

"Your name is Lee, Islander?" She waited for the Islander to nod. When he did, she continued. "Brewing Devil's Root is forbidden. There is a minimum of five years' time served for such a crime."

"Forbidden?" Lee repeated slowly. "You have my apologies, ma'am, I am not yet accustomed to the laws and ways of the Northern Federation."

Karin narrowed her eyes and lowered her weapon. "You bear the mark of a slave, yet you've made it into the North. Where is your master?"

"I was set free by a man named Jaspar," Lee said as he uncrossed his arms and puffed his chest out.

"I've heard that before," the hunter replied. "Slaves don't usually travel this far unless they killed their master. Slavery may be a crime, but so is murder."

"I am a free man, ma'am," Lee said. He made sure to clearly enunciate every word. "And I tell the truth."

"And may I speak to Jaspar, so that he may corroborate your story?"

"My apologies, ma'am, but that would be impossible. You must take me at my word."

"Tell me then," Karin commanded as her grip on the bident tightened, "how did you learn to brew? Devil's Root doesn't grow any farther south than the Clarion Swamp."

"If you struggle to believe that I am a free man, you will struggle with this as well."

"Try me," she said almost like a threat.

"From a book."

Karin stared at Lee for a long time. Fujin strutted toward the Islander and sniffed around him, but the badger quickly returned to its master's side when the hunter emitted a strange whine.

"You are right, Islander," Karin admitted. "I don't believe you. Explain."

Alberto heard a muffled snap. He looked over his shoulder at the wife trader, who was using his newly freed hands to cut through the aristocrat's bonds.

"Justice, by nature, is the lifeblood of man," Lee said quietly as he stared at Karin's weapon.

The hunter's eyes widened. She looked back and forth between the Islander and the runes etched into her weapon. Alberto heard another muffled snap behind him, and when he turned around, Mr. Bosely mouthed, "I'm sorry," to him. Then the two prisoners silently slipped off of the wagon.

Alberto hesitated a moment, but his conscience won out. He tore through his restraints with a roar and bolted after the other two. The wife trader fell behind his fellow escapee and Alberto pounced on him. He took the man down to the ground, but before either of them could get up, the hunter's bident sailed past them. It caught Mr. Bosely around the neck and tore his head completely off so quickly that his body continued for a few more steps before it collapsed. The man's head rolled along the ground, still blinking and gasping for air.

The wife trader had stopped struggling underneath the big man, and when Alberto looked down, he realized why. The badger had gutted him. There were four deep cuts that ran from the man's shoulder to his hip. He quickly bled out in Alberto's hands.

"What was all that?" Alberto blurted out. "I could have caught them both. You didn't need to kill them!"

"Escape is punishable by death," the hunter stated coldly.

"So that's how it works here?" Alberto shouted as he shoved the disemboweled body away from him. "You decide they should die, and so you kill them? Just like that?"

"It is the way of the hunter."

"It's buffalo shit!"

"I would watch my tongue if I were you," Karin warned. "Who's to say that you weren't trying to escape as well?"

"Is that a threat?" Alberto asked with a grin. "I've killed plenty of weasels on my farm, and you're no match for me without a weapon. Your overgrown fork is way over there, so let's be realistic about who's in control of what here."

Fujin hissed and made to slink past Alberto, but the big man stepped in its way.

"Enough," Karin commanded.

Her badger squatted and began licking its paws. Lee approached them cautiously and the hunter turned to him.

"Lee," she called, "You are free to go as you please. Your spirit is pure and your intentions are honest." Then Karin stepped toward Alberto and planted her hands on her hips. "But you," she told the redhead, "you're full of hatred and surrounded by death. You've not only broken the law, but you've broken out of custody as well. Why should I let you go?"

Alberto opened his mouth, but nothing came out. There was only one reason that came to mind. "My friend is in danger," he said. "I need to help him."

"I have told you that he is beyond your help, sir," Lee stated.

Karin walked toward Mr. Bosely's decapitated corpse. When she passed Alberto, he could smell the scent of pine tar on her. The hunter retrieved her bident and asked, "Is that your only reason?"

"You're a druid," Alberto said. "Shouldn't you already know that answer?"

Karin said nothing. He waited, but the hunter refused to drop her stare.

"I need to end this war," Alberto finally confessed.

Fujin let out a short howl, which seemed to relax Karin. "I believe the war has already officially ended," she said.

"If you believe those lies then you might as well cut my head off now."

"So you're the resistance I've been waiting for after all," Karin murmured.

Alberto watched as she set her weapon against a nearby tree.

He noticed light wrinkles at the corners of her dark eyes, and the aura of wisdom surrounding her told Alberto that she was older than her features let on.

Karin grabbed some kindling from the back of the wagon. Fujin led Lee and Alberto to join her as she started a fire.

"Don't just stand there," Karin snapped. "We need wood for the fire. Fujin will get our meal."

The badger purred and headed into the brush while Alberto and Lee headed toward the woods.

* * *

Once they had the fire started, they buried the two dead prisoners. Lee and Karin cooked a stew made from one squirrel and two rabbits that Fujin had captured. As they ate, Alberto caught Lee and Karin giving him fleeting glances. The big man ignored them and stretched out on the ground with a yawn. Then Karin cleared her throat and Alberto sat up with a scowl.

"Whatever it is that's on your minds, spit it out," he snarled.

"You don't find it strange that I was waiting for you?" Karin asked. "That I know exactly who you are? That I'm just letting you go?"

"I have nightly conversations with a man on the moon, strange doesn't even begin to describe the shit I've seen," Alberto answered. "But I'm sure no matter what I say you're going to explain it to me. I used to know someone like you."

The hunter took a deep breath and composed herself. "After decades of shifts in the druidic hierarchy," she finally explained, "one faction's practice of a corrupt, bastardized isotope of our lineage began to spread. For this reason, I feared and hoped for a revolution. Whitewater's silence during the war was a great sin and a dereliction of duty. I left—it was the final straw. How can I, as a hunter, dispense justice when the druids of Whitewater disregard their own law?"

"Mr. Bosely wondered the same thing—oh wait, you killed him in the name of justice. If you left, then what in Klyntar's name are you doing?" Alberto shouted.

"You misunderstood me," Karin said. "I will never abandon my title, my duty. I am not like those cowards; I have a purpose."

"Is that why you've been waiting for me, because of your

*purpose?*" Alberto asked.

"Yes and no," Karin answered. "I was waiting for a sign. There is something dark in the heart of Nordcross, something unnatural and fiendish, and it has spread to Whitewater. There are others who've felt it as well, but even united they wouldn't stand a chance in a revolt. Their fear binds them to their weakness…but that is not what I see in you."

Alberto shifted uncomfortably. "What do you see?" he asked.

She looked deeply into his eyes, but he didn't look away. There was something hypnotic about her stare, and he felt naked in front of her.

"You are a good man, Alberto Bluesummers of Westmore," Karin said solemnly. "Your dedication to the truth is both your strength and your weakness; you would suffer a thousand wrongs if you thought it was right."

Alberto placed a hand over the scar on his forearm. A part of him wanted to argue with the woman. Then his mother's voice rang out in his head.

*"Maxine was her own person who made her own decisions. If she had just asked for help instead of trying to carry the weight of the world on her shoulders, she may still be alive. And now I see you about to make the same mistake!"*

"You're right," Alberto finally said. "But I need to get back to Heatherbrook, my companions—"

"We were in Heatherbrook yesterday, while you were still unconscious," Karin interrupted. "If your companions were the two condemned men staying there, they did not wait for you. They managed to sell themselves to a slaver with the help of a man named Winston. I would have arrested all involved, but according to several witnesses, it was your companion's idea. His name was Howler, I believe."

"It would be," Alberto said with a laugh. "He isn't really the type to sit by idly for long. I don't suppose anyone told you where those two sons of buffalos were headed?"

"Padscott," Karin said with a smirk. "The same place we're heading."

Alberto grinned and looked up to the moons. "It would be."

# CHAPTER TWENTY-THREE: PADSCOTT

The Wall around the Federation came into view as the sun went down on the third day after Alberto had awoken as Karin's prisoner. They'd ridden in the wagon for the trip, and though it was slower than Alberto would have liked, he enjoyed not having to walk. He could still recall the last vision from Iggy. He was well aware that he was riding toward war.

At a certain point, the Wall stopped for a stretch and was replaced by a smaller wall. On the other side of the lower border, Alberto could just make out the pitched roofs of the city that lay beyond.

"We're not too late," Alberto said with a sigh.

"Too late for what?" Karin asked.

"It's a long story," the big man muttered. "I'd rather save it for later and tell it once."

They passed through the tall, iron gates in silence. Alberto's eyes widened in awe at the sight before them. Padscott was built into the side of a mountain on the shore of a giant lake. The city was the shape of a semicircle, cut in two by a large, half-frozen river that flowed down the mountain. The buildings were made of stone and steel, hugging the crooked streets. The paved roads navigated an assortment of slopes that led down to the banks of the lake. A series of waterfalls fell between a few of the steepest streets where buildings hadn't been erected.

The gates slammed behind them and Alberto was brought out of his short trance.

"Hunter," a guard said with a bow. "Luck must be on your side this evening! One more minute and those gates would have been locked for the night. We don't usually do that outside of wartime, but now that the *new* elder is here, we have some *new* regulations."

Alberto felt his neck creak as he turned to the guard. "The elder is still here? Where?"

"Sorry?" the guard replied with a confused look.

"You can trust him," Karin assured them. "If you couldn't, he would be restrained."

The guard nodded but his scowl remained. "Nobody sees the elder after dark—not even a hunter. Regulations."

Alberto noticed that each guard had a katana sheathed at their hip. He knew immediately that he would get nowhere with them. Karin snapped the reins, as if she had read Alberto's mind, and Fujin and their boarhound continued pulling the wagon into the city.

"We will stay at an inn for the night," Karin said. "At daybreak we will head to the Tower of Justice, which is where I'm sure the elder is staying."

A few turns later, they found themselves outside of a vacant inn bathed in the flickering, orange glow of a warm fire within. Karin parked her wagon and made a throaty purr. Fujin returned the noise and the hunter headed toward the entrance.

"The badger's staying outside?" Alberto asked.

"It is a matter of common courtesy," the hunter responded. "Not all of the inn's patrons will be as comfortable around Fujin as you or me."

"Welcome to the Puttit Inn, Hunter," a plump maid announced as Karin stepped over the threshold. Her voice was cheery, but Alberto saw a flicker of unease as she watched the druid darken her doorway. "There are two rooms left, and we still have room in the stables out back for—"

"My guide stays with my wagon, which is fine where it is," Karin commanded.

"Yes, ma'am, I apologize," the maid said hurriedly with a sloppy bow. "One room for you and your..." The woman eyed Lee and Alberto with a curious expression before she finished. "...your guests?"

Alberto opened his mouth to retort, but an angry shout from upstairs cut him off. Then they could hear someone stomping loudly down a hallway. The three travelers and the maid watched the staircase to their left, waiting for whoever was making the ruckus to reach them. Less than a minute later, a woman with long, black hair and strong, prominent features ran down the stairs and weaved around several tables. A red-faced man followed her closely, yelling so vehemently that spittle flew from his lips.

"That—that woman! I mean, I paid for one, but she's not...I'll kill her!"

The man stomped after the woman, but she managed to keep at least one table between herself and the man the whole time. As she passed Alberto, their eyes locked and she clung to his arm.

"Darling!" she said dramatically in a falsetto that seemed forced. "Oh, this man is harassing me! Do something!" She placed the back of her hand against her forehead and batted her eyes.

"Darling?" the man sputtered. "Are you behind this? Were you going to rob me during the night, was that it?" He swung at Alberto, who dodged instinctively and shoved him back. The man stumbled backward and tripped over his own feet, then shouted, "That woman has a dick!"

The room exploded with laughter and the angry man deflated a bit. As the din died down, more laughter echoed from the stairs. Alberto watched another woman stumble down the last few steps. She tripped over her heels as she tried to stand and she was forced to use the banister.

Blonde hair spilled out from beneath a curly, brunette wig that no longer sat where it should. When she finally regained her balance, Alberto caught a glimpse of the ancroas on her forehead.

"I told you," the blonde said between deep breaths and brays of laughter, "we should have ditched this plan when we got here, Howler!"

Alberto finally recognized the woman still clinging to his arm. His jaw dropped as he gawked at the Guildsman dressed in drag. The red-faced man began to storm around the room, shouting barely comprehensible rants, and Howler was forced to run again as the man strutted too close for comfort.

"Jake?" Alberto asked as the half-brunette, half-blonde woman approached him. "Is that you?"

"Just call me Kandi," Jake said with a grin as he pulled the wig completely from his head and added, "stud."

"You too!?" the angry man shouted. He stared at Jake, forgetting Howler for a moment, and he began to chase the blond.

"Let's just leave as quickly as possible," Howler whispered into Alberto's ear as he hid behind the big man. "I'd like to avoid any more complications."

The angry man walked toward Alberto, who raised his fists and braced himself for a real fight.

"Enough!" Karin shouted.

The entire commons fell silent.

"Human trafficking is punishable by twenty-five years' time served."

The man who had been so intent on hurting Howler changed from angry to confused to scared in only a few short moments. He took a step back as Karin continued.

"If what you say is true, then I will be forced to arrest all three of you."

"Hey, that's not fair!" Howler piped up. "He's the one harassing everybody and buying whores. We're innocent, I tell ya!"

Karin glared at them and Alberto elbowed Howler in the ribs.

"I'm sorry, ma'am," the duped man said hastily, "this is all just one big misunderstanding...I misunderstood...I'll, uh, I'll be going now, if you don't mind."

Karin nodded once and stepped aside. The man quickly skirted around the hunter, then paused when he reached Howler and Jake. He took a deep breath, thought better of it, and just left.

Karin turned to the maid, who hadn't moved once during the whole ordeal, and she said, "We will be staying in his room, thank you."

Minutes later, Alberto, Lee, and Karin sat in an elaborately decorated suite. Howler and Jake were in the bathroom, changing out of their dresses and removing their makeup.

"These are my companions from Heatherbrook," Alberto told Karin. "Meet Howler and Jake. They're going to tell us a story about why they're dressed in drag." He rounded on the two ex-cons. "I told Daniel to keep you two under control. Why didn't you stay in Heatherbrook?"

"We could ask you the same thing, mate," Howler said as he finished wiping his face with a hand towel. He discarded the rag and pulled on his coat. "We figured you buggered out on us, so—"

"So we had to come after you," Jake interrupted as he turned in a circle, trying to untangle the laces on the back of his dress. Howler stopped him and untied the knot, and then Jake continued. "We asked Daniel for a little bit of help. Took some of Gillian's clothes and makeup and sold ourselves to the highest bidder." The blond grinned and nudged Howler. "Looks like he bought more than he bargained for, though."

"Too right!" Howler laughed until he saw the frown on Alberto's face. "In any case, we're all together again. Does it really matter how it happened?"

"Right," Alberto mumbled. "Except you were here first. If you'd waited, I would have come back for you."

"I believe that about as much as that guy believed you two were *darlings*," Jake laughed. Then he frowned and added, "You think he's gonna come looking for us?"

"What's wrong, mate?" Howler asked as he inched closer to the kid. "You afraid he's gonna try to play tickle the pickle with you some more?"

"That's not funny," Jake whined.

It was impossible for anyone to take Jake seriously with half of his makeup still on and two sacks of oats hanging from his neck.

"You told me it wouldn't go that far!" the blond continued.

"Oi, how was I supposed to predict that my creepy new husband was gonna go after my cute, younger sister?"

"You really expected a man who bought a wife *and* her sister not to be a creep?" Alberto asked.

"You got a point, Red. Shoulda seen it comin'. I mean, look at that cutie…"

"Shut up, guys!" Jake shouted. He grabbed Howler's damp hand towel and stomped into the bathroom, making sure to slam and lock the door behind him.

"He'll be alright after a cold shower," Howler said dismissively. "More importantly," the suave ex-con turned and offered his hand to Karin, "who is *this* gorgeous blossom? My name's Robert Nader Quaashie Sibisi Henry Valerie Blue Hlimner Xanthippos von Banger the Fourth, and it'd be my pleasure to take you out and show you all that this city has to offer."

"I am the hunter known as Karin, and it would be my pleasure to show you all that the catacombs of the Tower of Justice have to offer."

Howler withdrew his hand immediately and stepped back. "Where's your bloody hellhound, witch?" he shouted. "I know your kind, you and those beasties never stray too far from one another!"

"Ah," Alberto mumbled. "You must get that a lot."

Karin rolled her eyes. "Witch, demon, hellhound, I've heard it all."

"She can get us into the Tower of Justice to see Harold in the morning," Alberto told Howler. "She's on our side."

"Right, and that's what the bloke at Whitewater told us too! All they'll help us with is finding an early grave."

"If I, or any druid for that matter, wanted you in a grave…" Karin paused for emphasis, letting the silence envelop them. "You'd already be there. Trust me."

Howler's face broke into a wide smile. He let out some of his obnoxious laughter and said, "I like her. I think I'll stick around just to see if she's always this funny."

\* \* \*

As the first lights of dawn carved streaks of ivory and jade across the sky, four men and a hunter rode in a wagon drawn by a boarhound and a badger. They made their way through the convoluted streets toward the border between the city and the lake. The roads all ended in a flat expanse that spanned the gap between Padscott and the shore. A black spire, about fifty yards into the lake from the center of the city's frozen docks, rose up through the ice.

The travelers left the wagon as they reached the border. They made their way toward the docks, and all but Karin were mesmerized by the size of the spire. Alberto had seen tall buildings, but he had never seen one with solid glass walls around its top.

There was a single bridge that connected the spire to the docks. It was only wide enough for two boarhounds to walk across side by side, and it was made out of a black, shiny stone that Alberto didn't recognize.

Howler and Alberto continued to stare up to the top of the spire, dotted with windows and ringed with four rows of gargoyles. The hunter reached the tower's doors first, where she waited with her arms crossed and Fujin at her heels. When they got close enough to the tower, Jake looked down and gasped.

"Look at what's carved into the wall!" the blond kid shouted. He pointed to a string of runes that wrapped around the entire lower level. Then he hopped up and down and smacked Howler in the back of the head. "Look, it's—"

"The Guild insignia," Howler finished.

The two ex-cons ran to catch up with Karin. Jake stopped in

front of the massive metal doors and trailed his hand along the wall. He tilted his head as he stared at another insignia that had been engraved on the doors. "What on Cygnus is this doing here?" he asked.

"I don't know, mate," Howler answered as Alberto and Lee caught up. "Maybe this used to be one of our buildings." He leaned over the railing and rubbed his hand against one of the black walls. "Blimey, the Guild really used to be something…"

"Would you two focus?" Alberto snapped. "We have work to do!"

He joined Karin at the heavy doors and the big man knocked loudly. When nobody answered, he knocked again, then kicked, and then he shouted at the top of his lungs for Harold.

The doors opened inward slowly and silently. A pale man in a dark green cloak stepped out from the threshold with a trident in his hands. The weapon bore the same markings as Karin's, but unlike the hunter, he lacked a spirit guide.

Karin held out her right hand and pulled up her sleeve. A bright gleam drew Alberto's eyes to her fourth finger, where a thick ring sat. It was white gold and had a raven carved into its top.

"Welcome back, Hunter Karin," the man said. He waved his hand and the doors finished opening. "Who are these men?"

"They are my guests for the moment," Karin stated, "and they seek an audience with Elder Harold."

"As your guests, they may enter the tower," the other druid said, "but I cannot speak for the elder."

"Many thanks, Warden Zelig," Karin said with a bow.

Lee and Alberto followed the druids into the lobby while Jake and Howler dawdled behind. The oval-shaped room could have fit several homes the size of Alberto's old shack in Arntim. Two staircases wound their way up the interior walls, connecting each floor to the next, but Alberto didn't care what lay beyond them. What caught his attention was the myriad of desks packed into the lobby.

Behind each U-shaped table sat someone who looked more ancient than the tower they occupied. Stacks of paper covered most of the desks, and even taller stacks had been shoved underneath them.

"Step forward," the worker nearest to them called out. "What is your business with the Tower of Justice?"

Alberto took a long stride forward, but Karin sped past him and answered.

"I, Hunter Karin, seek counsel with the elder."

The worker stared at her so intensely that his wrinkles twisted his face into something like a raisin. "Did you bring the proper paperwork?" he asked dryly.

"A hunter needs no paperwork to arrange an appointment with the elder," Karin barked. "When is he available? It's urgent."

"Laws change," Zelig said with a nod. "Due to recent events, all visitors must now present a formal request to meet with Elder Harold. Druids are no exception."

"Here are the necessary forms for a druid's counsel request," the worker said as he pushed forward a thick stack of papers. "You must sign here, initial here, sign and date here, here, and initial here," he added as he lifted some pages and pointed to several spots. "Then we will contact you if and when your request is approved."

Karin pierced him with a glare so intense that Alberto was surprised a hole didn't burn through the worker's forehead.

"Federation citizens must fill out these forms," he continued as he pushed a thicker stack of papers forward. "And non-citizens must file for temporary citizenship, pay a fee of seventy-five gold, and then complete the temporary citizen contract, release of liability, and request for counsel forms." He pulled a pile of leather folds from under the desk and placed them beside the other stacks of forms. "We'll also need one form of identification from each of you," he added as he stared at Karin's guests.

"Oi, that's bloody ridiculous," Howler whined. "We just wanna have a little chat!"

"This is our law," the old bureaucrat rasped. "You can opt out of it, but then you will not see the elder." He shrugged, bent over a mess of papers, and scribbled something on the top page.

"I heard Nordcross was booted outta the North," Howler muttered as the snapping turtle embossed on one of the forms caught his eye. "The bloody hell you guys still doing here?" The ex-con reached up and swept his hair in his face to hide his scar.

A door on the other side of the lobby opened and another old man in blue robes strode forward.

"The Tower of Justice deals with internal affairs as well as those of other nations," the worker answered. "The tower itself sides with no nation."

The other man made his way to the stairs without a second

glance at the newcomers.

"Now," the bureaucrat continued, "please take your paperwork and come back when you have completed the appropriate forms. We will notify you within a week of receiving your requests whether or not it has been approved."

"I believe I told you," Karin said, "that this is urgent. We must see the elder today."

"With the new regulations, that would be impossible," the worker explained.

The other old man hesitated at the stairs. His fingers paused just above the banister and trembled.

"You may expedite the processing time with an extra fee of fifty gold and a rush service order form."

"Unacceptable," the hunter growled.

"Karin," Zelig warned, "you'd best keep a civil tongue."

Alberto stared at the man on the stairs and called out, "Harold!"

The man didn't budge, but the redhead recognized him from his dreams.

"The elder is right here?" Karin hissed as she turned to the stairs. "Elder Harold, this matter involves the security of the Northern Federation," she told him.

The bureaucrat looked up from the scroll he'd been poring over and stared at Karin with dry, grey eyes that seemed unable to focus. "National security, you say?" He tapped the point of the quill against the table and hummed to himself for a moment. "That requires the NF-134, which you may retrieve from the third floor's archives. The request fee may be waived if you attach the NF-8133 with proof of citizenship."

Fujin growled in its throat. Karin held out a hand and her guide stopped, but its short snout still trembled.

"I don't believe we'll be filing any such paperwork," she murmured as she approached Harold. "But a hunter's presence is value enough for your fee. There hasn't been a druid birthed outside of the country for several centuries—we are, by definition, citizens of the Northern Federation. This counsel I seek is for national security, which has become of vital importance since the Paper Riots. According to both druid and Northern law, it is my duty to inform the elder of any imminent threat so that it may be handled with minimal collateral damage."

"Hunter..." Zelig scolded under his breath. "Tread lightly."

"To deny me access to Harold's chambers is treason against the North," Karin explained loudly. "Which is punishable by death. The Bureau of Justice is no exception."

"Blimey, Karin," Howler whispered appreciatively, "not bad." He clapped her on the back with one hand, then let it trail down her backside. Before he reached below her ribs, Fujin snapped at his crotch. "Easy, beastie," he muttered. "Heel. Stay. Sit?"

The badger only snarled until Karin snapped and called it back to her side.

Harold raised his eyes nervously and then turned to the others. "What could a hunter possibly want so early this morning? Don't you pray during the waxing and waning hours?"

"This matter should not be discussed so openly," she answered as she glanced toward the cluster of desks.

The old man licked his lips and sighed. "Fine. Follow me."

Karin, Alberto, and Howler did as commanded, but Zelig turned the other way, piquing Jake's curiosity.

"Where's your animal?" the blond asked.

"Years ago," the warden said quietly, "Alondra was called to return to the dragons. They believed that my journey as a hunter had been completed, so I offered my knowledge to the Tower of Justice."

"Young master," Lee said as he stepped out of a shadow and grabbed Jake's arm, "we are following the elder. Come."

The Islander led Jake away from the warden, who stared on with a stony face.

\* \* \*

Alberto followed Harold up the stairs from one floor to the next. He noticed that there were equally spaced doors around each level, and though he knew most of the rooms would be filled with paperwork, he couldn't help but wonder what else had been archived.

The stairs finally disappeared into the ceiling of the twenty-eighth floor, and for the second time that day, Alberto was stunned by the spire.

The room that Harold led them to was two stories high and surrounded by glass. The only thing that held the stone ceiling up, other than the glass, was a single, solid pillar in the center of the room. Alberto looked out of one of the walls and onto the grounds below. The frozen lake extended north into an expanse of ice and snow that stretched on in a blur of white. Glaciers rose up in the distance and ice jutted into the horizon like the frozen remains of a giant's hands.

"The Frozen Wastes," Alberto said to himself before turning back to the matter at hand.

Desks were scattered about in no particular order, and each had piles of papers scattered across them. Harold sat behind a large desk with three chairs in front of it as he wheezed.

"Still not used to that," he panted as he looked toward the stairs.

Despite his reddened face and heavy breaths, something had changed when the old man entered the room. He walked tall and with a purpose.

"Why are you here?" he asked as he folded his hands in front of him and caught his breath.

The elder's eyes traveled from Alberto, Fujin, and Karin, who stood next to him, to Howler and Jake, who sat at an adjacent desk. He watched Lee lean against the pillar and cross his arms before turning back to Karin.

"And why would you deliver a wanted terrorist to me without shackles?" Harold asked the hunter as he gestured to Alberto.

"I'm glad you recognize me," Alberto said with a grin. "That means you probably remember my friend Meyral."

Harold froze and blinked several times. "Why would you—"

The elder's words stopped as the sound of footsteps echoed to them from either side of the large pillar. Two people approached them from the other side of the room, one man and one woman. Though they wore identical black suits, the man had short, black hair and grey, piercing eyes, while the woman's hair was a tangled mess of brown and her eyes were two different colors. She yawned and her partner grinned.

"A terrorist who travels in the company of an Island slave, two condemned men, and a hunter requests a meeting with the elder. I wonder what the topic of discussion could be." The man sat on top of Harold's desk and motioned for everyone to sit.

His partner took a seat next to Howler and yawned again. It was the first time Alberto had seen him next to a woman without smirking or winking at her.

"Maybe they're chasing ghosts," she said. "Phantoms that don't exist, names that belong to the dead…"

"I'm Will," the man said, "and this is Farah. We're—"

"From the Nordcross Intelligence Bureau," Harold finished. "What are you doing in my war room?"

"Now, now, Harold, you sound like an emperor when you talk like that," Will said. "This place belongs to the people, or so I hear. To say that it belongs to the bureaucracy would be more accurate. Did you know there's a form you can fill out if you want to declare war?" He laughed loudly. "How absurd. And you're only acting as elder until the senate reassembles and votes you out of office. By the way," he leaned forward and inspected Harold's face, "what happened to your ear? That looks like a nasty cut."

"You know damned well what happened," Harold grumbled. "Answer my question. What business do you have in here?"

"Like we care about your questions," Farah snapped lazily. "We want to know about you, Ardänian," she said as she narrowed her eyes at Alberto. "What do you want with the Blue Bandit?"

"If you were hoping that the last person to see the Blue Bandit could enlighten you, prepare to be let down," Will added. "Even if he wanted to help you, he couldn't. See, before your recently popular friend left, Harold offered him traveling arrangements, but he refused."

"You mean 'they refused,' right?" Alberto asked with a sideways grin. "They ought to change your title, you two don't seem all that *intelligent*. His name is Meyral, so we can drop the bandit nonsense, and he's traveling with a woman—"

"Yes, yes," Will said as he raised an eyebrow, "a redhead, much like yourself. You seem to know a lot about your prey."

A long silence followed, like the two men were daring the other to speak first.

"Look!" Harold suddenly shouted. "I have a country to run, so if you all wouldn't mind leaving…" He made a shooing gesture and the two Suits looked at each other.

"But the Ardänian hasn't answered my question," Farah said. She stuck her bottom lip out and pouted.

"You already know the answer to that. I'm a terrorist, remember?" Alberto answered snidely. "My business with Meyral isn't quite as important as the information I have for the elder, though." He turned in his seat to face Harold. "Nordcross is planning to invade the North."

There was another long pause. Harold rubbed his eyes before he fixed Alberto in his gaze. The way the old man stared at him made the redhead feel like he was being studied.

"You know," Harold said, "I like a man that gets right to the meat of a discussion without all the trappings of decorum and politeness."

Alberto felt complimented and insulted at the same time.

"Well," Will replied with raised eyebrows, "that's a heavy accusation. In any case," he turned back to Harold, "our deal still stands. Should this accusation prove true, I imagine that would only make the offer look that much more enticing, don't you think?"

"This is boring," Farah complained with another yawn. "Let's go."

"We'll show ourselves to the door," Will said with a small bow. "Good day, Hunter. Elder Owl Harold, we require an answer in six days, eight at the latest. After that, the situation will be out of our hands."

When the agents left, Harold let out a tired sigh. He pulled out a bottle and a glass, and after he poured himself a double, he pulled out two thick files. Harold flipped them open and read quietly to himself as the others watched him in silence.

The elder finally looked back up and noticed his company was still with him. "Why are you still here?" he demanded.

Alberto leaned toward him and got a good look at the files he was poring over. The desk was covered in maps and charts with red lines and numbers scrawled all over them.

"You knew?" Karin whispered threateningly.

Alberto could feel his old serpentine friend crawling around in his stomach, threatening to rise into his chest; the anger was overwhelming.

"The truth is that for the last twelve years the senate sold off our defenses to Nordcross for their own selfish gains. When the senate was removed," Harold downed his drink and gestured toward Alberto with his empty glass, "Meyral said it was up to me to keep Nordcross out. I thought if I expelled them from our borders, the people would rejoice. I thought they'd be more than willing to help the North rise up anew."

Harold poured himself another drink and stood up. He started to pace, and his hand kept reaching toward his messy, grey hair in search of a mangled ear.

"But even with rooms of gold that I confiscated from the corrupt senators' families, I have yet to fill the ranks we once had. Soldiers, officials, even farmers. Anyone who used to be employed by the Federation in any way refuses to help, except for the paper pushers. The bureaucracy is the only damned thing running smoothly in the North and all it does is slow me down, as you witnessed this morning. But I can't change that without a senate vote, and right now I don't have a senate. Meanwhile Whitewater hides in its clouds, silent as a mouse..." Harold eyed Karin as he downed his second glass.

"The only people I've managed to recruit are scumbags that have nothing else to live for," the elder continued. "Drunks, old perverts, outcasts...but even with those standards, I've had to close most of the Gates. I can't rebuild; I can't even clean up! It's like the old senate left a scar across the North, and there's nothing I can do about it. I just don't have enough manpower. I've been going from town to town, trying to get the people back, but they don't trust the senate. They don't trust me." Harold looked at the others with sad eyes before he poured and downed a third drink. "And I don't blame them."

The old man sat back down and closed his files.

"A few months ago I overheard a conversation about a Nordcross invasion from a couple of bureaucrats with ties to the empire. After all, smart people 'keep their friends close and their enemies closer.'" Harold's face sagged. "Then a few weeks ago, I got my first visit from the Suits. That's when I knew it was the beginning of the end..." The elder stared into the bottom of his glass for a while, then poured another drink. "Look through that window and tell me what you see."

"There's just a frozen lake," Jake answered quickly.

"Correct. What should be there is the Eastern Fleet. It was the main reason I came here. I am the only thing that stands in Nordcross' way. They need to remove me before they can fully take over the North. I thought...I hoped that the fleet might still be functioning. Alas, it's not even here anymore."

"Oi, am I missing something?" Howler asked. "How in the hell is there supposed to be an 'Eastern Fleet?' That lake is frozen solid."

"Yes, in the winter the Great Lake freezes over," Harold

explained. "Someone could merely walk from the Clarion Swamp just south of here across to the Frozen Wastes themselves. That is, unless the NFS Odin and NFS Frigg are doing their jobs."

"The N...what?" Alberto asked.

"They're icebreakers," the elder continued. "Ships that plow through the ice and keep waterways flowing. The rest of the fleet was loaded with catapults and didn't really need to move to be effective." He waved a hand in front of his face. "It's all moot. They're gone now!"

"You must protect your people," Karin implored.

"You're right," Harold agreed as he stroked his trimmed beard. "That's precisely the reason I haven't left. I plan on surrendering."

"As a representative of Whitewater, I cannot just let you surrender this nation to Nordcross," Karin said coldly.

Harold laughed, but there was no joy in his wrinkled face. "That's rich. Where were you when all of this happened? Now you've got something to say? Well you can shove that up your druid ass!"

Karin's lips pursed and she ran a hand along the shaft of her bident.

"I won't lead my people to their deaths," Harold continued. "We can't win a war, and I don't need any divine powers to see that. If Nordcross has to cross the Federation to get to me, it would be a one-sided bloodbath everywhere they went. So I'm waiting at the first city that they'll come through."

The elder put his hands together and closed his eyes. Fujin began licking its paws as Alberto waited for Harold to continue.

"I'm taking the Suits' offer. If we surrender without retaliation, they'll show my people mercy."

"Coward," Karin said under her breath.

"Will you fight?" Harold rubbed his dry, wrinkled hands together. "Of course you will." He looked back at Alberto with fear in his eyes. "You strike me as the type, just like Meyral." Harold leaned over his desk and watched the big man through bloodshot eyes. "How did you know about Nordcross' plan?"

Alberto threw a sideways glance at Karin. The hunter nodded, and the redhead swallowed hard. "I had a vision," he finally announced. He braced himself for ridicule, but it never came.

"A vision?" Harold asked. "Tell me."

"A blond man on the moon. He showed me. He plays a

guitar…"

As Alberto spoke, the elder's face lost all color.

"That's preposterous," he whispered. "I have no idea what— please, just leave the North out of this. I can't let my people be killed because…because you're a damned loon!"

Alberto slammed his fists on the table and sent most of Harold's documents fluttering to the ground. "Then we need to leave the North as soon as possible. I'm one of Nordcross' most wanted, and my companions are two ex-cons and an escaped slave."

Howler and Jake shrugged and nodded.

"The Dew Drop Inn is up the road." Harold wrote a quick note and handed it to Alberto. "Tell them to put it on my tab, and I expect you gone in the morning. Stick to the main roads, no one will care who you are. Don't stop until you're on the other side of the Wall."

"We'll need a boat as well," Alberto added.

"Fine, that won't be a problem," Harold said. He scribbled another note, sighed, and handed it to Alberto. "Head west to Frazier Bay, they should be able to get you aboard a merchant ship. People do it all the time."

"What about you?" Alberto asked Karin.

Fujin whimpered and sat back on its hind legs.

"I am charged with protecting the Northern Federation," the hunter answered calmly. "I will not abandon that duty. I will stay here to ensure Padscott's promised mercy."

Alberto turned to Harold, expecting him to complain or argue, but he only shook his head and walked them to the door.

A twinkle appeared in Howler's eye. "Oi," he whispered to the elder, "your wife's cheatin' on you, mate!"

"I don't care about that old windbag, just so long as she leaves me alone," Harold said. "Now, good day." With that the elder closed the door between them.

"So what's our next move, Red?" Howler asked.

"The Dew Drop Inn," Alberto answered. "And then we leave for Frazier Bay in the morning."

"We're leaving already? Just like that?" Jake whined.

The kid's eagerness reminded Alberto of Meyral. They were just kids when they'd set out on their journey, and sometimes he could see a little bit of his old friend in Jake. A moment later the resemblance was gone, and all the memories with it.

*That was a different time and a different place. This is the eve of war.*

"Yes, Jake," Alberto answered, "Padscott can handle itself."

* * *

Later, Lee silently leaned beside a fireplace as Jake shined and polished his bow for the tenth time that night. Howler watched his friend from the other side of the room as he sprawled out on his bed. The kid's mouth never stopped as he jabbered away to Lee.

"Where exactly are we going, eh?" Howler asked. "I mean after Frazier Bay…"

Alberto opened his mouth, then changed his mind and turned to Lee. "Jaspar is in the Island Nations somewhere, right?"

Lee nodded.

"I'll bet that's where Meyral is headed…to find his dad."

"I told you," Lee said slowly, "there is nothing you can do for your friend, sir."

"I refuse to believe that," Alberto muttered as he grabbed a pointed twig from the nightstand next to his bed. He pulled out a dagger and began whittling it to an even sharper point.

"Bloody hell, Jake, put the blasted bow down!" Howler snapped. He wondered if bad moods were contagious, because he felt as on edge as Alberto looked. "So what are we basing our move on this time? Tea leaf readings? Astrology, perhaps? Or did you have another dream? Your first few visions have worked out well for us so far, haven't they?"

Alberto leapt to his feet, a dagger in one hand and a pointed stick in the other. Howler strode forward fearlessly and met him halfway as Jake jumped between them.

"He didn't mean it!" the blond pleaded. He turned from Alberto to Howler. "You didn't mean it. It's just nerves, that's all!"

Howler moved past Alberto and sat at the table near the fireplace. "Right, just nerves," he muttered as he pulled out a pack of cards.

Alberto hesitated for a moment, then returned to his bunk. "In the morning I'm heading out for Frazier Bay," he said, "and then the Island Nations. Come, stay, do whatever you want. I don't care." He set his weapons aside and pulled the blanket over him.

Lee headed into a corner and started his nightly meditation while Jake joined Howler at the table. Before long, the sound of Alberto's snores filled the air.

"What are we gonna do?" Jake asked quietly.

"Like I've been telling you," Howler answered, "I say we head back to ol' Misty alone."

He dealt the cards, and although they were worn and stained, he could still make out the naked ladies that had been painted on each of their faces. Howler set the two jokers aside and Jake chuckled at the female jesters. They wore nothing more than a silly hat and checkered suspenders that held up their hot pants and barely covered their nipples. Jake had played hundreds, maybe thousands of games with that deck, yet he still laughed every time.

The two ex-cons played a game while Alberto grumbled in his sleep. About an hour in, Howler laid his cards down in triumph.

"Gin!" he declared as he glanced at the sleeping man. "Oi, I bet he wakes up yelling about how if we could only attack Nordcross from the east they would fall, and then the whole world would be peaches and cream."

Alberto let out a yell and sat up, still half asleep.

"You alright there, big guy?" Jake asked.

Alberto opened and closed his eyes several times, like he was trying to focus on Jake. He gave up after a moment and rolled back over.

"He was right about the invasion," Jake muttered.

"You believe him?" Howler cursed and threw the nudie cards across the table.

"I'm just saying there might be—"

"I need some air." Howler stood and shoved Jake back into his chair as he tried to get up. "You stay here," he said before he shut the door quietly behind him.

"...hey, Lee," he heard Jake whisper, "wanna play cards?"

* * *

The emerald glow of the sunrise poured in through the windows as Harold made his way into the bathroom. He untied his robe and let it part as he began to piss.

"Stupid Nordcross convict, trying to cuckold me. Shoulda had

364

Zelig lock the bastard up…" He shook once and tied his robe back into place. "What does it matter? I'm signing over the last of my dignity to the empire."

Harold walked to the basin and turned the tap. He washed his hands with warm water, then splashed his face. When he looked into the mirror, his eyes immediately went to his mutilated ear.

"Guess you picked the wrong guy, Meyral. I failed you, me, the North…ah, shit. If those commoners down there refuse to fight, they deserve to get handed over. Hell, they oughtta build me a statue for avoiding all-out war."

The elder patted down his beard and fingered the crust out of his eyes.

"Pathetic. You're a lot of things, but pathetic isn't one of 'em. I'll write my own letter of surrender," he nodded as he walked back into his room and sat at his writing desk, "and damn what the bureaucrats have to say about it. My federation, my letter, my terms."

The sound of footsteps echoed down the hallway, subtle at first, then louder and quicker. Suddenly the doors to his chamber burst open and Alberto barreled in like a madman, his red beard frayed and swaying with his heavy breathing.

"We need to talk, old man!" Alberto yelled as he panted.

Two men ran in after the redhead with thick scrolls in their hands. Harold raised a hand and the secretaries promptly left without a word.

"Do you understand the headaches that come with these impromptu meetings?" Harold asked with a sigh. "Those goatless bastards downstairs are going to flood me with grievances and addendums from now until the day I die. I thought you were leaving, why are you here?"

"Things have changed," Alberto answered. "I can't just leave in peace. This place will burn to the ground if I go now."

"Is that a threat, Mr. Terrorist?" Harold bellowed as he rose from his seat, color filling his face. "You think you can just waltz into MY country and threaten me? Do not underestimate me, good sir!"

Harold shook as more footsteps echoed down the hallway. He wasn't sure if it was fear or something else, something he hadn't felt in a decade.

"Now *that's* the elder I've been waiting for," Alberto said with a puzzling smile, "but it's not a threat."

"Mr. Bluesummers," Zelig's voice called out, "I advise you to return to the lobby or you will be arrested."

"It's the truth," Alberto continued. "I had a vision earlier, and I have a plan now. It may be the only way to save your people."

# CHAPTER TWENTY-FOUR: SHOES

When Jake and Howler returned to the Dew Drop Inn, the sun was sinking and the streetlamps were just being lit. Jake collapsed onto his bed before Howler had even crossed the threshold. The kid immediately began snoring, and only the slightest shadow of a smile crossed his old friend's lips before Alberto walked in behind them.

"What's wrong with him?" the big man asked Lee.

The Islander hadn't left the room all day. Howler couldn't even recall if he'd seen Lee move. He had been sitting with his legs crossed in the corner meditating, so it wasn't a surprise to Howler when Lee didn't answer.

Alberto turned to Howler for clarification, but the Guildsman acted oblivious to the situation. He lay back on his bed and stared at the ceiling, enjoying the anger that he knew was building up in Alberto. First the big man cracked his knuckles. Then Howler could hear a low murmur. He waited until he heard Alberto practically huffing before he answered.

"We took Jake out to practice with his bow again, and the little tyke is turnin' into something amazing! I'm tellin' ya, he could—" Howler's face dimmed as he took a good look at Alberto. "That's a fancy shirt of mail," he said, pointing a dirty finger at the piece of chainmail draped over the redhead's shoulder. "Don't suppose you brought enough for the rest of us?"

"It's called a hauberk, and I don't even want this heavy piece of shit. It's all Harold's idea. When I mentioned you guys, he said, 'Archers have no need for armor!'"

"What about Lee?" Howler stared openmouthed. "Don't tell me it's some sort of slave thing, or so help me…"

"Can Lee even fight?" Alberto asked as he gestured toward their immobile companion. "Would he?"

Both men looked at the Islander, but he continued to meditate or sleep—they couldn't tell which.

"It's like talking to a rock with that bloke," Howler muttered. "Like it'll even matter, eh?"

"It will matter...it all matters." Alberto set the hauberk next to his bed and took a calming breath. "Look, tomorrow's the sixth day since the Suits left. We need to stay in the city from now on. If Nordcross shows up and captures any of us outside and alone, it'll be all over. You hear me?"

"Of course I hear you," Howler replied. "How could I not? You're the loudest person I know besides myself." He failed to maintain his scowl, and his face split into a wide grin. "I was meaning to find the undertaker anyway. Saw a nice plot in the graveyard by a tree and I was hoping to get a discount for buying early. Maybe we can get some kinda group rate...you want in?"

"No," Alberto said flatly.

"Too good to be eaten by the same worms as Jake and I, you armor-wearing tosser?"

"Go to sleep, Howler," Alberto grumbled as he lay down.

"Maybe I can convince some of these cowards to fight with us," Howler muttered. "Think I can?"

"No," the big man repeated as he pulled a blanket over himself.

"What about that druid broad?" Howler continued. "She seems...feisty. No doubt that demon pet of hers could take a few o' those buggers down. She might even want to order two graves, come to think of it."

"By the moons," Alberto said through ground teeth, "I know what you're trying to do."

"And what's that, mate?"

"You're trying to piss me off."

"Well, someone certainly has a high opinion of themselves," Howler said as he rolled his eyes. "It's not always about you, Bertie."

"You're scared," Alberto said as he turned onto his side. He fixed Howler with a serious stare. "If this is how you deal with it and it helps ease your mind, keep it up. Just leave the people of Padscott and Karin out of it."

Howler's brow furrowed as Alberto turned onto his back again.

"Really?" the ex-con asked quietly. "Sticking up for that witch and her hellhound? Blimey, Red, you gotta get a handle on those wandering desires of yours. How many ladies can you possibly be in love with at once?"

The only response he got was Alberto's heavy snoring.

"How in the hell..." The Guildsman shook his head and turned to Lee. "Maybe you could talk to him?" he asked, but the Islander didn't respond. Howler laid his head back against his pillow and murmured, "They're all insane!"

* * *

Howler tossed and turned, but sleep never found him. This wasn't the first night he'd spent lying awake while the others slept, seemingly unaware of the severity of their situation. With Nordcross' looming invasion, it was impossible for him to shut his eyes without reliving the horrors of his past. When he finally did get to sleep, he would wake up minutes later, terrified that the inn's exits had been barred and that he was once again imprisoned.

As he listened to the shifting patterns of his companions' snoring, his eyelids began to droop. His thoughts became fuzzy, nothing more than words smashed together without meaning, and then he could hear the heavy footfalls from the hallway that only meant one thing: the warden was coming. The smell of mildew, wet stone, and his own feces filled his nostrils and he had to clench his fists to keep from whimpering.

* * *

The sounds of Alberto marching around the room and spouting orders jolted Howler from his shallow sleep.

"Howler? Are you awake?"

"I am now, Red," the ex-con croaked. "What can I do ya for? Hold off an army? One-handed maybe? Perhaps—"

"Enough," Alberto interrupted. "We have serious problems we need to address. I've been trying to get a map of this damn city and I'm getting nowhere with these paper pushers. I need you to survey the area and find any potential advantages or weaknesses. Can you handle that?"

"You want me to wander aimlessly about town and take notes on what I see?" Howler asked dryly.

"It's not that simple. You and Karin—"

"That witch!" Howler yelled as he got to his feet.

"I wouldn't say that too loud if I were you," Alberto warned. "She's agreed to help out, and since she's familiar with the area, she'll be a great help."

"Fine, let's get going then. Jake, why don't—"

"Jake is with me today," the redhead interrupted.

"Now you're just playing dirty," Howler accused.

"I need you to pay attention and not play. That's why Jake and I will help out here around the docks while you scout."

"And Lee?"

"He'll…" Alberto looked over his shoulder to his still-meditating companion. "Lee will just try to draw as little attention as possible."

"Oi, did you just make a joke?" Howler asked as he wiped a thin layer of sweat from his pale brow. "I think our hardass leader just made a joke. Granted, Red, it bloody well sucked and we're all gonna die, but—"

"Shut up, Howler," Alberto growled. He cracked his knuckles and pointed at the door.

"You got it, mate." The ex-con gave a mock salute to Alberto's back before turning to Lee. "Let's go find us that pretty druid lady so she can buy our affection," he said with a wink.

* * *

At midday, Howler walked on one side of Lee with Karin on the other and Fujin trailing behind them. They had spent the morning walking the upper sectors of the city, mapping out weaknesses in the stout city wall. Unfortunately there weren't many to map, which left Howler bored.

His mouth never stopped moving. He talked about the advantages of asphalt as opposed to cobblestone streets, how dammed rivers in Nordcross had affected the fishing in his hometown, and even which flowers are edible and which could be sent to a woman for flattery. It was during the speech on flowers that Karin decided to walk with Lee between the two of them.

No matter the subject, eventually every conversation came back to Jake. He knew he kept doing it, but he couldn't help the anxiety that came when they were separated.

"…don't get me wrong though," he was saying, "canvas will make a fine sail, but if it's speed you're after, silk is the way to go. Ardänian would obviously be the first choice, but since there hasn't been any authentic silk stitched there in the last century, Svirdark is really the best option. There was one time Jake and I—"

"Another story about Jake?" Karin interrupted with exasperation. "If you miss him that much, why did you leave him behind?"

"Alberto told me—"

"Oh, so you always do what you're told?" the druid asked. "You didn't strike me as that type of person."

"Jake is still young," Howler said quietly.

"And you never intend for him to grow up so that you'll always be needed by someone?"

"Look," Howler snapped, "Jake's not even the problem here. It's your damned demon weasel, it makes me nervous! Do you have to take that thing with you everywhere?"

Fujin growled and Howler sped forward a few paces. His heart was racing, but it was worth it to change the subject. There weren't many promises that he had to honor, and the ones concerning Jake he would take to his grave.

"The Golden Gardens," Karin announced. "Here you'll find wide, clean streets, planted yards, and many windows from which one could strike."

"By the smell of it I'd say this is the richest part of Padscott," Howler guessed.

"I don't see how that matters," the druid said.

"You wouldn't," he muttered mysteriously. "For instance— look at the stonework on these homes. I mean, it really says a lot about the kind of people who live and work here. The joints are square and true, the blocks themselves are perfect...I can even see a hint of Nordcross influence here, too."

"A good, strong foundation," Karin agreed. "Sturdy enough to hold back the cavalry should they come."

As Howler mulled over the riches that undoubtedly sat behind those dark windows and closed doors, he stumbled right into two men riding boarhounds. The luggage strapped to one of the hounds clattered to the ground and landed on Howler's foot, pulling a profane insult from his mouth.

"Terribly sorry, gov'nah," Howler said as cheerily as he could through clenched teeth, his swollen toes throbbing in his shoes. "It would appear that my eyes were enjoying your lovely city too much to pay attention to where I was walking. Please forgive me, and let me get that for you."

"Don't bother," the younger of the two men said as he turned to Lee. "Why haven't you picked up my father's bags, you worthless piece of filth?" He pulled a stick from his lap and waved it threateningly at Lee.

Lee bent over to pick up the luggage and Howler grabbed his shoulder. "What are you doing?" the ex-con asked.

The Islander looked at him with a sad kind of confusion.

Howler turned to the two men. "Oi, he is NOT a slave!"

"The brand on his foot says otherwise," the old man huffed. "Now pick up my luggage before I—"

Fujin snarled and the hounds reared up. The men stared at the druid and her badger with sheer terror.

"A hunter!" the young man gasped. "Father, she—I, oh my, we didn't intend to—" His voice was cut off as his father's muddy bag crashed into his gut.

"There will be no bloodshed on these streets today," the hunter commanded coldly.

"We apologize," the son said. "We meant nothing by it, just buffoonery between men."

"Then ride on," Karin said.

"Yea, ride away!" Howler called to their backsides as their boarhounds led them away. "Get the bloody hell out of here before you really piss me off!" His hand was still in his coat as the two men rounded the corner.

Howler couldn't help but be impressed with their new acquaintance, even if she was a witch and bedded down with a giant weasel every night. When his newfound admiration faded and he remembered what had just happened, he turned back to Lee, whose head was down and eyes were closed.

"Why would you let people treat you like that?" Howler asked.

The look on Lee's face was unreadable.

"You're not a slave anymore! You don't have to take anyone's crap. Unless you're some kind of little girl that can't defend herself against the big, rich bag man and his big, shiny—"

Lee grabbed Howler by the coat and slammed him into the nearest wall. The former slave's eyes glowed purple and Howler cringed.

"A little help here, Karin!" the ex-con pleaded.

The druid only watched with her hands on her hips.

"As long as I have this mark, I am as good as a slave!" Lee shouted.

Howler's head snapped back to his friend's glowing gaze.

"What part of that is so hard for you to comprehend?"

Howler let out a bray of laughter. *"That's* what I'm talking about!" he shouted.

Lee pressed him harder into the wall as Howler continued to laugh.

"Look at you!" the Guildsman continued. "No sir, no master, we're equals right now! Two men squaring off! How does that feel?"

Lee's face shifted between anger and confusion as Howler pressed on.

"Good, right?"

The Islander nodded once.

"You keep that up and you'll be cured in no time. As for the brand...I think it's time I introduced you to shoes."

\* \* \*

Howler and Lee were the last to return to the Dew Drop Inn. As they approached the door to their room, they heard Alberto's voice coming from within. When they opened the door, however, all the shouting stopped. Alberto and Jake both stared for a tense moment, and then Jake exploded with laughter.

"What in the hell are those?" the blond finally asked when he caught his breath. He pointed to a pair of purple, shredded boots covering Lee's feet.

"Oi, I know," Howler explained, "I tried to tell this wanker that they were ladies' shoes, but he didn't care. Then the witch said something about him being a free man and walked off. Next thing I know, Lee's walking with her—wearing the shoes! The git left me to pay!"

"Why would you pay for trashed women's shoes?" Jake asked. Once it was out, he couldn't help but shake as he continued to laugh.

"Too right!" Howler exclaimed. "After I paid for 'em, I see this bloke across the way rippin' the boots apart. I nearly had a heart attack right there!"

"They are comfortable now," Lee said quietly.

"Yea, but what I'm wondering is why you're still half naked!" Howler yelled. "Why didn't you get a shirt too, eh? How can you stand this weather? It's bloody snowing!"

"Dammit!" Alberto threw his arms up. "I thought Karin would keep you in line, but it looks like I was asking the impossible."

"Your witchy friend tried her hardest, but I am a force to be reckoned with," Howler joked. "One day you'll realize it, Red."

Alberto's face flushed until it matched his hair. "Did anyone do anything they were supposed to do while they were out buying shoes and reading books?"

"Reading books?" Howler looked around, as if expecting to find stacks of books lying about.

"Apparently the spoiled Guild brat doesn't like manual labor," Alberto explained with a hint of accusation.

"Gave you the slip, did he?" Howler asked with raised brows. "That bugger makes me so proud sometimes."

"I finally found him in the library," Alberto added. He absentmindedly grabbed his dagger from the table by his bed and began fingering its blade.

"That's because I saw another building with the Guild insignia on it!" Jake explained. "I didn't know it was a library until I'd gone in and checked it out. I found a few books on Padscott and its history with the Guild and Nordcross."

Howler stared at the kid in disbelief. "Where did you learn— ah, never mind that," he said, "what did you find?"

Howler was genuinely interested, but Alberto scoffed and stomped toward the door.

"This place was the first Guild post back when the Frozen Wastes was actually a huge and powerful city," Jake began. "Nordcross was still just a small farming community. Turns out this place and the Guild itself were created to protect Nordcross from Venstrum, who controlled everything this side of the Wolke Mountains. Their leader Haat was apparently some kind of tyrant wizard or something." He paused, as if trying to remember what he was going to say, and then his eyes lit up and he grinned. "And get this! Once Venstrum fell and Nordcross rose to power, they were the ones who shut down the Guild. A nice thank you, don't you think?"

"How does that help us?" Lee asked.

It was a moment before the shocked silence was broken.

"No 'young master' this time?" Alberto asked.

"I must have cured him already," Howler answered loftily.

"Right…well, Lee, I'd just asked Jake the same damn question before you two arrived!"

"It—well, it doesn't. Not really," Jake said. "But think about it, Howler! This was the original Guild station! We've *got* to fight for it!"

"For the Guild?" Howler tugged on a strand of his hair. "I'll fight for the Guild. But not for the cowards that live here." He mimed spitting on the ground, much to Lee's disgust, then laid a neatly drawn map on the table. "The wall is strong," Howler explained as he pointed out the main features, "so they'll need heavy rams to break through. Unfortunately it's fairly short, which means it'd be easy for them if they bring ladders."

Alberto nodded along, but Howler didn't know what the big guy thought he was agreeing to. It was a bad situation.

"And then there's the Golden Gardens," Howler continued. "It's nothing more than a bunch of prissy aristocrats in big houses. They'd sell us out in a heartbeat and we'd be surrounded in seconds. And then," he dragged a finger across his neck, "lights out."

"Then we make our stand at the tower, just the four of us," Alberto said. "I can use the bridge as a choke point while you and Jake pick them off from higher up." The big man made his way back to his bunk and turned around. "I don't know if Harold can provide any reinforcement, but here's to hoping."

"Not a bad idea, Red," Howler said honestly. "Maybe there's actually a chance of surviving this!" He gave Alberto a thumbs up, but the big man still had his back to him.

"That's the spirit!" Jake gave a thumbs up as well and Howler smirked.

# CHAPTER TWENTY-FIVE: PUNISHMENT

It took Nordcross eight days to reach Padscott, just like Will had said. Alberto and Harold had been discussing precautionary evacuation plans on the top floor of the Tower of Justice since the sun had risen. A few hours later, Howler, Lee, and Jake joined them.

Jake had his face pressed against the enormous glass wall. His lips puckered so that they made a seal against the window and he puffed his cheeks out.

"Oi," Howler whispered to the blond, "it's not too late to bugger out, ya know. We still have time."

"Mmhmm," Jake hummed without removing his mouth from the glass.

"Red and that old fart—"

A loud pop interrupted Howler as Jake pulled his face away and gasped. "They're here!"

Howler followed the kid's line of sight and yelled something so profane that Harold knocked over his glass of scotch. Five lines of armored soldiers marched through the city streets. The gates were no longer manned, as per Harold's orders. No resistance would mean no bloodshed...until Nordcross was in front of the tower and safely out of the city proper.

At the front of the brigade, atop a stunningly white horse, was the Nordcross commander. His emerald- and feather-encrusted helmet reflected the sunlight back up at them.

"Well then," Jake said with an uneasy shrug, "looks like it's time."

"You don't think they're just here to borrow some sugar, eh?" Howler asked with a weak laugh.

"Alright you two," Alberto commanded, "come with me and then take your posts on the second floor. Lee, wait—"

"We know the drill, Red," Howler said with a sigh.

Jake bounded down the stone staircase and disappeared. Harold and Howler went next, followed by Alberto. Lee descended next, but he only made it down one flight of stairs before slipping into the shadows of the lower floor.

By the time Harold reached the entrance hall, the vanguard had already reached the bridge outside. As Alberto and Harold walked to the center of the black strip of stonework, the commander rode out from his ranks to meet them.

"I am the Northern Elder Owl, Sir Harold Prescott, and I do believe I have a right to know why you are invading our country!"

The commander took his gaudy helmet off and continued to sit sidesaddle on his horse. Alberto made a face like someone had just made him swallow acid. The man had perfectly curled, brown hair that reached his shoulders, and a long, thin mustache that Alberto immediately wanted to tear off.

"My sincerest apologies, *Elder*," the commander said in a borderline falsetto voice, "but I have my orders. The Northern Federation is to become assimilated into the majestic empire of Nordcross and become its Northern Frontier."

Alberto didn't need to look to know that Harold was shaking with fury.

"Of course, you could resist," the commander lazily waved a hand and blew a curly lock of hair out of his face, "but that would be so droll."

"Who the hell are you?" Harold finally shouted.

"Me?" the commander asked as if Harold had just insulted him. "Why, I'm the newly appointed Commander of the Northern Armies, De'rel. It's a pleasure, truly, to meet someone as prestigious as yourself, good sir."

Alberto heard Harold mutter something about De'rel being a disgrace to all men when Howler stepped forward with Jake. Alberto cursed under his breath and looked over at the ex-con.

*What in the moons are they doing down here?* Alberto thought. *They're gonna mess this whole thing up!*

"I knew it was him," Howler loudly told Jake while he ignored Alberto's frantic stare. The ex-con only had eyes for De'rel. "Didn't I tell you?"

"You called it," Jake responded happily.

"It's just that nobody else on this planet would ever dress so ridiculously."

"Agreed," the blond said with a nod. "It's those feathers, right?

They're just so over the top."

"So, Darrel," Howler called out, "how's life been treating you since your days as a warden?"

"How dare you!" De'rel shouted as his face flushed. He straightened up on his horse with his chest puffed out and yelled, "My name is De'rel!"

"Sure thing...Darrel," Jake said with a snicker. "You know, I've missed you. Hell, *we've* missed you!"

Howler put an arm around Jake, who brushed his hair back to reveal his ancroas. "Ring a bell, mate? You look like you've just seen a ghost or two."

"You!" De'rel said with an accusatory finger pointed at the ex-convicts. "Men, arrest these two criminals! How dare you flaunt your brands! When you are back under lock and key, I'll teach you some manners."

Jake set an arrow in his new bow and grinned. "Try it, fancy pants," he said as Howler reached into his coat.

Harold stepped between the three men. "You must obey the rules of engagement," he explained loudly. "These men came to us under a white flag!"

"Can it, pops!" Howler shouted. "Do you honestly think Darrel came here in peace?"

"I'd listen to him, Harold," Jake added with a nod. "Darrel is a real ass."

"Jake, Howler," Alberto hissed. "Enough! How do you two know this Darrel asshole anyway?"

"He was our host while we were prisoners of Nordcross," Howler answered. "I thought he sucked at it, considering we escaped, but apparently someone promoted him."

The new Nordcross commander, tired of being ignored and insulted, threw a tantrum on his horse. "MY NAME IS DE...REL! DE'REL!"

As De'rel's shrieks echoed through the city, Alberto noticed faces peering out at them from the windows of nearby buildings. As soon as he would make eye contact with the citizens of Padscott, they would duck down out of sight.

*Harold's right,* he thought. *There's no way these people could take on Nordcross.*

Alberto's concentration broke as soldiers rushed forward with their weapons drawn. Jake took a wild shot at De'rel and Alberto had to push him and Howler back toward the spire.

"Remember the plan," the big man hissed vehemently. "I need you in that tower now!"

The two Guildsmen turned and ran back with Harold while Alberto clotheslined the two nearest soldiers, sending them flailing to the ground. He threw his fists out wildly and dented several helms as spears stabbed toward him from all directions.

He kicked out and snapped one soldier's knee, then grabbed him by the head. He flung him at three more oncoming spearmen and knocked them over. A few spearheads grazed him as arrows began to whiz past from the other side. Nordcross soldiers fell one after the other without Alberto having to touch them.

*Jake and Howler must have made it to the second floor!*

Two men dropped at Alberto's feet with arrows sticking out from their stomachs, still screaming with their last breaths.

*He's still nothing compared to Maxi...*

A sound like a huge wooden door splintering echoed from the tower, and Alberto turned around as five more explosions quickly rang out. He expected to see some kind of struggle or the spire coming down, but all he saw was a cloud of grey smoke and Howler fiddling with his gun in a window. When Alberto turned back to the fight, the soldiers were all staring at six bodies lying on the ground with holes the size of fists through their breastplates.

*Damn, that's actually pretty impressive.*

"What are you all waiting for?" De'rel yelled from somewhere in the center of his army. "Attack! Attack!"

Alberto grabbed two distracted soldiers and tossed them at their comrades. He bowled them over the edge and into the frozen water below. It had been years since Alberto had fought like this—and goat farming was nothing like battle. At least a hundred troops still stood on the bridge while an army waited behind them, and Alberto was already panting.

The redhead ran on pure adrenaline as rivers of sweat poured down his face. He had gotten sloppy, and he was actually grateful for Harold's hauberk. He could already feel a few bruises forming from attacks that might have run him through without the armor.

Alberto held off two men on his left as another three came at him from his right. A spear swiped across his forehead and cut him deeply. In only a moment, his face was painted with his own blood.

Rage took over. He grabbed his assailant by the neck, raised him up, and slammed him back into the ground once, then twice, and on the third time, Alberto heard a loud snap and the body went limp.

De'rel saw his opening and kicked his white horse forward. The Nordcross commander darted past a pile of bodies as he drew a long, thin sword and pointed it at Alberto.

"You savage!" he called out. "You are through! Your archer is out of arrows and your little criminal tricks are no match for the mighty Nordcross army. Give up now, or face a fate worse than death!"

Alberto looked around, dazed and confused.

*Where in the moons is Howler? Jake's out of arrows? Shit, this is all too soon...*

Two more explosions let Alberto know that Howler was back in action. De'rel raised his eyes involuntarily, which was all the opportunity Alberto needed—he punched De'rel's horse right between the eyes and knocked it out. The beast fell and pinned the commander's leg to the bridge.

"Get him, you fools!" De'rel shouted from the ground.

Alberto ignored the shrill man and continued fighting. It only took a few moments before he was overrun, though. A small squad of four soldiers managed to sneak past him on their way toward the spire as he struggled against the sea of purple. He threw two more soldiers over the bridge, fighting his way out of a pile of troops.

Four more explosions echoed around him and the sneaking squad fell to the ground, as lifeless as a child's toys. Alberto dispatched the last of the soldiers around him before he knelt by De'rel to finish the job.

As he reached out with his hands, he felt a pair of thin, strong arms wrap around his neck. A knee lodged itself in the small of his back and pressed him against the ground. Alberto could see only an elbow wrapped in black cloth.

*An assassin!? How did they know I was here?*

"See what happens when you attack nobility, you horse's ass?" De'rel shrieked from beneath his steed.

Three soldiers ran forward and lifted the horse just enough to let De'rel free himself. He climbed to his feet, stabbed the horse through its neck with his sword, and then brushed off his green coat.

"You five," he called to a squadron marching his way, "get me those two little criminals. And someone find me Harold."

De'rel's voice was high and thin, but Alberto could taste the venom in his words.

* * *

Howler dropped back into the lobby and looked around. He was running low on ammo—though he'd never actually had any real ammo to begin with. He'd only ever used rocks and other small items.

Jake ran down the stairs behind him with some scavenged arrows held high. "I finally found more," he panted as he tossed a pearl necklace to Howler. "Is Alberto back yet?"

"Some guy in black pajamas got 'im, so you and I are gonna get 'im back!" Howler shouted with fire roaring in his voice.

The ex-con broke the necklace apart as he raced across to the other staircase. *Crossfire and confusion,* he thought, *an archer's best friends.* He stopped on the first stair, placed six pearls into the gun's small drum, and locked it into place. The rest of the perfect spheres went into one of his pockets as the footsteps outside grew louder. Howler opened the gun's main chamber and fiddled with the dimly glowing crystal inside.

"Shit," he grumbled, "I should have paid more attention…"

A group of five soldiers poured in through the entrance to the spire. Jake took aim at the tallest and broadest soldier in the lead as Howler aimed for the closest enemies who'd run right past him. They both shot at the same time and two soldiers dropped to the ground.

The other three enemies shoved their way past the falling bodies and continued the charge. Two had spears and the other one wielded dual swords. Howler shot four more times at the spearman heading his direction, but he was moving too fast and he missed.

Jake notched another arrow and let it fly. His spearman fell to the ground with an arrow sticking through his temple.

Howler narrowly dodged a swipe at his head and kicked the last spearman in the face. The swordsman reached the stairs, still pursuing Jake. The blond stepped backward up the steps and grabbed for another arrow, but he tripped. The soldier was practically on top of Jake when Howler shot. The Nordcrosser's head exploded in a shower of blood and skull fragments that painted the wall.

After a quick thumbs up from Jake, Howler walked to the door to check on the situation outside. Behind him, the young Guildsman started pulling arrows from the corpses.

"Check it out, Howler!" Jake shouted as he struggled to pull an ornate ring from a fallen soldier's finger. "This shit might fetch us some good coin after all this is done!"

Howler turned around to look, but instead of the ring in Jake's hand, his eyes were drawn to the spearman that he'd kicked in the face. The man's eyes were swollen shut and blood ran from his nose, but that didn't stop him from charging Jake with his spear. Howler raised the gun and pulled the trigger, but nothing happened. He shouted and ran, and with all his strength, Howler leapt between Jake and the Nordcrosser.

The tip of the spear found its way into the ex-con's flesh and ran through Howler's gut. Jake was sprayed with blood as Howler gasped for air. He silently wished that this was just another nightmare, that he was really tucked safely in his bed back at the Dewdrop Inn.

"Howler," Jake shouted, "no! No, stop it, stop bleeding!" The kid sobbed, but the damage had been done.

The pain seared through him, though, as if mocking his wish. He heard Jake's voice like he was a mile away. His vision began to fade as he bled out, but he knew there was still work to be done. Howler grabbed an arrow from Jake's hands and stabbed his murderer through the eye before going limp.

The iron, metallic smell of blood filled his nostrils, just like when he watched the royal guard kill his best friend. The dank smell of ancient stone, the moss that covered the damp depths of the prisons. The acrid stench of his own sweat and fear as he watched his wound expand and contract with every breath.

He was only vaguely aware of Jake kneeling at his side and screaming for help. The last thing he heard as his vision faded completely was the sound of heavy footsteps, the boots of the warden coming to see them. A weak whimper came from his numbed, parted lips.

* * *

Lee crouched behind a gargoyle and watched the battle unfold below. Alberto had told him to stick by the elder, and that if things looked bad, Lee was to pretend to be Harold's slave until they could escape. Harold agreed and they all assumed that the Islander had no objection, but as soon as the fighting had started, Lee disappeared.

He shifted slightly and continued to watch the fight. A man in black shimmied along the edge of the bridge and hung right beside where Alberto was fighting. The big redhead knelt by a fallen horse, ready to snap the neck of its trapped rider, but the man in black leapt up to the surface. He wrapped his arm around Alberto's thick neck and brought him to the ground before he could kill the commander.

Lee stepped out from behind the gargoyle—an ugly, winged dwarf with a beak the size of one of its arms. He put his hands on top of the statue and then jumped. The Islander launched himself into the air as De'rel ordered a squad of soldiers into the Tower of Justice.

The former slave plummeted to the ground like a javelin, his legs straight out, knees locked. He landed and there was a deafening thud as the ground around him cracked from the impact. Purple tattoos shined brightly from his dark skin, matching the blazing glow from his eyes.

The soldiers around Alberto faltered and stepped back. De'rel screamed again and roused his troops to action. They stepped forward with their spears ready as the Islander stood placidly in the mess of splintered stone.

Just then Lee leapt into the air and kicked the nearest soldier in the chest, taking him to the ground and denting his breastplate. As the soldier took his last breath, Lee pushed himself into a handstand and began a quick, upside-down dance. The soldiers stabbed at him, but his legs were too fast. He kicked away their spears and even snapped one's tip off with his feet.

Lee flipped back onto his feet and crouched down with his hands clasped in front of him. He began to hum and concentrate his energy as the soldiers stepped back to collect their fallen weapons. Lee could feel the runes pulsing on the surface of his skin, and he didn't need to open his eyes to know that everything in his sight had been tinted purple.

The soldiers froze, some still bent over with their spears resting only inches away from their fingertips. Even Alberto stopped resisting his captor as everyone turned to watch the glowing Islander.

"It's another trick!" De'rel shrieked. "Attack!"

Lee immediately snatched the nearest spear from its owner's

hands and used it to toss him over the edge of the bridge. When the sound of cracking ice reached his ears, Lee began to sway back and forth. The symbols on his body glowed brighter as a torrent of water shot from the lake into the sky.

"Attack! Attack!" De'rel repeated with such enthusiasm that spittle flew from his mouth.

A soldier near the commander dropped his spear and tried to retreat, but De'rel slashed the man's throat with his thin sword. He didn't even look at the body as it fell to the ground.

"Attack or I will kill you myself!" De'rel shouted.

Lee spun and maneuvered the jet of water toward the assassin holding Alberto down. When the airborne wave collided with the man in black, he lost his grip and slid along the black stone. Alberto rolled onto his hands and knees and gasped for breath.

"Where the hell do you think you're going?" Alberto grunted as he reached forward and pulled the assassin back.

Lee lifted his arms and summoned two more jets of water. He ducked and spun and turned the water into waves, which he used to sweep an entire squad of men into the freezing lake. When the only squadrons left were those surrounding De'rel, Lee pulled the water back toward himself. The liquid wound its way up his arms, covering his skin and causing the light from the glyphs to refract slightly. He exhaled and the water froze.

"What is this?" De'rel shrieked. He pulled the knight next to him off of his horse and mounted it, then rode back to the bridge's entrance.

All the fight seemed to have disappeared from the Nordcross troops as they shoved each other off the bridge in an attempt to escape the man covered in ice. All but the assassin retreated, and that was only because Alberto hadn't let him go. The man in black kicked Alberto in the face, but the redhead's grip didn't waver. He held onto the man's leg and dragged him back.

Another gunshot rang out and Jake's screams for help reached Lee's ears. At least fifty more soldiers waited on the other side of the bridge with De'rel, while another ten creeped forward cautiously.

Lee launched himself high into the air and spun wildly. Shards of ice burst from his body and shot into the soldiers heading toward Alberto. The assassin stopped struggling as Lee landed and nodded to the redhead, who let go and ran back to the tower. With one last motion, the Islander created a low, spiked wall of ice, barring the troops' path.

The symbols on Lee's body dimmed as he followed Alberto toward Jake's screams. When they entered the Tower of Justice's lobby, they found the young Guildsman kneeling over a bloody body.

Lee saw the long, plum spear sticking through Howler's torso and he heard Alberto moan softly. When he was sure they were alone, Lee tore the lizard-skin canteen away from his neck and pushed Jake aside.

"Howler, no!" Jake cried as he fell backward. "Don't die, please, just don't die!"

"Archers don't need armor, eh?" Howler mumbled. He grinned weakly as he looked up at Jake. A rivulet of blood ran from the corner of his mouth, along his jaw, and then down his neck, where it pooled around his collarbone.

Lee grabbed Howler's shoulder and pushed the spear the rest of the way through his body, earning him a slew of vulgar insults. The Islander flipped his canteen upside down and poured water into the gaping hole in Howler's stomach. Lee crossed his legs and held his hands over Howler's body as the bright glyphs returned to his skin. He began to hum loudly, one note, and something came out of his hands—it looked like the heat shimmering off of metal during summer. The water on Howler's torso began to work itself into his wound.

Jake and Alberto both gasped as the hole in Howler began to stitch itself back together and his breathing returned to normal. When there was no sign of the injury left, Lee's symbols disappeared. His eyes rolled up into his head as he fell back onto the stone floor, shaking and sweaty.

"What was that?" Alberto demanded with a mix of fear and awe.

"That," Lee panted heavily, "was Effreudia's Touch." He coughed into the air. "It is a difficult ritual…to perform…"

A blur of black appeared behind the big man and Alberto suddenly fell forward, landing face first on the floor. The assassin stood behind him with his fist cocked.

A heavy door opened from the back of the lobby and Zelig strode forward. Karin and Fujin followed behind.

"How dare you defile this tower," Karin bellowed in a voice that carried over the din of battle. "You are all guilty of murder. Your sentence is death!"

Zelig looked down at Lee with cold eyes as Karin pulled the Islander's arms behind him.

"No," Jake whined, "help *us*! Not them!"

"I am afraid I cannot do that," the warden said flatly. He lifted Howler's limp body onto Fujin's back.

Jake began to sob uncontrollably as Zelig bound his wrists.

"Karin, arrest the Ardänian," the warden commanded.

De'rel finally entered the tower as Harold descended the main staircase. Both the elder and the commander wore looks of triumph.

"Well," De'rel exclaimed with a pointed look at Harold, "it looks like daddy betrayed you. Who knew rats would eat their own when backed into a corner?"

As the commander stepped forward, Zelig leveled his trident at De'rel's throat.

"What is the meaning of this?" the flamboyant man asked with disbelief. The joyous look on his face immediately disappeared.

"Commander, these are prisoners of the Northern Federation," Zelig announced mightily. "They are to be detained in the Tower of Justice until a proper hearing can be scheduled and their sentences carried out."

"You just said they were sentenced to death," De'rel spat. "Let Nordcross help its friend, the druids. You don't need to worry yourselves over this filth."

"I disagree," Harold cut in. "I would, however, be willing to negotiate their release into Nordcross custody," he added smugly.

De'rel looked around the room. He seemed to be weighing his options as his mouth worked silently. The stink of cowardice overpowered Lee's senses, and he already knew what the commander would say next.

"What do you want, *Elder*?" he finally asked. The spite in his voice was enough to sour the air around him.

"The Northern Federation is willing to become a Nordcross territory so long as it is allowed to maintain its own government and a standing army," Harold began. "In return, we will pay whatever tribute Nordcross deems fit."

"You cannot be serious," De'rel hissed. "Those wretched fools attacked us and we won, as Nordcross is wont to do. We shall be taking them as our prisoners. There is *no* need for negotiation."

"That is where you are wrong," Zelig interrupted. The druid's face remained expressionless, but Lee noticed a glimmer of pride surface in his eyes. "You are not only intruding on land that belongs to the Northern Federation, a nation that far outranks yours in age, but the land of the druids as well. Although we are not as presumptuous to lay claim to what rightfully belongs to the planet, we will still enforce nature's laws to their fullest."

De'rel fixed the warden with what he might have thought was a menacing stare, but he only looked to Lee like a man who was inches away from soiling himself. The Nordcross commander pulled a scroll from his pristine coat and made a show of breaking the wax seal.

"The Commander of the Northern Armies shall assume the mantle of Elder of the Northern Federation and will replace the entire senate as he sees fit," De'rel announced as he read the parchment. He paused as he considered something. "There would be a place in that senate for you if you started to play nicely, Harold. I'd hate to see innocent citizens die for an old man's pride." He grinned and the light caught a silver cap on one of his teeth.

"Like I said," Harold continued, "we will pay tribute so long as the North remains. Under these terms, we will surrender peacefully."

Karin's hand twitched, but De'rel didn't notice. Lee locked eyes with the druid and felt her pain radiating from her. He shook his head slightly and willed her to hold on.

"Excellent! Now, what should we do with you?" De'rel asked as he turned his sights on the four prisoners.

"There is a dungeon in the catacomb—"

"You will address me as Elder De'rel," the prissy commander snarled, interrupting Zelig.

"Elder De'rel," the warden corrected, "the dungeon below could serve as their prison until suitable transportation to Azrael can be arranged."

"Yes," Harold added, "I'm sure the high court is waiting to parade their prize in front of the emperor."

De'rel sniffed the air and looked directly at Alberto, who remained unconscious. "As acting Elder of the North," De'rel said as he stepped over Howler's motionless body, "I do believe our justice deserves some form of autonomy. Don't you agree, Senator Harold?"

Lee watched Harold grapple with being addressed by his former title. He quickly responded with a well-rehearsed, "Yes,

Elder."

"And do the druids concur?" De'rel asked.

"Yes, Your Eldership," Zelig agreed as he bowed.

De'rel turned his back on the Northerners and looked from Jake's brand to Howler's, and then he turned to Alberto. "Separate cells, in the deepest, darkest ward available. We'll just keep them here until the emperor comes to claim these prizes. I don't want Sera to have all the fun when she executes them anyway. Take extra precautions with that one," he added as he motioned to Lee and exited the tower.

* * *

In the dungeon, the four travelers lay trapped in dingy cells. Chains coated with mold and fungus hung from the ceiling and rats scampered across the damp floor. Each cell had a plank of rotting wood chained to the wall as a bunk and no other furnishings.

Howler lay on his bed in a near coma. His eyes were shut and his face was pale and covered in sweat. He moaned quietly as Lee continued to watch over him from across the hall in the opposite cell.

Lee reached up and tugged fruitlessly at the collar that the assassin had strapped onto him. He only got one look at it before it disappeared under his chin, but it was all he needed to recognize the ivory ring. It was the same collar that was used in the Islands to restrain slaves—the ivory interfered with their ability to use magic. For the fifth time since they'd been locked away, Lee tried to manipulate a water droplet stuck between the stones in the wall. As he expected, it didn't budge. Although he didn't have much energy left after healing Howler, being imprisoned in the middle of a lake would eventually have put him at a great advantage.

"Lee," Jake pleaded. He gripped the rusted iron bars in front of his cell and pressed his face against them to try to see into the next cell, where the Islander resided. "You saved Howler. You saved him. How did you..." He whimpered quietly and stared longingly at the other Guildsman. "How did you do that?"

"The Islands have had slaves for many generations," Lee responded quietly. "Our masters buy and sell us based on our abilities. Those of us who are more adept at manipulating the elements are forced to mate with others like us. Those who refuse to teach their children magic are tortured…" He paused and took a deep breath. "And the children who show no affinity are either killed or sterilized. I used the power of my people and the natural properties of water to heal Howler."

The Islander looked to Alberto, who occupied the cell next to Howler's across the way. The big man was still unconscious, but he was muttering to himself as he slept.

"You know this is your fault," Lee added.

Jake flinched and knocked his head against the bars. A loud clang resounded and he could hear the kid openly begin to cry.

"You were careless and you put someone who loves you in danger," he continued. "Had I not intervened, Howler would have died…and it would have been your fault."

Footsteps from the stairs echoed down to them. Lee let his head drop and rested his chin against his chest.

"I-I…you're an asshole!" Jake screamed.

"Prisoners of Padscott," Zelig's voice boomed through the hallway. "Be silent."

Jake dropped down onto his wooden cot and sobbed loudly.

\* \* \*

Almost three hundred feet above his prisoners, Harold sat at a desk with a bottle of whiskey. Nordcross had taken the Northern Federation and he had failed as the new hero. He thought about what the Blue Bandit would do if he found out that the man he spared had betrayed and imprisoned his old friend.

The old man realized that his fingers were caressing the ear that Meyral had cut as a reminder. He took his trembling hand away and reached for a glass. He poured himself a shot, stopped, then made it a double and downed it in one gulp.

Imagining the Blue Bandit's punishments wasn't nearly as terrifying as thinking about De'rel or Sera ordering him around for the rest of his life. He sighed shakily and stared into the mouth of the bottle.

# CHAPTER TWENTY-SIX: HARBINGER

"Yiddi thinks that your injury has set you back," Rubi said. She had taken to soaking in the spring with Meyral regularly, and she always started the conversations. "Is that true? Because I think it has more to do with you being called the Harbinger of Death."

Meyral nearly jumped. He was always amazed at how accurate Rubi was at guessing his feelings and he hated it. "I've just been thinking a lot," he answered after a moment.

"Maybe talking to someone might help. Someone like me." Rubi moved closer to Meyral. "It always helps me when I get things off my chest..."

"Like when you helped Maxine?" Meyral knew it was a cheap shot, a secret that his eye gave him that no one should have known. He just wanted to catch her by surprise like she had done to him so effortlessly. "I'm sorry, I didn't mean that," he added apologetically. "You're just...it's like you're in my head sometimes, you know? It's weird."

"Forget about it," she answered, still blushing. "After all, you're the tzęprön. That's a lot to struggle with."

"That's what Yiddi says, anyway," Meyral muttered darkly.

Rubi's eyes went dark. The redhead chewed her cheek, which Meyral knew meant that she had something on her mind. One part of him hoped she would just go to bed without starting another fight, but another part wanted the chance to listen to Rubi more.

"So what do you do with the yid art since you're still broken?" Rubi asked Meyral.

"Who?"

"Never mind," the redhead said with a laugh. "I'm talking about Yiddi."

"We sit in the dark and try to *feel* things. Mostly I just sit in the dark and get bored. And then I *feel* pissed." Meyral splashed the ground. "Meditation...boarshit is what it is."

"You mean like the meditations we used to do under the almond tree with Taryn?" When Meyral didn't respond, she added, "I wish I could join you."

Meyral slipped under the thick water and resurfaced with the same surprised look on his face as when he'd gone under. "Why?"

"Maybe it'll jog your memory if I'm there. Or, I don't know, maybe I miss life in Mantrych…"

"So why don't you?" he asked. "I'm sure it'd be okay with Yiddi. Maybe training with you really can help me remember what I used to know."

"I'd like that," she said with a smile. Then she made a circling motion with her finger and Meyral turned around.

He slowly peeked over his shoulder as Rubi pulled on a dress that revealed a good amount of her freckled skin. Meyral knew that she had borrowed it from one of the lizard twins, and he wondered what they had looked like before the sinking.

* * *

Yiddi was at their door early the next day. Meyral already forgot that he had invited Rubi, but he wasn't upset when she joined them in the tunnel.

"How is the arm?" the old lizard asked.

"Still broken," Meyral answered curtly.

When they reached Grey Lake, he sat in his usual spot and started to empty his mind while Rubi and Yiddi continued to discuss the finer points of meditation. For the first time, Meyral was having trouble with the emptying part. He kept going over what Rubi had said and comparing it to his broken memories.

*The orb brings in a topsider, then death follows. These scars all over my body…the people I've killed…destruction follows me everywhere I go. But where's this orb they're talking about?*

*Maybe I'm not the 'tree-pond' thing everyone talks about. They've been wrong before. Maybe I'm just some regular guy. My eye isn't even acting up anymore. What if the senate was all I was meant to do, and now I'm supposed to live a normal life?*

*But that ghost…Shraka. 'When you give up, come and find me.' Isn't that what he said? I wish he had been wrong, or better yet, not real. Just a figment of my stressed imagination…*

As his thought process continued, images of blue, glowing orbs, his father in chains, and a young man with curly, brown hair danced through his head. In darker, more obscure corners of his mind, a certain redheaded beauty danced as well.

*As long as I run, it can't catch me,*
*When I'm done, I'll become the enemy.*

Meyral had a flashback to burning tents exploding in the desert. A powerful wave of shame accompanied the memories. He tried to push them out of his head, but rather than forget, he surrendered to the grief that had plagued him. Tears burned his eyes, and suddenly he felt something else. It wasn't much, but it felt...cold.

He quickly let go of the feeling to check his surroundings, sure that someone or something was approaching. But once he opened his good eye, all he could feel was the same subterranean warmth he'd felt for the last few months. Even his sorrow was gone.

He restarted his meditation and was able to reach out to the cold feeling immediately. As he held the object in his mind, other sensations became apparent. Wet, fear, hunger. They felt strange and new coming through this fresh channel, but he knew what they meant.

Meyral had finally done it. He was reaching out with his mind and had found a fish. He wanted to yell at the top of his lungs, but as soon as he thought about it, the connection disappeared.

"The tzęprön has completed a connection," Yiddi announced. Somehow he knew before Meyral had a chance to tell him. "Do we have an idea of what we were in contact with?"

"It was a fish," Meyral said, barely concealing a grin. He knew Rubi was staring at him, but he was too focused on Yiddi to answer her surprised look.

"Did the tzęprön see the fish?"

"What?" Meyral asked. He was crushed. He thought he had just completed the impossible, but instead it looked like he just learned a small part of a much larger thing. "...no. I didn't."

"Then we must continue with our training."

Rubi scooted closer to Meyral and leaned in close. "What did it feel like?" she whispered.

"Wet," Meyral answered with a wink.

Rubi laughed, and a moment later, silence enveloped them all again. Meyral tried to reach out with his mind to the fish in the lake, but something had changed. He couldn't focus on Grey Lake at all.

* * *

"Six months underground and I'm still struggling," Meyral grumbled as he soaked in the hot springs, absentmindedly rubbing his fully healed arm.

"Yiddi says you're making progress," Rubi said soothingly.

"All I can sense are feelings of simple animals with all the complexity of a catfish!" he shouted.

"Well sometimes you can feel other things, right?"

"That's not enough. I'm supposed to be the tzęprön!" Meyral's mood was awful, even for him. His training with the lizard brothers had gone worse than usual that day.

He was able to survive his sessions with Kirth and Luka without being knocked out. He'd gotten better at dodging hits, feeling his opponent's movements, and once he even parried one of Luka's attacks. Meyral saw it as improvement, but the others weren't so optimistic.

"We've still got plenty of time. You'll get better," Rubi said, though she crossed her arms.

* * *

Days later, Kirth and Meyral made their way toward the springs with Luka trailing silently behind them.

"If we can't hit our opponent, what kind of snít'n would that be?" Kirth asked for the hundredth time. "Your lamö seems to be doing much better," he continued, changing the subject before Meyral could snap back. "I haven't seen her limp in weeks. I hear she even defeated a golem."

This was the first time since Meyral had met Kirth that he had attempted small talk.

"Call her Rubi," Meyral grumbled. "And she's not my lamö."

"The topsider can finally speak properly."

Meyral was aware of the insult, but he didn't take the bait. His mind was occupied by Rubi. He'd spent so long convincing himself that he didn't love her, but all he'd really done was fight the inevitable.

"Syndell tells us that the female kasmömig talks about you almost nonstop. Why would she do this if she is not your lamö?" Kirth tilted his head and Meyral knew he was probing his emotions.

The problem was that he knew that they could never be together, no matter what ridiculous fantasy he created in his head. The latest one was that he could convince Yiddi to let them stay down there forever. Then he and Rubi could have a life together, without fear of being torn apart. Unfortunately, he was the tzęprön, whose sole purpose in life was "to deliver finish."

Rubi was everything Meyral couldn't be. She radiated beauty, she was caring and pure, and she had nothing but love and hope for the world. He didn't want to sacrifice that for some selfish reason. Those crystals would strip her of her beauty, but he would strip her of everything else.

The short walk to the springs had become a long journey as questions continued to swirl around in Meyral's head.

*Should I run? Should I take Rubi with me? Maybe I could hide somewhere down here. Does Rubi...has she moved on from Liz? I have to know. But do I want to know? What if she hasn't? ...what if she has?*

Meyral gave the lizard brothers the slip and headed into the city instead. Yiddi always knew when to show up to stick his snout in Meyral's business, and he was hoping that the old lizard would do just that. As he rounded a corner onto a dimly lit and desolate street, he heard an unusual string of familiar beats—one step, two step, clomp.

"Ah, Meyral!" Yiddi stopped and spread his arms when he got close enough that Meyral could see him. "No springs tonight? Raysnít'n went well then?"

"You already know the answer to that," Meyral grumbled. "Just like how I knew you'd find me."

"You understand more than you give yourself credit for." Yiddi waved his cane for Meyral to follow as he continued down the road.

"Then why do I feel so useless?"

"These things take time, but soon the tzęprön will—"

"There!" Meyral stopped and pointed a finger at Yiddi. "That name, how do you even know that I'm the one?"

"Daz kas'n foretell of—"

"Yea, the green fury and all that. But there were two before me, weren't there?"

Meyral waited for Yiddi to answer, but he only continued with his leisurely stroll.

"Ręxoo tur rù zo," the old lizard called over his shoulder.

"Rexoo tur antęza."

"What does that mean?" Meyral asked as he started to follow again. He didn't know if Yiddi had actually answered or was just rambling, but something about what he said struck a chord with him.

"Destiny is yours to control," Yiddi answered. "Fate is not predetermined."

Meyral's face contorted in concentration as he tried to remember where he'd heard that same saying before.

"There were two kasmömig before you, yes," he continued when Meyral caught up. "The kasprön and the antzęprön. Either one could have been the tzęprön. It depended on them and their choices, just as it is now. They failed to truly see our light!"

"I guess that makes me failure number three then," Meyral muttered.

"It sounds like we have read the first chapter and have already finished the story." Yiddi smacked his cane on the ground twice and growled. "It is all in the head. The tzęprön has the passion, but he lacks the determination. He must go back to his lamö and—"

"SHE IS NOT MY WOMAN!" he shouted.

The word "woman" echoed around them for several moments and they both waited in silence.

Yiddi muttered something that sounded suspiciously like "passion," and then he snickered. "Perhaps she is not just a lamömig. She is much more than that." The old lizard nodded and slipped into an alleyway shrouded in darkness. He left Meyral standing in the middle of a broken road with dilapidated shops on either side of him.

Meyral stayed where he was for a long time. He had no idea what was happening. During the brevity of his second life, he had always had goals or destinations. Discovering his identity, disbanding the Northern Senate, finding his father...but now he felt like a ship tossed out in a storm.

New emotions assaulted him that his addled mind didn't seem capable of processing. Doubt, fear, love, hope...they all felt so foreign to him, even after what seemed like a lifetime of meditating in the dark.

He heard two sets of heavy footfalls and a low slithering, and he knew the lizard brothers were searching for him. Meyral sighed and briskly walked the other way, back to the apartment where he knew Rubi would be waiting.

\* \* \*

When he opened the door, she looked more beautiful than he could remember, if that was at all possible.

"Training went well?" she asked. For the first time in six months, her daily question didn't irritate him.

"I heard you landed a kick," he said with a smirk as he closed the door.

"Where did you hear that?" Rubi asked. She brushed an auburn lock of hair out of her face.

"A little lizard told me. So is it true?"

"It was an accident really. I was training with the twins and I kicked Sascha while trying to dodge Syndell."

Meyral laughed. "Don't be so humble. I've been at this for over half a year and I haven't landed a single blow in the dark, even by accident!"

"It seems like time has gone by so quickly." Her eyes darkened and she looked toward the door. "And soon you'll be gone…"

"And out of your hair, you mean," he finished for her. He knew who she was thinking about.

"I'm being serious, Meyral." Rubi looked back at him with worried eyes. "I just feel like something bad will happen if we're not careful." She reached out and rubbed a hand down his arm. "I don't want to be separated from you again…like before. It was awful."

Instinctively, Meyral wrapped his arms around her. She leaned her head against his chest and he buried his head in her silky hair.

"I know," he whispered. "That's the last thing I want to happen." He pulled her closer and sighed. "We could…we could stay here, you know. Away from it all."

"Your father is still out there," she said as she dropped her arms and stepped back. The light of hope shone faintly behind her eyes, and Meyral silently cursed his fate.

"As far as I'm concerned, he died like everyone else in my past…aside from you." Meyral fumbled over what to say next, torn between his desires. More memories had come to him in the last few months, but most of his past was still a mystery to him. All he knew was that it was filled with loss.

"That's not true and you know it." Rubi shook her head with a sad smile. "You'll find him if you look, and you have to look. It's in your nature."

"There's no reason to go back. There's nothing out there for us," he whispered quietly as he reached for her again. Before he could pull her back into his embrace, she began to quietly sing.

*"Love departed from this world,*
*Speeding like the cry of a crow*
*But still our hearts beat on.*
*Never again this face*
*Did a smile touch."*

Rubi trailed a hand along Meyral's scarred cheek as she spoke. "I've been reading your book," she explained, catching the almost fearful look in his eye. "I hope you don't mind."

Meyral stood silently. Rubi dropped her gaze, and when she looked back up, he kissed her. She pushed him away and he stared into her eyes, fearing her reaction. Without warning, she grabbed both sides of his face and returned his kiss with several years' worth of pent-up passion. She let her hands slide down and explore his bare torso, and then she dragged him toward the bedroom. Just before they reached the bed that Meyral had yet to use himself, she turned around and let go of his wrist.

"Rubi…"

"No," she said as she held a finger to his lips. "Don't spoil this." She trailed a light, soft hand across his face, lingering for a second on his scars. "You're not a monster, Meyral." She ran her hand down his neck, down his arm, and across his chest. "And it doesn't matter if you're the tzęprön. You're perfect." Rubi kissed the places her hand touched.

Chills ran down Meyral's back and his heartbeat began to speed up. He could hear it easily, as if the walls around him were pulsing along.

"I love you," she whispered in his ear as she nipped his neck. "I should have told you so long ago."

"I—"

"Shh. I told you to shut up."

Meyral helped her out of her clothes, all the while kissing her gently. Once her blouse was off, she wrapped her arms around his neck and kissed him. He'd found his thoughts wandering in this

398

direction from time to time, but actually living it, experiencing it…it felt unreal.

She stepped back to remove her pants as her perky breasts glistened with a light sheen of perspiration. Meyral's eyes followed a bead of sweat as it rolled down her chest, her stomach, and finally disappeared at her waistline just before the last of her clothes dropped. He wanted nothing more than to study her, to memorize her every curve.

Meyral stood and pressed Rubi's warm, sleek body against his. As she nuzzled his neck, her hands dropped from his chest to his waist, where she untied his pants and let them drop. He pulled her into another kiss, and another, and then worked his way down to her navel. His lips brushed her bare skin and he rubbed his hands up her thighs. He wrapped an arm around her and stood, then laid her gently onto the bed.

He joined her on the bed and Rubi arched her back in anticipation. A light moan escaped her as he crawled toward the headboard and slid his body over hers. Meyral put his left hand behind her neck and kissed her lightly, and as he braced himself with his scarred arm, Rubi reached between their bodies. She slid her hand down and softly wrapped her fingers around his pulsing shaft, then guided him inside her.

Rubi gasped and Meyral could feel her muscles tense. Her breath came as a quick pant, but she relaxed and pulled her right leg around his torso. She used her heel to push him forward and she cried out. Her nails dug into his back as she started to writhe against him.

Meyral's mind barely registered the scratching against his back. They locked lips and rocked against each other as the world seemed to brighten several shades. For the first time in months, the lizards and his role as the tzɛprön were the furthest things from his mind.

\* \* \*

The hot wind was back, blowing sand in his face. How long had it been since he'd seen the light of day? He didn't know. It didn't matter. He was standing in the middle of the desert again, his own personal hell that he would never escape. He heard the cry of a vulture above him, but he couldn't see any living creature around him.

The ground beneath him shifted like water, although he didn't sink. It made him dizzy and nauseous, and then his head started to hurt. He reached out for something, anything, but there was nothing near him for miles. The ground steadied, but he could smell something horrible wafting up from below. He refused to look—he was terrified of what he might find. Instead he raised his eyes to the horizon and scanned all around him.

There was a tree in the distance. He willed with all his might, and suddenly he was right beside it. He vaguely remembered the dream so long ago, before he woke up knowing his name, when he first saw the tree. Its flaky bark cried out to him and its roots reached up out of the sand, as if it knew that its only hope was to leave the desert. When Meyral walked toward it, the wind died down and he saw something he hadn't seen in the last dream.

A sapling that reached his knee had sprouted up from the unforgiving soil, as vibrant and green as any plant Meyral had ever seen. He felt a bright glimmer of hope rise inside of him; even the dying tree in the desert had been given a second chance.

\* \* \*

Meyral awoke in a daze. He didn't know how long they'd been holed up in their room together, but the air was thick and humid. Rubi had fallen asleep on his arm, facing away from him. He gently lifted her head and pulled his arm out from under her. She shifted and rolled onto her back, but she didn't wake. Her red hair, darkened by the lack of light, fanned out across the pillows in a sea of crimson beauty.

As he quietly set his feet on the dusty floor, there was a knock from outside. Meyral made his way across what had started to feel like home, and before he let the chunk of quartz close, he took one last look at the bedroom. For a moment he stood still and watched Rubi sleep. Reality set in and he was glad that it wasn't just another dream.

He found Yiddi waiting for him in the tunnel when he opened his green door. The old lizard wore a wide grin that stretched his scaly snout back. His razor-sharp teeth, some of which were missing, gleamed in the dim light.

"Is the tzęprön ready to resume raysnít'n?"

"Resume?" he asked. "What do you mean?"

"The tzęprön has been absent for two days." Yiddi's smile left and he gained an air of impatience. "So again—are you ready to resume raysnít'n?"

Meyral didn't even bother responding. He grabbed his pants and left for Grey Lake.

* * *

His mind wasn't easy to empty. It kept wandering back to the naked beauty he left sleeping in his bed.

Yiddi coughed quietly and Meyral was pulled back to the task at hand. He reached out with his mind and he immediately explored the lake for a fish.

Something was different. The rolling boil of emotions that had plagued him since Rubi and Liz had fallen into this dark place quieted for the first time. He felt a kind of click in his mind, and the visual of a bright yellow line floated up in his empty head. He didn't understand, but for some reason he knew that this was the same fish that he had first made contact with.

The line began to twist and writhe and change colors, and soon enough he had a perfect image of the creature. The fish was about the length of his arm, and green with a tan belly. Its blank, stupid eyes stared off into the distance, completely unaware that he was watching it glide through the thick, black water.

Testing his limits, he opened his eyes and tried to stay focused. His eyes set on the still, glassy surface of the lake, and although he couldn't see the fluorescent fish, he could still sense its presence and visualize it in the back of his mind.

Wanting more, Meyral pushed his mind out a little further. Before long, he felt another fish, and then another, until he could feel the whole lake teeming with aquatic life. He shifted his senses upward and found a young bat flapping around the rocky ceiling. Meyral followed the bat all the way back to its resting place. He could feel something else—some weak force pulling his mind even further. Letting the force guide him, he found an entire horde of bats nestled in a crevice in the ceiling.

As he let his mind wander into the dark depths of the top of the cavern, he wasn't even aware of Yiddi tapping his head with his jade cane.

"Our time has ended, Tzęprön."

"Yiddi, I did it! I could see fish...and bats...I saw it all!" Meyral motioned toward the lake, but it was as black and still as ever, and his new senses picked up nothing.

"We have made progress, yes, but there is still much to learn."

"By the moons, I told you I can do it!" Meyral fumed as he punched the soft ground.

"Then the tzęprön can show us us tìksävv when he spars with Kirth and Luka, yes?"

"Gladly," Meyral growled. He was only partially aware that he had just agreed to a highly handicapped two-on-one battle, but his attention was somewhere else—back with Rubi, in fact, probing her life force with his mind and feeling her with his soul.

He stood up to leave and his world turned even blacker than it already was. A crashing sound met his ears, and it seemed like ages passed before he realized that it was the sound of his head hitting the rocks.

\* \* \*

When he opened his eyes again, he was in the bright torchlight of his apartment. Yiddi and Kirth were looking down at him with their milky-white eyes while Rubi held his head, which rested on her soft thighs.

"How'd I make it back?" Meyral asked. "I feel like I just went ten rounds with Luka's feet..."

"Turns out using your brain like that takes as much energy as using your body—maybe a little more, in your case," Rubi answered with a giggle.

Meyral tried to sit up, but Kirth held out a clawed hand and stopped him.

"You know," Meyral told Rubi, "you never giggled much before we got down here. I think you like it—"

"Rest," Kirth interrupted. "You will need it for tomorrow."

Meyral opened his mouth to argue, but Yiddi interrupted him. "Dra lödran," the old lizard said as he shoved a goblet of green liquid into Meyral's hands. The tzęprön drank it all in three large gulps and laid his head back onto Rubi's lap.

\* \* \*

He awoke and Rubi was gone. Instead, Pläblé was watching him silently by the couch. Meyral had fallen asleep without realizing it, and he had slept through the night. He swung his legs off of the sofa and jumped up, much to the displeasure of his pounding head.

"I'm glad you're so eager today," the female lizard said softly.

"You don't even know. I have a few lumps to pay back to your ręxlamig."

"While that threat displeases me, I am glad that the tzęprön is beginning to accept his ręxoo. Follow me, if you will."

As they walked the black tunnels, Meyral mulled over a question that he hadn't been able to answer himself. "How do relationships work down here?" he asked, and as soon as it left his mouth, he cringed.

"What does the tzęprön want to know?"

"Well," he continued, unsure where to start, "I don't know many liz—people down here, but as far as I can tell, you and Kirth are the only married couple."

Pläblé laughed. The sound wasn't entirely unpleasant, but it sounded strange to Meyral considering that the mouth it came from housed teeth he once thought belonged to a monster.

"There are plenty of couples in lamäch. Perhaps the tzęprön should wander more, like his lamö."

"So what's with the twins and Luka?" Meyral asked. "Why aren't they la-macked?"

"*Lamäch*," Pläblé corrected. "Sascha and Syndell were young when the city sank, and Luka is a klynlön."

"And…" Meyral prompted.

"There has not been a lamäch since Ardan sank. It's not that the love went out of this place, but something did change that day. Finding one person to spend the rest of your life with just lost its meaning. It seems as if we'll *all* spend the rest of our lives with each other now."

Meyral was sure that if he could see, he would find tears on Pläblé's cheek.

"Well, we are here. Please take it easy on my Kirth. He is a good mig." With that, Pläblé left.

Meyral entered the torchlight of the sandy arena where Yiddi and the lizard brothers waited for him. Kirth started talking as Meyral tried to enter a light meditation.

"Unfortunately, Yiddi wants you to take it slow today," Kirth announced. "We will go easy on you." The last part was directed at Luka.

Meyral reached out and felt Kirth a few steps in front of him. He watched as Kirth's tail swept back and forth. The torches went out and Meyral was able to hold the image of the lizard. He balled his fists and waited for a perfect opening. Just as he was about to strike, something collided with Meyral's head and he felt a familiar crunching.

"I wasn't ready, you tactless son of a bitch!" Meyral shouted at where Luka had been.

"Is that what you're going to say to the enemy?" Kirth called. "Wait, give me a chance, I'm not ready?"

A fist found its way to Meyral's gut and another landed on his shoulder. Meyral dropped to his knees.

"We thought the tzęprön was going to show us something," Luka gloated. "I think you've gone soft. We told Yiddi that more time in the arena was what you needed…"

As the lizards taunted him, Meyral stayed on the sandy ground and again reached out. He found Luka, small and packed with muscle, standing and laughing. Wrong lizard—Meyral wanted Kirth. He moved his line of focus to his right and found the captain of the guard.

Kirth was completely oblivious that Meyral's fighting spirit was far from gone. When the lizard approached him, Meyral launched himself from the ground and punched Kirth twice in the face. The captain fell back—out of surprise or pain, Meyral couldn't be sure—but Meyral had already redirected his focus to Luka. A fist, a foot, a tail—Meyral was able to dodge them all.

"Enough!" Kirth yelled as he got to his feet. "I am proud to say that the tzęprön has finally landed a punch. This is an important milestone. You're finally able to use ká'ahan in a battle situation."

Luka strolled over and clapped a hand on Meyral's back. "Yiddi taught you to crawl, it seems." He barked laughter, but it was not unkind.

Meyral let his guard down. Just then, a fist slammed into his kidney and sent him to his knees.

"Now we'll teach you to run!"

\* \* \*

He woke up in Rubi's arms hours after the training session. Yiddi stood at the side of the springs and Meyral could sense pride rolling off of him.

"That ká'ahan shit is distracting," Meyral complained. "I got my ass handed to me! I could at least dodge them before." His bad mood was back and in full swing. Something he seemed to have learned about himself was that he actually didn't enjoy getting the shit beat out of him.

"Do we blame the hammer if the barn falls apart?" Yiddi asked.

"What does that even mean?" Meyral was trying to figure out if he was just insulted, but his foggy mind was barely working.

"It means that the new senses you're learning are just tools," Rubi answered.

"When we first pick up the blade," Yiddi continued, "can we do more than swing it blindly?"

"Do all yid art speak in nothing but riddles?"

There was a sharp intake of breath from Rubi, but Yiddi only chortled.

"Where did the tzęprön learn such language?" the old lizard asked.

"Rubi," Meyral said without hesitation. He noticed that the redhead's face now matched her hair.

"Did we bother asking what it meant?"

"No."

Yiddi laughed again. "Curiosity is perhaps better than nothing. You just called me an 'old fart,' by the way."

Meyral sighed and rested his head against the stone wall. "I'm sorry."

"We know," Yiddi said quietly. "But do not fret. The tzęprön will continue to improve, we are sure of it."

"In the next three months, when I've only made it this far in the last seven? Why do I only get a year? What's the point of all this?"

"We do not question daz kas'n."

"Well this tzęprön does!"

Rubi actually cringed at the ferocity in Meyral's voice as he pulled away from her arms. Meyral's time with the lizards had gone by so slowly to him, but now that he had Rubi, he wanted more.

"At least you can pronounce your title now," Yiddi said with a trace of irritability. "We raysnít again in the morning. Rubi may come, if you would like." There was silence as Yiddi limped away with the aid of his cane.

When Meyral spoke again, he had regained his composure. "Let's get out of here tonight," he whispered to Rubi. "We could go back to the North as Christophe and Jewel, and we never have to look back."

"I told you what Roke said. There's no getting out of this place," Rubi said darkly. "Besides, Jewel is gone. That life…"

"Then we'll find a nice dark tunnel and become lizards, just you and me. You'd still be the most beautiful creature to me."

"You used to want to fight."

"Yea, but I don't even remember why." Meyral sat back and frowned. "I was wandering the desert, fighting something I couldn't see and following a light. All I wanted was my past…but you are my past. *You* are what I've always wanted."

Rubi kissed Meyral's neck, heating him up more than the springs ever could. There were tears in her eyes when they broke apart.

"I'm sorry, Meyral." She shook her head and bit her lip as she got out of the water. "I know you aren't lying to me…just yourself. We're staying, and you're going to learn what they have to teach you. There's a reason Liz died and we're here."

With that she disappeared and left Meyral to stew with his thoughts.

\* \* \*

Those same thoughts followed him all the way back to the apartment, where Rubi was already asleep. They hounded him through a sleepless night and continued to follow him during their walk to Grey Lake in the morning. Rubi made no mention of their previous conversation.

Then Meyral got an idea, but he wasn't sure if it would work. He wasn't even sure if it was morally sound, though he wanted to try it regardless. He sat down on the rocks next to Yiddi and cast his mental fishing rod, but he didn't send it into the lake. Instead he turned his mind toward Rubi.

Her energy was easy to find; it was like a bright ray of moonlight in an eternally pitch-black midnight. First her outline appeared, just like Kirth's and Luka's had the day before. It was a dim silhouette against the shifting blackness of his closed eyes. Slowly it filled in with a cornucopia of colors.

Unlike the fish and the bats, the colors in her aura were constantly changing. They flowed around her while she sat next to him, eyes closed and legs crossed. But they weren't random and spontaneous. They were patterned. Meyral vaguely wondered what others' looked like.

He left Rubi for a moment to check Yiddi's aura, but his energy was nowhere to be found. Meyral reached out a hand and felt his scaly arm, but he still couldn't sense him. He shrugged and ignored it, then sent his mind back to Rubi. He studied the patterns and his mind began to understand.

Memories started to form in his head that were not his own. There were bits and pieces at first, like a teddy bear or a small room, but Meyral kept at it until complete thoughts came.

He saw a blond man in shining blue armor march in a parade of similarly dressed men. They looked like they were heading off for war as they held banners on poles that bore the Raven and Moons of the North. Sadness filled his heart and he was certain that it wasn't his. Since his time in the desert, most emotions, aside from anger, were rare for him to feel.

Meyral continued probing her aura for more memories until he came across one of himself. Outside of a city's gate, an old man spoke to him, Alberto, and Maxine. He noticed that he looked a great deal younger and much more fragile and weak than in his own recollections. As he focused on the scene, he noticed that Alberto and Maxine also looked different.

*Is it possible that people could recall the same event so differently?*

Alberto's hair was almost blood red, and his nose was much more bulbous than Meyral remembered. Maxine looked taller, slimmer, older and...attractive. She didn't have that motherly sheen that Meyral's mind automatically imbued her with.

When he looked again at the younger version of himself, a sliver of embarrassment wound its way into his mind and the vision began to blur.

*Does she really remember me as such a weakling?*

As he thought this, another memory presented itself, one of

407

him and Rubi sparring in Taryn's garden. The younger Meyral wasn't quite as frail this time; he had his shirt off and his muscles seemed overly defined. And, he noticed, there was a lot of focus on his butt.

Like the sadness before, he felt someone else's emotions fill him. This time it was contempt, mixed carefully with a certain degree of lust. He smiled to himself, but it wasn't what he was looking for.

He delved deeper.

As his mind whirred through her memories, flipping through them like the pages of a book he hadn't yet read, he saw a flash of Maxine and Rubi holding each other. The emotion that touched him was warmer than anything he'd ever felt. For a moment it was like liquid gold had burst from a dam in his heart, and it disappeared with the image before he could even think about it.

That one flash was so strong and intimate that he finally realized what an invasion of privacy it was to be intruding in her mind and feelings. He tried to leave and forget the whole thing, but before he pulled out, a new memory pulled him deeper.

Liz lay naked on a mattress with bright, white sheets. The room around them took form and Meyral recognized it as their home in Nasabin. Rubi slinked into the room, stark naked, with her left arm held across her chest modestly. As she made her way toward the bed, she caught her reflection in the dark window. She reached for a lock of her shoulder-length hair and caressed it with her right hand, and Meyral felt her comfort in her new identity. A smirk appeared on her lips as she bent her head down and slipped between the sheets. Her hands disappeared beneath the silk covers and Liz covered her mouth with her own.

The emotions weren't as strong as they were with Maxine, but he recognized them. She loved her...as much as she could let herself, anyway. Then he watched as the room transformed into a dark cavern, and suddenly Liz was shoving her away. She disappeared under a pile of boulders, but for a split second, Meyral saw blue armor covering Liz and a banner in her hand.

Pain struck him and he moved along until he found another memory of himself. It was the night after the Blue Bandit had slaughtered the senate. Rubi watched as two Meyrals started a fire. One was a mangled monster, scarred from head to toe with both eyes gleaming white in the night...but the other was the childish Meyral from her past. There was no judgment in her memory, only understanding. Meyral paused for a long time, mesmerized by the two versions of himself overlapping and kindling a flame.

*Is this why I can't be with her? She sees me as two halves of a demented whole. One a nightmare, and the other a piece of her childhood...*

Meyral watched as a recent memory floated to the surface. Although it was still out of focus, he knew he had finally found what he really wanted; not memories of his past, not the piece of himself that he'd been missing, not the things he was wandering the desert for. He wanted to know why he couldn't have his lamö now.

The images started to sharpen, but then it bled into another one...and then another...and another as heavy emotions attacked his heart. Her dad marching away in his armor, Tyler stomping off into a sunset, a tearful goodbye with Maxine, Meyral leaving Mantrych, Taryn facing off with a man in black and that evil blonde woman, Liz being crushed, and then...

Nothing.

* * *

Meyral awoke, once again dazed and confused on the stone couch in the main chamber.

"You passed out...again." Concern lined Rubi's face as she peered into Meyral's eyes.

"The tzęprön pushes too hard," Yiddi said. "We must pace ourselves. The ká'ahan is a treacherous skill." The old lizard handed him the healing tonic with a knowing look and left.

Meyral sat up and drank it before turning his attention to Rubi, her emotions echoing in his heart. "I'm not leaving you," he said suddenly.

"What?" She stared at Meyral, her eyes wide.

"I won't let you be alone ever again." Meyral grabbed her hand.

"Excuse me?" The worry in her face disappeared as she took a step back. Meyral could see a hint of fear in her eyes.

"Your whole life, people have left you," he explained. "I've even done it before. But I won't let it happen again, I promise." He grabbed her other hand with his scarred one. "Never again."

Tears filled Rubi's eyes and Meyral reached for her face. She slapped his hands away and retreated to the far wall. "It's not your decision," she whispered. "War happens, death happens…there are things you can't control! You can't make that promise! No matter how hard you try, something will happen. You'll leave." She brushed her tears away and turned for their room. "Everybody does."

"I left you once, but I came back. I will always come back. I swear it." Meyral stood, ignoring the lightheadedness that swept through him.

Rubi stopped and turned slowly. "The Meyral who left me never came back."

He froze. He remembered those words and how she saw him as two separate halves.

*But that was before. I thought things had changed.*

A moment later, a soft hand caressed his scarred face and tilted his chin up. His eyes locked onto Rubi's orange ones, full of love and softness.

"It's not this," she explained as she kissed his scars. "It's not even you. I love who you are now. But that optimistic kid I once knew is gone. If you leave again, I cringe to think what will come back to me."

Rubi pecked him on the cheek, and in an instant she was gone. The quartz door shut quietly behind her as Meyral tried to steady himself. He slumped down onto the sofa and prepared for a night of interrupted sleep.

# CHAPTER TWENTY-SEVEN: FORSAKEN

Two more months passed and Meyral was amazed to find that he was quickly becoming everything that Yiddi had told him he would. The ká'ahan came as easy as breathing now. Sensing life and consciousness was something he could do without focusing. He was also able to, much to his enjoyment, dodge the lizard brothers with ease. It had been a whole month since they'd even landed a blow, and Meyral found a dark pleasure in sending the brothers to the hot springs instead of the other way around.

Things had changed since he had probed Rubi's memories. He hadn't pried into anybody's mind, and he and Rubi never mentioned their conversation from that night, but something was different. They no longer spoke of the future—instead they focused on each day's training as if it were all that existed. By burying his anxieties and hopes, Meyral was able to apply himself fully. He was happy, but if he stopped, he would remember that it was only fleeting.

When Meyral trained with Yiddi, the two of them tested his limits. The old lizard sent him on a mission with ants, which he found to be much more difficult than he had anticipated because of their shared consciousness.

Rubi spent even more time wandering the sunken city and its many tunnels, but she always took a guide and she never dug too deeply. She also kept coming up with excuses to not attend meditation with Yiddi. Meyral got the feeling that she feared his new powers. He hoped she didn't know he'd already used them.

Meyral was only worried about one last detail.

"Why can't I sense you?" he finally asked Yiddi during the ninth month.

"So are we right to assume that the tzęprön can do more than sense life?" Yiddi asked with pride.

"There's a lot I can do. I've been able to get inside certain people. Inside their minds, their memories, their feelings…"

"Indeed. It is a powerful tool, and we must learn to use it sparingly. It is a dangerous road we walk on."

"You didn't answer my question."

"No, we didn't, but don't we understand the lesson that is in the question?"

There was silence as Yiddi waited for Meyral to put things together.

"Shit! If I can see people, then people can see me!" He panicked when he realized that Yiddi, Kirth, and even Luka could have probed him just as he'd done to Rubi.

"That is correct." The old lizard nodded. "But do not fret, for there are few who know what the tzęprön knows. Even less understand enough to do as we have undoubtedly already done."

"Have you poked around in my head?" Meyral asked with a hint of anger.

"Yes."

Meyral suddenly felt like he was naked, more than he'd ever felt even when he really was naked. Yiddi let out a croaky laugh.

"Are you doing it right now?" Meyral yelled.

A low chuckle was all the response Yiddi gave.

Meyral closed his eyes and acted on impulse. Instead of reaching out, he strayed backward into his own mind. The logical part of him doubted it was even possible, but he tried anyway. And then, there he was—he saw himself, whole and raw.

His aura was dry and broken, a dull shade of blue mixed with grey. When he dove in to see his thoughts and memories, he found that most of them were washed out and shattered. His mind was as badly scarred as his body. As he wandered through his broken mind, he came across something that felt wrong. He pursued it as if he was scratching an itch. As he pressed in on it, the intruder pushed back. He felt it moving, watching, feeling.

Meyral's fury began to get the better of him and the intruder seized its opportunity. He felt the outsider growing stronger, pushing him out of his own head, and then Meyral understood that Yiddi was feeding off of him. He tried to clear his mind again, but it was too late. Yiddi nearly launched him out of his own mind.

When he opened his eyes, he was covered in sweat and panting, but the old lizard next to him looked as peaceful as ever. Meyral squeezed his eyes shut and restarted his meditation. He knew Yiddi was still in there. He re-entered his head and pushed, but he was distracted by something else.

In a shadowy corner of his mind, he saw something watching

him. Feeling his way into the darkness, he sensed a familiarity in it. It crawled out of the shadows and Meyral realized that it was him—or, rather, a part of him.

Its body was the same as his, but all of its skin had been charred. Its hair, eyelids, and lips had been burned away completely. All that was left was a shell of a human. He was terrified by what he sensed. The monster that Rubi saw that night was there in his mind, waiting and watching.

The burned shadow continued until it was only a few feet away from Meyral. He watched as it paced back and forth in front of him, and then he realized the thing was trapped behind what looked like a veil of clear glass. The monster lay dormant, at least for the time being, so Meyral turned his attention to the new intruder. His issue was with Yiddi, and now there was a more important matter at hand. He didn't want the old lizard to see what was truly inside of him.

Meyral calmly gathered all his strength into one single point and he stabbed at the glaring emptiness, the void that he knew was Yiddi's consciousness. He felt himself winning, like he was about to break through, and then something in his mind seemed to burst and his shattered memories flooded back at him.

As he drowned in his own thoughts, Meyral understood that Yiddi was using his own memories against him like a weapon. When he couldn't take it anymore, he passed out, something he hadn't done in months.

* * *

When he woke up, he was back in the bathhouse. It had been days since the murky water had run over his skin. Yiddi sat near the entrance with his cane across his lap.

"You fought me...with my own mind." Meyral croaked. He didn't have enough energy to be angry.

"The tzęprön impresses us with his abilities, but we are not yet equals. Let not our minds be troubled, for even in defeat, we can always learn something."

Meyral nodded. He had just seen firsthand how to create barriers and block intruders. His goal now was to block Luka, Kirth and anyone else from ever gaining access to what few memories he still held so close.

A line from that poem resurfaced in his mind as his thoughts wandered back to the creature hiding in the dark depths of his consciousness.

*The creature inside my head,*
*The It that wants me dead,*
*It fills me with dread.*

* * *

Meyral woke the next morning to an empty bed. On the table in the main room he found a note:

*I wanted to watch you get beat up, but I still can't see in the dark so I'm visiting the Thalamus Library with the twins instead. I promise not to wander off alone. See you in the springs tonight.*
*—Rubi*
*P.S. Try to have some energy left for me!*

Meyral was still holding the letter when the captain of the guard came to fetch him.

"What does it say?" Kirth asked.

It appeared he could sense the letter, but not what was written. Meyral had a feeling Yiddi would have known, however.

"It says kiss my ass," Meyral answered with a smirk.

"The tzęprön is in a fiery mood today. I assume you're ready for today's raysnít'n, then?"

As Meyral walked, he used the ká'ahan to sense the things around him: bats, mice, a few spiders, the faint outlines indicating walls and rocks, and two lizards. His companions' auras spiraled around their bodies.

Rubi's aura had been a watercolor of pastels, beautiful and poetic. It flowed freely around her like a colorful funnel cloud. Pläblé's had the same fluid grace of Rubi's, but her colors were darker and more subdued. The loud greens and golds of Kirth's aura were hard to ignore, and the patterns were much more aggressive, almost jagged. Luka's purple and blue perfectly complemented Kirth's, and his patterns were strangely similar.

In his mind he thought of them as equal parts tormentor and

teacher, and he wondered if his own bias affected the auras he sensed with the ká'ahan. As Meyral contemplated this, his mind slipped into a memory of one of his trainers. It was a wedding. A young man in gleaming armor waited by a man in a richly patterned robe as a single violin played. The armored man had strong, chiseled features. His thick, brown hair had been pulled back into a braid and his pale eyes scanned the chamber. Meyral knew he was looking at Kirth before the sinking, before he became a lizard.

There was movement behind Meyral and Kirth's face immediately split into a wide smile. When Meyral turned, everyone was standing and a woman dressed in white slowly made her way down the aisle.

Pläblé's human form was not what Meyral expected it to look like. She was squat and rotund, but she also had an undeniable grace about her. Pläblé's eyes sparkled with the color of ripe limes, and her alabaster skin seemed to radiate light. Her face was round and her features were soft, and despite Meyral's infatuation with Rubi, he found Pläblé similarly beautiful.

They began the ceremony, and although it was recited in the old language, Meyral could hear the translation in Kirth's voice. He realized he was doing exactly what he'd vowed never to do again and he left the memory. As he brought himself back to reality, Meyral wondered how angry the captain of the guard would be if he had been aware of his intrusion.

A moment later, Meyral was walking through the familiarly uneven sandy arena. He slowly began to slip into his own mind. Kirth and Yiddi started to discuss something, but Meyral was too busy to pay them much attention. He found his broken conscience oddly comforting, like returning home after a long journey. Meyral was able to exist simultaneously in his head and in reality while being aware of both. Then he finally felt what he had been waiting for.

Three consciousnesses that weren't his own slowly entered his mind. Two were so familiar that he didn't have to spend any time to know they were Luka and Kirth. The third one was like the feeling of being watched when no one was there, and he knew that that one had to be Yiddi.

As Kirth called out, Meyral felt the other lizard brother's excitement. Luka attacked with a jump kick that would have knocked Meyral out if he hadn't ducked.

"Not bad, whelp, not bad!" Kirth continued while Luka leapt again.

Meyral was able to avoid that attack as well as the next one. He even managed to avoid Luka's next three attacks through the ká'ahan, but Meyral wanted to do more than dodge and punch a couple of times. He wanted his trainers, his tormentors, to feel a measure of the haplessness he had felt for months.

Meyral cartwheeled to a far wall and focused. While Luka yelled something to Kirth, Meyral finally reached his goal. He shoved Luka and Kirth out of his mind with surprising ease.

"By the moons!"

Meyral could feel the panic building inside Kirth, and he used that energy to strengthen his own defenses. He quickly built a wall around his mind until the lizard brothers could no longer sense him at all.

"Did he run?" Luka asked frantically.

"No, but the tzęprön has learned a new trick," Yiddi muttered happily.

Meyral took great pleasure in punching the defenseless Kirth right in the snout. The lizard yelled with rage as he struck out at nothing.

"If you weren't so reliant on your ká'ahan, you would have seen such a rudimentary attack," Meyral chanted mockingly.

Luka dove for Meyral's voice, but Meyral easily sidestepped him and jammed his knee into the side of the lizard's face. Meyral let out a triumphant laugh, and then a flash of blue light blinded him.

After a moment, he regained his senses and found himself trapped in his own broken mind. Something had changed, though. He no longer felt comfort there. Meyral found nothing but dread and malice. He pushed, but he was stuck. Panic took him in an instant. An aura, like a dark fog, fell over him, and he heard glass shatter.

*The monster!*

He pushed back and tried to regain control, but he still couldn't. Something gave way inside and he watched a memory fly toward him out of the fog. He watched as Alberto held a bloody corpse in his arms, howling at the sky. The pain filled his heart so clearly it was as if he'd just probed into Alberto's mind.

Using the pain like adrenaline, he burst out of his thoughts with a final push and watched as his foot slammed down on top of Kirth's leg. Maniacal laughter reached his ears, and for a moment he didn't realize that it was his own.

Meyral stopped himself, but not before he heard a loud snap come from Kirth's leg. The captain of the guard whimpered as Luka pushed Meyral aside and picked up his old friend. He hauled him away and threw a furious glance over his shoulder as he left.

Silence enveloped Meyral, as thick as the darkness that had overtaken his sight for so long.

"Did you help me find that memory?" he asked Yiddi quietly. He knew the old lizard was standing behind him in the shadows. "I-I lost control of my body. Why...? How?"

"The tzęprön knows full well that there is something foreign inside of his mind," Yiddi answered quietly.

"I thought I had it restrained," Meyral whispered.

"For a time, yes," Yiddi continued. "But there are few things in this life that are d'sävv. The anmäch inside was weak, yet the shadow was not."

"Why?" he asked simply.

"It could be a number of reasons," the old lizard said. "It seems that the soul has been split, and one such part no longer truly belongs to the tzęprön."

"Get it out of me then!" Meyral's pain and rage masked the shame he felt, but Yiddi wasn't fooled.

"Let us sit and meditate. Perhaps...perhaps it is possible."

Meyral entered his head quickly and sensed Yiddi already there. He looked for the monster that he knew was still inside of him, somewhere. When he finally sensed the evil, it was too late—the scarred demon attacked him from behind. He was used to feeling emotions, but this was the first time that being mentally elsewhere caused him physical pain.

*"Let me out!"* the thing shouted in a voice that Meyral could only parallel to the darkest of his nightmares.

Its hands stopped just inches away from Meyral's neck. The monster struggled against an unknown force as Meyral backed away from the thing's still-outstretched fingers. It took a step toward Meyral, and then another before it was again overcome. The demented version of himself struggled on as the outline of Yiddi slowly appeared behind it.

The old lizard was so focused on battling the monster that his defenses were faltering. Meyral watched as Yiddi's outline filled in and then exploded in his mind.

Maybe it was a consequence of having a wall up for so many years or the stress of the battle, but Yiddi's memories and emotions flooded into Meyral with such force that he couldn't have stopped them if he'd tried. They smothered him, and soon he was engulfed in centuries of information.

Lines of text ran through his mind in languages he couldn't comprehend. Men and women, dressed from head to toe in armor and some in rags, marched across a snowy landscape. A beautiful woman with black hair and incredibly blue eyes looked down at him with a warm smile.

Then he found himself in the courtyard of a castle, in the middle of three men. Two stood together, their staves raised and ready to attack. The man at the point of the triangle raised his hands and shouted at the other two.

*"You should have stayed where you were, klynmig! There is nothing here for you but death!"*

The sorcerer summoned a green staff out of thin air. The youngest wizard spun and hurled lances of ice toward him.

A large wall of stone burst from the ground and took the impact of the frozen spears. The third wizard summoned a flaming dragon from the tip of his own staff, but it was swallowed up as the stone barrier burst into a flurry of sand that extinguished the deadly fire.

*"Your apprentice has gotten better while he was away. Perhaps it was you, Svaark, who was holding him back!"*

Svaark clapped his hands together and froze the taunting man, who Meyral guessed was Spencer, in a thick block of ice. By the apprentice's command, a boulder formed from the pile of sand on the ground and he maneuvered it up into the air. He dropped it on the frosty coffin, shattering it and covering the courtyard in slush.

The sky began to dim, and it was a moment before Meyral realized that it wasn't the vision fading—the moons above were aligning and blocking out the sun.

A manic laugh brought Meyral's attention back to the courtyard. The slush had melted, and the resulting pool of water flowed behind the other two wizards. It rose up and created a liquid outline in the shape of a man, and then the water turned into flesh and reformed Spencer. He picked his staff up and a ring of fire immediately erupted from his weapon. Molten rock burst from its tip and Spencer shot magma at his opponents.

Svaark grabbed his brother as he dove to the ground, and they both burst into a swarm of insects. The millions of bugs easily avoided Spencer's attacks, and he feebly swatted at them as they bit and stung every inch of him they could find.

Spencer fell to the ground, but Meyral knew he wasn't finished. A high-pitched screech filled the courtyard, and both Svaark and Saul fell out of the air as the bugs vanished.

When Spencer's mouth closed, the noise stopped. As the two grounded magicians reoriented themselves, Spencer used those precious few seconds to heal the bites that had left him blinded and grotesquely swollen.

It seemed that no matter what Saul or Svaark threw at him, Spencer was always able to counter it. His skills were unmatched, but seeing as he was outnumbered, Meyral thought the battle might continue on in a stalemate.

As the last of the sunlight disappeared from the sky, darkness enveloped them. Yidtar, the largest moon, blocked almost all of the sun. Sintar and Klyntar entered their larger counterpart's circumference and the sky turned brilliant cobalt. A glimmering, aqua aura burst around the aligned satellites.

Saul began to convulse violently, and a bright blue glow came from his coat. An orb of sapphire burst from one of his pockets and seemed to be sucking the life right out of him. Small flashes of lightning arced between the orb and Saul, and an intense energy filled the courtyard.

Svaark froze. He had no idea what was happening or what to do. He reached out to pull the orb away, but when he touched it, a jolt of electricity sent him flying across the yard.

*"I tried to warn you,"* Spencer muttered as he raised his staff.

A bolt of black lighting struck the young magician in the chest and he slumped to the floor. The orb lost all of its animation and clattered to the hard ground as its host lost his life.

*"You murdered him! You...you fiend!"* Svaark yelled as his brother left him for the second time.

*"I saved us, you fool—"*

*"Liar! I'll kill you!"*

Spencer only scoffed in response and raised his jade staff. A moment later, after nothing had transpired, Meyral realized he was waiting for the grieving wizard to make the next move.

Svaark twitched and closed the distance between the two magicians with impossible speed. The terrible but beautiful dance that was the wizard's duel quickly devolved into something no more respectable than a brawl. Fists and elbows and knees flew at random. Their staves lay abandoned nearby, and all magic had been forgotten as they regressed into a battle of raw strength.

The orb rolled back into the midst of the fight, unnoticed by the two preoccupied men. Svaark slammed Spencer's face into the ground and dropped onto his knees, pinning Spencer on his stomach.

Spencer bucked Svaark off and they both lunged for their staves. Spencer grabbed his and whipped it around as Svaark did the same. The two weapons collided and the tip of Spencer's staff broke, sending out a burst of energy that separated the two men and disarmed Svaark.

Spencer pointed his now shortened rod at Svaark menacingly. Black lightning shot out, but it curved to the side and Spencer watched with horror as the sapphire absorbed his attack.

Svaark either didn't notice or didn't understand why Spencer had stopped, and he summoned his staff back to him. He launched spell after spell at Spencer, casting the courtyard in an eerie glow that meshed with the newly azure sky. Each spell that Svaark summoned deviated from its target and found its way back to the crystal lying innocently on the ground.

*"Fight back, you coward! Just die already!"* Svaark shouted, enraged by what he thought was a protective shield.

He continued to cast spells with incredible speed and carelessness. Spencer held up a hand and shouted something that was lost in the chaos of the battle. For the first time since the apprentice's death, Spencer was hit by magic. A bright, orange pillar of light pierced the side of his torso and left a smoking hole in his robes. A trickle of blood seeped through and stained his cloak.

He resigned himself to finishing the battle and fired back spell after spell. The ground beneath them started to quake, and the orb rose into the air as the spells that it swallowed energized it. A blue beam shot toward the sky and expanded until it filled Meyral's vision.

* * *

Rubi stared into his good eye when Meyral regained consciousness.

"What did you guys do to him this time?" she asked with a sigh.

"It is the captain of the guard who has a broken leg," Yiddi murmured.

"What the hell was that?" Meyral gasped.

Yiddi stepped forward and laid a scaly hand on the redhead's shoulder. "Rubi, would you excuse us please?" he asked at just above a whisper.

Rubi hesitated and watched the old lizard warily. It was the first time he'd ever asked her to leave them alone. When Meyral gave her a nod, Rubi kissed his forehead and left the apartment.

"We were unable to remove the creature inside of you, but he is now restrained. We understand that these dark urges have plagued the tzęprön ever since he woke up in the desert, and we applaud the strength and dedication it took to fight them."

"Forget that! You...you're Spencer! You...you..." Meyral panted and swung his legs over the stone couch, readying himself for a fight.

"You are the second man to find this out." Yiddi sighed heavily. His voice was desperate and sad as he dropped to his knees in front of Meyral. "Yes, we were once Spencer. When we woke in the middle of Ardan and found a rock ceiling where the sky should have been, we were grateful for the dark. We hid in it with the orb. We knew it had caused the city to sink, and we hoped we could reverse it somehow and atone for our part. But the damned stone never responded to us, so we did the next best thing—we kept the danger out of reach of others. Or that's what we told ourselves, at least.

"The truth was that we were afraid. We were terrified of what would happen to us if people knew we were still alive. Perhaps they would kill us out of spite or even justice. That mindset lasted until the day a new threat forced us into action, forced us to rescind our hopes for returning and embrace our progress into the future of Ardan.

"The golem that Rubi destroyed was once our salvation, in a way. It had been conjured by a man who had not been down here with us. Many once believed this man to be a simple thief, but seeing the golem still operational, there is little doubt that he knew what he was looking for. He came for the orb, but he was the first; this was before the kasprön first visited. That golem acted as his distraction while he escaped, and it took every trick we could manage to seal it into that tunnel, much like we had to do with your other self.

"Enough people were so grateful to be alive that we began to rebuild our society. Spencer…I was shunned by all, except for my sisters, Sascha and Syndell. The only other person that refused to spurn me was the only friend that I had ever had on the topside…Kirth. Then deformity overtook us so no man remembered what the other looked like. Those three helped me, and in that time, Yiddi was born.

"We always knew that if Spencer survived, then Svaark probably did as well. It was lifetimes ago that he came to Ardan as someone else, and much like the way the tzęprön did, Svaark figured out who we were. But his mind was too weak to cope with our energy…and we couldn't save him. That was the first time anlön visited our underground prison. Because that is what Ardan has become. A prison. And it is our fault.

"Our second visitor from the world above was the kasprön, the Harbinger of Dreams. She did what we had all forgotten how to do. She dreamed. She dreamed the same dream for three years, and after her visit, we dreamed it as well: a topsider driven by a green fury comes to us, and we are supposed to train him for a year, so that he may take our technique to the ręxpol and end our suffering."

"End your suffering?" Meyral asked.

"Only the power of the tzęprön will free our souls."

"The tzęprön…that's my destiny?"

"Of course, dear boy," Yiddi said as his snout peeled back to reveal his sharp teeth. "That has always been your role to play. But, ręxoo tur rù zo. Ręxoo tur antęza."

Meyral was speechless. Maybe the training had given him some insight into empathy, but he actually felt pity for the murderer that sat before him. He reached out his scarred hand and lifted Yiddi to his feet.

"I don't know what all you did, but I do know you didn't sink Ardan. It wasn't your fault. And I know that if this is truly my destiny, then it will all be over soon."

Tears filled Yiddi's milky-white eyes as the lower part of his snout quivered.

# CHAPTER TWENTY-EIGHT: LIGHT

"Everybody, we found it!"

"We found the Crystal Cavern!"

"The orb is back!"

Everyone was shouting and running all at once. Meyral looked up, along with Luka and a freshly healed Kirth. He could hear the lizards muttering to each other before they set off, a sense of dread and excitement pouring off of them. A quick scan let Meyral know that Rubi wasn't in the mass of dark figures heading for the northwestern tunnels. After a moment's hesitation, he turned away from the excitement and headed for the apartment.

He ran into the dark, which was no longer a problem for him, and didn't stop until he found the granite door that marked what had been his home for the last year. Rubi lounged on the couch inside, reading the book of poems. For a second he could have sworn it was dimly glowing as blue as the crystals in the tunnels.

"What's wrong?" she asked Meyral as he panted for air.

"They just found the room with the orb!"

Rubi didn't even bother with a response. She pushed past him and was halfway to the main tunnel before Meyral realized she was gone. He looked longingly at the book she abandoned, but he left to follow his lover.

A minute later he was right behind Rubi. She stopped suddenly and Meyral slammed into her.

"This orb that everyone's so excited about..." She bit her lip. "It's weird, isn't it? The year is up in what, a few days? And just now they find this mysterious cavern? It's all just...too much of a coincidence."

"You heard Yiddi," Meyral said. "It was all in the dream. And those dreams...you have to take those seriously." He smirked, but he doubted if Rubi could see it in the dim lighting.

"Shut up, Meyral." She took his hand and he didn't need any extra senses to feel the love coming from her. "This could be...the next step."

"To what?"

"I don't know. You're the tzęprön!"

"There's no need for name calling," he muttered before they started running again.

By the time they reached the opening of the new cavern, the whole city was already there. The crowd parted to let Meyral and Rubi through.

There was a line of workers standing smugly by their new hole at the front of the crowd. In the center of the line was Roke, whose pride shone like a beacon.

Meyral leaned into Rubi's ear and whispered, "Looks like your favorite klynlön was the one who found the entrance."

In the dim light that emanated from the cave, Rubi could make out the faces of the front line of lizards and she let out a giggle. "Looks like he's not too worried about the Harbinger of Death anymore."

The whole cave became still as Yiddi calmly stepped forward and cleared his throat. "This marks the day that our träg returns to its former glory," he announced.

Cheers resounded off the walls.

"The final cavern has been restored," the old lizard continued, "and as we predicted, the orb has been located. So let the celebration begin!"

The cave came alive with excitement as the throng of lizard-people headed back to Ardan. Rubi grabbed Meyral and pulled him to the side.

"Tonight we ought to celebrate, too. It might be our last chance before—"

"Tomorrow is tomorrow. We'll worry about that then."

"Then let's focus on tonight," Rubi whispered into Meyral's ear.

She looked up at him with her gorgeous, orange eyes, and chills ran down his spine—for once not from fear, but from excitement.

As the lizards celebrated below, Meyral and Rubi found their way back to their apartment and made love. Without even trying, Meyral kept slipping in and out of Rubi's mind until their two consciousnesses became as one. The connection that they created rocked through the both of them in an immense wave of pleasure. Years of forgotten emotion filled him as he and Rubi became a single entity. Meyral had never felt so alive.

He fell asleep holding Rubi against his chest, his face nestled in her hair. The fact that it wouldn't last no longer mattered to him. Rubi was what he wanted, and he would hold onto that for as long as he could.

\* \* \*

"Wake up."

Meyral awoke in the middle of the night to a commanding voice in his ear.

"Wake up!"

He rolled over onto his side, trying to ignore it.

"*WAKE UP!*"

He opened his eyes, but he couldn't see a thing in the darkness. He reached out with his mind like he'd done so many times before, but he couldn't sense any life around him, save for Rubi's sleeping body.

"It's time for you to come and find me."

Suddenly, without seeing him, he knew who it was. The curly-haired phantom that kept visiting him the year before was finally back.

"You've forgotten something. It's time to get it back."

Meyral reached out again. He'd never tried to sense something that wasn't alive, and the amount of concentration it took was exhausting. As he expanded his mind, he was distracted by a simple wooden chair. It had once been a tree by a lake until it was cut it down. He focused harder on the object and he felt every scrape and cut that had formed it. Meyral was fascinated that he could feel the history in something inanimate.

"We have no time for this!" the bodiless voice commanded impatiently.

Meyral made one last attempt to connect to the apparition, but he felt it disappear as his mind rubbed against it. For a split second he felt cold and empty, like he felt when he'd woken up in the desert.

He pulled his clothes on haphazardly and left the apartment without waking Rubi. Meyral felt just as he had on his first day underground—lost. Trying to use the ká'ahan while following a voice he could only hear in his head proved difficult. His mind was open, still trying to sense the apparition, and the walls around him came alive. He could feel the axes and shovels that created them, and at one point he was able to catch a glimpse of the faces of those people whose sweat was forever imbued within the dirt. When he realized that he could see beyond the rocks themselves and into the people who formed them into tunnels, an odd thought struck him.

*What would I be able to sense from that orb?*

Meyral ignored his thoughts and ran until he was just outside of the newest cavern, where a smell like copper filled his nostrils. He stared at the freshly formed entrance, and the crystals embedded in the walls around him began to glow brighter and brighter until the phantom came back.

"Don't do it, Meyral," the voice pleaded. "Just take it and go! Trust me!"

Meyral wasn't listening. The glowing blue pulse of the cave was mesmerizing. As he reached out with his mind, something took hold of it. An invisible hand gripped his brain and rocked his head back. His senses exploded in a whole spectrum of colors and sensations.

He was vaguely aware of the shallow water that reached his ankles as he stumbled inside the room. With each step he felt himself fading from the cave and his consciousness took flight to a time long past.

\* \* \*

He was running through the Vigrid Desert, the very same place he'd wandered through for eight years. He came to a stop as two men ran by in hooded cloaks.

The shorter of the two slowed as he pointed to a chunk of marble a few feet away. "You think that's the rock Lady Taryn told us about?"

"Sure," the other man muttered. "It couldn't just be another rock, like the hundreds we've passed already. Why the hell isn't Taryn out here searching? What are we, her henchmen...her servants?" He approached the rock and did a mock bow. "Yes ma'am, let me get that for you. And while I'm at it, why don't I polish your ass!"

"Derek, be quiet."

Something about the way the shorter man spoke struck Meyral as oddly familiar. He lowered the hood of his cloak and a flood of shoulder-length, black hair spilled out, obscuring his face. The second man did the same and a thick braid of green hair fell down to the middle of his back.

Meyral didn't know who Derek was, but he could sense vanity and greed pouring off of him and he instantly disliked it…but something in his features looked so familiar that Meyral couldn't help but wonder where he'd seen the man before.

"This kind of work is beneath Lady Taryn," the first man continued. "It is best suited for her students. They should do it and then thank her for the opportunity to prove themselves."

It was then that Meyral realized who the first man was. Although much younger in this vision than Meyral had ever seen him, he knew it was his father.

"Sure, sure, boss. Whatever you say," Derek said with another bow. "Now let's find this oasis that our great teacher was talking about so we can get outta this shithole." He felt his blistered lips with his fingers. "I hate the desert!"

The sour look on Derek's face made Meyral slightly nostalgic. It reminded him of how Maxine used to look at Alberto whenever he'd fart or talk about women.

"Calm down," Jaspar said with exasperation.

Derek shut his mouth as Jaspar leaned over the chunk of marble and rapped on it with his knuckles. The rock made a hollow sound.

"This is it! Now we head southeast…"

The world spun once and Meyral found himself on a large sand dune. Below him was a single palm tree that marked the edge of a beautiful, crystal-blue lake. Large, flowery reeds grew in bunches around the banks, connected by swaths of high grass. Little, yellow birds hopped around in the foliage and bathed in the shallow water.

The two men from earlier ran by Meyral just as he began to question why he was there.

"Right, this must be the oasis," Derek drawled. "I think I'll just wait here. Y'know, in case it's a trap."

Meyral was already sick of Derek. He was a lazy coward, the very kind of person that Jaspar had raised him not to be.

"What's that?" Jaspar asked sarcastically. "You're volunteering to go first?" He grabbed Derek by the back of his neck and forced him toward the water's edge.

The green-haired man spun and started to wrestle with Jaspar.

Meyral didn't understand; the two men were rolling around and fighting in the sand, and yet there was no malice in them. The only emotion Meyral felt was happiness.

Derek let out a yell, followed by laughter. "Alright, alright, I'll go first. But I know it's only because you hate the water!"

They walked to the shore together and Jaspar stared at its surface. "Taryn said what we're looking for is at the bottom of this. She said there should be a whole system of caves down—"

"I was there when she was giving the orders," Derek mumbled. "She failed to mention how, though. Are we just supposed to dive in? Maybe strap ourselves to some rocks and risk drowning while we look for some piece of junk that she lost?"

"Don't have much of a choice," Jaspar said as he stripped his clothes off and waited.

Derek dove in and Jaspar followed. Meyral slid underwater and watched his dad flail around and try to work his way deeper. Derek passed him easily, and Meyral watched with some embarrassment as Jaspar struggled to keep up.

The water got deeper and darker, and Jaspar eventually surrendered. He floated to the surface, and a second later, Derek joined him.

"There's a huge hole beneath us," he told Jaspar. "It just keeps going."

Meyral's father nodded solemnly. The two men took deep breaths and submerged themselves again. Derek still surpassed Jaspar, but the two stayed somewhat close as they neared the dark cavity in the ground.

The light quickly disappeared as they used the rough walls of the cave to pull themselves farther along. After a few moments, Meyral could feel panic rippling off of both men. It wasn't until he saw Jaspar clawing at his neck and being dragged down into the hole that he realized why. An intense sense of vertigo gripped him and the vision faded.

When Meyral returned, the world was still darker than night. The only sounds were the heavy breathing of his father and Derek.

"Did you know…that current would be there?" Derek asked. Meyral didn't need any extrasensory perception to note the accusation in the green-haired man's voice. "We could have drowned!"

"But we didn't. Have some faith, Derek."

"It's the tzęprön," someone nearby whispered.

The voice startled both men and Meyral finally realized where they had ended up.

*Grey Lake!*

"Did Taryn mention anything about people living down here?" Derek whispered.

Jaspar slowly shook his head, but it was too dark for Derek to see. Again the world turned and Meyral felt unnerved with what the vision presented him.

His father, Derek, and Yiddi all sat around a small, clay table in the very same apartment he'd slept in with Rubi for a year.

*It's just like my first night in Ardan...*

"...so he's the tzęprön? Then what am I?" Derek asked.

"Daz kas'n foretold of the harbinger led by a green fury," Yiddi explained calmly.

"Daz kas'n...your dreams?"

"Only a few have dreamt since kìtanarr," the old lizard continued. "Each is the same, a tale of a kasmömig arriving to free us."

"That would be you," Jaspar answered. "Derek, you're the green fury. You led me here."

"Like hell I did!"

"However!" Yiddi cut in. "The tzęprön must remain here for a full year, so that we may teach him to see the ká'ahan before he can fulfill his ręxoo."

"We accept this honor, Master Yiddi," Jaspar said as he bowed his head.

"Hold on! What is this *we* crap?" Derek shouted as he stood up from the couch. "Apparently I'm just the guide, so I did my part. I want out of this black hell! I want to see again!"

For a moment Meyral was confused, and then he realized that Derek was reacting exactly as he had. He was beyond ashamed that he had acted more like Derek than his father.

"That would be impossible," Yiddi responded calmly. "The only way out is through the tzęprön. His destiny—"

"What? This is buffalo shit!"

The world shifted and Derek's arguments faded while a new world took shape. From the smell alone, Meyral knew where they were, even in the dark. The healing waters of the springs had a distinct and unpleasant odor that he would never forget.

"I don't like talking here," Derek murmured. "You never know how many of those scaly bastards are hiding in the dark, but you need to hear this."

Meyral reached out with his mind in an attempt to sense Derek's thoughts, but he could hardly sense either of them.

*They must have learned to shield themselves already.*

Meyral felt a dull anger rising up inside of himself. Not only had he reacted like a selfish coward, but Derek had learned everything he had.

"While you've been training with those two lizards in the arena, I've been looking for the staff. And I found it...or at least part of it. I found a cave made of crystal in the northern tunnels, and I saw a bright sapphire sitting on a dais in there. That's gotta be what Taryn sent us here for. Unfortunately there's a guard at the entrance...I say we finish what we came here for and put this place behind us!"

"It has only been five months. My training is barely halfway done," Jaspar responded nonchalantly.

*My father and that anray'n Derek have only been down here for five months and they can already block off their minds?*

"We didn't come down here to train," Derek hissed. He climbed out of the water and lit a torch. "We came here for the jewel!"

Jaspar's head rested against the rim of the pool and his eyes were mostly closed. He slowly turned and looked at his friend.

"Look," Derek sighed and rubbed his eyes, "Lady Taryn didn't mention any of this lizard prophecy training garbage. For all we know this is a trap! We need to finish what we came here for!"

"You're right." Jaspar nodded solemnly. "We will inform Lady Taryn and decide on our next plan of action."

Meyral's stomach dropped. He felt torn that his father could so easily abandon Ardan and his duty as the tzęprön.

A second later, he found himself standing in a massive, rocky cavern with a shallow layer of water at the bottom. A round dais sat in the middle of the cave and a large sapphire sat on a pedestal at its center. Meyral looked around and realized that the walls were made of solid crystal.

*This is the same cavern I left in my time.*

Turning back to the dais, Meyral watched the young Jaspar grab the orb with his right hand. He pulled the blue crystal up, and a long wooden pole emerged from the stone with it.

"We've got it! Let's go!" Jaspar whispered.

Meyral spun around as the sounds of a struggle reached him. Derek was at the entrance of the cave, engaged in hand-to-hand combat with Kirth. Three other lizards, one of whom Meyral recognized as Luka, lay unconscious just beyond the captain of the guard. The farthest one lay face down in the water.

As Derek dodged a kick from Kirth, he ran up the beginning of the crystal wall, flipped, and landed behind his enemy. He reached around his neck and caught him in a chokehold.

"You're not so tough in the light, are you, lizard boy?" Derek growled.

Meyral could hear the malevolence behind his words.

"Derek, stop!"

The command in Jaspar's voice was undeniable, and Derek grudgingly dropped Kirth. Meyral was certain that he would have killed the lizard if Jaspar hadn't intervened. Derek sprinted across the cavern before Kirth could recover, and he grabbed hold of the staff with Jaspar. The two men braced themselves as cobalt flames engulfed their bodies and they vanished.

When the images settled, they had the same vivid quality as before. Meyral found himself back in the desert. The last of the day's light had gone, and Klyntar was the only thing in the heavens aside from the stars. Thin, dark clouds drifted across the sky, occasionally blotting out the light. Derek lay on a bedroll, watching the sky, and Jaspar sat up with the staff in his lap, scrutinizing it.

"Do you remember what Taryn called this oasis?" Jaspar asked Derek without looking up.

"Chanteclaire." Derek seemed distant, and Meyral knew he was reliving the battle with the lizard.

"It's a beautiful name…fitting." Silence overtook them for a moment. "What happened back there?" The accusation in his voice was heavy. "The guard was practically asleep. If you'd closed off your mind a little better, we wouldn't have alerted anyone—"

"Enough with the lectures!" Derek cried. "We're not in that abyss anymore. You aren't the tzęprön. Just let me have my fun. Besides, you know better than to think you can survive this life without shedding a little blood."

"I don't take pleasure in fighting!" Jaspar stared incredulously at his companion. "Battle should be something we have to do as a last resort, not something enjoyable that we strive for!"

Once again Meyral felt a certain amount of shame as he remembered the joy he got from hurting the lizard brothers. As the fire died down, a beam of moonlight fell across the staff. An inscription carved down its side glowed in response.

"Look at that," Jaspar said suddenly. His wonderment overpowered his concern. "Can you read this?" He picked the staff up and pointed to the now glowing inscription. "I wonder what it means."

Derek propped himself up on one elbow. "Forget about it. Can't we just—"

Meyral stopped paying attention when he realized the two men weren't alone. He could sense others lying in wait—three of them.

*Something's off. Their life force seems...torn.*

Before Derek could start what promised to be another well-worded complaint, three figures burst out of the sands around them.

"Assassins!" Derek cried. He was on his feet in a flash and he reached for a belt that wasn't there. He realized his belongings were on the other side of the fire and Meyral could feel his fear increasing.

"Nordcross scum," Jaspar muttered. Everything about him was calm and calculated. He stood slowly and grabbed the massive broadsword that lay next to him. Then he stuck the staff in the sand before unsheathing a small axe from his belt with his free hand.

Meyral watched as the warriors moved in. He groped around with his mind and found that they were all devoid of any feelings except one—pain. A pain so black and deep that it was excruciating, and he had to turn off his extra sense to stop the screaming in his head.

The biggest of the assassins moved toward Derek. He was twice as tall and three times as wide as the green-haired man, and there were massive blocks of steel like the heads of warhammers where his hands should have been. The assassin was bald, and a fissure-like scar ran from the back of his neck, over his head, and down his face, splitting his features in two halves that didn't quite line up. The scar ended between his nose and upper lip, creating an odd triangle of exposed gum. He wore a simple, black leather trench coat, an outfit that Meyral had seen others wear in the desert during his travels.

An assassin wielding two steel fans stood next to Meyral. This one was female, and everything about her was pure, primal animal. The bone chest piece was molded to the curves of her oversized breasts, and black fishnets covered her arms and legs. A mess of sickly pink dreadlocks grew from her head, and her mouth had been sewn shut with a thin leather cord.

The last assassin was covered from head to toe in a familiar black garb. He was armed with a long, spiked flail. Meyral recognized him from the Great Moon Temple during the massacre, even though most of him was completely obscured.

The one thing they all had in common were their eyes—solid black with a thin ring of red surrounding their giant pupils. Those eyes were lifeless and dead, but their bodies had no problem functioning. They were organized as they moved swiftly and silently in the sand. Meyral could feel the tension rising.

Derek attacked first. He reached into his shirt and let loose a barrage of throwing knives. One assassin blocked the blades with his flail and the woman dodged with ease. The huge assassin took three blades in the chest without even flinching. He brushed the knives aside, breaking the tips off while they were still embedded in his flesh, and then he began his assault. Despite his hulking mass, the assassin's attacks were fast, but Derek avoided every swing effortlessly.

"You'll never hit me at that speed, you useless dope!" he shouted with a laugh.

Derek looked and fought so much like Maxine that Meyral began to wonder if he was her father.

*Did my dad know their father? Why didn't he ever say anything?*

Derek dodged one punch, then another, then finally slid between the assassin's arms and sprinted forward and up the man's chest. He kicked off at the top of his head and landed in a neat roll. When he popped back up, Meyral saw him holding a knife so large it almost qualified as a sword.

"Now let's dance, ya hammer-handed asshole!"

The sound of metal on metal rang out and Meyral turned to watch his father fight off the other two. He was impressed—Jaspar slashed with speed and accuracy unmatched by anyone Meyral could remember. The flail-wielding assassin was also unnaturally fast, considering the bulk of his weapon, but Jaspar managed to block each strike while simultaneously parrying the deadly dance of the woman's fans.

Meyral could hear Jaspar's mind yell with frustration as he hooked one of the fans with his axe and dragged the woman forward.

She stumbled and he plunged his blade into her gut. The gambit left him unbalanced, and the other assassin kicked Jaspar's stomach and sent him sprawling into the sand.

Jaspar's attacker abandoned his flail and pulled the huge blade out of his comrade, ignoring the female's muffled shriek. He swung the sword around and held it above his head, his sights locked onto Meyral's father.

Jaspar glanced at the small axe in his hand. It was his only weapon, and with no way out, it was his only hope. The man in black slashed down in an attempt to hack his body in two. Jaspar rolled and dodged his own sword, barely managing to pop back up in time to cut the assassin. He aimed for his unprotected throat, but a blow to his cheek was the best he could do. As the two broke apart, the black mask fell away from the assassin's face, revealing skin that was the color of bile and a wound that didn't bleed.

A blood-curdling scream brought Meyral back to the battle. The huge assassin was panting. One of his hammers lay on the ground as black blood slowly oozed from his truncated elbow. He bled from about a hundred different places as well, but his injuries didn't seem to slow him down. The heavily wounded assassin turned his attention to Jaspar. Derek intercepted him and lunged in between the two fighters, but the assassin's remaining hammer caught him in the chest and knocked him to the ground.

"By the moons, why don't you just die?" Derek cried out, but the mountain of a man didn't even acknowledge him.

Panic gripped Meyral's stomach as he turned back to his father. The young Jaspar knelt with an air of defeat. Several wounds dripped blood into the sand, and sweat-soaked hair hung in his face. The assassin slowly used Jaspar's own blade to tilt his head back. Both warriors locked eyes and Meyral could feel the hope draining from his father.

As the assassin raised his sword, he took a moment to grumble something incomprehensible. That delay was all Jaspar needed to speed around him and jump onto his back. Once he had a good grip, he buried the hatchet between his shoulder blades and then kicked off, sending his would-be executioner rolling down the dune.

Just as Jaspar landed, his bloody axe still clutched in his hands, Meyral heard a loud splintering sound that made him flinch. He spun and saw Derek on the ground, clutching his leg.

"You broke my leg, you fat shit!"

Blood began to pool around him, clotting the sand where he sat. The one-armed assassin continued his silent advance and he raised his remaining fist to finish the whimpering man at his feet.

Derek closed his eyes and a flood of terrified, pathetic promises, littered with vulgar insults, suddenly invaded Meyral's mind. He quickly closed the connection, disgusted. He may not have been begging for his life out loud, but what Meyral sensed was a man willing to do absolutely anything for his own gain.

Then the assassin's head split in two, right down his scar. Jaspar stood behind the giant man, clutching the handle of his axe tightly. The giant fell to his knees and then slumped onto his side. Jaspar pulled on his weapon, but the handle broke off, leaving the blade jammed inside the monster's skull.

A familiar, muffled shriek grabbed Meyral's attention. The female assassin, whom Meyral assumed had died, ran toward his father's now unprotected back. She jumped and spun and kicked out, but Derek caught her in midair with his huge knife. The blade found its way directly between her breasts and entrenched itself in her heart. She dropped to the ground like a limp doll.

Jaspar and Meyral spun around at the same time, but the last assassin disappeared into the shadows of the night, still wielding Jaspar's blade. When Meyral turned back, Jaspar extended his hand to Derek.

"Thanks, brother," Jaspar said.

"Keep your thanks." Derek slapped his hand away. "This blows goats. There's no way I can walk in this condition."

Jaspar frowned, then hoisted Derek up onto his back.

"Easy, I'm injured here!" Derek yelled as he grimaced.

With one arm still supporting his friend, Jaspar pulled the staff out of the sand. "I could leave you here and come back with help. It'd only take a week or so," he said with the slightest hint of sarcasm.

"No thanks," he replied. "We could try to teleport," Derek added with a nod to the staff.

"That could very well get us both killed."

"Yea, well you could at least be more careful. I have a friggin' bone sticking out of my leg!"

The vision faded for a moment, and then it returned. Meyral was still in the desert, and Derek was still on Jaspar's back. Night had gone and the bright, red rays of the morning sun poured out from over the dunes. Jaspar looked well enough to go on, but Derek was pale and had dark circles around his eyes.

Long shadows streaked across the sands as a small army of men on camels came over the dunes surrounding the two men. Their armor was unfamiliar to Meyral, and he wondered where they had come from.

"How many people are looking for this *secret* staff?" Derek whispered into Jaspar's ear as he set his friend down.

He looked terrible, but he wasn't delirious yet. Jaspar reached for his belt, but his weapons were gone. He hesitated for only a second before he brought the staff around and held it above his head.

"You cowards want this?"

The warriors let out battle cries and charged the two men. Jaspar leveled the staff at the army, readying himself to attack.

"Jaspar, what are you doing!? She told us…" Derek's voice was drowned out by the screams of the attackers.

There were maybe twenty of them in all, and they attacked from all different directions. One by one they rushed forward, but blue bolts of fire shot out from the tip of the staff and blew the strange men away. As Jaspar became overwhelmed he raised the staff, causing a shield of sand to whirl around him and Derek. The miniature vortex threw the men and their beasts into the air.

Jaspar released the spell and the sands fell, but the staff was still raised high. The ground began to quake and Derek crawled away as fast as he could. Bolts of blue lightning rained down from the sky, frying the men and blasting the sand into small tornados of molten glass. The staff began to shake Jaspar violently and then it dragged him into the air. Derek screamed, but his voice was lost in the sounds of thunder as lightning struck and dark clouds swirled in the skies above.

Jaspar shouted as the staff pulsed bright, brilliant cobalt. He lost his grip and was shot back onto the desert floor. Having lost its vessel, the staff fell powerlessly to the sandy ground.

"That witch!" Derek yelled. He glanced around, but there wasn't a single enemy left alive.

Jaspar lay on the ground not far from him, and Meyral felt a flicker of anxiety in Derek.

"By the moons, what kind of weapon is she having us bring

back to her?" Derek's pain and fear mingled to give him a look of desperation. "I'm done with...with all of this. When my leg heals, I'm leaving Ardänia for good. You can tell *her* I'm out," Derek shouted to nobody in particular, "ya hear? I'm out!"

The images began to break apart. The red sky melted away and was replaced by dark stone. Meyral drew a deep breath. He had forgotten that he was underground—the vision was so strong that he had forgotten everything for a moment. He rested on the banks of the shallow pool, letting reality sink back in.

"I bet that was fun. Maybe now you'll start listening to me?"

Meyral looked up and saw the same dark-skinned man dancing on the dais, beckoning for him to join.

"Seriously, hurry up. You take so long to get the simplest of tasks done."

Meyral waded into the room as the water reached his knees. *Am I making the same mistake as my father?* he thought.

When he looked up from the water, he had reached the dais. As he climbed on top, a small earthquake shook the cavern. Dust fell all around him, but he thought nothing of it until he felt panic filled the tunnels. A second quake hit and he could just make out the shuffling of feet and muted cries in the dark.

None of that mattered now. Meyral was focused on the pulsing light in the center of the cave, the source he'd been searching for. He finally stood next to what had been calling him for so long.

Meyral heard water splashing and he sensed Kirth and Luka, side by side, but he didn't turn around. He was too close. The pedestal was within reach.

The sound of cracking rocks and splintering crystals echoed as the ceiling of the cavern broke apart. A marble boulder crashed onto the dais to Meyral's right before it rolled into the thick water. Two raspy voices shouted at him and he felt their fear that he would be crushed and buried—fear of not only losing the tzęprön, but a friend.

Meyral shut the feelings out. He grabbed the orb with his scarred hand as the light of day poured into the cave. The pool shone dark crimson, as if the cavern was filled with blood. Then he felt a new presence. It was faint, but it was there.

He sensed a dull layer of pain, but as quickly as he had felt it, the feeling disappeared. If it hadn't been for the shadow that moved in the pillar of light, he wouldn't have known that someone else was there with him.

*Is it Yiddi? Who else can make a barrier that strong?*

Meyral risked a glance behind him and saw Kirth go down like a bag of rocks. He saw an unarmed assassin appear over Kirth's limp body. Luka attacked, but the assassin seemed to have the advantage in the lit cave and was able to outmatch the lizard.

The man in black punched Luka twice in the stomach, dodged a jump kick, and then punched him so hard in the head that Luka slammed into the crystal wall and lost consciousness. Meyral jumped down into the pool, ready to join the fight, but a new presence made his heart stop.

The newcomer exuded pure lust. Its absolute desire was so raw, infantile even, and entirely selfish. It was a hedonistic hunger that permeated every one of his senses. The foulness filled the cavern and hampered Meyral's ká'ahan. What horrified Meyral most was that he knew exactly what the person was: his replacement. It was the Blue Bandit, and he was coming for Meyral.

A foot collided with Meyral's jaw and sent him face down in the water. He rolled to avoid several more strikes that he barely sensed, and then he got to his knees in time to catch another well-aimed kick. He tried to protect his mind from the repulsive flow of cravings as his eyes finally adjusted to the new light.

Meyral saw the assassin's next attack coming and grabbed his leg. He wrestled the man in black down into the water and held his head under. The assassin thrashed his arms but Meyral didn't let up. His struggling slowed, and as Meyral looked up, he saw the Blue Bandit less than ten feet away from him.

It looked like it had once been a man, but Meyral wasn't sure that anything beyond a shadow of what it once was still existed. The monster wore heavy boots and thick woolen pants that hid whatever horrors waited below its belt. Its chest was bare and heavily scarred, and burns of various sizes had left rivers and circles of marred flesh in their wake. There were too many badly healed cuts and punctures to count, but Meyral could sense the pride with which the thing wore its scars.

*Who would do that to themselves…and why?* he thought.

Dull pieces of metal pierced the Blue Bandit's arms, in through one side of its bicep and out the other, over and over, at least a dozen times. Meyral could feel every gratifying moment that it had experienced while doing it. He could feel every self-inflicted wound and every burst of pleasure the thing had ever experienced.

The arms were skinny and pasty, yet heavily defined with muscles like cables wound impossibly tight. Both appendages ended in almost complete stumps—there were fingers missing from each hand, most of which had been chewed down to the first knuckle. Meyral's stomach churned as he felt the sexual release the Blue Bandit had felt with each and every bite.

Its hair grew in patches and clumps, but not from balding. Yet another feeling of unwarranted satisfaction surged through Meyral as he looked at the raw skin where it had pulled its own hair out. The Blue Bandit caught his gaze and grinned. Meyral felt every blacksmithing tool that it had used to sharpen its teeth over the years, and every nibble, bite, and scratch that it had performed to tear away its lips and ears completely. He cried out in pain, but that only made the thing's grin widen.

His replacement's eyes had been clawed out of its skull. Meyral knew that it took the thing three nights to fully tear its left one out, but after that, it only took it an afternoon to pluck its right eye. Scabbed, vacant holes sat on either side of its nose, and a long horizontal slash stretched from ear to ear. Pinpricks of blue light shone from the bloodied pits on his face, yet the body in front of him could never match the horrors that surrounded the monster's being. His victims had been women, some children, some elderly, some even handicapped. It didn't matter to the Blue Bandit; all it desired was pain.

In the seconds it took for Meyral's senses to become overwhelmed, the assassin had stopped struggling. The Blue Bandit, however, stood right next to him. He let go and jumped to his feet, but not before he sensed Rubi running through the corridors. She was heading straight for the cavern. The thing kicked the backs of his knees and ran toward the entrance of the cave, where it caught Rubi with its misshapen arms.

Rubi spun and kicked the Blue Bandit squarely in its face, then punched it in the ribs twice. Meyral lunged through the water to join the fight, meanwhile wondering frantically how to fight something whose sole purpose was to experience and deal pain. The bandit stumbled, but it recovered quickly. Meyral felt it smile before he saw it.

The ground shook again and the sunlight dimmed as sand poured in through the hole like water. The mound poured directly in front of the cavern's opening, blocking access from the only people that could help him.

He heard splashing from the other side of the cave and realized that the unarmed assassin was still conscious. Before he could help Rubi, the man in black attacked him. The assassin threw sand in Meyral's face. His eyes burned and he was forced to open his mind again. The cave was easy enough to keep in focus, but the hate and lust from the Blue Bandit nearly overpowered him. The most Meyral could feel of the assassin was akin to a shadow, and close to nothing when he tried to keep track of Rubi, Luka, and Kirth as well.

The assassin was fast, strong, and hard to track, but Meyral was able to keep up. There was only one enemy, and he'd grown used to fighting two lizards at once. The man in black parried as fast as Meyral hit; neither could gain the advantage over the other.

The chaos behind him quieted and Meyral could sense Rubi in the Blue Bandit's chokehold. Its forked tongue licked the redhead from her collarbone to her temple as she gasped for air. Arousal stirred Meyral, although it wasn't his own. The rage that boiled inside of him was his, however. Crystals strewn throughout the walls pulsed with his emotions and he kicked the assassin directly between his legs.

The man in black dropped to his knees and rolled over in pain, carefully leaning to keep his face above the water's surface. Meyral turned away from his assailant and the two unconscious lizards to help Rubi. He lunged again, half running and half swimming. The monster held Rubi against its body with one of its mutilated hands across her chest. It dragged her backward through the water as Meyral continued to charge forward. With every heave, the Blue Bandit squeezed Rubi's breasts and tugged at her clothes.

As Rubi's consciousness faded, the monster wriggled its hand into her pants. It stopped playing keep away as it became enthralled in humiliating Rubi, and it worked; she let out one sob before passing out and falling limply out of its grasp.

Meyral finally reached her as he felt the assassin's shadow fall across Kirth's body. He risked a glance over his shoulder and watched in horror as the assassin jumped into the air and landed with both feet on the lizard's chest. He knew he couldn't save both, so he made a choice—the unconscious captain of the guard was on his own.

As Meyral approached the Blue Bandit, the monster dislocated Rubi's arm and dropped her at its feet. Meyral punched and kicked, but the pain it felt quickly dissolved into ecstasy. Meyral felt the Blue Bandit's jaw give with his next punch, and a satisfying crunch reached his ears. Meanwhile, across the cavern, the assassin held Kirth underwater. A few seconds later, the lizard-man's body sank. The faint pulse of life emanating from the captain of the guard dwindled, and Meyral knew that Kirth was dead. Luka screamed inside Meyral's mind. The lizard was still unconscious, but somehow he knew that his friend was gone.

Luka's rage boiled inside of Meyral and acted only as another distraction. A knobby fist collided with Meyral's face, then his ribs, and then his throat. As he wheezed and panted for breath, he could hear the monster's elation between its own sputtering gasps.

Suddenly Meyral was dragged to his feet and held against the thing's body. A skinny arm wrapped around his neck as its twin snaked down his chest. It rubbed against his crotch as Meyral felt a bulge press against his back. He struggled in vain as a forked tongue licked blood from his face.

The ground shook again and Meyral was pulled out of the way of another falling boulder that missed Rubi's stirring form by inches. He continued to fight, but he was forced to watch as the assassin grabbed Luka's body and dragged it over to the dais. Then the hand was back at his crotch, fumbling with his belt. The deformed fingers found it difficult to grab hold of the small buckle.

Meyral tried to retreat into his mind. His breathing slowed as his vision started to fade to black. He wanted all of it to be a bad dream, and then he heard a voice that only amplified his terror.

*"It's okay,"* the darkness inside of him cooed. *"I'll take care of everything. Just let me out."*

Meyral was only slightly aware that his pants were now around his ankles.

*"Let me out, let me out, let me out!"*

"No!" Meyral roared.

He turned and headbutted the monster. The Blue Bandit's nose broke and blood flowed down its face, pooling in its lipless mouth. Meyral yanked the metal entwined in the bicep around his neck and grinned at the pain he felt from his enemy. He brought the arm down over his shoulder and snapped it at the elbow.

*"Let me out, let me out, LET ME OUT!"*

His willpower faded as he spun and grabbed a fistful of woolen pants.

*"Find pleasure in* this,*"* the other voice snarled through his mouth.

He pulled with all his might and the sound of tearing flesh reached his ears. The Blue Bandit made a gurgling sound, and then the blue pinpricks of light in its eye sockets dwindled. Its body fell to the ground and disappeared under the water. Meyral pulled up his pants and searched for his love, but when he turned around, he realized that Rubi's body had joined Luka's on the dais.

The assassin pulled the lizard and the redhead up by their necks and turned back to Meyral. While holding both captives, he made a slight bow and disappeared in a column of green fire.

It was a long moment before the silence set in and Meyral realized that, once again, he was all alone. Reality tried to creep in. He could feel it on the edge of his consciousness. He fought against it, knowing that he didn't want to face a world where he just watched his love get violated and then dragged away.

Meyral heard digging from the tunnel and knew that Yiddi, Pläblé, and the twins stood just on the other side of the blocked entrance. He only had seconds to decide what would happen next.

"You only have one choice," the phantom voice said, full of panic and desperation. "Take the staff and use its power!"

Meyral could hear an undertone of insanity, of undeniable pleading. It scared him because he knew that the phantom was right. He approached the dais.

"That's it."

He turned around and put both of his hands on the sapphire.

"Take it! Use it!"

Meyral pulled up, and as he did, its fine wooden handle appeared from underneath with the same inscription that he'd seen in his vision.

The ghostly man exploded in a rain of color, and Meyral roared in pain as his consciousness was filled with a myriad of memories: a young man hit by a column of black fire as his master watched in horror; an emaciated man with a sapphire in his chest howled under a thick sheet of ice; a bald man with tan skin screamed in the darkness as a blue light hung just above him, out of his reach; a man with black hair and a sword stuck through his chest, surrounded by troops in fur armor; Derek crawled on the desert floor while Jaspar floated in the air and bolts of cobalt lightning struck the ground; a younger version of himself held a staff on the edge of a cliff, then erupted into an azure inferno. Each vision exploded in a flash of brilliant light. And then he watched as it all suddenly disappeared.

He opened his eyes.

*What the hell was that?*

Another tremor shook the cave, but this time every stone, boulder, and grain of sand flew up into the air and replaced itself to its former home. Lizard-people flooded the cave, but Meyral could barely see their outlines. He knew Pläblé held her shattered husband while the twins tried to console her, and he knew Yiddi was the only one staring at him.

*"Run!"* It was another voice inside his head, but this time it belonged to Yiddi. The old lizard turned away and redirected people back into the tunnels to avoid being buried, but Meyral could feel him searching and probing his mind. *"This is your rexoo. Go! Fulfill your duty as the tzęprön!"*

Meyral raised the staff in his arms and concentrated. There was only one thought in his mind as he channeled all of his energy into his new weapon.

*Rubi!*

The cave filled with blue light that caught the Blue Bandit's body on fire. As the flame incinerated the monster, a final quake shook the tunnels. The walls collapsed, resealing the Crystal Cavern, and Meyral disappeared.

# CHAPTER TWENTY-NINE: SHRAKA

A feeling like death had overtaken Meyral as his body became nothing. He could hear voices all around him. He saw blurs of colors and random images of buildings and people from all different times and places.

The feeling stopped and he opened his eyes. In front of him was a large pyramid made of stone that was covered in vines with large, pink blossoms. The strong and dark scent of honey reached his nostrils.

He lifted his foot to step forward, but a high-pitched screech stopped him. A blue light appeared to the east, the same warm light that he had followed for so long. But Rubi was the most pressing matter, so he took another step forward. He trusted the staff—somehow he knew that it had taken him right to her.

The screeching continued to oscillate in rhythm with the pulsing light, but he ignored it and continued toward the building. As he pushed on the huge stone door, a memory came back to him for the second time in his life.

He was walking down a corridor lit dimly with emerald torches, following a figure in red. When she turned around, she tossed something at him and attacked with razor-sharp talons. He wasn't sure what she had thrown, or who she was, or if it was even real, but he knew that he'd seen it before.

Meyral shook his head to try to clear it, but more fragmented images continued to flood his mind. Ever since he'd touched that staff, memories had been assaulting him, and most weren't even his own.

When he finally came back to reality, he was lying on a stone floor on the other side of the mighty door. He noticed that the awful screeching had quieted down, but he could still hear it.

The inside of the pyramid was warm, humid, and devoid of light, no longer lit by green fire. It was as dark as Ardan, but that meant nothing to him now. He opened his mind and searched the temple first for Rubi and then Luka.

The place was a giant labyrinth of tunnels and hidden rooms, but it was surprisingly empty. There was one room that his mind refused to enter. It was as if someone had set up a barrier, much like that assassin had. He figured the others would be in that room.

*It's one thing to mask your own consciousness, but an entire room? Whoever did this certainly isn't a novice…*

Meyral continued to walk, and soon he could hear the sounds of metal hitting metal and the cries of battle. He followed them through passage after passage until he eventually found a large, wooden door with thick chains across it. He grabbed the staff and pulled it close to him, then closed his eyes and focused his energy on what lay beyond the door. Meyral could just make out figures moving in the room in front of him, but they didn't feel right. He ignored the odd beings and continued to feel around the room until he found what he was looking for.

Hanging from the ceiling by chains were Rubi and Luka. They were both alive, but Luka wasn't doing so well. His blood dripped slowly from his feet and tail onto the floor below.

Meyral opened his eyes and turned his attention to the door. He concentrated on the chains until he heard the clicks of the locks that bound them. The metal in his way dropped to the ground with a clatter. Steadying himself for a fight, he pushed on the door, which swung open much more easily than he expected.

A catwalk that overlooked a large pit lay before him. Below was a small battalion fighting amongst themselves with a strange assortment of weapons, some Meyral had never seen before. Across from him, hanging in midair, were the hostages.

He walked slowly into the lit room while keeping an eye on the combatants below. Not a single head turned in his direction. The fighters were so intent on the battle that even the sound of the huge door slamming behind him didn't faze them.

Meyral looked at Rubi, expecting to see relief on her face. He was confused to find disgust and outrage until he followed her gaze. He realized why the warriors hadn't felt right when he first sensed them. They were only kids, none of them any older than he'd been when he left Berrywillow.

Meyral reached out again with his mind, looking for the twisted bastard that was in charge. The drab stone floor and walls that were lit by green torches came alive.

The room had existed for lifetimes and had seen thousands of deaths. Those memories that filled the chamber rushed his mind all at once, the ghosts of tortured souls begging to be heard. He couldn't stop them once they started, and they pulled him deep into a layer of his subconscious that he wasn't even aware existed.

There was a boy who had lost his parents and then spent four years in the dungeon before killing himself. A girl who thought she had been saved from a lifetime of prostitution was stabbed to death as she slept only a week later. A countless number of memories of twins who were forced to fight each other, and each time the victor was killed by their master.

*Who did this to you?*

Meyral concentrated on the question until a boy in his teens appeared. He was given a black bandana by a shadowy figure.

*"This is your final test,"* a distorted voice echoed from the shadows.

An assassin wielding a chain-whip stepped forward and the young man attacked. It was a close fight, but in the end the man in black wrapped his weapon around the boy's neck and snapped him like a twig.

*Assassins...you're assassins?*

No matter how hard Meyral focused or how much he probed the memories, none of them would reveal their master. It was as if, even in death, they were still terrified.

A group of Ardänian children were crying in a corner as the oldest girl yelled, *"We'll never turn our weapons against our own, you wench!"*

The girl was cut down, but her executioner was submerged in shadow.

Meyral probed deeper and the torches suddenly burst in his mind. The emotion was so powerful that it knocked Meyral onto his back. As he fell, one last vision lingered. The vision was blotched, like a watercolor painting, but the voices were perfectly coherent.

*"I see something special in you, young lady. So I'll give you a choice that I've never given anyone before you."*

*"What would that be?"*

*"Serve me as my lead assassin and command the fighters that I've trained here. The power, the control, it can be yours...should this deal not appease you, you can be free. Take your pick."*

*"Lady Sera, you have my unending gratitude for liberating me,*

*but why would I leave one prison to join another? I would never subject myself to that kind of bondage again."*

*"I can bring out your true potential. Let me show you who you truly are!"*

*"You have my answer."*

*"Then it is truly a shame to not have you with us, Aldomein."*

Finally the visions stopped, but the resounding scream that came from Meyral's own mouth continued, and he was helpless to cut it off. Rubi's eyes filled with fear as he finally regained control of his body, but the damage was done. Every head in the room snapped up at the same time to find the source of the noise. Meyral looked down into their haggard faces and cringed.

*They're so young, but they have the features of the old men I used to see in the desert.*

In an instant his pity transformed into rage as the kids drew their weapons and attacked. He dodged three different types of arrows and a crossbow bolt before diving to avoid several spears. A large axe flew by his head and cut through a length of chain that held the catwalk up. He and the metal flooring crashed to the ground and Meyral had to execute a series of rolls and flips to avoid a barrage of blades.

He stood up and he could feel the monster waking inside of him. He raised the staff, its presence simultaneously soothing and terrifying. A thin veil of cobalt light rose up in front of him and a batch of arrows that had been heading his way exploded in midair. A puff of sawdust fell at his feet and he laughed.

Meyral started to lose himself in the battle as all his energy was channeled toward the young assassins. Power began to pulse through the staff, vibrating his arms. The children backed up, still eyeing him suspiciously.

*"They were innocent, Maxi!"* Alberto's voice echoed in his head from a decade before. The grief, the pity, the regret…those old emotions rose up to combat the monster that was taking over his mind, just like they had after he attacked Kirth. Grimacing with concentration, he redirected the power flowing through him.

As the blue light washed over the young warriors, they became paralyzed and their weapons clattered to the ground. A few moments later they disappeared. Meyral dropped the staff as if it had been burning hot.

"Are you two okay?" Meyral yelled up at Rubi as he picked the staff back up. He aimed and blasted her chains away, then caught her as she fell from her suspended prison. There was a brief moment where he thought she was going to kiss him, but then she pointed up to their scaly friend.

"I'm fine, but Luka is hurt. We need to hurry!"

He eased Rubi down before turning back to the lizard-man. He demolished the chains and caught Luka with Rubi's help before he hit the ground. Luka still wasn't awake, but Meyral could sense the faint trace of life that was still in him.

"Is he dead?" she asked.

Meyral looked up at Rubi. "No, but he needs—"

"What did you do to those kids?" Rubi asked with anger and trepidation.

"Hear that?" He paused and cocked his head. "They're down in the dungeons. They'll be fine."

As Rubi listened, she stared at Meyral. In the firelight, her eyes scanned his face in the usual way—follow the scars from his neck around his ear, then to his eye. When Meyral reached up, his fingers felt the damaged tissue on his face that now reached all the way down to the corner of his mouth, tilting one end in a perpetual kind of smirk.

"Where the hell did all those kids come from in the first place?" Meyral asked slowly.

"All over the world," Rubi answered. "Most of them spoke foreign languages. My guess is that she's been kidnapping people and forcing them to fight here as training."

"By the moons…" Meyral muttered solemnly and looked back toward the entrance. He could still hear the screeching in the distance. "Rubi, you need to take care of Luka. Get him to safety and—"

"Are you kidding me?" Rubi knelt by Luka's head and glared at Meyral. Her lips were pursed and Meyral knew she was furious. "You're just going to leave again? Do you have any idea what's going on?"

"Wh—huh?" he stammered.

"You're a moron, Meyral!" She slapped him across the face, rocking his head back. "Look, Sera and Nordcross are behind this, but Sera isn't here. She went back to the capital—something big is happening! The guy that took us left to get her."

When Meyral slowly shook his head to tell her that he still didn't get it, she grabbed his face.

"They found your father! Jaspar is coming back to the mainland and the entire Nordcross army is gathering in the desert to meet him! *That's* what you need to be doing—saving your dad!"

Meyral opened his mouth and quickly closed it again. The mind-splitting screech and the blue light had returned. He had to find the source before he could join his father in the desert. Without any explanation, he pointed the staff at the ground and a sapphire bubble formed around the three of them. They floated up and Meyral guided them through the tunnels until the screeching became too much to bear. He dropped them all to the ground and pressed a hand against the side of his head.

He felt something cool against his face, and when he opened his eyes, Rubi was kneeling by him. Her hand caressed his cheek and the screeching started to fade.

"Rubi, get Luka to safety and hide until this is all over."

"What's happening? What aren't you telling me?"

Meyral paused, once again impressed with her intuition. He stood and turned away.

"You ass!" Rubi yelled, her patience long forgotten.

Meyral didn't need to invade her mind to know that there was an inferno inside of her, ready to scorch him.

"You think I'm going to sit back and let everyone else fight, after all I've been through?"

He turned around reluctantly.

"Give me the staff!" she shouted.

"What?" He tightened his grip on the weapon instinctively.

"I may not know how, but I know that thing can heal Luka. If you won't do it, I will." Her voice had softened.

Meyral looked at the staff with wonder. "How do you know what it can do?" he asked slowly.

"Magic isn't just for killing," she answered.

Meyral had only ever viewed the staff as a weapon; he never once thought to use it to heal someone. He walked back and pointed the staff at Luka's motionless body. He concentrated, and a beam of cobalt light shot into the lizard. A feeling like cold water ran up his arm, a response he couldn't remember having gotten from the staff before. The screeching receded and the light dimmed as Luka's chest began to rise and fall more rapidly.

"I feel like...I've been dragged all over Ardänia by a herd of buffalo," Luka coughed feebly as his eyes opened, "and then mauled by a mountain lion."

"Hold onto him," Meyral said as Rubi gave him a questioning look. "Just trust me for once."

She pulled Luka up as Meyral stepped forward. "Meyral..." Rubi leaned in and kissed him. "Be careful."

He nodded and laid his left hand on her shoulder. "Concentrate on someplace safe," he whispered.

Rubi reached into her pocket and pulled out the shard of crystal she kept from the tunnels. She closed her eyes and Meyral noticed the tears forming under her beautiful lashes.

Blue, semitransparent flames licked their way down the sleek, wooden handle of the staff, up his right arm, across his shoulders, and finally down his left arm, where they engulfed Rubi and Luka. Her eyes opened and Luka stirred weakly. Then, in a quick burst of light, the two disappeared.

\* \* \*

Meyral returned to the entrance hall after a short break to catch his breath. The staff seemed to be getting easier for him to use, but it still knocked the wind out of him. When he reached the entrance, he pointed the staff at the stone door and blew it away. As sunlight poured into the room, Meyral could already feel his anger receding.

*How long was I in there?*

Once he crossed the threshold, the screeching stabbed into his head and he dropped to his knees in more pain than he cared to remember. The flashing light was so strong that he could no longer see anything else. He stabbed the staff into the ground with desperation and tried to focus on anything other than the deafening screech and blinding light.

When it had finally stopped, Meyral opened his eyes. The noise faded and the light went with it. He looked up to the two peaks on either side of the small valley, and then at the forest that now surrounded him. Off in the distance, he could just see the top of the pyramid. He reached out with his mind, but there was nobody in the woods aside from him. He let out a deep sigh, and as he did, the sound of water caught his ear.

Moments later he emerged from the trees and found himself on the shores of a giant lake which seemed carved out of the mountains themselves. A thick forest of redwoods stretched around the entire shoreline. The only mark that mankind had left was a single, two-story house, its wide windows looking out over the water and heavy vines climbing up its walls.

In the center of the lake, a small island peeked over the surface, its turf dotted with small boulders and dwarfed trees. At the north end, a vast network of waterfalls danced their way down the face of the mighty mountain and into the beautiful body of water.

He felt so strange being there. Dreams that he had forgotten returned to him, although dim and faded. Once more, memories that didn't belong to him came to the front of his mind. He'd never been to the lake, but he knew it intimately through someone else's thoughts. His eyes wandered back to the house, certain that he'd seen it before, but nothing specific came to mind.

Something in his subconscious reached up and tugged at him, and all he wanted to do was get behind a particularly wide curtain of water toward the top of the falls. Meyral pointed the staff at the lake and ice immediately began to form on its surface. He formed a path, then made his way carefully across the makeshift bridge, running as fast as he could without slipping. Finally, he would see who or what had been calling him for so long.

At the end of his path, he raised the staff and the waterfall parted. He leapt through the part and landed on a small ledge, but the claustrophobia didn't set in until the water sealed itself back into a liquid wall behind him. He could still hear sounds from the lake and the forest, but they were twisted, like they were coming from another world.

He followed the ledge as it rose high into the mountain, weaving in and out of the rocks and behind several of the waterfalls for what seemed like miles. He came to a landing in front of a gaping cavern, and unlike the others he'd seen on his way, this entrance was dry and maintained.

He turned to face a wall of water that by some mechanism was a constant, steady sheet as translucent as glass. Meyral had a perfect view of the landscape before him.

To the west was green and lush land with a single blue ribbon leading toward the center of the kingdom. There the river branched off into two separate waterways, one leading north out of view and the other leading southwest into the ocean.

To the east was a land of rolling hills dotted with small lakes. Ribbons of steel outlined and ran through the entire area, connecting cities that were taller than life. The copper and bronze monuments rose up against the green sky, ringed by blankets of dark smog. Long, wide patches of farmland stretched between the cities, replacing the forests and meadows.

"Nordcross," Meyral whispered with disdain.

It wasn't wholly unpleasant, but there was something wrong about the way nature had been pushed aside for the sake of mankind.

Meyral turned around and headed into the cave. He tapped the staff on the ground and his own light shone around him. It bounced off of a system of mirrors, and in an instant the entire rocky hallway was bathed in blue. Symbols had been carved into the walls, and they seemed to glow and pulse as the light from the staff reached them. It was as if the cave was reacting to its power.

There were rooms that branched off from the main tunnel. The first three Meyral came to had straw on their floors and strange devices hanging from their ceilings. The acrid smell of rotting meat and overripe fruit hung in the air.

The fourth room lacked the mirrors, so it remained a black hole until he entered. There were several bookshelves along one wall, each covered in centuries of dust and cobwebs. In a corner was a desk piled high with thick tomes and a model of Cygnus with its moons. In the center was a large table with various vials, tubes, pots, burners, and other bizarre instruments that had been set up and abandoned.

As the light of the staff reached the contraptions on the table, everything came alive, glowing in various colors and gurgling with whatever fluid remained. He heard a raspy cough come from farther in the cave and he returned to the main hall. Deeper in, the carvings on the walls became more cramped and complex.

Meyral turned right, his eyes trained on the symbols and runes, and he nearly dropped the staff when he noticed a corpse standing next to him. Its skin was shriveled and burned, and each of its eyes was a solid white. Like Meyral's skin, the heaviest of the scars shone bright cobalt. Ropes of dirty, black hair hung down in front of its scorched face. The thing stumbled forward and reached a hand out.

"Who are you?" Meyral asked, trying to hide his fear and disgust.

"Do you really need to ask?" his own deep, raspy voice echoed back to him.

Meyral stood, paralyzed, while waves of demented pain and hunger rolled off of the apparition.

*The monster inside my head,*
*The It that wants me dead,*
*It fills me with dread.*

*"MEYRAL!"* the thing yelled.

Meyral jumped and the staff went dark. He lost his balance and fell backward onto the stone ground. Fear slipped its icy fingers around his throat and he started to crawl on his hands and knees.

When he finally regained control of himself, he relit the staff. The thing was gone. In its place was a man—a man so emaciated that he looked like a skeleton with a thin layer of skin stretched over it.

"I've been waiting centuries to finally meet you," he said.

Meyral stood slowly, ignoring the man as he looked around frantically for the demon.

"It has been a long trip, I'm sure. Welcome…to the beginning of the end."

"What did you…where did it go?" Meyral asked.

"My boy, there is nothing in this cave but you and me," the man said sadly as he shook his head.

*Did I imagine it?*

"You are my guest. Please…" The ancient man motioned for Meyral to follow him into the last chamber.

When they entered the room, torches along the walls lit themselves and shed natural light throughout the room. It was not overly decorated, but the furniture that was there was curiously exquisite. A huge bed took up most of the space, along with a wardrobe and a low dresser. A table sat in one corner with a small, leather couch and an armchair on either side.

The man stood by the armchair and gestured for Meyral to sit on the couch. "Young man, if you would, please tell me your name. I have never known what to call you."

Meyral made eye contact, but he hesitated to sit.

*I know that voice from somewhere, but where? And how in the moons is a person supposed to have been waiting centuries for me?*

"Meyral...my name is Meyral." His curiosity got the better of him and he sat down, although still uneasy. "I followed the—"

"Yes, yes, the light."

In the dim glow of the torches, Meyral could see his host with much more clarity. Earlier he thought the man was constantly smiling—but now he realized that he simply had no lips. He was wrinkled like a prune and his teeth were forever exposed.

"Meyral...my dear boy..." He reached out a hand and ran it across Meyral's face, finally coming to rest on his scarred cheek. "I need something from you."

"Why should I help you? I don't even know you." Meyral swatted the man's gnarled hand away.

His ancient body made several cracking sounds as he sat down. "I know," he continued. "It's incredibly selfish of me, after all I've done. You've been through hell and back, and then I ask you for more." His yellowed, sunken eyes made Meyral's stomach turn.

"Who...what are you?"

"You really don't know?" The man seemed a little disheartened.

"I don't remember much at all. For the past decade I've been wandering, trying to find my past..."

"Of course, how could I forget?" He feebly smacked a skinny hand to his head while he continued to stare at Meyral's scars. "The ability to use that power...it certainly comes with a price, doesn't it? Here, let me give you a gift." The man gestured for Meyral to lean forward.

Meyral hesitated again before moving to the edge of the seat. The man rested a cold hand on his forehead.

"This might be a bit...uncomfortable." He closed his bulging eyes and grimaced.

For the second time that day, Meyral's mind was filled with a million memories and voices all at once. His head felt like it was splitting apart. Then something changed. He was able to control the flow of information. He could hold onto individual memories and study them. His jumbled mind, old memories, new memories...they all came together and fit into place like the pieces of a puzzle. His brain worked like it never had before—everything became clear and he felt elated.

The panting skeleton removed his hand and sat back. Meyral slid from his seat and dropped to the ground. He vomited on the stone floor before he looked up.

"Not so bad, right?" the ancient man asked. "Now tell me, do you know who I am?"

"Sh-Shraka…" Meyral slowly climbed back into his seat. "You're Shraka. I remember…everything."

"Well, that's fantastic," Shraka said. "And now it's your turn to help me."

Meyral nodded. All the humor left the face of the mage and insanity twinkled in his eyes.

"First, let me tell you something." Shraka cleared his throat. "In my youth, I did impetuous things, stupid things. I've done so much wrong in my life that I can't fix, so many things that I regret. I have done what I can to make reparation, but no matter what I do, there are evils that I cannot undo. Evils that, no matter how much I repent, I will never be forgiven of."

The sadness in the old man shot straight to Meyral's heart—it was almost crippling. Meyral felt truly sorry for him.

"The first is that I can't die. I have futilely sought my own demise for so long. I haven't eaten a single thing in nearly a century, but my body just keeps going." He held his arms out as if to emphasize his lack of diet. "I've hidden myself away in the mountains and haven't seen the slightest glimpse of moonlight in ages. I thought perhaps without Klyntar's interference, my body might return to its natural state, but alas…"

Meyral coughed impatiently. Shraka looked up with a hunger in his eyes as he glanced at the staff.

"Only the staff has the power to undo what it has done," Shraka said with a shaky sigh.

"Why?" Meyral asked with a raspy voice. "Why would you curse yourself?"

"Why, you ask? Boy, that is the same question I have asked myself for centuries. Why indeed. Why would anybody seek to become an affront to nature? Better yet, why would somebody force it on two innocent girls? Greed…vengeance…we are a vile and repulsive race, we humans, and I got carried away with it all. Our only saving grace is that we can feel remorse. Humans are at our most beautiful when we feel sorrow. It is only then that we help others. Only then that we lay aside our own little schemes and desires for one second and focus on someone else.

"I have felt that sorrow for too long now. I have tried for a quarter of a millennium to help, but all I seem to do is hinder. All I long for now is oblivion."

"Wait," Meyral said as he reached toward his pants. Where his hand expected a pocket with a leather fold or a book, he found only emptiness. "I want to know what...damn!"

A look of confusion surfaced on Shraka's face.

*"For only the first bright star of the dark, dark night catches the eye,"* Meyral murmured. He looked back at the ancient man, clinging to the thinnest thread of hope.

"By the moons," Shraka rubbed a wrinkled hand over his face, "that's my poem. I wrote...I..." He let out another shaky sigh. "I am glad that it found its way into the hands of at least one other person who appreciated it."

Meyral pulled the staff around and lowered it at the mage's chest. Shraka reached his hand out and clasped Meyral's wrist.

"Before I go, you must promise me that you will restore the balance. Let the true Keeper guide you."

"How do I do that? What is the Keeper?"

"Promise me!" Shraka shouted as he squeezed his wrist.

Meyral hesitated. The manic look in the old sorcerer's eyes told Meyral that it wasn't up for debate.

"I promise," Meyral replied solemnly.

A small wave of light washed over Shraka. The former court magician closed his eyes and a tear ran out of each. His body seemed to inflate and he became the handsome young magician that Meyral had seen in his first visions.

A smile formed on Shraka's face as he burst into a cloud of dust and ash. Meyral pulled the staff back to his side as the old man's voice rang out for the last time.

*"Destiny is yours to control. Fate is not predetermined."*

A blinding flash of yellow light overtook Meyral's vision and he felt himself being pulled in every direction. The old man's laughter filled the cave.

*"One last gift."*

# CHAPTER THIRTY: MEMORY

When Meyral regained consciousness, he found himself in a dimly lit corridor with stone walls and a sleek, marble floor. A burgundy rug extended its entire length and large paintings covered the walls. Two men stood about halfway down the hall, shrouded in darkness, completely still.

As Meyral approached them, he immediately recognized King Thessius, but the other man's face was hidden beneath a brown hood. He held a walking stick in his hand. Instinctively Meyral's eyes searched for the sapphire, but it was nothing more than a wooden pole. The two men stood in silence for a long time, until two more people approached them from the opposite direction.

"Brother," one of the new men threw out his hands in greeting as he approached, "this isn't like you."

"Shhh!" Thessius looked terrified. His face was pale and a light sweat had broken out on his forehead. "Theron, I need your help."

"Relax, Thess," Prince Theron replied. "Nobody's around this late at night. Not here anyway." He smiled, revealing a mouth full of perfectly straight, white teeth.

The man next to Theron shifted uneasily, and Meyral recognized him as the knight named Malachi, who would later be framed for Thessius' assassination.

Thessius nervously wrung his hands as he continued. "I have made a large…error in judgment—"

"The king, make an error?" Theron's voice was wrought with sarcasm. "This must be some kind of farce. You're practically the king of judgment. What did you do, tax someone that deserved it?" Theron and Malachi chuckled, but no one else shared the joke.

"My wife," the king said, then stumbled over his words for a moment. "She is with child."

The man in the brown cloak twitched, but nobody else moved. It was several seconds before anything happened.

"Congratulations!" Theron embraced his brother in a hug that went unreturned. "So much for being barren, right?" He pulled away and winked at his brother. "This is a joyous occasion which calls for a month's worth of celebration. Malachi, go and—"

"Silence, you buffoon!" the fourth man said, speaking for the first time. He walked in front of a low-burning candle just in front of Thessius. He had a sour look on his face, but Meyral recognized him immediately: Shraka.

"Your mage needs to learn his place, brother," Theron said. He stepped forward and poked Shraka in the chest.

"That's right," Shraka sneered, "have your brother fight all your battles. He already fixes all of your messes."

Malachi took a step forward threateningly, but Thessius raised his hand.

"Enough, the both of you!" the king commanded. When he spoke again, his voice was composed. "The chambermaid, Louise," he told Theron. "She is also with child."

Theron scratched his head for a moment, and then looked from Shraka back to his older brother. Then his eyes grew with realization. "Oh-oh! That's something I'd expect from me." His mouth worked for a few moments, trying to find the right words. "If you needed a quick fix, you should have just asked. I know these women...I tell you..."

"The king would never need, nor would he want, the services of a whore," Shraka interrupted again.

"Tell me, brother, how does this *thing* know your needs and wants?" Theron asked.

"You bring up old transgressions, Prince!" Shraka's words were measured, but his hands shook with rage.

Theron sneered at the mage before turning back to his brother. "Then do you want me to take care of it?" He drew a finger across his neck and Thessius' face flushed.

"This is impossible! Do we need to draw you a map?" Shraka snapped. He poked Theron in the chest, just as the prince had done to him earlier. "I've met children with more intelligence than you."

Malachi made a movement so swift that nobody had time to react. The wizard found himself pinned to the wall with a dagger to his stomach.

"Do not touch Lord Theron again, you glorified trickster," he growled.

Thessius rested a hand on Malachi's shoulder and the knight backed away. Meyral caught a look of pure hatred on Shraka's face and he half expected him to attack Malachi right then.

"I need you to marry Louise," the king said suddenly. Theron opened his mouth to protest, but Thessius talked over him. "Marry her and claim the child as your own. The child can never know the truth. It would devastate it, and the monarchy...the people would revolt!" Thessius' eyes dropped as he finished.

Theron considered this for a long time before he sighed heavily and said, "You know I'd do anything for you. Besides, with all the things you've done for me...I guess it's time for me to pay it back some." He clapped a hand on Thessius' back, and the king looked up with a brighter demeanor. "Although I think everyone will be surprised that I've finally settled down and gotten a wife—and a kid!"

Shraka shook his head.

Theron let out a hearty laugh and then turned and walked back down the hall, still chuckling. "I wonder what the wedding night will be like...wait, don't tell me, I want it to be a surprise." He laughed again as he beckoned his bodyguard. "Malachi, come. It seems we have an engagement party to plan!"

Malachi kept his eyes on Shraka until Theron was a safe distance down the hall. Then the knight turned and walked away, following the still-laughing prince.

When they were out of sight, Shraka grabbed Thessius' shoulder and turned him around. The look of relief vanished from the king's face.

"Thessius, we cannot trust your brother," Shraka whispered fervently. "He runs a damned prostitution ring. There's even talk of slave trading!" His eyes seemed to be searching for something that wasn't there. "Don't you remember what he did? He used your secrets against you! Against *us*! With all due respect, this is a terrible idea!"

Shraka was pleading and, for once, sincerely worried. Meyral was oddly comforted to see that he had had empathy for Thessius at some point.

"Shraka, after all we've been through together..." Thessius put a hand on each side of the sorcerer's head, his fingers entwined in Shraka's thick and curly hair, and he kissed his forehead. "What was that about old transgressions? Trust me. He's our only hope of keeping this under control and avoiding a civil war."

Shraka grabbed each of Thessius' wrists and said nothing. At long last, he let go and followed Thessius down the hall as everything faded to black.

When the candles were relit, Meyral was in another room. Once again, Shraka occupied a shadowy corner. This time, however, his staff had a sapphire in the tip.

Across from him was a large, luxurious bed, on which an emaciated man lay, his pallor sickly and green, and patches of colorless hair surrounded his face. At his side sat a teenage Marguerite. A chambermaid placed several small bottles on the bedside table and exited the room with a tray of blood-soaked rags.

"Father...are you feeling any better?" Marguerite asked through her tears.

"Marge...you know...better than that." Theron's breathing was labored. His whole body shook as he coughed up blood into a fresh rag that his daughter held for him. "Are we alone? I can't see very well."

Marguerite turned to look at Shraka. The wizard bent his head down and stared into her eyes.

"Yes, Father," she lied.

Theron reached out with a weak arm and Marguerite took his hand. "Do not hate me for this..." He coughed again and Marguerite wiped his mouth. "I raised you with all the love I had...but..." Theron's body shuddered. "You have been deceived."

Shraka didn't move a muscle, but Marguerite nearly jumped backward. "Daddy? What do you mean?"

Theron flinched. Marguerite squeezed his hand tighter. He coughed so hard this time that Meyral wondered if he would be able to continue.

"Thessius...my brother, the king...he is the one who impregnated your mother."

Marguerite's eyes filled with fresh tears as she let the bloody rag drop onto the bed. Another bout of coughing racked Theron's body.

"You're...not my f—"

"No! I am your father! I will always be your father..."

A large smile spread across Shraka's face.

"I love you, I raised you, I would die for you...you know that." Marguerite nodded.

"But there is more." Theron's body shuddered as Marguerite's stiffened. "You are three days older than Marie...which means..."

"I'm first in line for the throne." Marguerite's tears were gone and her eyes took on a dark and greedy glow. She stood up and dropped Theron's hand, which stayed suspended over the edge of the bed.

Marguerite waved to Shraka, who followed her out of the room as Theron coughed for the last time. The lights faded again and Meyral heard Marguerite say one final thing.

"Shraka, we need to have a little talk about my coming of age..."

As Meyral tried to piece together all of his new memories, another vision invaded his mind.

Sera stood in a circle of rocks at the base of a mountain. A large man was with her, wearing a black, weatherworn bandana on his head. He knelt before her with his left fist on the ground and his right resting on his knee. Sera stood with her arms crossed and her blonde hair tied back in a high ponytail.

"Milady..."

"Have you found her?"

"Yes," the man answered. Meyral heard a hiss from the back of Sera's throat. "I believe she is staying in Tem, and she's trying to call some kind of meeting."

"A meeting...whatever for?" Sera's eyes turned into slits.

"I do not know, Milady."

"Well then, you know what I need from you. Take back your post as a knight, by whatever means necessary—"

"You know I can't! Once you've turned your back—"

His words were cut off as Sera wrapped a strong hand around his throat. "Do you think that because I was banished that I'm no longer royalty? That you can treat me like ordinary scum?"

The man shook his head pleadingly, her hand still around his throat.

"Then never interrupt me again!" She let the former knight drop to the ground and he immediately resumed his kneeling stance. Sera crossed her arms and glared at him.

"My deepest apologies, Milady."

"Then go on."

"If I show my face I will be executed!" he pleaded.

"I do not want your excuses, and you do not want to fail me, Nicholas."

"N—no, Milady..." Nicholas sputtered.

A figure dropped down from a boulder above. He landed in front of Sera with his brown cloak trailing behind him.

"Shraka, what a pleasant surprise," Sera said lazily. "How did you know you were just the person I was looking for?"

Shraka smiled, but it was empty. Dark circles hung around his eyes and a thick layer of unkempt, patchy beard obscured most of his face. His curly locks of hair were gone—his head was completely bald.

"Just a hunch, Lady Marguerite," Shraka said.

"I told you, my name is no longer Marguerite. That was a name given to me by an imposter, a fool of a man. My name is now Sera." Her eyes locked onto the staff in Shraka's hand. "Is that…?"

"Yes," he answered. "It never leaves my side." This time Shraka's smile had something in it—the desperate insanity that was already in his eyes.

Meyral felt a tinge of pity for what would become of him.

"That changes today," Sera said. "Shraka, give me the staff," she commanded as she held her hand out.

Shraka didn't answer. He looked at her with wide, fearful eyes.

"Shraka? Are you alive in there?" Sera asked. She knocked on his bald head, but he hardly moved.

"Last time…but…it's…why?" Unable to create a complete sentence, Shraka backed up a few steps to take the staff out of her reach.

"I am Ardänia's queen, I am the one who should be rightfully ruling. Now, give me the staff." When Shraka didn't comply, she snarled, "My wretched sister will pay!"

"You still mean to end Marie's life?" Shraka asked.

Meyral thought he heard honest sorrow in his voice.

"Yes, I will kill her," the banished queen answered. "But we both know what is necessary to do that…after all, it was by your hands that I'm in this mess!"

"Kill…Marie?" Shraka scratched his neck so hard that he left red trails where his fingernails touched. "I swore my loyalty to the royal family of Ardänia. I could no more kill her than I could kill you."

"I would do it myself, but that enchantment she cast is so complex that I haven't even begun to figure out a way back into Ardänia. That's why I need you…unless you think you can resolve my banishment."

"I'm not that powerful, Lady M...Sera." He hung his head and held the staff out, but quickly brought it back by his side.

"You are starting to outlive your usefulness, Shraka." She sighed and looked back and forth between the two men before her. "No matter, there are ways around the rules...aren't there, my old teacher?"

Sera grabbed the staff from Shraka, and by the look on his face, Meyral thought he was going to attack her. She paid no attention to the former court magician and she walked back to the disgraced knight, who was still kneeling. She pulled a blade from inside her dress and held it out to Nicholas. The dagger shone in the sunlight and the engraving of a ram in its hilt was easily discernible. As it caught Shraka's eyes, he twitched.

"Something wrong, Shraka?" Sera tittered. "Maybe you recognize this. You gave it to me around the same time you gave Marie that silly book of poems. It's amazing how well you've lied to everyone in your life...even yourself." She turned to Nicholas. "Take this and hold it up."

Nicholas did as he was commanded. Sera held the staff against the dagger, then closed her eyes and began humming. As he watched, a coating of azure light appeared around Nicholas' weapon. The knight didn't dare move, and the look on his face was that of sheer terror. Shraka turned away from the ritual entirely. Meyral could feel the mage's disgust and anxiety.

"This should break the immortal enchantment that Shraka cast so long ago," Sera muttered. "By this weapon, she will die."

Nicholas held his blade up and marveled at the blue glow coming from it.

"I expect you to finish the job," Sera said. "Bring me Marie's head. If you disappoint me again, it will be the last thing you do!"

The knight nodded and walked away in a daze.

"And take this waste of space with you!" Sera grabbed Shraka and leaned forward to whisper in his ear. "Don't get any ideas," she said. "The dagger will only work on Marie—I made sure of that."

"As I told you, I can no more kill—"

"—her than you could kill me, blah blah blah. I heard! You're only there to vouch for my assassin." Sera let him go with a little shove.

As the two men walked away, Nicholas seemed pleased, but

Shraka kept nervously looking back at the staff with every few steps he took.

The vision dissolved as another took its place.

Shraka and Nicholas knelt before a tall, radiant woman with short, blonde hair. She wore a red, Ardänian-style dress that reached her calves, and she stood in front of an ornate temple, beyond which the Errigan River flowed.

"I apologize for being late, Lady Marie," Shraka said as he took her hand.

Her red eyes were soft and compassionate as she looked down, a complete contrast from her sister's menacing gaze. "Think nothing of it, dear Shraka," she said. "It's good to have someone else from the old system with us today." She motioned to the temple behind her and sighed. "Everyone is waiting inside to begin the meeting."

The two men entered the temple with Marie. The ornate double doors of the structure were guarded on each side by war-hardened men. They both sat in chairs with their swords across their laps.

The temple itself was made of thick stones and high, stained-glass windows. There were no entrances except for the front, and with all the torches lit, the giant room lacked any shadows. The furniture was kept to the dozen or so benches and a few chairs.

This was the most defensible space Meyral had seen. There were no hiding places, yet an assassin had still been able to find his way into the meeting. Meyral watched the former knight take a seat in the front next to Shraka and glance furtively around.

The whining of a short fat man with bright red hair brought Meyral out of his musings. "Do you really think it's wise, abandoning the monarchy?" he asked. "It's worked just fine so far."

"We need something more flexible," Marie announced from her spot on a low stage. "Something more encompassing of the people and their needs as a whole."

The determination in her words was so powerful that even Meyral felt roused. The only person that seemed unmoved was an old warrior with a scar that cut through his left eye. He sat just behind Marie on the stage. His white hair was pulled into a ponytail on top of his head, which didn't move. Only his one brilliantly blue eye swept back and forth as he surveyed the audience.

Meyral's attention was again captured by Marie. She was gorgeous; the light of the moons poured in through the open door and she seemed to glow in it. Shraka seemed transfixed by her as well. While she spoke, the entire room became still except for Nicholas. His hand slipped from his knee, a movement that drew the old warrior's attention.

Nicholas wrapped a black bandana around his head, and Marie's knight stood at the same time he did. Just as the old warrior opened his mouth to bark an order, Nicholas yelled, "You're a fraud!" He pulled the dagger from his boot and lunged to finish the job that Sera had started so long ago. "Long live Lady Ser—"

Before he could reach the queen, a bright, yellow flash filled the room and blinded Meyral for a moment. When his eyes refocused, the assassin lay crumpled on the other side of the stage. His head had been split in two vertically, spattering blood all across the stage. Without hesitation, the old warrior kicked the body from the stage, then turned his sword on Shraka, who stood panting above the dead body.

"What was that?" Marie's knight asked. His voice sounded as scarred as his face.

"The son of Malachi dares to speak to me," Shraka spat.

All eyes were on Marie and two people ran forward to help. She raised a steady hand and everyone stopped. Meyral was mesmerized by the aura of power surrounding her.

"Shraka, what is the meaning of this?" Marie addressed her old friend as if he'd just told an inappropriate joke.

"Lady Marie, I...you must die." Shraka's voice was low and filled with emotion.

"You're not the only one to think that," she said. Her voice was sad but strong. "Your old vow, taken so many years ago, prevents you from spilling royal blood."

Meyral couldn't understand how Marie could be so calm.

"I wonder how you got around that to kill my father," she added.

"You knew?" Shraka gasped. His eyes darted between her and the knight.

"You mistake my kindness for weakness." Marie stared intensely at Shraka for a moment before continuing. "Fear not, my old friend. I relinquish my power over you. There is no royal family anymore." She brushed her hand along her neck, motioning to her freshly cut hair. "I have cut ties with the past, as I hope everyone will be able to do in the time to come. Ardänia is changing, and it's up to us to see it through. Shraka, your vows are no longer binding."

Shraka shifted and Marie's knight pushed the tip of his blade into his neck, drawing a trickle of blood.

"Elohim, let him go," Marie commanded.

He hesitated for a second before lowering his sword. Elohim stepped back, but his eye never left Shraka.

"I still love you, Shraka," Marie said through a voice clogged with emotion. "I would do so much for you—but I cannot allow myself to be killed. That is imperative. Marguerite…there is something wrong with her. I fear that one day I will have to be the one to put an end to her madness. No good can come of my death today, I assure you."

Shraka didn't respond.

"You could come with me, Shraka," Marie said as she reached for him. "Help rebuild Ardänia. I was not lying when I said it was good to have you here with us."

Shraka's eyes shifted for a moment from Marie to the dagger on the ground and back to Marie. Elohim's muscles tensed as he let out a low growl. Every torch in the temple suddenly flared up and exploded in emerald fire, casting a dark light all around them. Then Sera's voice echoed from above, causing everyone to scream.

*"Ardänia's name will be synonymous with pain!"*

As Shraka disappeared in a column of green fire, so did the vision of the temple and Marie. It was replaced by the mountainous scene Meyral had seen earlier. Shraka was back in front of Sera and panting, his brown cloak smoking slightly. Nicholas' decimated body lay in the rocks nearby.

"Why did you stop me?" Shraka asked between breaths. "She was within my—"

"Don't lie to me, fool," Sera snapped. "I know you wouldn't have done it."

She kicked him in the chest, but Shraka continued to kneel.

"I always knew you were a sneaky, double-crossing snake of a man. All those things you told me…you really were in love with her. The moons be damned, you still are!" Sera grinned and Meyral could feel the waves of sinister malice coming from her. "And yet you let my flames call you back, tisk-tisk. Still trying to play both sides, are we?"

Shraka could hardly conceal his contempt at this point. His jaw was clenched and he was trembling, but Sera took no notice.

"In any case, I think I want her to live. I want her to suffer. I want her to watch as everything she loves so much falls to pieces. The kingdom, the people, her friends...anything she creates, I will take it away!" She cackled and ran her hand along the staff, fingering the inscription.

"Just like she took away your throne and your father?" The Shraka that now stood in front of Sera looked like a wild animal that had be let out of its cage.

"Who do you think you are? I'm still of royal blood." She made to kick him again, but he deflected her foot and she landed on her back.

"Did you not hear?" Shraka snarled. "The royal family has been absolved. I am no longer bound by anything!"

There was a slight hint of fear in Sera's eyes as she quickly regained her footing. Shraka leapt at her, reaching for the staff. She pulled back quickly and yellow light filled Meyral's vision again. When the world came back into focus, Sera was on fire, rolling and screaming in the dirt. The staff was only about a foot away from her.

Shraka lunged, but Sera grabbed his legs with her burning hands and pulled him back. The flames died down and Meyral watched as her burned and disfigured skin began to knit itself back together. Shraka got back to his feet and the two faced each other.

"How...dare...you..." Sera panted. "I am royalty! I am the true queen of Ardänia! You are my servant!"

"I would never—never—serve you!" Shraka ducked under his cloak as a jade inferno enveloped him. He howled in fury, clutching his burning cloak. When the flames receded, he looked disheveled but otherwise unharmed.

Sera was only inches away from the staff when a golden whip of fire slapped her back into the rocks. A second later, the flaming whip wrapped itself around her neck and dragged her into the air and back to the ground with a thud.

As Shraka turned around, one hand on the whip and the other reaching for the staff, Sera grabbed the golden fire and yanked. She pulled Shraka forward as the whip exploded in a rain of green and yellow fire. Sera stood back up and walked over to the staff as Shraka lay face down in the dirt. Victory was hers.

When Shraka rolled over onto his back, Sera had the staff

pointed directly into his face. He scrambled backward, dragging himself through the dirt, and Sera let out a laugh that chilled Meyral to the core.

"Where would you go?" Sera smacked him in the face with the blunt end of the staff. "You've committed treason and, like me, you will never be able to return to Ardänia…to her." A quick jab to his gut made Shraka stop moving. "And now you won't work with me?"

"You were once my puppet…" Shraka managed to say through the blood in his mouth.

"I guess the student has become the master!" Sera knelt beside him and whispered in his ear, "In this world, there are two types of people: those who are confused, spineless, and controlled by useless compassion. These are the weak, the ones who believe that it's honorable to die for a cause, to sacrifice for love.

"Then there are those who are like me—purified by apathy and logic. It gives us the power to do the things that the weak cannot. Without us, this world would be empty. Full of people, maybe, but like sheep without a shepherd, they would be living a wandering, useless existence."

Her eyes gleamed threateningly. Blood dribbled down Shraka's lips and onto his chest.

"Which are you, Shraka?" she asked, her breath hot on his ear. "Are you weak and fueled by emotions? Because I can sacrifice you right now for whatever ill-conceived love you think you're fighting for. Or are you able to make decisions based on reason?"

She waited for his answer, one hand holding the staff and the other extended toward the former court magician.

"I am…nothing…" Shraka's face darkened as he pushed himself into a kneeling position, his left fist on the ground and his right resting on his knee. "If not yours to command."

He bowed his head and the vision faded to black once more.

\* \* \*

Meyral woke up in the dark with his head resting against the cool leather of the chair. The staff lay across from him in a pile of ash on the couch.

*"You must restore the balance."*

472

Meyral reached down and picked the staff up. He turned and faced south, where he knew the enemy was gathering. An aura of blue light engulfed him and he disappeared with a gust of wind, scattering the wizard's ashes.

Don't miss the next book in
The Old Kingdom Ardänia series,
Timeless Tundra!


Take a peek at what's in store…

# CHAPTER SIX: BETRAYAL

\* \* \*

The sound of ice cracking around them grew louder and the ground began to quake. Hugo and Thessius drew their swords and stood back to back. The others spread out to minimize damage as they waited for it to stop.

There was a heavy thud as the frosted ground beneath them shook and cracked apart. Pillars of icy water shot into the sky, and something burst forth from the frozen lake. Thessius and Hugo were launched into the air, along with thick chunks of ice. A deafening roar imbued with the might of a thousand beasts surrounded them.

Shraka dove to avoid a flying iceberg. He landed next to Faylen and they both scrambled backward.

"Charybdis!" she shouted to Shraka. "Northern legend tells of a creature that haunts the Frozen Wastes—"

The beast roared again, drowning out Faylen's voice. The airborne debris settled and Shraka gawked at the giant lizard, veiled in a blizzard of shadows and snow. The beast looped through the air on massive wings made from living ice, and it roared into the setting sun. Two massive horns like upside down icicles protruded from its head. His curiosity piqued when Charybdis shot lightning and ice from its long snout.

Shraka and the two priestesses rushed forward. Thessius had landed, but he and the Guildsman lay languidly where they were. Charybdis landed on a glacier and watched them hungrily. It sniffed the air noisily, then turned its long neck toward Thessius.

The great beast sprang into the air and the pillar of ice crumbled beneath it. Faylen and Shraka started to chant and a thick shield of rock surrounded the king.

Charybdis changed course and aimed for the other priestess, but Thorn only closed her eyes and stood where she was. As soon as the beast came close enough, she opened her eyes, which shone blazing red. She spread out her hands, and from them an inferno of blood red flames erupted, the size and intensity of which Shraka had never before witnessed. Charybdis flew right into the deluge of fire, but the flames bounced right off of the dragon's crystalline hide. The diverging flame melted several nearby glaciers. Chunks of ice and torrents of heated water spilled over the lake's surface, creating a thick mist over the ground.

Thorn's screams were all Shraka could hear as he tried to navigate through the fog. Charybdis roared and the priestess' cries stopped. The beast blew a torrent of icy mist at the ground, clearing the stubborn mist. Thorn's raw, eviscerated body lay in a thin layer of red slush underneath the ice dragon.

* * *

As the rock shield around him dissipated, a loud scream reached Thessius' ears. A fallen glacier had pinned Hugo by his legs only a few feet away from the king. Thessius' sword was too far away for him to grab—they were both easy prey.

Charybdis circled once in the sky as Faylen stepped in front of the king. She splayed her hands out in front of her and yelled, though the strong winds from the dragon's wings drowned her voice out before Thessius could hear her.

He felt a pair of firm hands pull him to his feet. Shraka motioned for him to follow as he ran toward Hugo. The Guildsman's eyes were wide with fear as the ice dragon circled around him, occasionally blotting out the sun. Shraka placed his hands on the ice pinning Hugo and he chanted quietly. Yellow flames appeared in his palms and melted the small glacier. Thessius helped Shraka lift the Guildsman, but as soon as Hugo's legs shifted, he grimaced and screamed in pain.

"Get away…minion of…darkness…" Hugo managed while feebly slapping Shraka.

Charybdis slipped right through one of Faylen's voids, then almost instantly flew out of the other side. Charybdis let loose another torrent of icy mist and she dove to avoid its attack. The dragon looped through the sky again, its eyes staring hungrily at Faylen. The pink-haired priestess howled with rage as she summoned another void near Charybdis' head, but it only batted it away.

"Sister Faylen!" Shraka shouted, but she only knelt in the icy slush with her hands in her hair.

"How did it—"

The words had barely left her mouth when Charybdis swatted her aside with an icy claw. Shraka heard an audible crunch as Faylen was launched through the air. He pushed Hugo along the ice and dove out of the way as the beast stomped past him, carving deep ruts in the tundra underfoot.

Thessius watched as the ice dragon dove, attacked, and took flight. It kept that pattern consistently, keeping its prey at a distance. Charybdis reached the swirling snowstorm where Faylen had landed, but it couldn't find her.

As it stooped to sniff along the ground, Thessius charged at the beast's backside. It turned and Thessius was forced to jump onto one of its massive feet to avoid being crushed. The king drew his sword, then leapt into the air and stabbed upward. Charybdis thrashed as it felt the steel of the king's sword pierce between its scales.

Thessius dropped and rolled as he hit the ground. As he tried to regain his footing, Charybdis breathed another plume of deadly frost. Shraka sprinted forward and tackled him, then covered the young king with his body.

"Shraka!" Thessius yelled.

The rogue mage's face contorted with pain. He locked eyes with the king, and Thessius watched Shraka's eyes go dark. He climbed out from under his savior and his heart grew heavy with pain. Shraka's entire backside had been decimated, leaving his ribs and spine exposed to the cold air.

Thessius didn't know how long he had been staring at the shredded flesh of his old friend, but he became aware of popping noises all around him. Black voids appeared and disappeared all around the dragon, and Charybdis persistently batted the balls away. Each time he slashed, he sent one crashing into the ice. Glaciers were sucked away and gaping holes were left in the icy floor.

Faylen appeared from the settling cloud of snow, clutching her chest and panting.

"Priestess, stand down!" Thessius roared. "Magic doesn't affect it!"

She continued conjuring voids, and each one was marked by

another popping noise. Charybdis hovered around in circles, just above the snow, as it desperately swatted some away and bit the others.

*By the moons, she's brilliant! She's distracting it!*

Thessius didn't waste his chance. With one last glance at Shraka's corpse, he sprinted toward the dragon and leapt into the air. He timed his jump just right and caught hold of Charybdis' thick tail. The king pulled himself up and climbed onto the dragon's snow-covered back.

"Oh Klyntar, give me strength," Thessius muttered to himself as he drew his sword and continued to climb.

Charybdis flapped its giant wings, forcing Thessius to hang onto the icy spikes that lined its back. The dragon's snout peeled back and it snapped at the king as it climbed the sky.

When Thessius finally reached its long neck, Charybdis reared back. One of its frozen horns pierced Thessius' leg. The king screamed into the freezing wind whipping around his face, but he held on.

He pulled his leg from the spike and blood spurted from his wound. The drops that fell onto Charybdis' neck instantly froze, and within moments his leg had gone numb. The dragon clawed at its head, but Thessius dodged its deadly talons as they swiped at the scales around him. He rolled, nearly falling from the airborne lizard, and then raised his sword high. He plunged his blade deep into the creature's left eye.

Charybdis screeched and thrashed about, throwing the young king from its back. As Thessius fell toward the frozen tundra, he watched the dragon dive to the ground. Its tail knocked Faylen across the ice as it climbed back into the hole that it had emerged from.

Just before he hit the ground, Thessius saw Shraka's body move seemingly on its own. His vision faded, and all he knew was darkness.

# About the Author

Preston Robison was born and raised in the Central Valley of California. He received his Bachelor's degree in physics from the University of California, Santa Barbara. His previous jobs include small-time acting in L.A., farm work in Lancaster, security in Santa Barbara, and teaching in Bakersfield. For several years he worked at a zoo, where he became inspired to begin writing his first novel. Preston enjoys death metal and smooth jazz, terrible horror movies, and getting lost in the wilderness.

Find him on Facebook, Tumblr, and Twitter:

www.facebook.com/prbison
www.prestonrobison.tumblr.com
www.twitter.com/prestonrobison